Seduced
In the Dark

C J Roberts

Photo credit: Kurt Paris

Cover design: Pixel Mischief
www.facebook.com/PixelMischiefDesign

Edited by: Emily Turner (dpemily@gmail.com)

A Note to the Reader

If you're reading this and you haven't read *Captive in the Dark*, turn back! You'll be lost.

For the rest of you: Hello again, I'm glad you decided to continue this journey with me. As of January, 2013, *Captive in the Dark* has sold over 70,000 copies. That's incredible! It's a goal I never thought I would reach, and honestly, I've been humbled by all of you.

You've made my dream come true.

I have faced adversity. I have had my share of rejection and heartbreak. I won't say it's all been worth it; there are some things I would give anything to undo. However, looking forward, I can honestly tell you: I have never had more hope.

Thank you.

"I am thankful to all those who said 'No' to me. It's because of them, I did it myself."
– Albert Einstein

This book is dedicated to:

My daughter. This book took many months to write. There were days I couldn't play. There were nights I couldn't tuck you in. You're too young to understand why mommy had to work, but you forgave me anyway. Your love has changed me forever, and I will always aspire to be worthy of you. You are my legacy.

My husband. There are times when I try to express how much I love you, but words fail me. You're a part of my soul and I cannot imagine my life without you in it. Suffice to say, if you ever leave me – I'm going with you.

My mom. When I think about what it means to be strong, I think of you. Thank you for never giving up. I know I wouldn't be a fraction of who I am without the love and support you give me. You're my inspiration.

M. McCarthy. Keep writing, little sister. Your day is coming. I love you.

K.A. Ekvall. You kick my ass girl and I love you for it. I can't wait to return the favor, so please, write!

A. Mennie. A compliment from you is like rain in the desert: rare and precious. Thanks for believing in me.

M. Suarez. You had me at 'I read *Captive in the Dark* as a result of losing a bet'.

My brother, Scott. Thanks for the amazing trailers, little brother. This *almost* makes up for all the spankings I took because of you as a kid. I love you. ;)

Pixel Mischief. Your knowledge of graphic design transmogrification is only outmatched by your zest for kung-fu treachery!

R. Welborn, Y. Diaz, and J. Aspinall. I can never say thank you enough for the love and support you've given me. You have catapulted my hobby into a career. The friendship that has blossomed between us is one I hope to continue to nurture in the years to come.

Rilee James. What can I say, I f**king love you. Someday, we're going to turn the camera on and the world will never be the same.

Lance Yellowrobe, and Johnny Osborne. With friends like you, I never know where my husband is, LOL! Love you guys.

These blogs: SamsAwesomness.blogspot.com, TotallyBookedBlog.com, Maryse.Net, you have been instrumental to my success and you deserve every follower you've earned!

Independent Authors. When the publishers won't have us, we have the fans. Special thanks to Shira Anthony, Anthony Beal, Daisy Dunn, Rachel Firasek, Colleen Hoover, Sonny Garrett, Tina Reber, and K. Rowe.

Vino 100/The Tinderbox, Rapid City. Thanks for the good times, the great conversations, and the endless supply of quality booze.

Emily Turner – avid fan and grammar nazi. Thanks!

Prologue

"I've been doing this a long time – manipulating people to get my way. That's why you think you love me. Because I've broken you down and built you back up to believe it. It wasn't an accident. Once you leave this behind...you'll see that." – Caleb

1

Sunday, Aug 30, 2009
Day 2:

Vivisected. It's the only word I can think of to describe how I'm feeling – vivisected. As though someone has cut me open with a scalpel, the pain not sinking in until the flesh begins to separate and my blood bubbles out. I can hear the crack as my ribs are flayed open. Slowly, my organs, wet and sticky, are pulled out of me one at a time. Until I am hollow. Hollow and yet, in excruciating pain – still alive. Still. Alive.

Above me, there are sterile and industrial fluorescent lights. One of the bulbs is threatening to go out and it flickers, buzzes, and struggles to stay alive. I've been transfixed by its Morse code for the last hour. *On-off-buzz-buzz-on-off.* My eyes hurt. I keep staring. Following along with my own Morse code: *Don't think about him. Don't think about him. Caleb. Don't think about him.*

Somewhere, I'm being watched. There's always someone here. There's someone to tug on my various cables. One to watch my heart, another my breathing, one to keep me numb. *Don't think about him.* Cables. They extend from my hand, where I receive my liquids and my drugs. They wind from my chest to monitor the beating of my heart.

Sometimes I hold my breath, just to see if it will stop. Instead, it beats harder and faster in my chest and I gasp for breath. *Buzzzzz-on-off.*

There's someone who tries to feed me. She tells me her name, but I don't care. She doesn't matter. No one does. Nothing really matters. She asks me my name as though her kindness and gentleness will move me to speak. I never answer. I never eat.

My name is Kitten and my master is gone. What could possibly be more important?

In the corner of my mind, I see him, watching me in the shadows. "Do you really think begging is going to work?" asks Ghost Caleb. He smiles.

I cry. Loud, horrible, sounds come out of me, so violent they shake my whole body. I can't make it stop. I want Caleb. I get drugs instead. The food comes through a tube while I sleep.

There's always someone watching.

Always.

I want to leave this place. There's nothing wrong with me. If Caleb were here, I'd walk out of this place, happy, smiling and complete. But he's gone. And they won't let me grieve for him in peace.

***

Day 3:

I close my eyes and open them slowly. Caleb is standing over me. My heart races and tears of pure joy flood my eyes. He's finally here. He's finally come for me. His face is warm, his smile broad.

There is a familiar tilt to his lips and I know he's thinking something naughty.

A familiar tingle spreads throughout my belly and creeps down toward my pussy, making it swell and throb. I haven't had an orgasm in days and I've become very accustomed to them.

"Should I let you go? You look so sexy when you're tied down," he says through a smile.

"I missed you," I try to say. My mouth is unbelievably dry. My tongue feels heavy and dead in my mouth. My lips seem to have fared no better. They are chapped, and when I scrape my tongue over my bottom lip, I can't help but think of sandpaper.

The tube they have been using to feed me is crammed up my left nostril and fed down the back of my throat. It itches. I can't scratch it. It hurts. I can't shake it free. I feel it every time I swallow and it tastes of antiseptic.

"I'm sorry," Caleb says.

"For what?" I whisper. I want him to tell me he's sorry for not telling me sooner…that he loves me.

"For the restraints," he says.

I frown. He loves restraints.

"As soon as we can be sure of your mental state, we can remove them."

This is wrong. Really wrong.

It's the drugs.

"Do you know why you're here, Olivia?" a woman asks, softly.

I am not Olivia. I'm not that girl anymore.

4

"I'm Dr. Janice Sloan. I'm a forensic social worker for the Federal Bureau of Investigation," she says. "The police were able to identify you from your missing person's report. Your friend Nicole reported your abduction. We've been looking for you. Your mother has been very worried."

I'm tempted to speak, so I can tell her to shut the fuck up. I can practically feel my skin crawling. *Stop! Stop talking to me.* But she won't. There will be more questions, the same questions, and this time I might have to answer them. I know it's the only way they'll let me go. They keep me strapped down and pumped full of drugs; they say I tried to hurt my nurse. I tell them they tried to hurt me first. I never asked to be brought to the hospital. The blood wasn't mine and the original owner wouldn't miss it. I was fairly certain he was dead. I should know – I killed him.

"I know this can't be easy for you. What you've been through…" I hear her swallow. "I can't imagine it," she continues. It reeks of pity and I don't want it. Not from her. She reaches her hand out to touch mine and I instantly recoil. The harsh clang of my hands smacking against the railing of my bed is like a threat of violence. I am more than willing to inflict violence if she tries to touch me again.

She holds up both her hands and steps away. My breathing begins to settle and the black ring surrounding my vision dissipates, until the world is once again in high definition, color. Now that she has drawn my attention, I notice she isn't alone.

5

There is a man with her. He cocks his head and stares at me like I am a riddle he wants to solve. The look is heartbreakingly familiar.

I roll my head toward the window, staring at the light filtering through the horizontal blinds. My stomach clenches. *Caleb.* His name whispers through my mind. He used to look at me that way. I wonder why, since he seemed so capable of reading my mind. My body aches. I miss him. I miss him so much. I feel tears again, sliding down the corners of my eyes.

Dr. Sloan doesn't relent. "How are you feeling? I've been briefed by the social worker who was present during your initial exam, and I've been apprised of the events witnessed by the Laredo Police Department."

I swallow hard. Memories assault me, but I fight them. This is exactly what I didn't want.

"I know it doesn't seem like it, but I'm here to help you. You're being held on charges of assault against federal border patrol officers, possession of a weapon, resisting arrest, and suspicion of felony murder. I'm here to determine your competency, but also to assist you. I'm sure you have your reasons for what happened, but I can't help you if you won't talk to me. Please, Olivia. Let me help you," Dr. Sloan says.

My panic is rising. Already my chest is heaving and the world is black around the edges. Tears choke me around the tube in my throat. The fucking pain of the post-Caleb world is endless. I knew it would be.

"Your mother is trying to find someone to take care of your brothers and sisters so she can come see you," she says.

NO! Stay away.

"She should be here in the next day or two. You can talk to her on the phone if you'd like."

I am whimpering. I want her to stop. I want them all to go away – this woman, the man in the corner, my mother, my siblings, even Nicole. I don't want to hear them. I don't want to see them. *Go away, go away, go away.*

I scream bloody fucking murder. I won't go back!

"Caleb!" I scream. "Help me!" My body wants to curl in on itself but can't. I am bound, like a caged animal on display. They want to know what's wrong, but they will never, and can never, understand. I can never tell them. This pain is mine to keep.

I scream and scream and scream until someone rushes in and presses all my magic buttons.

The drugs take over.

Caleb.

***

Day 5:

I'm fully aware I am in the psych ward of the hospital. I've been told many times. I can't help but laugh inwardly at the irony. They will let me go once I'm able to tell them to release me. But I won't

7

speak. I am literally holding myself hostage. Maybe I *am* crazy. Maybe I belong here.

The bruises on my wrists and ankles are an angry shade of purple. I suppose I fought pretty hard. I miss the restraints. In a way, they allowed me the freedom to writhe and flail. They gave me something and someone to fight against. Without them...I feel like a traitor. No longer a prisoner, I seem to be allowing them to keep me here.

I eat when they bring me food, to keep me from having that fucking tube in my nose. I shower when they say I must. I get back in my bed like a good little girl. I float away with the drugs. Oh, how I love the drugs.

But they never leave me alone. There is always someone here, watching me like I'm a lab experiment. Whenever the fog of the drugs lifts, they are here: Dr. Sloan, or her 'associate', Agent Reed. He likes to stare at me. I stare back.

The first one to look away is the loser.

Often, it's me. His glare is unnerving.

In Reed's eyes, I see a familiar determination and a cunning I have never been a match for.

"Are you hungry?" he asked, soft and low.

I feel as though he is telling me I have no choice but to break. Eventually, he'll get what he wants from me. I taunt him with my silence. Sometimes he smirks at me. And then, Caleb's specter seems much more pronounced.

When I failed to respond, the fingers of his right hand trailed across the underside of my right breast.

On this particular day, he looks away from me first and returns his attention to the laptop in front of him. He types, and then scrolls through information I can't see.

I took a sharp breath and leaned away from his touch, forcing my tightly-shut eyes into the skin of my upraised arm.

Slowly, he reaches for his briefcase on the ground next to his chair and pulls out a few brown folders. He opens one and makes some notes while furrowing his brow.

His lips caressed the shell of my ear...

I know.
I know Caleb is not here. I'm fucked in the head. Factually, I take stock of the fact Agent Reed is a very good-looking man. *Not as handsome as Caleb.* Still, he strikes me as equally intense. His pitch black hair seems a little too long for his profession, but he keeps it impeccably groomed. He wears the A-typical, movie G-man outfit: white shirt, black suit, dark-colored tie. He makes it look good though, like he'd be wearing it even if it weren't a requirement. I wonder what he'd look like without it on—

Caleb has made me into this. He admitted it. I am everything he wanted me to be. And in the end, what did I get in return?

I knew he smiled, though I couldn't see it. A shiver, so strong my body nearly jerked toward his, ran down my spine.

"Your mother should be here today," says Agent Reed. His tone is detached, but he keeps glancing at me sidelong. He's eager for my reaction.

My heart stutters, but the jolt is over quickly and once again I simply feel...nothing. She is my mother; I am her daughter. It's inevitable. Eventually, I will have to see her. I know I'll have to say the words when I do. I'll have to tell her I don't want to go back with her. I'll have to tell her to forget all about me.

I've been grateful for the reprieve, but really – it's taken her five days to get here? Perhaps telling her to leave me alone will be easier than I thought. My feelings are ambiguous on the subject.

"Tell me about where you've been for almost four months. Tell me where you got the gun and the money, and I'll see to it your mom walks you out of here today," Reed says. His tone is salacious, as though he wants me to buy what he's selling.

No thanks. They know about the money – it didn't take them long. I look at him with confused eyes and an innocent head tilt. *Money?* He stares at me for a second, then looks down at his folders and writes something mysterious. Agent Reed isn't buying my bullshit. He isn't impressed. At least he isn't a complete fool.

His lips caressed the shell of my ear. "Are you going to answer? Or must I force you again?"

Tick-tock – I can't hide behind my silence forever. There are some pretty serious charges against me. I guess one does not simply walk into the U.S. from Mexico. I know I should cooperate, tell him the story and get him on my side, but I just can't do it. If I break my silence, I will never be able to leave this behind. My entire life will forever be overshadowed by the last four months. More than that, I don't know what the fuck to say! What can I say? For the hundredth time today, I miss Caleb.

Something drips onto my neck and I realize I'm crying. I wonder how long Agent Reed has been watching me, waiting for me to break down and give in. I feel lost, and his flicker of concern suddenly seems like a lifeline. It's hard not to see Caleb in his stead.

"Yes," I stammered. "I'm hungry."

It is a few long, tense, seconds before he breaks the unending silence. "You may not believe me, but I have your best interests in mind. If you won't try to help us help you, things will get out of your control. And quickly." He pauses. "I need information. If you're afraid, we can protect you, but you have to give us a sign of good faith. Every day you say

11

nothing, your window of opportunity shrinks." He stares at me, and I can feel him willing me with his powerful, dark eyes to give him the answers he is looking for. For a moment, I want to believe he really does want to help me. Could I afford to trust a stranger?

What did he want from me that he couldn't just take?

My mouth opens; words are crouched on the tip of my tongue. *He'll hurt him if you tell.* My mouth slams shut.

Agent Reed looks frustrated. As well he should be, I suppose. He takes another deep breath and delivers me a look that says, 'Okay, you asked for it.' He reaches down and grabs one of the brown folders he was looking at earlier. He opens it, stares at it, then at me.

He leaned forward and held the delicious smelling morsel to my lips.

For a moment he looks unsure, but then determined. He removes a sheet from the file and walks toward me, the paper held loosely in one hand. I almost don't want to see what it is, but I can't help it. I have to see. My heart lurches! Every fiber of my being is suddenly singing. Tears sting my eyes and a sound mimicking both sorrow and joy bubbles out my mouth before I can keep it in check.

It's a picture of Caleb! It's a picture of his beautiful, scolding face. I want it so badly I reach for it, fingers stretching to get closer to his image.

With an almost unabashed relief I opened my mouth, but he snatched it away.

"You know this man?" Agent Reed asks, but his tone makes it obvious he knows I do. This is his game. It's a good one. Through choked sobs, I reach for the photo again. Agent Reed keeps the photo just out of my reach.

"You son of a bitch," I whisper hoarsely, staring at that one piece of paper. If I blink, would it disappear?

He offered again.

I don't reach for the photo again, but I can't keep from looking at it. Caleb is younger in the photo, but not by much. He's still my Caleb. His blond hair is being blown up in the back, and his Caribbean-blue eyes are glorious as they scowl at the camera. His mouth, so full and perfect for kissing, is set in an annoyed line across his perfect face. He wears a buttoned-up shirt, in white, and the obviously-billowing wind offers tantalizing glimpses of his sun-kissed throat. It's my Caleb. I want my Caleb. I glare at Agent Reed. With my rage in every syllable, I break my vow of silence. "Give. Me. That."

Agent Reed's eyes go wide for a fraction of a second. Smug satisfaction is there, then gone. Round

13

one goes to the Agent. "So you *do* know him?" he mocks.

I glare at him.

He steps closer, picture held out.

And again.

I go for it, and he pulls it back.

Each time I crawled closer and closer, until I was pressed between his legs, my hands on either side of his body.

Caleb taught me a few things about starting fights I can't win. He would want me to use my head and exploit anything I have to offer to get what I want. I force myself to portray calmness and sorrow. The sadness comes easy.

"I...I *knew* him." I purposely stare at my lap and let my tears fall.

"Knew him?" Agent Reed asks curiously. I nod and let sobs fill the room.

"What happened to him?" he asks. I want him curious.

"Give me the picture," I whisper.

"Tell me what I want to know," he counters. I know I have him where I want him.

"He...." I am overcome by grief. I don't have to manufacture my pain...I am my pain. "He died in my fucking arms." My mind immediately recalls seeing Caleb, expression blank, his body covered in dirt, and blood. It was the moment I lost him. Only

14

hours before, he'd held me in his arms and I had thought everything was finally going to be okay. One knock on the door...and everything changed.

Agent Reed takes a tentative step forward. "This isn't easy for you, I can tell, but I need to know how, Miss Ruiz."

"Give me the picture," I sob. He takes another step.

"Tell me how," he whispers. He's played this game before.

I look up and glower at him from under my tear-soaked lashes. "Protecting me."

"From what?" He steps closer, so close, and so eager.

"From Rafiq."

Without another word, Agent Reed turns away to remove another photo from the file and turns it toward me. "This man?"

I hiss. Actually, fucking hiss. We're both shocked by my reaction. I never knew I could be so feral. I rather like it. I feel capable of anything.

Suddenly I threw my arms up around his hand, wrapped my mouth around his fingers to get the food away from him. Oh my god, so good.

Agent Reed is close, and he isn't prepared when I grab him by the collar of his suit and crush his fucking mouth with mine. He drops the folder.

Mine!

15

Despite his shock, Agent Reed is able to wrestle me onto the bed. He snaps his cuffs on my wrist and secures me to the bed. Before I can reach for the folder, he snaps it away.

He moved quickly; his fingers found my tongue and pinched viciously while his other hand dug into the sides of my neck.

Confusion and anger twist his features. "What the hell do you think you're doing?" he whispers and wipes his lips slowly, looking at his fingers as though the answer is somehow written across them.

The food fell from between my lips to the floor, and I howled around his fingers at the loss.

When I try to speak, I scream my frustration instead, tears of anger filling my eyes.

"You're very proud and very spoiled, and I'm going to beat it out of you twice."

When the nurse scrambles in, bewildered and a hand to her heart, Agent Reed politely tells her to get lost.
"Better?" he asks me, raising a brow.
I stare at my cuffed hands. "Not even close…"

Vivisected. On-off-buzz-buzz-on-off. Caleb, I miss you.

16

"Help me catch him, Olivia." He pauses; his expression is calculated, but he needs something too. "I know I'm not a nice guy, but maybe you need someone like me in your corner."

Caleb.

Go away, go away, go away.

My heart aches. "Please...give me the picture," I plead.

Agent Reed steps within my line of sight, but I only stare at his tie. "If I give you the picture, will you tell me what happened? Will you answer my questions?"

I suck my bottom lip, running my tongue across it as I hold it between my teeth. It's now or never, and never isn't truly an option. The inevitable is upon me. "Uncuff me."

The agent's eyes flicker over me. I know his mind must be racing with ideas on how to make me talk. Trust is a two-way street. Show me yours, and I'll show you mine. He steps toward me, slowly, and cautiously removes the cuff from my wrist. "Well?" he asks.

"I'll tell you. Only you. In exchange, you'll give me any pictures you have of him and get me out of here." My heart is beating a frantic tattoo in my chest, but I gather my courage. I'm a survivor. I hold my hand out. "Give me the picture."

Agent Reed's mouth twists with disappointment at the knowledge he cannot win this point from me. Reluctantly, he gathers his folder and hands me the photo of Caleb. "You'll have to tell me what you know first, and then I can talk to my superiors and make a deal. I promise I'll do whatever I can to protect you, but you have to start talking. You have to tell me why it looks like you're more involved in this than any eighteen-year-old-girl has any right to be."

No one else exists as I stare at Caleb's face. I sob and trace the familiar lines of his face. *I love you, Caleb.*

"I'm gonna go get some coffee," says Agent Reed, his voice resigned but still determined, "but when I come back, I expect answers." I don't notice when he leaves, or care. But I know he's giving me time to grieve in peace.

He walked out of the room and shut the door. This time I heard the lock.

For the first time in five days, I am left alone. I suspect it will be the last time, for a while, Caleb and I will have to spend together. With trembling lips, I kiss him.

18

2

It seemed to Caleb that the nature of human beings revolved around one empirical truth: we want what we *cannot* have. For Eve, it was the fruit of the forbidden tree. For Caleb, it was Livvie.

The night had been a fitful one. Livvie whimpered and trembled in her sleep, and Caleb's chest seemed to contract with every sound. He had given her more morphine, and after some time, her body seemed to quiet down – though there still seemed to be frenzied movement behind her eyelids. Nightmares, he assumed. Without fear of awkwardness or reproach, he felt a compulsion to touch her. He held her close and comforted them both, but he could not get Rafiq's text out of his mind.

How soon would he land in Mexico?

How would he react to Livvie and her broken condition?

How long did he have with Livvie before she was taken away from him?

Taken. Away. Strange, horrible, and foreign words. He closed his eyes and set his mind to reality. *You're giving her away.* He opened his eyes. *And the sooner, the better.*

He couldn't argue with logic. It had kept him alive for longer than he could remember. He was cold and efficient. He did not dally with questions of morality. Still, he *wanted* to argue with logic. He wanted to find reason in what he felt to pacify the hardened man inside his head. But he couldn't. The truth was – he wanted her. The truth was also that it was never meant to be. He pulled Livvie even closer, careful not to crush her ribs or injured shoulder, and buried his nose in her long hair, trying to smell her scent.

He had told her he wasn't her Prince Charming, but what he hadn't said was he wished he could be. Once upon a time, he may have been...normal. Before he had been stolen, before the beatings and the rapes and the killing – he could have been something different than what he was. He had never thought like this, never wondered about the roads taken or not taken. His life was lived in the present and without the angst of fantasies. But he fantasized now. He fantasized about being the sort of man who could give Livvie all she ever wanted. The kind of man she could....

But you're not that man, are you?

Caleb sighed, knowing the answer. The fantasies of others had never confused him, but his own left him dissatisfied with the life he'd accepted and even enjoyed from time to time. He wanted it to go away, the longing, and the feelings of regret. He wanted to live for the hunt and kill – it had been the only thing to make sense to him for so very long. Even in those moments of darkness, when his drive had flagged and he questioned the possibility of ever finding Vladek – he had never thought to be anything other than what he was.

Yet, in just three and a half weeks with Livvie, most of which she spent locked in a dark room, it all seemed to be evaporating. It was stupid, naïve, and dangerous. A person was incapable of changing fundamentally in such a short period of time. He wasn't different. And yet, he *felt* different and not even logic could alter that. If it hadn't been for the memories, those awful, fucking memories of Narweh, beating and raping him. If he hadn't seen Livvie, covered in blood, bruised and shuddering in that biker's arms – he wouldn't feel like his entire world was caving in on him.

God! What he'd done to make them pay. It had been the kind of rage he hadn't felt in a very long time. He didn't regret it either. He'd savored the look on those bikers' faces as he'd plunged the knife deep into Tiny, spraying blood all over himself, the walls, everything.

Revenge! That was his purpose.

It felt good to have a purpose. He was certain he'd feel the rush again. He'd feel it the second Vladek's eyes dawned with realization, and it would carry through until Vladek took his last, gasping breath. Caleb shivered. He wanted to feel the satisfaction of that moment. He wanted to feel it more than anything. He wanted it more than he wanted the girl.

She'll hate you. Forever. She'll want vengeance.

"I know," Caleb whispered into the darkness of the room. Unable to resist the numbness sleep offered, he let himself be carried into the dark.

21

***

The boy refused to bathe.

"Caleb, I will not tell you again! You stink! You stink, horribly. It's been days and you're still covered in blood. Someone will see you, and then you will have real trouble on your hands, boy."

"I am *Kéleb*. Dog! I've ripped my master to pieces. I've tasted blood and I like it! I will not wash it off. I want to wear it forever, as a badge of honor."

Rafiq's dark face became drawn, eyes narrowed.

"Bathe. Now."

The boy squared his young shoulders and glowered at his new master. Rafiq was handsome – much, much, more so than Narweh. The trained whore in him was stirred by this. Rafiq was also much stronger than Narweh, capable of more damage, but the boy would not allow himself to be afraid, to cower before a man set on being his new master. He was a man now, a man! He could make his own damn decisions about when he'd wash the blood from his face.

"No!"

Rafiq stood. His eyes were hard and menacing. The boy swallowed deep and hard, and despite his best efforts, he could not deny the fear he felt. As Rafiq approached, the boy quelled his desire to shrink away. Rafiq's calloused hand landed firmly on the back of the boy's neck and squeezed with enough force to make him wince, but not enough to trigger his fight or flight instinct.

22

Rafiq leaned and growled into the boy's ear, "Wash yourself now, or I will strip you down and scour your skin until you would never dream of defying me again."

Tears stung the boy's eyes. Not because he was in pain, but because he was suddenly very afraid and wished Rafiq was not angry with him. He had no one else. He was still young, unable to truly fend for himself. His race and appearance put him at a sharp disadvantage with the locals. Unless he wanted to be a whore again, Rafiq was all he had.

"I don't want to," he pleaded with a whisper. The hand at the back of his neck loosened a little and the boy screwed his eyes shut to stave off the threat of tears. He refused to cry.

"Why?"

"I want to know he's dead. It was over so fast, Rafiq. It was over so fast and he...he deserved to suffer! I wanted him to suffer, Rafiq. All the pain he put me through, all those things...I wanted him to feel all those things. If I wash away the blood..." The boy's eyes pleaded with Rafiq.

"It will be like it never happened?" Rafiq said, softly.

"Yes." It was a choked sound.

Rafiq sighed. "No one knows how you feel more than I do, Caleb. But you *cannot* continue to defy me; you cannot continue to act like a petulant boy! You are not *Kéleb* any longer. Wash. I promise you, Narweh will still be dead when you are finished."

The boy pushed away from the grip on the back of his neck. "No! No! No! I won't do it."

23

Rafiq's face went from cautiously warm to stone cold. "Have it your way, *Kéleb*." His grip on the boy's neck intensified, and as Caleb winced with pain and tried to struggle away, Rafiq's other hand came down with a meaty thud across the boy's face. Caleb was not new to pain – he could easily take a harsh slap to his face – but he was stunned nonetheless. He tried to stagger away from Rafiq, but he was held firmly in the older man's grip.

"Bathe!" Rafiq growled with enough force to vibrate Caleb's head.

"No!" Caleb cried, tears falling down his face.

Rafiq bent his body, threw his shoulder into Caleb's stomach, and hoisted him over his shoulder. Ignoring the pounding fists on his back, he strode purposefully into the bathroom and all but tossed the boy inside. He ignored the angry screaming and invective curses coming from Caleb's twisted mouth and turned the knob to release cold water into the tub.

Caleb's body jolted at the feeling of cold water soaking his clothes and touching his skin. Unable to resist and full of anger, he managed to punch Rafiq in the face and scramble halfway out of the tub. He had only ignited more of Rafiq's rage. He felt Rafiq's hand fisting in his hair, then the pain on his scalp and in his neck as he was wrenched backward. The bathtub filled around him as Rafiq pressed him to the bottom of the tub.

Fear and dread gripped him.

24

"You will obey me, boy! You will! Or I will drown you, here and now. You belong to me. Understand?"

Caleb's mouth and nose filled with water. He could not make out words clearly, and he heard only the angry shouting of the man holding him prisoner in the water. The feeling of impending death held him paralyzed with fear. Anything. He would give anything to never feel this brand of fear again.

Air!

Caleb gasped and heaved as he was pulled up, his arms scrambling for purchase and finding Rafiq's shoulders. He pulled himself toward the warmth and safety of Rafiq's body. He fought the arms trying to shrug him off. Caleb thought nothing of his panicked cries – he only wanted out of the tub. He wanted only to breathe and to be warm.

Strong arms gripped his shoulders and shook.

"Calm, Caleb. Calm. Breathe," Rafiq said. His tone was soothing despite its intensity. "Be calm, Caleb. I will not put you in the water again if you're prepared to listen. Still!"

Caleb worked hard to do as Rafiq asked. He held firm to Rafiq's shoulders, telling himself over and again he could not be thrown into the water so long as he held on. Caleb stilled and shuddered, taking his first calm breath. He took another and another, until at last, only his anger remained. Slowly, he released Rafiq's shoulders and slumped into the tub. He shivered at the cold, his lip trembling, but he wouldn't ask Rafiq for hot water.

"I hate you," Caleb spat, teeth chattering.

25

Rafiq's eyes were calm and collected. With a smirk, he stood and left the room.

Caleb's eyes stung with angry tears and because he was alone, he let them fall. Sure Rafiq would not return, he turned the tap for the hot water and huddled close to it, hoping it would warm him all the faster. He dragged his sopping wet clothes over his head and threw them in a heap on the bathroom floor with a sense of satisfaction over the mess he was making.

Pure, unfettered anger rolled through his body like a physical thing. Pulling his knees to his chin, he bit into the flesh of his knees, scraping them with his teeth. The tears would not abate! They continued to leak from his eyes. He felt weak and pitiful. He could not stop Rafiq from doing this to him. He bit harder, longing for the physical pain to release him from his suffering.

He wanted to scream.

He wanted to hit things.

He wanted to kill again.

He scraped his fingernails along the flesh of his arms, simultaneously feeling pain and relief as his skin broke and small drops of blood appeared on his flesh. He repeated the process – more pain, more release. In the water, Narweh's blood swirled with his. He didn't know what to feel at the sight of it. Numbness assailed him. He stared, transfixed as the blood of the man who tortured him for so long dissipated into the water surrounding him.

Who was he now?

He was no longer *Kéleb*, no longer Narweh's *Dog*. It was the only name he had ever known, the only thing he had ever been.

He's dead. He's truly dead.

His thoughts returned to Tehran, returned to the night he murdered his owner, his tormentor, and his caretaker. *Kéleb* had lifted the gun, and Narweh's face had registered shock, then fear – only for a moment. Then, he had given *Kéleb* the look – the one to remind him he was less than human in Narweh's eyes – and then *Kéleb* squeezed the trigger. He was thrown by the force of the powerful weapon.

He missed it.

He missed the moment of Narweh's death.

Bits of gore sprayed his hair, face and chest, but he did not register them. He scrambled toward the body. No gurgling, no gasping…only a corpse. And he felt…sorrow. Narweh had never begged. He had never knelt at *Kéleb's* feet and begged his mercy and forgiveness.

No, Narweh had never begged, but he was dead. And under the sorrow, there was blessed relief.

But you have a new owner now, don't you? Caleb.

He screwed his eyes shut for a moment and took a deep breath. Then, he did as Rafiq asked and washed his old life from his skin.

***

27

Caleb woke, startled and anxious. He reached for the dream as it raced to abandon his conscious mind. There was something...something important. It was gone. Frustrated, it took him a moment to realize Kitten's eyes were scanning him. She looked like shit. The bruises on her face were much more pronounced than they had been the night before. Her eyes were swollen and purple against her russet skin. Her nose, free of tape, also looked inflamed. Under the damage, he could still see Kitten, surviving despite it all.

His heart again – it seemed to pinch in his chest. He kept it from registering on his face. He struggled for words. After their encounter last night and still reeling from Rafiq's text, what could he possibly say? All he had to offer was more bad news.

He settled for stating the obvious. "It's morning."

Kitten's brows furrowed and she winced from the effort. "I know. I've been up for a while," she said morosely.

Caleb glanced away, feigning interest in his surroundings. He'd nearly fucked up—nearly fucked her. That could *never* happen. A sense of urgency filled him. They had to leave this place, as soon as possible, but he couldn't make himself say the words. The night had been intense.

"Are you...in pain? Can you sit up?" Caleb whispered.

"I don't know. I'm in too much pain to try," Kitten whispered just as softly.

They stared at each other a second too long, gazes touching too closely before they both quickly, almost frantically, darted their eyes away, choosing to look anywhere but at one another.

"Or maybe I'm just too terrified to think about what's going to happen today. Or tomorrow. Maybe I just want to go back to sleep and wake up from my life." There was pain in her voice and he knew it wasn't physical. Caleb glanced in her direction and noticed she wasn't crying. She was simply staring off into space, too numb for tears, Caleb supposed. He knew the feeling well.

And now this. Limbo. A state of existence he'd never experienced. He felt immobilized by what had happened, about everything, because as fucked up as it had been before, he'd been in control and removed. Now, their situation was untenable. Their continued existence around each other would only cause more pain and agony. Caleb scratched his face, digging his fingers into his stubble as if, by distraction, he would never have to look at Kitten again, never have to tell her they had to leave, and that despite last night…she was still his prisoner. He was still her master.

"Fuck it," she huffed, her voice strong, as though awakening from the numb void and becoming vibrant and willful again. "Let's get this over with, Caleb. What the hell happens now?"

Caleb. He just looked at her. There it was again, the use of his name. He knew he should correct her, force her to address him as Master and restore the delineation, the barriers between them, but he just couldn't, fucking, do it. He was exhausted! So, damn, exhausted.

"Breakfast, I suppose. Afterward, we have to leave. Beyond that, I don't care to discuss it," he said. He tried to force some semblance of levity, but it fell flat and Kitten knew it.

"And last night?" She tried to keep her tone neutral, but Caleb knew her too well now and he didn't have to guess at what she was really asking. She wanted to know if she meant something to him, if the fact they'd almost...*fucked*, changed his mind about selling her into slavery. The answer was yes... and no. Vladek still needed to pay, and Kitten still had her part to play. They were past the point of no return.

"I told you everything you wanted to know." He paused, tempering his tone. "I'm not saying any more. So, stop asking." He bolted out of bed and rushed toward the bathroom. Inside, he avoided his reflection and searched for a toothbrush. Two of them sat near the sink. He chose the least chewed and put some toothpaste on it. Germs were the least of his concerns. Although he'd showered only hours ago, he turned on the hot water, only the hot water, and set about stripping from his borrowed clothes.

The water scalded him, and his own body fought to remove itself from the punishing temperature of the water – but Caleb wouldn't allow it. He forced himself to feel the stinging pain. He gritted his teeth and ignored the fact his skin would probably blister in places. Placing his hands against the shower wall, he let the torrid water and multiple shower heads beat his confusion out of him. His back felt tight, already sensitive. The scars he wore tingled and came alive.

It was the feeling he was looking for. The scars reminded him who he was, where he'd come from, and why he needed to move forward with his mission. The water stung against his ass and his genitals, and he felt the lump in his throat building and rising into his mouth. He would never let it out. He would swallow it down and keep it prisoner in his chest. He allowed his hands to come down and shield his cock and balls from the punishing heat of the water.

There was a knock on the door and Caleb's head whipped toward it. Kitten had stepped inside, announcing herself with a knock but not waiting for his answer. Shock assailed him. He couldn't keep it from his face and without thinking he scrambled to turn the cold water on. This was private!

Well, at least she didn't run. But where would she have gone, anyway?

Kitten looked at him…everywhere. Even through the intense amount of steam, he could see her fierce blush. Blushing virgin or not, her eyes did not deviate from his person.

Their eyes finally met.

"I…" Kitten cleared her throat and began again, but nothing came. She wasn't blushing anymore.

"Did you need something?" Caleb snapped. He'd been trying to rebuild his composure, but her interruption left him feeling exposed somehow, even vulnerable, and he didn't like it. However, she was also naked, never having dressed again since last night, and that was confusing as well. His eyes took her in, inch by inch, and all sense evaporated. Beneath his hands, his cock stirred. He wanted to wince at the stinging sensation of his punished flesh stretching and expanding, but it didn't hurt as much .as it should have because pain and pleasure were suddenly almost one and the same.

Kitten straightened her spine, her posture confident. "Yes. I need something. Lots of somethings. Where do you want me to start?"

He stared at her, shocked. Had she really just said that? To him? He knew he should be angry, but instead, he turned his head to hide a smile. This banter was familiar, and oddly, it quelled whatever distracting emotions had just been storming through him moments before. He knew this part of the game —it was his game, no matter how much Kitten participated. He spoke to the shower wall and tried to keep the amusement from his voice. "Well, can it wait until I'm at least out of the shower?" And because he couldn't help himself, he added, "Unless you're looking to climb in here and return last night's favor?" He hazarded a glance in her direction.

She blushed heatedly, but held herself high. "Actually? Sort of. I mean...no, but...." She huffed, "I would like to take a shower and since I'm practically crippled, I could use your fucking help. But not if you're going to be an asshole about it." She nodded, as if to say: *There, I said it.*

Caleb couldn't resist laughing, his mood much improved, and he decided to let her antics amuse him. It was much safer and less complicated. He knew his reaction was counter to the one he would have normally had, another day, another situation, another girl. But right now, he was just fucking relieved to feel something similar to joy, instead of what he'd woke up to. He grabbed it and held on tight.

He opened the shower door and gave her his best and most salacious smile. "Well, come on in, then. I'll try my best not to be an asshole."

She didn't smile back, opting instead to hold on to her anger. It was a sort of challenge to him and he accepted it, because one day her hate for him might keep her alive. She needed him, and he was determined to do what he could for her. He owed her *at least* that much.

He stepped backward into the shower as she approached. Her head was down and her cheeks were tinted with pink, but also hues of purple, green, yellow and blue as she carefully maneuvered toward him. Suddenly, flashes of her beaten and bleeding body, and of his own past, merged like one vision, like one person reliving a horrible memory. Powerful emotion swept through him, and he was glad the steam of the shower and the sound of the water pounding against the walls hid it all.

Caleb blinked, fighting the thoughts and voices streaming through his brain. When Kitten reached out toward him, using his arm and shoulder as a brace, he only saw and thought about her.

"Jesus, it's like a sauna in here," said Kitten. She looked up, her expression strained. "Can you make it so it isn't so hot?"

"I don't know. Can you say please?" Caleb's tone still held humor, but unease was creeping its way back in. The feeling of *differentness* between them hung heavy and dense in the air.

Kitten finally gave him the tiniest of smiles, just a quirk of her full lips, but her eyes were direct. "*Pretty please*, Caleb?" And instantly, she was the girl from the night before: seductive, predatory... Livvie.

Caleb slowly sucked in a breath and turned to adjust the water. He didn't realize his error until he heard her startled gasp and felt her hand on his back. "Don't touch it," he growled and turned to face her. Her eyes were wide, filled with both terror and horror, and her hand covered her mouth. Caleb clenched his fists and she turned her face away from him. It hurt, the idea she believed he would hit her with a closed fist. He strained to unfurl his fingers from his palm, but it became easier as he watched her relax with his progress.

When he finally stood in front of her, hands open at his sides, his face one of deliberate calm – she finally brought her hand down from her mouth and smoothed the fear and horror from her eyes. She studied him warily, looking for a way to approach him without setting him off. Cautiously, she reached for his hand. Her fingers brushed against his, silently asking permission.

He pulled his arm back slowly, a few inches, issuing his denial of the intimacy between them. He watched as she stared down toward her feet but inched forward and traced her index finger along Caleb's wrist.

"Come on, Caleb," she whispered softly. Her head remained down, allowing him the privacy of his reaction.

His skin crawled. If she weren't so injured, he might have pushed her away. Instead, he let her keep coming. Two fingers touched him now; they trailed slowly from his wrist toward his hand. He allowed it. With a deep breath, he let her fingers find his and interlace. Caleb stared over her head.

His hand was lifted. He felt his fingers brush against Livvie's ribs. And then her shoulder. And at last, her cheek.

Here.

They hurt me*, here.*

Caleb's body swayed a little.

"Kiss me," she whispered. It was an offer of distraction.

He took it.

Caleb's chest rattled with the force of his sigh and his lips swept down to meet Livvie's upturned face. They moaned into each other's mouths. *Fuck! Yes!* He wanted nothing more than to hoist Livvie up into his arms, slam her against the shower wall, and fuck her until he forgot all of his frustration, anger, lust, and remorse.

Unlacing their fingers, Caleb reached for Livvie's breasts with both hands and squeezed. His touch was rough, needy, but she responded with equal intensity. His thumbs traced her areolas. Her flesh puckered beneath his skilled touch. The pebbled tips of her nipples dragged across the pads of his thumbs and she keened softly into Caleb's ravenous mouth.

Livvie's trembling hands found his waist. Her fingers gripped his hips and her fingernails dug into his sensitive flesh. It was Caleb's turn to groan. His flesh was tender from the hot water, but he welcomed the pain, especially when it mingled with the pleasure. He wanted more. He wanted it all.

Caleb stepped forward. Livvie stepped back without breaking their feverish kiss. It was a dance their bodies already knew. She nipped at Caleb's tongue, his lips, stunning him for short seconds before she slid her tongue along his. With her back against the wall, Caleb took the opportunity to come closer, kiss harder. His cock brushed her belly and he thrust against soft, slippery flesh.

"Ow!" Livvie cried. She broke the kiss and braced her arms around her body, bending slightly as she processed her pain.

Caleb instantly backed away. "Shit. I didn't think," he panted, clenching his hands with his arms by his side. "Are you okay?"

"Yeah," she said, but didn't sound it. "I'm okay, just give me a second."

Caleb felt silly, hovering over her with his massive erection between them. What the fuck was he even thinking?!? He shouldn't be doing this. He vacillated between what he should be doing and what he wanted to do. He should stop. "We need to stop."

One of Livvie's hands reached up and Caleb gave her his arm to use as a support. He wasn't expecting it when her other hand wrapped around his cock and squeezed. Caleb groaned loudly.

"No," she said. Her tone brooked no argument. "I don't want to stop. I don't want to think. I want to stay here and pretend nothing's waiting for us when we get out." Livvie's words seemed to touch something deep inside him, something he couldn't touch on his own. Of course, there was also the very physical touch of her palm against his cock.

He hissed through his gritted teeth. Her hand was wrapped tight around him, her fingers not long enough to touch. She squeezed again. More pleasure. More pain.

"We can't. I'll hurt you," Caleb said.

Livvie's hand released him, just barely, and the sensation of blood rushing toward the head of his cock was almost enough to make him thrust into her hand. He moaned as her fingertips skimmed his hard flesh. "Well, I can *see* that, Caleb. Are they all…like this? I mean…are all men this big?"

Caleb put his hand over hers and held it still. "Don't talk about other men right now, Livvie. Not when you have my dick in your hand." He wasn't jealous. He wasn't the kind to care enough for jealousy. But her question reminded him how much he knew about other men and he didn't fucking like it.

"Sorry," she whispered and blushed. "I guess no one would like that, would they?"

Livvie smiled at Caleb cautiously, beautifully, despite the bruises.

My tough girl.

Livvie's brown eyes still drew his interest, more than ever before. As he let himself take his fill, her eyes seemed to do the same. Her fingers twitched beneath his hand and against his cock. He moaned and watched her pupils dilate, deepening the depths of her stare; he wondered if his did the same.

Caleb watched as her kitten tongue slid slowly across her bottom lip. Slowly, the supple flesh disappeared into her mouth and he watched as she bit down. He swallowed hard. "No," he said, his voice hoarse, "especially when in this sort of position." He smiled at her. "Still, I assure you, my dick is very special."

Livvie grinned. "I can't believe...you had this in me."

Caleb's hips rocked forward at her words. His cock remembered fucking her in the ass – it recalled the tightness, and warmth, waiting inside her. He remembered her whimpers and sighs, the way she undulated against his chest when she came apart under him.

"I can't. We can't." Caleb was surprised to hear the rasp in his voice. He wanted this bad and he was doing a poor job of hiding it.

Livvie stepped closer to him, until her head touched his chest. Caleb's arms went around her, as if by instinct. "I want to make you come," she whispered against his chest. Shyly. Seductively. Her hand still held him and she slid her hand up and down his length.

Caleb went up on his toes and groaned, unable to resist the delicious friction of her hand, but he fought the urge to thrust against the softness of her breasts as they met with the head of his cock.

"Keep doing that," he rasped. He placed one hand against the wall behind Livvie, his arm extended as a reminder not to crush her. His other arm held her loosely against him. He noted her injured shoulder was braced against him, her hand on his tender, scalded hip.

She stroked him. He opened his mouth and silently drew breath to keep from moaning, his stomach tightening sharply. Her touch felt inexperienced, disjointed – like heaven one second and an assault the next – but he was enjoying it. She was touching him because she wanted to, and for no other reason. *What the fuck are you doing to me, Livvie?*

The next minute, his mind went blank. Unable to resist, he rocked into her hand, his hips snapping forward to touch his cock against Livvie's amazing fucking tits.

You're ruining my life…

So soft. She was so fucking soft.

"Oh…god," escaped his mouth, but Caleb didn't give a shit. Against his chest, Livvie panted with her arousal and exertion. The fingers against Caleb's hip tightened and pulled his hips closer and then pushed them back.

More. Oh fuck! Please, more.

"Harder Livvie, hold me harder," he panted. Livvie complied, sending Caleb into a state of nirvana. He felt like he was going to burn from the inside out. "Don't stop. Just like that."

"Oh, god, Caleb. You're so hard," Livvie's voice was pure lust. "I want you to come. I want to watch you come." She tried to pull back, but Caleb held her closer.

He shook his head. "Don't watch me, watch my cock. Watch it come all over you."

Livvie's hand tightened and sped up.

Caleb couldn't hold it in any longer. With a cry, he rose up on his toes and came all over Livvie's bountiful tits. As he panted and tried to keep from passing out, Caleb listened to Livvie squeal in shock.

"Oh. My. God!" She whispered and laughed. She looked down at her body, her expression priceless. "It's all over the place. Eww. Caleb – it's...*sticky*."

Caleb laughed and watched as she poked at his semen and tried to wash it off.

He snickered. "It's stickier when it's wet," he warned. He turned and reached for the soap. He stilled at the touch of her hand against his back. He sighed deeply. In the glow of his orgasm, he didn't have the energy to argue or fight.

He tensed as she came closer. He shut his eyes while she traced the harsh white lines crisscrossing his back. His skin was red from the heat of the water and he knew the scars were more pronounced because of it. This wasn't the first time anyone had seen his scars. He wasn't necessarily ashamed of

40

them, and it wasn't like he hid his body from lovers. But he never talked about it, not ever.

"What happened?" The whisper was so soft, Caleb might have missed it if he didn't know it was coming.

"Fucked up childhood," he said tonelessly.

Livvie's breath skated across his skin. She kissed his scars.

Livvie got in the car and slammed the door. She tried to hide it, but Caleb saw the way she winced and rubbed her collarbone.

"Happy? Have we taught the door a lesson?" Caleb taunted through a gentle laugh.

Her eyes narrowed in his direction, her rage unmistakable. "I can't believe what you did to those people, Caleb. You're just...never mind. Can we just go please?"

Caleb's ire, dormant because of his unexpected orgasm earlier, now rose to the surface. "Which part can't you believe?" he snapped, jamming the key in the ignition of the stolen car and turning it. "The part where I rescued you from a bunch of would-be rapists that beat you half to death? Or perhaps the part where – at great risk to myself – I kidnapped a doctor to help save you? Which part is it, because I'd like to know which of those things I should never do for you again?" He threw the vehicle in gear and took off. For a moment, he didn't care Livvie had been jostled in her seat.

Silence.

Caleb sat back, satisfied. It wasn't like he killed them. The doctor and his wife were free to live their lives, no worse for wear. Livvie had been mortified to find the couple exactly as he had left them the night before – taped to their dining room chairs. Granted, the fact they had urinated on themselves during the course of the evening was distasteful, but they were otherwise unharmed. In a different situation, he might not have let them off so easy. He wondered how Livvie would have reacted to such a thing.

"Thank you," Livvie muttered from the passenger seat.

"For what?" Caleb was still irritated.

"For saving my life. Even if you're just going to put it in danger again," she whispered.

Caleb had no response. It was exactly what he was going to do. Drive her to Tuxtepec, bring her to Rafiq, train her, sell her…lose her forever.

And kill Vladek. Don't forget that part.

The thought didn't assuage the guilt taking up residence inside him. His heart was heavy, his thoughts scrambled. Still, he couldn't allow himself to show weakness. All the turmoil within him had to be hidden, from everyone.

"You're welcome, Kitten," he scoffed. From the corner of his eye, he watched Kitten swipe at her eye and flick her tears toward the floor of the car. *Ruining my life!*

Things had been so much easier in the shower, easier when it was just the two of them and the outside world seemed irrelevant and beyond the reach of his thoughts. The world was in the car with them now, and it was Kitten who seemed beyond reach.

After she'd made him feel more pleasure than he'd ever had – with a hand job, no less – he'd reveled in soaping her skin, watching intently as water sluiced over the taut peaks of her nipples, down the slopes of her tan belly and hips, and descended past the raven triangle between her thighs. He'd touched her there as well, sifted his fingers through her sparse hair until he felt her slippery flesh part under his fingers. It was like opening a flower, her petals pink and vibrant, shiny with dew and lust.

He'd knelt before her, worshipful. She'd opened for him, hungry, full of want. His every sense had been engaged and focused on her. He could smell her arousal; he could see the way her flesh darkened, and against his fingers he had felt her tremble. He had heard her soft whimpers. She had begged him to taste her. Slowly, he had licked her tiny bud.

Oh! How she had wanted him.

She'd spread wider, placed her fingers in his hair and pulled him closer.

"Beg me." He'd whispered the words against her.

"Please, Caleb. Please, lick me."

He'd obeyed. One long, wet lick across her open petals.

She sobbed, "Again. Please. Again."

"Say you want me to lick your pussy."

She gripped his hair tighter. "Caleb!" she'd grated.

"Say it. I want to hear more filth from your mouth."

She hesitated. Her hips rocked toward his mouth, but he'd do no more than kiss her with his lips.

"Please, Caleb. L-lick my…pussy."

Nothing had ever turned him on more. He'd pushed her legs wide, cradling her thighs on his shoulders, and pressed his face into her pussy. Lick her? He fucking devoured her.

Pain had no longer seemed to be an issue for her as she undulated and rocked her hips against his rapacious mouth. Her hands held his head, pushing him deeper, demanding more, even as he gave and gave.

When she'd come, her pussy had gripped his tongue. Wet, pulsing flesh fluttering against wet, pulsing flesh. Her juices saturated his mouth, a rush of honey he not only swallowed, but sucked from her flesh long after she had begged him to stop.

But that had been then. This was now.

Caleb sighed heavily, frustrated by the turn of events. More bothersome than Kitten's demeanor was the prospect of Rafiq's impending visit. He had tried to call Rafiq earlier, while Kitten was getting dressed and combing her hair, but there had been no answer. Caleb could only assume Rafiq was either on his way or ignoring him. He hoped it was the latter. The last thing he needed after what was sure to be a very long and taxing car trip was a confrontation with Rafiq.

Their relationship was beyond complicated. Rafiq was many things to Caleb. At one time, his guardian. Later, a friend. Now? Rafiq called him *brother*. But Rafiq was also much more. Rafiq held a power and a sway over Caleb he'd never felt comfortable with. Caleb had been a difficult teenager. After Narweh, he was left with a lot of fear

45

that had turned to anger. There had been times when
they had argued and Caleb had seen things in Rafiq
he wished never to see again.

Rafiq would stop at nothing to have his plans
carried through. Everyone was expendable; anyone,
collateral damage. If it ever came down to it, Rafiq
would kill him – therefore, Caleb had to be prepared
to strike first. The truce lay in the fact neither of
them would relish the task.

As Caleb made his way through the narrow
roads, he spared a thought to think about what he
would do if Rafiq were waiting for them in
Tuxtepec. He gripped the wheel tighter. He knew.
That was the problem. He knew exactly what would
happen.

Prepare her.

"It's going to take us all day and part of
tomorrow to reach our destination." He relaxed his
grip on the wheel and leaned into the back of his
seat. He had to stop being soft with her. He had to
make her tough, make her hard, and he knew better
than most how the coldness of reality would sober
any wide-eyed hopeful. The first step had been
telling her the truth about her future, but he had to
push her further. He had to make her understand.
There was no future for them. "I suggest you take
the time and wrap your mind around the seriousness
of your situation. I forgive you for running away, but
only because fate has done a better job of punishing
you than I could." Caleb kept his eyes forward,
refusing to acknowledge the heartbroken girl next to
him. He didn't have to see her to know how much

his words hurt her. An echo of her pain seemed to reverberate through him. At least, that's what he wanted to believe it was – an echo.

He recalled the press of her lips against his scars. *She kisses my scars and I create new ones for her.*

"You're still going through with it?" Kitten's tone was anguished, but also angry and determined.

He told himself over and over: *She's plotting her revenge already. She'll never care for you.* If he reminded himself enough, perhaps he could get the truth through his head. So, he repeated the words like a mantra. *She's playing you. She's just biding time until she can be rid of you.*

"I never said otherwise, Kitten. I've broken no promises to you," Caleb replied, his tone harsh and unyielding. He had to slam the door shut on everything between them. It was the only way to move forward and ensure her survival. *It's your survival, too.*

Caleb expected her sobs at any moment. It was their dance: she fought him, he hurt her, and she cried…he felt like shit. Repeat. He was surprised to hear the steel in her voice when she snapped at him.

"You promised me if I did as you asked, I would always come out better for it. Do you still believe that, Caleb? Do you really think selling me into sexual slavery will make me better?"

"It's done," he said.

"Fuck you," she spat.

Anger surged and flared on the heels of his guilt. He had promised her, but not in the way she proposed. "I mean to teach you how to survive this. I have always intended to arm you with what you'll need. In that way, *yes*," he hissed, "I'll keep my promise. But I've made other promises as well – to someone who has earned my loyalty."

"Am I supposed to earn your loyalty, Caleb?" she sneered at him. "Why? What about *my* loyalty? What have you done to earn *that*?" Caleb clenched his jaw. "You're worse than those bikers," she spat, her body tense and coiling, ready to attack. "At least they knew they were monsters. You're pathetic! You're a monster who imagines he's something else."

Heat surged up Caleb's spine and radiated down toward his fingers. He held the steering wheel in a white-knuckled grip. His first instinct was to hit her, to release the wheel and slap her across the face, but what would it prove? Only that she was right, which of course she was. Only a monster could do the things he'd done. Only a monster would have the instincts he had, and only a monster would feel indifferent to his nature or try to rationalize it.

"I know what I am," he said, calmly. "I've always known."

He gave her a quick up-and-down look. She slouched back in her seat, as though his gaze were venom.

"It's *you* who thinks otherwise," Caleb said. He watched Kitten flinch. His words apparently hurt her feelings, but they were the truth. The truth stung them both. She had seen him as something else, something she deemed better. For a little while, he'd shared her imagination. He had never realized how much it meant to him, until it was no longer true. No one had ever seen him as someone capable of being more, and he had just hurt the one person who did.

It was just as well. He wanted to return to the time before he had ever known she existed, a time when his life was black and white, and the gray didn't matter. He ached for the simplicity of his life, free of moral quandaries, guilt, shame, overbearing lust, and the worst sin of all—longing. He wanted to go to bed at night and know exactly what to expect when he woke up. He wanted Kitten out of his life and out of his head.

The space inside the vehicle was silent, but loud and clear. Caleb was glad to stare out of the windshield as stretches of road disappeared under them, taking them thousands of kilometers from that shower, their confessions, and all the possibilities of what might have been between them.

After a while, they finally ventured onto paved city roads. Civilization surrounded them. Caleb didn't miss the way Kitten sat up straighter in her seat, her head turned to view everything passing her window. She raised her uninjured arm and pressed her palm to the window.

Caleb swallowed and ignored her, eyes front.

The sun was shining brightly, burning off what was left of the morning chill. Caleb reached for the air conditioner and set it low. He would roll down the windows when there weren't quite so many people around to hear Kitten's impassioned pleas for help. He had to get rid of the vehicle as well, just in case the doctor didn't keep his word and the

Federales were already looking for them. He had a few hundred U.S. dollars on him, and a few hundred pesos, courtesy of the doc. It wasn't enough to bribe a cop, but plenty for your average trouble maker. Regardless, the sooner they arrived in Tuxtepec, the better. Caleb pulled into a roundabout and took the exit leading toward Chihuahua. He'd have to stop and get everything he needed near the city.

"I can't change your mind, can I?" The soft spoken words pulled Caleb back into the car. He didn't want to do this anymore. He didn't want to talk. "This is all really happening. Isn't it? And you're going to let it happen…aren't you?"

"Try and go to sleep, Kitten." His voice was detached, wooden. "We have a long way to go."

She wouldn't relent, though her manner was casual and airy, as though she were only speaking aloud – not expecting an answer. "I admit…at first I thought…" She shrugged. "I thought you really *were* my 'knight in shining armor'. Stupid, I know."

Her ironic sadness, as she repeated Caleb's words, tried to make him feel guilt. Instead, he worked to ignore her. He didn't want to give her the satisfaction of badgering him into an argument.

"I was so shocked when I saw you again. Shocked to discover…I thought you were a monster then. You terrified me. But now? Now, I don't know how I feel about you," she whispered.

Caleb gripped the wheel tighter with one hand and flipped on the stereo, flooding the vehicle with loud *Banda* music.

Kitten turned to face him, the once far-away look gone from her face and replaced by narrowed eyes and a mouth set into a stern line. She reached for the knob and switched the radio off. "So that's your answer?"

Caleb took a deep breath and tried to control his anger. "You think you're so fucking clever, don't you?" He gave a mirthless, condescending laugh. "Do you honestly believe for one second I'm not aware of what you're doing? You're trying to make me feel guilty, trying to make me believe you have feelings for me." She winced, her jaw clenching. "You know you're trapped and you're trying to find a way out. Trying to seduce me with your show of caring and sharing won't work on me." He scoffed when he saw the way Kitten feigned surprise and hurt. "You can drop the act. I'm not impressed. Your attempts are laughably transparent."

He anticipated her rage, braced for it, but he hadn't given her enough credit. Instead of invective, Kitten attacked him with cold and resolute reason.

"You're right, Caleb. I *am* trying to seduce you. I *am* trying to find a way out of this fucked up mess you've gotten me into. What else can I do? What would you do in my place?" There were no tears in her eyes, nor was there anger. There was only truth, and the truth was always more powerful. And painful, too.

Caleb knew exactly what he would do in her place, because he'd done it. There were times when he had tried to get men to help him, free him, and deliver him from Narweh's treachery. He'd listened to the men who bought his body swear they loved him. He'd allowed himself to put stock into the endearments they'd whispered in his ear. But when it was over, when they'd taken all they could from him, they'd betrayed his trust to Narweh. He remembered the way his heart had broken when Narweh had used his own words to taunt him as he was beaten.

"I'm sorry I'm so bad at it. I'm sorry you find my attempts *laughable*, but I don't know how to do it any better. You're all I know. For what it's worth, I'm not trying to make you believe anything. I've never lied to you. When I asked you to make love to me, it wasn't a ploy, and it hurts like a bitch to hear you think otherwise, because –" Her voice finally broke, tears bursting past her façade.

Caleb felt panic. He had no idea what to do. Her words, her presence, and her pain, affected him. He hated it. His memories, the ones he worked so hard to push deep into forgotten recesses of his mind, banged on the door of his consciousness. They connected with *Livvie*, they connected to her suffering, and together, they threatened to undo him.

A shuddering breath and Kitten seemed in better control of herself. She wiped at her eyes, took another breath and retreated to her side of the vehicle, her eyes once again focused on the world passing her by. Every now and again her chin trembled, and she would take another breath to will her tears away.

She had more dignity than even she was aware of, and Caleb decided he would never again say otherwise. He wished he had never said it in the first place. His heart was racing, banging harshly in his chest and creating a thumping in his temples that made his head ache. His stomach was also affected, a strange kind of tingling pain churning in his gut.

He had an impulse to offer Kitten comfort, to tell her the truth: her attempts were anything but laughable. However, he knew telling her would be putting himself at an incredible disadvantage. Just acknowledging how much he wanted to comfort her was disconcerting. Still, the thought of hurting her any more than he already had was too much – too much by far.

"Kitten, I –"

She leaned over and twisted the knob for the radio, and the annoying voice of the announcer cut Caleb short. She avoided his eyes as she returned her focus to the window.

Caleb sighed in relief. He had no idea what the hell he had been about to say. The important thing for him to focus on was there would be no more talking for the moment. He wished he could say the same for the next twenty-four hours they would spend together on the road.

***

It had been an exhausting day. What should have been a nine-hour drive had turned into twelve because Caleb had had to stop for Kitten every so often. With her bruised ribs and collarbone, she needed to stretch frequently, so he stopped along scouted roadways. When they reached the city of Zacatecas, Caleb had breathed a weary sigh and decided he could finally stop for the night and get some much needed sleep.

Kitten had spoken very little during the drive, which proved to be a great relief to Caleb. He had traded the doctor's luxury sedan for a sturdy, but dented, farming truck and some groceries. It would offer quite the profit for the farmer, so he asked as few questions as possible – going so far as to pointedly ignore Kitten and her bruises.

She slept most of the way. The drugs in her system seemed to numb her pain, though it left her drowsy. Caleb made sure to keep a bottle of water next to her. He made sure she drank from it whenever she was awake.

Zacatecas was a full-blown city, filled with hundreds of thousands of people – many of them tourists. Caleb took great care in finding a motel for them to spend the night. Kitten had said she wouldn't run from him again, but the look in her eyes whenever they passed American tourists with families spoke differently. She would run again, given half the chance. Not that he could blame her. "I need to take a shower," Caleb said into the silence of the room. "You can either sit in the bathroom with me, or I can tie you up. Option's yours."

Kitten stared at him hard. "Don't trust me?" she taunted.

"Not when you're looking at me like that, no."

She sat stiffly on the edge of the bed, her anger emanating off of her like a toxic fog intent on choking him. "I told you I wouldn't run. Go take your fucking shower and leave me alone."

Caleb closed his eyes and took a deep breath to settle himself. They were back to this. Well, he thought, this was just as good a time as any to reestablish the rules between them. When he opened his eyes, a warm tingle drifted down his spine and he finally felt like himself again. His gaze fell on the girl and he smiled when she flinched.

"Get up," he said calmly, the threat in his voice muted but still present. The girl looked at him for a moment and swallowed harshly. It was obvious her anger had quickly turned to fear.

"Caleb?" Her voice was small, meek.

"Get up. Now."

Slowly, Kitten cast her eyes toward the floor and stood on trembling legs. In fact, her entire body trembled. Caleb, at last, felt no remorse, no pity for the girl in front of him. She was his to do with as he pleased. The thought was an aphrodisiac on its own.

"Strip," was his command, and the girl flinched, though his words had been softly spoken. A whimper escaped her lips, but she didn't hesitate to follow his command. Slowly, she reached for the waistline of the flowing skirt Caleb had selected for her to wear and pushed it down over her hips until it pooled at her feet.

She ignored the panties and slid her trembling fingers to the top button of her blouse; there were more whimpers, but Caleb ignored them. He watched, painfully aroused by the adrenaline coursing through him as she gingerly let each button slip through its hole until she reached the bottom. The fabric parted, exposing a tantalizing line of flesh between her naked breasts. She looked up at him briefly, eyes pleading.

"Off with it."

"Caleb…"

"That!" he growled with menace, "is not how you address me. Do it again and I'll not forgive you."

Kitten began to weep, but still stood. "Yes…. Please…don't…."

"I gave you a choice. If you cannot make it, then I will make choices for you. Understood?"

She sniffled, "Yes…Master." The words seemed painful for her to say, but Caleb cared nothing for her pain at the moment. She had defied him for the last time. He watched dispassionately as she slid the shirt from her shoulders and the panties from her legs. She stood, shaking and sobbing, but finally compliant.

"Kneel!" he barked for the sake of watching her scramble to obey. He smiled as her knees hit the threadbare carpet and her hands went to cup her breasts to hide them from view. His heart raced and he nearly groaned at the touch of his palm against his erection, trapped inside his pants.

He stepped slowly and deliberately toward her, watching with sadistic pleasure as she closed her eyes and her lips moved; she made no sound. He pulled at the tie holding her hair back, letting her long, dark mane cascade down her naked body, but hiding nothing.

"Do you remember what happened the night you decided to scream out my name?" he asked casually. The girl sobbed as she nodded. He lifted a piece of her hair and wound it around his hand, each turn bringing his hand closer to her scalp and tugging softly, but with ominous implication. "If I wanted you to nod, I'd move your fucking head myself. Answer...please."

Kitten's chest heaved with the force of her sob, but the answer came through. "Yes, Master." Caleb undid the top button of his pants – jeans, pilfered from the good doctor. "Oh. No. Please, no, Master. Please, no."

"Don't speak unless it's to answer a question you've been asked!" Kitten became silent, lips pressed together. "Breathe through your mouth; the last thing I want is for you to pass out without my permission." She gasped, but didn't speak. "How did I punish you?"

The words seemed to affect her like a physical blow and she pulled away from his hand, panicked, but with no place to go. Caleb pulled her hair hard enough to force her back into position, but not hard enough to injure. "Answer me."

"You...you...I can't!" she sobbed.

"Answer the question!"

"You fucked me!"

Caleb slid his zipper down slowly, drawing the moment out for the benefit of them both. "Yes, I fucked you. Right in your sexy little asshole." She gasped at his words, her face a puffy mess from her open-mouthed sobbing. "Did you like it?"

She shook her head. "No, Master. No."

Caleb tsked and brought her head toward his erection, still secure in his underwear but undoubtedly hot against her skin nonetheless. "Liar. You came more than you had a right to. I know because I felt you, hot and clutching at my cock, begging me to come inside you. Isn't that right?"

The girl shook her head no, but she whispered, "Yes, Master."

Memories played through Caleb's mind as a series of erotic flashes. He remembered how good it had felt to be buried inside her and feel her push against him. It would be so easy to have her again, to have her in any way he wanted and to bring her to the heights of unbearable ecstasy until she no longer knew how pain or pleasure differed. However, he had a different point to make.

"What is your name?"

"Kitten!" she shouted without hesitation.

"To whom do you belong?"

"To you," she sobbed.

"Yes. To me. Now, tell me what I could do with you?" His tone was urgent.

"I don't know!"

"You *do* know! Tell me."

"Cal–"

"Don't you dare! I am not your lover. I am not your friend! Who am I?"

"Master! You're my…. I want to stop. Please make it stop."

"Answer my question – what could I do with you?"

58

"Anything! Fucking anything!" she sobbed wetly.

"Yes, I could do anything to you. I could throw you face down and fuck you until you couldn't stand and there would be nothing you could do about it. You're beaten, bruised and damn near broken. I could kill you. Those bikers could have killed you, but you keep provoking!"

"No! No, Master."

"Are you prideful?"

"No, Master."

"No?"

"Yes! Yes, Master, I'm prideful. I'm sorry!"

"Is your pride worth the situation you are in?"

Caleb let her go and watched as she placed her hands on the floor and cried with her head bowed. "No, Master."

He'd done what he set out to do. "Exactly, Kitten. Your pride isn't worth it. It's not worth the pain. It's not worth the torture I, or anyone else, could put you through. It sure as fuck isn't worth your life. Be smart! Fight the battles you can win and accept the ones you can't. That's how you survive." *That's how you avoid being tied to a fucking mattress and soaked in your own blood.*

"I'm sorry! Please…just stop. Don't be this way anymore. I can't stand it! I can't stand being with you and not knowing who you are from one moment to the next!" Kitten cried.

Caleb buttoned his pants and crouched with one knee on the floor, pulling Kitten into his arms. She offered no resistance; her arms wound around his neck as though she had been desperate for them to be there all along, and she sobbed into his neck.

"I like you so much better when you're like this," she whispered as she pressed her lips to his neck softly, over and over as though she sought to calm him, when it was her in need of calming.

"What you like or don't like is irrelevant, Kitten," he answered, gently. She went still – not tense, just lax. "That's what you need to start expecting." Without another word, Caleb lifted her into his arms and carried her into the bathroom. They both needed to rinse the day away.

They would start fresh in the morning.

Day 6:

I look around the room and feel let down by the lack of darkness and sterility. I had an image of what an interrogation room might look like: two-way mirror, scratched metal table, a high-watt bulb lighting my face and making me sweat. Instead, the room looks more like a kindergarten classroom, with art projects and motivational sayings glued onto bright construction paper on the walls. I am sitting on a plastic chair, staring at Reed across the round, faux-wood table in front of me.

"Okay," Reed says. He releases a breath. "Just to get the chronology right: After you were kidnapped, you spent approximately three weeks locked in a dark room, in a city you can't recall. You escape the man known as 'Caleb' and are, almost immediately, held for ransom by a man named 'Tiny' and his motorcycle gang. You contact your friend, Nicole Freedman, and ask her to obtain your ransom of one hundred thousand dollars and meet 'Tiny' in Chihuahua, Mexico, to exchange your freedom for the money. You never make it to the drop because you are *rescued*, by 'Caleb'. In the morning, you discover he has kidnapped two people and held them hostage in their home. He leaves them alive but steals their car. He drives you to Zacatecas,

Mexico. You are there for *approximately* three months."

There is a long pause, as though he expects me say some other thing that will amaze him. He'll be vastly disappointed. He ought to start expecting disappointment.

"Is that all correct?" Reed asks.

"You look like you want to spit every time you say his name," I say without inflection.

"My feelings are irrelevant," Reed says.

"They're relevant to me."

Reed shakes his head and can't seem to stop himself from giving me his two cents. "He's a human trafficker, Miss Ruiz, a murderer, and a rapist. He didn't *rescue* you. He *captured* you. There's a wide distinction between the two. Have you considered you might have Stockholm Syndrome? Otherwise, I can't see how you can defend him on any reasonable level."

My vision is blurry. "He was a lot of things, that's true enough," I say. My voice is raspy and my lips tremble with the force of my sorrow. "But he was also more than what you've written in your damn reports." I blink, and glare at Agent Reed. "It was the bikers who tried to rape me. It was the bikers who nearly beat me to death! If Caleb hadn't stopped them, I'd probably be dead."

"Is he the one who killed them?" Reed asks insistently.

I take a deep breath and lean back in my chair, wiping the tears from my face. "How would I know?" I shrug. "I was unconscious."

"I'm not defending what those men did to you. Especially if it happened the way you said it did."

"Are you implying it didn't happen that way?"

Reed lets out an exasperated breath. "I didn't say that. I'm interested in the truth and nothing more." There's a long pause, both of us regrouping. "The auction. When is it supposed to happen?"

"Caleb said about a week from now."

"Where?"

"I don't know. Pakistan, somewhere."

Reed's questions come at me quickly. I have no choice but to answer just as fast. I don't want him to mistake my pauses for answers. Worse, I don't want him to think I'm taking time to form a lie – which I am. "So, according to Caleb and Muhammad Rafiq, Demitri Balk – also referred to as Vladek Rostrovich – is supposed to be there?"

"I guess," I grind out.

"Will Rafiq be there?"

"How the fuck would I know?"

"Will Caleb be there?"

"Caleb's dead!" I pound my hand against the table. "How many times do I have to say it?" Reed sits back, unconvinced. "How did he die?"

"I told you already!"

"Tell me again."

"Fuck you!"

"Whose blood was on your clothes when they brought you in?"

"His."

"How did it get there?" He leans toward me.

"I told you! He died in my fucking arms."

63

"And it was all very romantic. Who killed him?"

I burst out of my chair and throw it behind me, knocking it into another table and littering the floor with art supplies. "Stop asking me! I've answered already."

Reed stands quickly and circles the table. Before I can run, before I can even react to the fear racing through me, he has me face down on the table with my arms behind my back. I feel the cold from his cuffs and then hear them click as he cinches them around my wrists. It occurs to me I should never have asked to be alone with him. There's no one to watch him. There is only my word against his.

I struggle, but he holds me very easily. He's obviously done this before. Caleb would be impressed. I am less so. "Get the fuck off me, you asshole!"

His voice is calm, but filled with authority. "I'll let you go as soon as you calm down. I don't like being threatened, Miss Ruiz."

"I didn't –" I start to say and am interrupted.

"You can't throw the furniture around. I take that as a threat." I am furious! But his tone is so calm and collected. I know if I don't settle down, he'll hold me like this forever. It's almost tempting, but I force myself to let my body go soft. This is a battle I can't win.

Reed releases his hold on me in degrees – the calmer I am, the looser his hold, and soon I am free of him and standing. He's much taller than me; I don't even reach his shoulder, so I have to crane my head all the way back to glower at him.

"If you spit at me, you won't like what I do next," he says very seriously, but I can see the barest trace of a smile. *Caleb.*

"What about what I asked for?" I whisper the words, taking advantage of our closeness. I'm not nearly as bruised as I used to be and I know what men like him, men with power, like from beautiful women like me. I sway my body toward him, trying to make it seem incidental.

He frowns and gives me a strange look. Slowly, his hands come up to rest on my shoulders. They're warm. I wonder if his mouth is too. I lick my bottom lip and his eyes track my tongue. He reminds me. He reminds me so much of him. It's been days since someone has touched me in a way I might enjoy.

He pushes me back gently. This man is all business. "Entry into Witness Protection isn't guaranteed," he says. He grabs the chair I threw and motions for me to sit. "This crosses international lines, not just federal. The DOJ is currently reviewing this case, and it depends on other complicated factors." He sets it down where he wants and looks at me. "Sit down."

I look at the chair and raise my arms from behind my back, wiggling my fingers.

"I'm going to leave those on. Forgive me if I don't trust you."

I force a smile just to piss him off. "I won't sign anything until you come through. I'll say I lied about everything."

He steps closer. "Have you been lying, Miss Ruiz?" His gaze is hot and smoldering – intimidating as hell. If it weren't for the fact I've been with Caleb for so long, I'd probably piss like a puppy – but after Caleb, Reed's threats feel like a caress. "Sit. Down," he orders less nicely.

I sit slowly, giving him the sultriest look I can muster. He holds my eyes the entire time, trying to maintain his authority, his control. I slowly lean over and spit on his shoe. I look up at him, lips wet, and smile.

His hand wraps around my bicep with enough force to make me wince and he hauls me to my feet. "We're done for today. You can go back to your room." He shoves me toward the door and I go without a fight.

I want to go back to my room. I'm too close to falling apart and I don't want Reed to see it. I don't want anyone to see me falling apart.

***

Day 7:

The ache in my chest is ever-present. I dream of Caleb whenever my eyes are closed. I can touch him in my dreams. I can run my hands along his smooth, sun-kissed skin. He's always so warm; he has so much heat inside him.

I press my nose to his chest and inhale deeply. There is a familiar tug of arousal as my nipples pebble and my pussy swells. Standing up on my toes, I press my lips to his. He won't open his mouth to me. He wants me to beg. My Caleb loves it when

I beg. With him, I always have a reason to. I hear myself whimper softly and then I brush my nose against his. Against my lips, I can feel him smile. He opens his mouth and lets me sweep my tongue inside. *Mmmm.* I could spend a lifetime trying to describe the decadence of Caleb's mouth. He tastes like everything I've ever wanted to eat. Unlike biting into a tender, warm, juicy piece of meat, Caleb's flavor never fades. It builds. I want him more with every slide of his tongue against mine. I whimper louder. Beg harder. *More. Please, give me more.*

I can hear him. He moans against my lips. Softly, he inhales and exhales as we kiss. He never stops kissing me; he simply continues to steal my breath, returning it to me only when he's infused it with his essence. Pure lust lives inside him. Every breath I take should come from his lungs.

This is what it's like to dream of him.

This is what I lose when I wake.

***

The situation is uncomfortable, to say the very least. In fact, it's closer to insufferable. Agent Reed is not here. His invitation has been revoked by Dr. Sloan. I can't say I'm unhappy about it. Still, it means I am alone with Dr. Sloan, and I *can* be unhappy about that.

She found me crying yesterday. Gripping Caleb's picture to my chest and rocking.

I rather like rocking. I'm doing it now.

67

She asked about the photo of course, asked about what had happened between Agent Reed and me. I refused to respond to her questions – she had nothing to offer me, no photos to dangle in front of me. I haven't said a word since I was brought back to my room yesterday.

Agent Reed returned this morning, ready for another round of what he calls an interview and what I refer to as an interrogation. Dr. Sloan got here an hour before he did. I watched, detached, as she asked Agent Reed to step outside with her. He gave me the stink-eye as he turned to leave. I guess he thinks I'm a rat. I don't really care though, because it means I can keep quiet a little longer. When Dr. Sloan returned, she was obviously tense. Whatever was said left her in a huff. If I weren't so grief-stricken, I might have smiled.

She's much calmer now. She has shut the door to my room, entombing us, but she hasn't asked me any questions…yet. I rock back and forth, cradling Caleb's photo in my hands as I sit on my bed. He is so beautiful. I love him so very much.

Dr. Sloan is sitting in a chair near the corner, knitting a sweater of all things. It's a strange design – unless she has a pet octopus she likes to put clothes on. A few times, I've been tempted to ask her what the fuck that is about.

She catches me watching her.

"It gives me something to do with my hands," she says through a rueful smile. "A lot of times I am the last person people want to talk to. So I just sit down and knit. I understand the mechanics of it, but

I haven't really learned how to make anything. I guess you could call it 'free-form knitting'." She laughs at her own joke.

This woman is ridiculous.

For a moment there is a pause and I think we've reached the end of our one-sided conversation, but then she sighs and keeps right on talking.

"I never really had anyone to teach me how to knit. I think most people learn from their mother or grandmother, but I grew up in foster care, so I had to learn on my own. I picked it up a few years ago when a friend of mine suggested I get a hobby. A mindless hobby. I'm a bit of an over-thinker. If I don't find a way to shut my brain off, I just keep thinking and thinking and thinking. Mostly about work. My job can be pretty thankless sometimes." She glances up at me and smiles again.

I roll my eyes. She's obviously trying to annoy me to death.

"See, told you. Thankless."

For the love of Christ, shut – up! Let a bitch enjoy her mental breakdown in peace.

"I liked it so much I picked up a few other hobbies."

Oh god. Please don't.

"I make my own beanie babies. Well, not really my own, because we already know I can't knit or sew worth a damn, but I like to buy them, take them apart, and then put them back together in some pretty interesting ways. I like to call it 'interpretive taxidermy'."

Kill me. Just, fucking, kill me.

69

"It's a little redundant I guess, since most taxidermy involves putting things together in an interpretive way. Still, I'm the only one who calls it that. It's my own little spin.

"Do you have any hobbies, Olivia?" She looks up at me.

I can't help the way my eyes narrow. I wish she'd stop calling me that.

"You don't like it, do you? When I use your name?"

I give an infinitesimal shake of my head that isn't really voluntary. The moment I catch myself do it, I scowl and stare down into my lap, at my handsome Caleb.

Caleb.

Don't. Don't think about him.

Once again, I am a fragmented person. I am divided between the soft, sentimental girl who loves Caleb at all costs and the hard, logical version of me determined to survive – even at the cost of pushing Caleb from my heart.

"Would you prefer Livvie? Your mom says everyone calls you Livvie."

Tears sting my eyes as I look up toward Dr. Sloan. She is studiously avoiding eye contact, focusing on yet another 'arm' of her strange outfit.

I wonder, against my will, if my mother is here. I don't want to see her, but…why hasn't she come to see me? Everyone I love betrays me.

Oh, god. Caleb.

Yes, him too. Don't think about him.

"I spoke with her a great deal yesterday; she wanted to see you," Dr. Sloan says casually. My heart is skipping every other beat. Panic is rising, but I breathe through it. Barely. "But when I stopped by to ask if it was something you might want...." She frowns and shakes her head angrily. I know she's thinking about Reed. "I figured I'd wait for you to tell me what you want to do."

I nod shallowly and feel manipulated when I see her nod too. She's getting in my fucking head and I haven't even said anything.

Caleb says all your emotions are on your face for all to see.

Shut up and stop thinking about him. Be smart for once. Listen to me.

I sigh. Thinking about Caleb hurts, but trying to move beyond my love for him hurts more. There's no getting past the pain. There is only a different brand of pain available for my eager consumption.

"Do you want to see your mother?"

I don't know whether the question is real, or a threat. I carefully abstain from signaling my emotions through my body language or facial expressions. I suppose it works, because Dr. Sloan resumes her ridiculous monologue about her hobbies.

"I know what you must be thinking."

You have no fucking idea.

"That I'm a silly woman with ridiculous hobbies."

Or maybe you do.

71

"Though, you'd be surprised to learn, I'm not all free-form knitting and interpretive taxidermy. I have a dark side."

Hmm...doubtful.

"When I'm really frustrated with things," she giggles, "I like to get online and change things in Wikipedia!"

This bitch...is *weird.*

"I once made up a whole entry based on someone called the Christmas Amoeba. You see, I'm not much of a baker, and I made these holiday cookies for the people at the office. They came out horribly deformed. They tasted fine, mind you, but they were misshapen. Not a round cookie in the bunch."

I look at her octopus sweater. I'm fairly sure nothing this woman does with her hands is meant for people to see, let alone consume.

"So I left a note next to the cookies. It was a story explaining how a small village near K2.... You know that big mountain, right?" She looks at me to make sure I'm following along.

I lie down on my bed and huff at the ceiling. Where the hell is the nurse with my drugs?

"Anyway, they made a movie about it. Not my cookies," she cackles, so fucking amused with herself, "...the mountain. Can you imagine if they made a movie about my cookies? So, I made up this story about how this village near K2 celebrates someone called the Christmas Amoeba instead of Santa Claus. He sneaks in undetected – amoebas are microscopic, so it stands to reason someone who's an amoeba would be very stealthy – on Christmas Eve and leaves presents for everyone. In return, the people of the village leave a variety of oddly-shaped cookies for the amoeba to eat. Amoebas come in a variety of shapes, so it makes sense."

She can't see my face, so I don't feel like a traitor for smiling at this preposterous woman's story.

"Well, the people in my office are just sticklers for the truth. You know, everything must be verified, blah, blah, blah. So sure enough, they do a Google search and – BOOM – up pops my entry on Wikipedia about the Christmas Amoeba."

She dissolves into peals of laughter.

Oh my god, she really is crazy. I bite the inside of my cheeks to keep from laughing. She is laughing so hard. It's infectious, but I resist it. My shoulders are trembling with withheld laughter. I shut my eyes to assist in the effort.

Caleb is there the moment I shut my eyes.

Joy turns to grief and before I can control it, my emotions just spill over. I open my eyes and bolt up in my bed. I laugh for a second before I burst into tears.

I can hear Dr. Sloan moving. Her steps are coming toward me, cautiously. I don't care. I'm too *tired* to care. After so many months of being careful, and hiding every emotion as best I can, and fearing the future, and not knowing what's going to happen next, and thinking I might die, and fighting for my life, and hating Caleb, and loving him….

For fucksake – I watched a man die!

When Dr. Sloan silently puts her arms around me, I crush her to my body. I hold on to her with all my remaining strength. I cry all over this ridiculous fucking woman.

She doesn't say a word, and I'm grateful. *Please, just hold me. Please, just hold me together.*

I'm so tired of holding myself together.

She rocks me.

I rather like rocking.

Back and forth we sway for endless minutes while I cry and sob all over Dr. Sloan's suit jacket. She smells nice. Her scent is light and almost fruity. It is distinctly feminine, and therefore far removed from Caleb. With this feminine scent saturating my nostrils, my brain cannot connect to memories of Caleb and the way he smelled when he held me. It feels nice, being free of the pain of missing him.

Reluctantly, I pull away from her. I am still humming with shame. I don't know what's come over me. I wrinkle my brow in confusion and shake my head.

Caleb's scowling face is staring up at me from the photograph in my lap. I feel a pang of longing. Dr. Sloan pushes my hair from my face and I can't help but think of it in a sexual way. In another time, I'd have thought nothing of it, but now all my interactions seem tainted by my newfound lust. Caleb trained me well.

"I want to help you, Livvie. Talk to me," she says, softly. I know she doesn't want to startle me, but already I feel the tension creeping back into my shoulders. She's standing too close, and the fact she's talking to me makes me feel cornered.

She must be able to tell, because she backs up. I relax, just a little.

"I would like to see the charges against you dropped, but you have to talk to someone. Agent Reed is…" she searches for the word she wants to use, "very good at his job, and despite his behavior yesterday, he's a great guy. However, his first priority is solving his case. My first priority is you. He shouldn't have pushed you the way he did."

I look up at her from beneath my lashes. I wish she would hold me again.

"I'd like a lawyer," I whisper.

"Of course. If you're ready to talk, I'll find a lawyer for you. But, Livvie, the things you need to talk about go far beyond the legal charges. I'm here to help you with that."

I nod, but say nothing else.

Dr. Sloan returns to her chair and sits. She looks at me expectantly with her green eyes. She's pretty, in a very down-played sort of way. With her red hair, the brown suit she is wearing does her no favors. Still, there is something about her, something warm and pleasant.

When it becomes obvious I won't be the one to keep our little conversation going, she reaches for her knitting and resumes the mindless design.

Dr. Sloan presses her lips together, searching for words.

"Do you want to see your mother?"

I don't hesitate. "No."

She stops knitting. "Livvie, the people who love you accept you for who you truly are. No matter what has happened to you."

"Well there you go. My mother doesn't love me, Dr. Sloan. She wants to love me, I think, but...I just don't think she does."

She nods, but I can tell she doesn't believe me. What would she know?

"I think your mother loves you a great deal."

I stare down at my picture of Caleb. I thought he loved me. Could it be the one person I discounted loves me more than the one I trusted completely? My heart aches. It's a question I am not prepared to have answered.

Slowly, I crawl under my covers. I want to go back to sleep. I want to be with Caleb again. In my dreams, there is never a reason to doubt my heart. In my dreams, he is everything I want him to be. He is mine.

As if on cue, Dr. Sloan stops asking me emotionally-charged questions and once again regales me with tales of free-form knitting and interpretative taxidermy.

5

Day 8:

I'm feeling somewhat better today. I still miss
Caleb; I don't think the feeling will ever go away,
but I can get through several minutes without
wanting to break down and weep for him. It's
progress. Dr. Sloan says one day I'll make it to an
hour…a day…but that's as far as I let myself hope.
The thought of one day not thinking of him at all is
just too much for me. It feels like a betrayal to ever
hope for such things.

Once again, I am sitting in the dreadfully cheery
room they use to interrogate kindergarteners. This
time, I don't have to do very much talking. I have a
lawyer to do it for me. He and Agent Reed have
been battling it out for the last hour. David, my
lawyer, isn't much to look at, but he's very smart
and incredibly aggressive. There's something super
hot about watching the two of them argue…or
maybe I just like Reed when he's unsettled.

His hair is somewhat disheveled from where he's
run his fingers through it so many times to keep
from punching David in his face. Every now and
again, his eyes flick to me and I feel a dark thrill just
thinking about what he'd like to do to me if only he
could. If he were Caleb, I would assume a spanking
is most certainly in order!

"When exactly did you imagine yourself as...? My lover?" My heartbeat vibrated my skull. "Was it the first time I made you come with my mouth? Or one of the many times since that I've put you over my knee? You seem to like that."

And there he is – Caleb, in my thoughts, in my blood. I can feel my face getting warmer, my stomach getting tighter, and already there is the drumbeat of my arousal pulsing between my legs. I squeeze them together and get so lost in my thoughts it takes me a second to realize Reed is still staring at me. When our eyes finally meet, I blush – hard. I smile when he blushes too.

Agent Reed clears his throat and takes a drink of water. It's enough to bring back his control. I sigh through my disappointment.

"Agent Reed," David says, reclaiming Reed's attention, "my client is being held on ridiculous charges that would never stand up in court. She was living with her mother and attending high school at the time of her kidnapping. Even though she's eighteen, the U.S. Attorney would be hard-pressed to try her as an adult. If she's considered a minor *and* involved in a human trafficking case, under Section 107 of the Trafficking Victims Protection Act of 2000 she's protected from the FBI's tactics of investigation. There's no point in us even sitting here. I should be talking to the U.S. Attorney, not you."

Reed does not look happy, but he doesn't look beat either. "Your client has two hundred fifty thousand dollars in a foreign bank account. How did it get there? She won't say. Also, she's been living with suspected terrorists. She's admitted to it. Then, there's the small matter of her knowledge of a meeting between enemies of the United States taking place in less than a week! We need information, and her refusal to give it qualifies as an obstruction of justice –"

"What terrorists!?!" I yell at Reed and move to stand, but David calmly pushes me back into my seat.

"Muhammad Rafiq, Jair Baloch, Felipe Villanueva, and of course *Caleb*," he says. "Do you or do you *not* also have information about Demitri Balk?"

"I never said I knew him!"

"You said you knew where he'd be," Reed says with a raised eyebrow.

"Miss Ruiz, please stop talking and let me handle this," David says in an irritated tone.

"By the way," begins Reed anew, ignoring my lawyer and focusing on me, "Balk is suspected of having ties to arms dealing and narcotics trafficking. And until I know how you," he jabs his finger in my direction, "are involved, you're a suspect too. You can deal with me or I can let the DEA and Homeland Security in here, and when they use Patriot Act against you, don't say I didn't warn you."

"That is enough," David said firmly, glaring at us both.

"Caleb is not a terrorist. I don't know about the rest of them, but he's not a terrorist! And neither am

I! And–" A cold wave crashes over me. *Felipe.* I never said anything about Felipe. Reed knows things he's not saying.

Caleb! Fuck!

I can't breathe; all of the oxygen is suddenly being sucked from the room, from my fucking lungs! I keep taking deep, deep breaths, lots of them, but I can't get any air.

My heart is racing.

I can't breathe!

"Olivia?" says Reed, and I can hear him shuffling around.

"We're done here, Agent Reed. I'll be speaking to your superiors." David reaches for me and tries to get me to stand. I don't like his hands on me. I can't breathe! He's suffocating me. I need to think. I need to breathe.

"Shut up! Everybody just shut up!" Reed and David go silent and I ignore them as I put my hands on the table in front of me and try to catch my breath.

You fucked up, girl. Don't make it worse.

I squeeze my eyes shut and will myself to breathe slower, deeper, calmer. My heart starts to slow in degrees, until finally I feel only a fraction of my panic. Without looking up, I think about what I need to do.

How does Reed know about Felipe? Does he know more about Caleb? Is he really going to charge me with murder? It was self defense!

I have a feeling Reed would be a lot more amenable if my lawyer weren't here. Still a prick, but less likely to push this hard. Dr. Sloan said he was a good guy and would do right by me. I don't have much faith in anything anyone says to me lately, but a glimmer of hope is better than none. I take a sip of water when Reed slides the paper cup beneath my face. I hope he feels guilty, the son of a bitch.

David puts his hand on my shoulder and I shrug it off. "Don't touch me."

"I think I should take you back to your room now, Miss Ruiz," he says.

"I want you to leave," I whisper with my eyes still fixed on the table.

"Excuse me?" David says, indignantly. "I don't think that's a very good idea, Miss Ruiz. I strongly advise you to keep silent and let me do my job."

"She wants you leave," Reed says. He knows he's won this round. He boxed me in a corner and I let him. I realize I should have assumed he knew a lot – not just about me, but other things too. I feel stupid, and angry, and scared. But right now, I need time to think and Reed is the devil I know.

They argue for a bit, puffing their chests at each other in some *National Geographic* display of machismo. In the end, David gathers his things and leaves. Reed and I are alone again. I have a feeling it's what he wanted all along.

He sits quietly, relaxed and patient, unwilling to break the silence. He doesn't want to lose ground. He wants me to come to him, and I know it's exactly the way it's going to play out. I need him on my side. Just the way I once needed Caleb.

My voice is soft on purpose. I need him to see me as fragile again. I need to bring out the alpha male in him. I need him to believe I'm his to protect, even if I already belong to someone else. Caleb would have been proud. I remind myself that I am now my own master. "You wouldn't really let them take me to jail would you? After everything?" I let the threat of tears simmer beneath the surface of my words.

Reed exhales deeply through his nose and I hear his fingertip tapping softly against the table. "I would never put an innocent person in jail, Miss Ruiz, but I still need you to convince me you're not guilty."

"I thought I was innocent until proven guilty, not the other way around."

He chuckles a little, but it doesn't quite reach his eyes. He really is stunning. "I think most people subscribe to the better-safe-than-sorry philosophy these days." He leans forward, conciliatorily. "The truth is, I think you're just a girl who got caught up in a whole lot of awful shit. I think you did what you had to do to get back home, and I think that makes you incredibly smart, and incredibly brave. You don't have to be brave anymore, Miss Ruiz. You don't have to protect anyone. You'd save yourself, and me, a whole lot of grief if you'd just tell me the truth so I can make sure what happened to you doesn't happen to someone else."

It would be so easy to believe him. I'm more tempted than I've ever been to just spill my guts to Reed and let him figure out what to do. It's no wonder he's so good at his job. "I wish I could trust you, Reed, but I know I can't."

His brow furrows in confusion, but there is a wry tilt to his lips. "Why?"

I give him a small smile of my own. "You think you're different from men like Caleb. You see everything in black and white. You don't care about the whole story; you don't care about the gray. Some stories aren't black and white, Agent Reed."

He shakes his head a little, obviously amused, but still professional. "In my experience…the only time a woman wants to tell you 'the whole story' is when she wants you to make a decision based on emotion instead of logic."

My eyes narrow and I stare at the surface of the table. The scars are not visible at first glance but become clearer as I stare, unblinking. "Maybe," I begin, my voice hollow and far away, "but if it weren't for emotions overriding logic, I wouldn't be here."

Reed's smile is gone, his gaze intent. "Meaning?"

"Caleb. It wasn't logic…what he did for me." The words are a revelation. I hadn't been expecting to say them, but I know they're true. Caleb might not love me, but he cared. He kept his promise to keep me safe, even if it meant we couldn't be together.

It makes the pain so much worse.

"I've been doing this a long time
– manipulating people to get my way.
That's why you think you love me.

83

*Because I've broken you down and
built you back up to believe it. It
wasn't an accident. Once you leave
this behind...you'll see that."*

*"Please. Please, Caleb. Don't
make me do this – don't make me go
back to trying to be someone I don't
know how to be anymore."*

"It's time for you to go, Kitten..."

Reed's voice jolts me back into reality. "What
did he do for you?"

I wipe my eye, sweeping away the tears pooled
there. "Everything," I say through a pained smile.
"But it had nothing to do with logic and everything
to do with emotion – revenge, honor, betrayal, lust,
even love...all of these things stem from our
emotions." I paused. "I'm sure you're not doing
what you do without some kind of emotion, Agent
Reed."

"You made your point," Reed says softly and
leans toward me, "but I've been around and seen
some shit."

"Why should that matter to me? Is that supposed
to make me trust you?"

Reed shrugs. "What other choice do you have?"

"How do you know about Felipe?"

He smiles. "I thought that might get your
attention. I'm good at my job, Miss Ruiz, and I've
been digging through anything I can find on
Muhammad Rafiq. What I've found so far is pretty
damn disturbing. Looking through his known

associates and cross-referencing with those in Mexico, it didn't take me too long to find Felipe. As far as I can tell, the man is quite...eccentric."

Eccentric wasn't quite the word I would have used. "Wait...if you know where he is, why haven't you—"

"Mexico isn't the U.S., Miss Ruiz – we can't go rounding up every criminal in another country based on suspicions we can't substantiate. Also, he's left the country and gone who knows where. Maybe Pakistan?"

I look up and shake my head. "Hard to say." I wonder if they're all dead: Felipe, Celia, Kid, and Nancy. I'd like to believe Caleb wouldn't hurt Celia, but then I remember the blood and I wonder if...no, I can't handle it.

"Miss Ruiz, where's the auction?" Reed's words are sharp and serious. This is his end game. I really would have to make a choice.

"I don't really know, Reed. I don't. Not specifically, but I could probably give you an idea. Maybe if you listened to the whole story you could figure it out for yourself. You probably know more than I do."

"Okay. Tell me."

It's my turn to smile and shake my head. "No. Not without some concessions."

He's exasperated. "WITSEC. I told you, I can't guarantee it. More than that, I don't think it's the right move for you. The last thing you need is to be separated from everything and everyone you know. It's a cop-out."

"I don't care what you think it is. I want to disappear. I want this whole mess behind me, and if and when I ever decide to deal with it – that's my business. Not yours."

Reed and I go around for a few minutes as I lay out everything I want in exchange for my story. It isn't pleasant. Reed is a scary bastard when he wants to be, and I would be lying if I said he didn't intimidate me, but I'm willing to take him on. There are things I will not bend on. There are battles I'm determined to win.

"I know what I want, Reed, and if you can't give it to me…you're shit out of luck. After what I've been through, I don't care what you think you can do to me."

Reed's jaw is clenched and I can hear the subtle pop as he grinds his teeth. He stares long and hard at me for a while, and even though I want to, I don't shrink under is gaze. "Start talking."

"Will you help me?" I whisper, but keep my chin up, my eyes level on his.

He exhales slowly and unclenches his jaw. "I'll do my best. If you get us there, get us to the auction, I'll help you."

My heart is in my throat. I want to leap over the desk and hug the hell out of him. He's given me hope. Hope for all the things I want most in the world. With great care, I lick my lips and prepare to tell Reed what he wants to know.

***

Where to begin?

So much was different between Caleb and me.

So much remained the same.

He was still the man who had hired ruthless men to kidnap me. Still the cruel person who had locked me in the dark for weeks, forcing me to become dependent on him, crave him, rely upon him, until even my own instincts stood no chance. He was the man who had saved my life, and the one who had put it in danger. Finally, he was still the man who planned to sell me as a sex slave. A whore.

He'd had his own reasons for wanting me back and they'd had nothing to do with my well-being and everything to do with revenge. Did I know why he wanted revenge? No. Trust did not run both ways between us. There were certain things I had no choice but to trust him with: keeping me alive, fed, safe, and – unless it was him – untouched. It didn't leave much, but I refused to trust him with the most important thing of all: my future.

I guess things between us were the same and the differences didn't matter.

What mattered was *I* was different. The naïve girl in me had been bitch-slapped into womanhood. I'd been razed by pain, grief, loss and suffering, and honed by lust, rage, and an acute awareness of my need to survive.

I understood things I couldn't fathom before. I understood Caleb's need for revenge – because the seed had been planted in me. I recognized how he often turned my body against me – because the desire for him had always been there. Above all else,

I had learned the one thing every person has to learn to make it through life: the only person you can truly count on is yourself.

I was still reeling from Caleb's display of dominance over me when he finally laid me down to sleep. I should have been angry with him, and in a very real way I was, but the way he had unleashed on me made me realize how thoughtful and gentle he had been before. Dealing with Caleb was all about perspective. You couldn't appreciate his kindness until you'd felt his cruelty. I had felt it, but even I was smart enough to know he'd still taken it easy on me.

He didn't have to explain himself to me – he'd made it plain. However, I knew he wanted me to understand the danger I was in. He wanted me to think before I acted. He wanted me to pick and choose my battles, even if those battles were with him. He wanted me to survive. He'd told me as much in the car, but then he'd shown me. For Caleb, that was kind. He dosed me again and I drifted, thoughts swirling in my mind and none of them comforting. Then Caleb was there, and his long, warm body was like a prayer I held onto as I tried to stay awake and did not succeed.

I woke up crying. I could hear the shower running and it was sickening how the relief washed through me, knowing he was close. I forced myself to lie back down, to find a position less aggravating to my injured shoulder or cracked ribs.

I didn't feel comfortable without his arm around me. I couldn't sleep without knowing he was near.

He'd done this to me. He'd made me afraid. He'd made me need him. And if he thought he was suddenly going to abandon me and clear what was left of his shriveled conscience, he was sadly mistaken.

A strange noise drew my attention away from my thoughts. Regardless of my renewed fear, it was a welcome distraction. I wondered for a moment if Caleb had hurt himself, slipped in the shower or something, but there was no loud crash – only a muffled sound. I listened intently, waiting for the noise to repeat itself, and was annoyed by the apparent loudness of my breathing.

"Uh!" That was the noise. Like a grunt mixed with a whimper. "Uh!" Something inside my belly tightened, muscle memory. I should have ignored it, but I couldn't. In spite of everything that had happened to me, and everything Caleb had put me through by deed or design, I still thought him the most beautiful thing I'd ever seen.

"Min fadlik!" he sighed loudly, but I didn't know what it meant. Whatever it was, though, it sounded…needy. What did Caleb need? And why did I find the idea of his need so intriguing?

I needed him to touch me. Not want, because I didn't want him to… I *needed* him to. Only his arms wrapped around me could make the nightmare dissipate; only the smell of him made me forget the fetid breath of the men who had attacked me. Only his. I was always grateful for his presence and resentful of it.

More sounds came from the bathroom and I couldn't resist. I couldn't stop the rush of adrenaline coursing through my veins, urging me into some kind of action – anything that would reveal to me what was happening behind the closed door. *What if he's fucking someone in there?* The thought stopped me cold, a wave of something akin to nausea clogging my throat and tightening my stomach. "He wouldn't," I whispered to myself in the darkness of the room. For whatever reason I just couldn't make it a possibility in my mind. *He's done it before. Remember? Remember him fucking that woman while you were tied up in the other room.* The voice in my head was cruel. I had to know! I had to know if he would do something like that to me again. *Bastard!*

I forced my steps toward the bathroom door. My body trembled and my palms were wet with sweat, but I couldn't stop myself from knowing.

"Fuck…" The obscenity was little more than a whisper beyond the door as I pressed my ear against it. "Oh…yes baby," then something in another language, then "open your pussy." I nearly fell against the door as my knees went weak. Between my legs, I felt a gentle throbbing keeping pace with my heart. *Please, please don't be fucking someone else.*

I could hear the fan was on, which might have been why he felt safe making sounds. If I hadn't been awake, I wouldn't have heard him. Forcing bravery I didn't really feel, I pressed on the latch to open the door. I gripped the latch in my fist until sweat seemed to squeeze between my fingers. The shower was to the left of the door, and I worried I wouldn't be able to see without opening it fully and making my presence known, but there was a mirror to the right where I might be able to see his reflection. I could only pray he wasn't directly facing the door or mirror.

The door opened, just a crack, barely enough to get a finger through, but my heart felt crammed into my throat for those breathless seconds. I waited, hoping not to hear him yell at me or make a startled sound. I heard his heavy breathing and those same groaning sounds from before, accompanied by a wet staccato rhythm. I knelt on the floor, not trusting my legs to support me as I pressed my cheek flush with the door and peeked inside. The room was steamy and it aggravated me to no end. I waited while some of it cleared, but all I could see was a shape in the mirror.

I dared to open the door a little wider, my adrenaline pumping through me in proportionate degrees to the opening in front of me. More steam drifted out of the room and settled on my face and neck, dripping like sweat into the well of my breasts before being absorbed by my shirt. The mirror was much clearer, and I could finally make out the image in the shower.

I gasped, but Caleb didn't hear me. I was sure he couldn't. He was much too absorbed in what he was doing alone in the shower, only a few feet away from my prying eyes. I should have felt embarrassed or guilty, but there was no way I could feel those things. All I could feel was the throbbing between my legs and the sharp pang of lust that punched me in the belly. He was fucking…perfect. Sooo fucking perfect.

He was facing the shower, so I could only see him in profile. His skin was pink and white from the intensity of the water. One arm was braced against the wall, his long legs spread for balance as his head dipped toward his chest and he panted. His other arm was rigid, the muscles tense while his large hand held his enormous erection in his hand. I swallowed hard and licked steam from my lips.

The head was thick and a deep dusky pink as it slipped through his fist. His shaft got thicker toward the base, until his fingers had to grip hard to keep him contained. I remembered his weight in hand.

He didn't shuttle his hand up and down the length of it. He rocked his hips into his fist, making the well-muscled globes of his ass hollow on each side as he thrust forward, his large, heavy-looking balls swaying between his splayed legs in a fluent rhythm. His cock was the arrow, and his fist, the quiver.

I couldn't tear my eyes away – didn't even try. I wondered how much come he held inside those large balls and if he'd given me all of it when he'd come in my hand and on my breasts. I thought about the only time he'd been inside me and I could remember the sound of them slapping against the wet flesh of my pussy as he held me bent over and drove his meaty cock into me. The throbbing between my legs was intense. My own thoughts had me panting and wet. My thoughts were dirty and sexy and they flooded my body with every sensation imaginable.

"Make him love you," Ruthless Me whispered. *"Make it so he can't live without you."*

"I can't," I whispered back. *"I tried. He said my attempts were laughable. He doesn't care."*

"He will."

"Uh…mmm…come on." Caleb's eyes were shut tight, his beautiful mouth open, and the sexiest sounds I'd heard in my life were coming out of him. I wondered what he was thinking about. I wondered if it could be me. Could I be the one driving him toward this frenzied display of lust?

"Yessssss," Ruthless Me shuddered.

My nipples were tight and painful, scraping against the suddenly-rough fabric of my shirt. I wanted to take them out. I wanted to touch them against something cool. I pressed my breasts against the door, rubbing them against the hard wood as I continued to watch Caleb in all of his masculine and somehow vulnerable glory.

I leaned back and pressed the palm of my hand against my mound, rubbing in tiny circles I feared wouldn't get me where I wanted to go nearly quick enough. I didn't want to get lost in my pleasure. I wanted to watch Caleb. I wanted to see him come. The thought made me press against my clit even harder, the circles smaller, tighter and faster. I felt a flutter in my belly, then a warm tingle spread from my spine out to all my limbs until finally I felt my pussy clench tight, then release and clench again. I let out a small cry before I sucked in my lips and bit down on them to keep in any other sounds. It hardly sated me. It was a sneeze compared to how Caleb made me come, but it was enough to force my focus toward Caleb.

His hips were thrusting faster, the cheeks of his ass flexing up and down as he put real effort into reaching his climax. He leaned his body forward, resting his forehead against his forearm as he gritted his teeth and pumped that monstrous thing he called a cock back and forth through his wet fist. Rivulets of water fell from all over his gorgeous body, and I was suddenly so thirsty. I wanted to kneel at his feet and lick water off of him, especially his impressive cock. I wanted to lick water off of it and suck it.

I was thinking of all the things I wanted to do when he let out a grunt, followed by a painful whine as ropes of thick semen burst out of his dick and covered his large hand before dripping down toward those heavy balls and eventually the shower floor. It was a lot of come, and yet his balls didn't seem any smaller.

Caleb was panting hard, his shoulders rising and falling with the effort. His beautiful face was red with exertion, but, if possible, it made him look even more handsome. I wanted to continue to admire him, but doing so felt like a betrayal – of me. The facts were still the facts. He didn't really care about me. He was using me.

My passion was quickly cooling, and finally I slowly shut the door and crept back into bed to nurse more than my physical injuries.

Sometime later I heard the bathroom door open

and the soft scrape of Caleb's feet against the carpet as he made his way toward the bed. I felt the bed dip as he got between the covers, making sure no part of him touched any part of me.

"I woke up and you weren't here," I whispered with my back toward him. I knew he tensed, but I can't say how – perhaps it was the air between us that was tense.

"Have you been up long?"

"No, just a few minutes." I felt him relax into the mattress.

"Another nightmare?"

"Yes," I lied, but felt completely justified as his warm chest, covered in soft cotton, met with my back and his fingers, the ones covered in his semen only minutes before, traced along my arm to soothe me. A vision of his powerful, sleek body straining toward orgasm made its way into my mind's eye. His fingers were long, influential, and still damp as they charted their course along my flesh, leaving me tingling in their wake. I touched his skin. "You're wet."

He sighed heavily. "I'm sorry, Kitten. I needed another shower." His voice was low, dopey with fatigue, but sincere nonetheless. One mention of the word shower and my throat was dry thinking of all the water sluicing off his perfect body and from that beautiful organ. I wondered what he would taste like.

"It's okay," I whispered. My throat was hoarse.

"Anything I can do to make you feel better?" All sorts of answers flitted around in my lust-filled head.

It was tempting to fall back on reliable tactics and pretend things were…perfect. To pretend he was only a boy and I was only a girl and we desired each other. I wanted him to hold and kiss me and pretend he would do anything to protect me. I wanted to pretend he felt a fraction of the things I couldn't seem to stop myself from feeling for him.

My heart hurt. As much as my shoulder and ribs screamed with pain, they were eclipsed by the sorrow in my heart. I couldn't pretend anymore. The time for it had passed; there was only the reality of things left to deal with.

Yes, Master," I said, trying not to sob, "there's so much you can do to make me feel better." His body pressed deeper into mine, and for a moment I just let him be close. "You could not sell me… I could stay with you… be with you?" Caleb gripped me tight – not because he wanted to hurt me, but because I'd shocked the hell out of him. I'd shocked myself, too, but I'd been through too much not to just tell shit the way it was. He swallowed audibly, fingers tentative as they loosened their hold.

"Kitten…" His forehead pressed hard against the nape of my neck. "You ask for impossible things." I wanted to ask which parts were impossible, but I knew the answer. He couldn't let go of his revenge, but he could let go of *me*.

6

Matthew tried very hard to concentrate on the computer screen in front of him, but as he typed, his mind couldn't help but wander off. Olivia Ruiz was most certainly suffering from Stockholm Syndrome, pining over her lost lover, her kidnapper, and abuser. Matthew didn't care for abusers – not one little bit. They were all the same. His mother used to try and apologize for beating him by taking him to the park. The best abusers could make you believe they felt guilty for what they'd done, right up until you got in their way.

Still, he would be lying if he didn't admit, at least to himself, Olivia's storytelling abilities were quite…compelling. For four hours he'd listened to her talk about her relationship with Caleb, and he'd watched as her cheeks had colored and her skin flushed with what he knew was arousal. How could he not be affected?

Yes, he'd grown hard – painfully so – but he didn't like it. What kind of person got a hard-on while listening to a victim talk about her abuse? It made him feel sick. He was sick.

And it wasn't necessarily a new problem. He had a long history of strange sexual proclivities. It was the reason he was thirty-one and still single with no viable prospects on the horizon. He was afraid of someone seeing him for what he was. Being alone didn't mean he was lonely, not really. He kept very busy with work at the Bureau. However, he often thought it would be nice to have someone to come home to, someone he could talk to that wouldn't make him feel like a freak – even though he knew he was. And like attracted like.

He was attracted to damaged and fractured women as much as they seemed to be attracted to him. Olivia Ruiz seemed to be no different. She was drawn to him for some reason, he could intuit that much, but he knew it was an attraction that could only run the one way. He would never compromise an investigation, never take advantage of a witness, and never try to save someone who was so obviously broken. He'd learned his lesson all too well.

He would do his job. That's why the Bureau kept him on board – because at the end of the day, he could be counted on to do what needed to be done. He was a closer. Nothing got in the way of that. No one got in his way.

Bringing his attention back toward his screen, he continued to type up Olivia's statement about her time in captivity. He tried to remain impassive as he typed, but certain sentences continued to jump out at him:

"He made me beg for food..."
"Spanked me repeatedly..."
"...forced me to come."

His report was reading more like an erotic novel than a case file. His mind was beginning to wander again, this time toward his last girlfriend, the one who couldn't come unless he called her a whore. He was starting to get hard again—*Stop!*

He saved the file and decided to take a much-needed break from Olivia's relatively useless memoir. Opening his browser, he searched for more information on Muhammad Rafiq. Matthew suspected Muhammad Rafiq was the lynchpin of the entire investigation.

According to the witness, Caleb had reported his involvement with Rafiq began because they needed to kill Vladek Rostrovich, A.K.A. Demitri Balk.

"Why?" Matthew whispered to himself and then remembered the comment about Rafiq's mother and sister. Were they dead?

Doesn't matter, he thought. The important thing was the auction – everything else was inconsequential. So why couldn't he get it out of his head? Why did the story seem relevant? It was motive, sure, but how did it lead to the location of the auction in Pakistan?

Matthew let out a deep sigh and got up to pour himself another cup of coffee. He'd heard the local cops gripe about the coffee on an almost-daily basis, but unlike them, he actually enjoyed the coffee in the office. It was likely true the coffee machine had never been cleaned, but maybe the grit added something. He smirked. Back at his desk he grabbed his notepad and started digging through his notes to find a starting point for his research.

Olivia's jerk-off story didn't provide much of a jumping off point, but he did manage to learn *min-fadlik* meant 'please' in Arabic. Caleb apparently spoke Arabic with so much ease he used it in private. He would guess people typically spoke their native tongue while alone, and certainly while engaged in that particular activity. Lord knew he'd never yelled out in Mandarin while in the throes of ecstasy. Of course, he didn't speak Mandarin.

He flipped through more of his notes and found Caleb also spoke Spanish, and his English was spoken with a strange accent, one characterized as "…a mix of British, Arabic, and Persian…*maybe* on the Persian." Matthew pulled out a map of Pakistan and tried to narrow down an area with such a mix. It seemed highly unlikely he would find it. Still, an accent meant Caleb was either born or immersed long-term in an area where he'd have heard those languages on a daily basis. Afghanistan, India, and Iran all surrounded Pakistan and each of those would certainly have similarities in demographics and social conventions. The Brits obviously had influence in each mentioned country, but he knew their influence would be more pervasive in India. Caleb was obviously not Indian, and if he had grown up there, he would have picked up the dialect.

He needed to narrow the list of possible locations for the auction and he had little more than experience, old case files, and the internet to work with. Pakistan was making strides toward reducing or eliminating the number of human trafficking crimes committed within their borders. However, Pakistan remained a long way from succeeding in any that would impact their society or politics. Slavery was very popular there, though most of it came from an indentured work force made up of women and children.

People were bought, sold, and rented in an almost casual way in Pakistan, and it was about time the U.S. Government started to take notice and work with the U.N. to do something about it. Matthew was not naïve; he knew the reason the U.S. had decided to take point on the change throughout many Middle Eastern regions had more to do with the resources abroad. Still, if it meant fewer women and children were sold into sexual slavery or bonded labor, then he was all for it. Oil and freedom for everyone.

The Sindh and Punjab provinces were large hotbeds for human trafficking activity, but he temporarily opted to exclude them, as the area was mostly agricultural and the slavery predominately bonded labor. Certainly not the location for the world's elitist playboys and terrorists to arrange for a lavish pleasure slave auction.

Fuck! It was going to be a very long night.

Matthew checked his watch and decided to order his dinner before his favorite Chinese restaurant closed for the night. He was practically salivating over the thought of garlic noodles and crunchy eggrolls. There had been a time when he'd have ordered for two, but it had been nearly a year since he'd had a partner to share the long investigative hours with; these days, he worked alone. It was just as well, since he wasn't really good with people. He was much too honest and people just didn't appreciate him for it.

He was good at his job and people respected him, but it didn't mean they jumped at the chance to work with him or wanted to go out for beers after

Seduced in the Dark   CJ Roberts

work. Still, they did what he asked them to do and he couldn't fault them. If he'd asked one of the analysts to stay behind and help him do some research, they'd have begrudgingly done it and kept their disparaging remarks to themselves until the next time they found themselves in better company.

Matthew had asked for a special task force to assist on the case. There was a potentially short turn-around and the possibility of an international incident if they had a raid in Pakistan. Still, his boss refused to get a decent task force together unless Matthew had concrete proof suspected terrorists and political targets would be at the auction.

If he didn't know any better, he'd accuse the Bureau of purposely letting this case fall between the cracks. Olivia Ruiz's face was splashed all over the news, complete with grainy surveillance and camera-phone videos of her standoff with the border patrol. Something like that didn't go away easily.

He scrolled through the information he had available on Muhammad Rafiq and his accomplices. He was a Pakistani military officer and a high-ranking one. He had fought beside U.S. forces as part of the coalition during *Desert Storm*. He was highly decorated and was rumored to be very close to the former Major General who assisted in the 1999 coup that overthrew Pakistan's president. In short, the man had some very powerful people in his circle.

If he wanted someone dead, he couldn't imagine it would be difficult for him to carry it out. Of course, he would have to do it without embarrassing himself or his superiors in front of the international community. Could his involvement be the reason the Bureau was hesitating on attacking this case full-force?

Matthew picked up his pen and wrote down a list of things he needed to gather information on: military bases in Pakistan, air strips near or on such bases, customs locations, and refueling stations. One thing was for certain – Rafiq wouldn't be flying in or out through commercial means. He'd need a private plane, one that wouldn't have to contend with customs officials. It wasn't much, but it was a start.

The intercom buzzer startled him. His food had finally arrived. He took the elevator to the first floor and met the delivery guy, gave him a healthy tip, and trudged back upstairs to enjoy his greasy, delicious treats.

Several hours later, Matthew decided to call it a night and drive back to his hotel. He planned on getting up early in the morning and going to visit Olivia in the hospital again. She'd be expecting news on her request to join the witness protection program and he had no additional news to offer, but he still needed to get the rest of her statement.

If her information delivered the results he had proposed to his superiors, her request would likely be granted, but not for the right reasons. What the girl needed was justice. She needed the men responsible for her kidnapping, rape, and torture to pay for their crimes in the public arena. She needed for those men to be judged and found wanting of basic human decency – only then could she pick up the pieces of her life and move forward.

However, if he was correct in his assumptions, the Bureau would be more interested in the national security elements, rather than justice for one eighteen-year-old girl. There would be no official arrests, no public trials. Any evidence of involvement in human trafficking by wealthy and powerful military leaders, heads of state, and billionaire moguls would be an invaluable asset in the hands of the U.S. government. Especially if the persons involved remained in power.

It was somewhat of a moral conundrum as far as Matthew was concerned. Olivia was running away. She didn't want to face her former life or its inhabitants, and it was a sentiment Matthew understood well but couldn't agree with. At the same time, he was the last person to give advice on how a person should move beyond their personal traumas. He was still damaged, still sick in the head, no matter how many therapists he had talked to as a teenager. His records had been sealed and for all intents and purposes he was fit for duty, but he knew his own mind. He knew his own limitations and biases. He supposed it counted for something; his knowledge of his own shortcomings afforded him the semblance of perspective when dealing with his job.

He entered his hotel room and set his briefcase down on the table provided. He emptied his pockets, careful to stack any loose change by denomination and place them in a row by size. His keys, wallet, and watch were also placed with care. He unbuttoned his suit jacket and hung it up in the closet. Next, he sat and removed his shoes and socks, followed by his shirt and tie. Finally, he removed his belt, wound it, and placed it on the table with his other things before he removed his underwear. He lined up his shoes under the bed and placed the other items in the hotel's dry-cleaning bag. It was his nightly routine and he took comfort in the repeated actions. Order was important.

He stood naked in the warm, slightly-humid Texas air and ignored the tingling sensation of his penis becoming more erect. He knew why he was getting hard and he wished he weren't. He'd been unable to resist the temptation of perusing his interview notes, despite the promising information he'd garnered through researching Rafiq in greater depth. That much of the girl's story was filled with violence was regrettable; that the violence was a direct result of sexually-charged circumstances was contemptible, but the way she recounted the story with such devious and manipulating zest and obvious arousal was enough to put him over the edge. It pushed all of his buttons, and on the heels of his distaste was the undeniable quickening of his pulse.

He wouldn't do it though. He wouldn't fantasize. He wouldn't masturbate. He wouldn't seek out sexual gratification. Doing so would be a step in the wrong direction for him, because he knew it would lead to the debilitating guilt that inexorably followed.

Instead, he got down on the floor and proceeded to do as many push-ups as he possibly could. He was tired and his muscles protested. Two in the morning was not the time for exercise, his muscles screamed at him, but it was better than the alternative. He pushed himself until sweat ran down his back and his stomach quivered, until his arms threatened to give out...until there was not a chance in hell he could inspire his lust. Then he took a shower and got in bed.

He slept peacefully and without dreams.

7

Caleb couldn't sleep. He'd done everything he could think of: he'd taken a hot shower, he'd masturbated, and he'd sat in Rafiq's library and looked through his books. He couldn't read, but some of the books had pictures in them. He'd walked around the house and discovered the snacks in the kitchen. He'd eaten all the *gulab jamun*, and even now his fingers and the corners of his mouth were sticky. He still couldn't sleep.

Where was Rafiq? he wondered. His heart began to race at the thought of the older man. What if he didn't come back? What if something had happened to him? Caleb's stomach hurt. He'd never been alone before. There was always someone near him – if not the other boys, then Narweh, and if not him, then perhaps a patron.

Caleb stood and pushed his pillow and blanket onto the floor; his bed was too soft. He lay down on the thick carpet and swaddled himself in the blanket he'd been provided. Outside, the wind howled. Why would Rafiq leave him alone? He drew his knees up to his chest and rocked. He wished RezA were with him. RezA was one of the British boys who often shared his bed. If he had a friend at all, it was probably RezA.

For the first time in a week, he let himself think of someone other than himself. With Narweh dead, what had happened to the others, to RezA? It was true they often fought and sometimes threw one another into Narweh's angry path, but it didn't mean there was not affection there. Whenever one of them was mistreated by a patron or after a particularly savage beating, they would often comfort each other by applying bandages or offering arms that consoled instead of harmed. Caleb was smaller, younger probably, but he was a fighter, whereas RezA was more amenable and easily manipulated.

"Why do you anger him so often, Kéleb? You know what he will do," he'd often whispered to Kéleb in the dark and applied ointment to his skin.

"I hate him. I'll let him kill me before I become his little lap dog. A dog I might be, but not his."

"You're not a dog, Kéleb," RezA kissed his forehead. "You're a stupid boy."

"And you're a lap dog," Kéleb countered with a half-hearted laugh.

RezA laughed too and put the cap on the ointment. He stood quietly and tip-toed toward his own bed on the floor.

"RezA!" Kéleb whispered.

"What?"

"I'm going to kill him one day."

After a long pause, "I know. Goodnight, stupid boy."

Caleb had done exactly as he'd promised. He'd killed Narweh in cold, efficient blood. But he hadn't bothered to look for RezA, nor had he told everyone they were free. He never told them to run. He would like to say it was because the thought had not occurred to him, but that wasn't true. He'd been afraid. He'd been afraid they'd turn on him, because without Narweh, many of them would have to choose between poverty and a new and unknown master – perhaps even the drudgery of bonded slavery. He had also been afraid Rafiq would decide all of it, including Caleb, was too much of a burden, and he would have to face the fate of the others. So he'd simply let Rafiq lead him away. He'd let himself be shocked and traumatized over what he'd done. He'd let himself be the victim. He deserved to be abandoned in return.

A noise startled him from his self-deprecating thoughts.

He was stone-like in his stillness, listening for any sounds to indicate whether or not he was alone in the house and furthermore, if a presence equated to danger. He heard the door shut somewhat gently and then heard the familiar shuffling sounds of someone removing their shoes and placing them near the door. Casual noises were a good sign, Caleb supposed, since someone intending harm would likely not care enough to remove their shoes.

Caleb wanted to leave his room, he wanted to investigate, but the fear he felt still lingered strongly. Rafiq was a stranger and his moods could be erratic. He remembered with perfect clarity the way he had been tossed into the bathtub and held down by Rafiq's strong arms. He shuddered.

Footsteps neared his door and Caleb tensed even more, his muscles quivering from being held so tight. The door opened slowly and he shut his eyes tightly. If Rafiq tried to rape him, he would fight back. Somewhere in his mind a voice whispered he should just do whatever was expected of him. He'd survive. He'd want to die, but he could survive it again.

"Caleb?" Rafiq's voice whispered into the darkness.

Caleb held his breath and didn't answer.

"Boy? Are you sleeping?" Rafiq whispered again, and he seemed in control – not angry or predisposed to violence.

Caleb refused to answer, though. He kept his eyes shut and tried to breathe as quietly, shallowly and as evenly as he could, until finally his door shut and Rafiq was gone. Caleb instantly felt relief, but also loss. He was alone again. Alone and frightened in a strange, dark room.

What was his life now? He'd killed someone. He'd murdered. He didn't feel bad about doing it – he would do it again given the chance – but what was he to do with his life? Who could he be? Who was Caleb? He had always told himself one day he would be free, but he didn't realize freedom could feel…too vast, too open and uncertain. Now that he was free, he felt devoid of purpose, and without a purpose what did his life amount to? He owed a debt to Rafiq and he would honor it, but once his task was complete he would find himself in exactly the same place.

Caleb swallowed his fear and tossed back the blankets, determined to seek answers from the one person in his life who might have them: Rafiq. He slowly opened the door and tip-toed toward Rafiq's room. He hesitated at the door, but then tentatively knocked.

"I'm not in there," Rafiq said from behind him.

Caleb whirled around and stared into Rafiq's intense gaze. "I-I-I'm sorry," he stammered. "I was awake when you came in, but I...." He looked at his bare feet. "I wasn't sure what you came looking for." Caleb swallowed.

Rafiq smirked. "And what did you decide?"

Caleb shrugged. "I don't know. I thought...I'd get it over with and simply ask you."

Rafiq's loud sigh caused Caleb's shoulders to tense, but he didn't move to walk away from the older man. "That is very brave of you *chab*, but you have no need to be wary of me; I intend you no harm."

"What do you intend?" Caleb bristled at being called a boy.

"I would hope I've earned your loyalty by now. I only meant to see if you are well? I've been gone since very early and I feared my absence was... stressful for you."

Caleb shrugged half-heartedly, but in reality he wanted to weep with gratitude. No one in a position of power had ever concerned himself with his well-being. No one had ever come to his room for the sole purpose of checking on him. He took a deep breath and pressed his emotions down into his stomach. He did not wish to appear weak in front of the one man offering to make him strong. "It was strange to be alone. Before, with Narweh, there was always someone, but...it was...I don't know what to say. I ate all of the *gulab jamun*," he confessed sheepishly. "I was also in your library. I've never seen so many books! You must know a lot of things. But don't worry!" He was suddenly nervous. "I can't read. I wasn't trying to invade your privacy. I only looked at the pictures. I'm sorry."

Rafiq laughed and the sound put Caleb at ease somewhat. He relaxed further when Rafiq's hand landed on his head and ruffled his long, blond hair. "It's fine, Caleb. This is your home now. The food was left for you and you are welcome to the books. I will teach you how to read them."

Caleb shut his eyes tight to keep his tears from surfacing. Without warning, he lunged toward Rafiq and wrapped his skinny arms around him. He wanted to express his gratitude. He wanted Rafiq to know how much Caleb felt indebted to him.

Slowly, and with shaking hands, Caleb reached up and pulled the older man's head toward his and pressed his lips to Rafiq's. The older man stilled, but didn't stop him when his tongue slid across the opening of Rafiq's mouth. Caleb had done this many times with men he hated; surely he could do it once with someone whom he respected.

Caleb's youthful body responded to the kiss and he pressed forward, chasing Rafiq's mouth, his taste. Rafiq pulled away.

Caleb panicked. If Rafiq rejected him, he would die. He would die of shame because he was a whore and knew no other way.

"Caleb, no."

"I won't fight you. I'll do as you ask," Caleb whispered. His words were shaky and full of fear.

"Do as I tell you, now, and stop this." Rafiq's tone held the slightest bit of contempt.

Caleb pulled away and tried to run past Rafiq, but his path was blocked and soon Rafiq's firm grip held his arm. "I'm sorry! I didn't mean to. I won't do it again." This time the tears were present in his voice. He couldn't hide his shame.

Rafiq pulled him to his chest and held him tight. "You are Kéleb no longer. You are not a dog, and no one's whore. You don't owe me that. You owe it to no one."

Caleb cried and held tighter to Rafiq. He couldn't speak.

"Have you ever been with a woman, Caleb?" Rafiq whispered above him.

Caleb shook his head. He had seen them, of course – there were female whores Narweh kept, but they were separated from the boys and never shared with them. He'd caught glimpses of their bodies and wondered what it would be like to touch them, but it was a pleasure he'd never experienced.

Rafiq led Caleb toward his own room and opened the door. Slowly, he released Caleb and urged him inside. Reluctantly, Caleb loosened his arms and meekly stepped toward the bed he'd made for himself on the floor. "Tomorrow, then," Rafiq said casually. "Tomorrow you'll begin to learn how to take your place at my side. You'll have your choice of them." He smiled as Caleb stared at him in shock, and then he shut the door.

Caleb still couldn't sleep, but now the reasons were different. For the first time since he could remember, Caleb was excited about what the morning would bring.

***

Caleb's eyes opened in the dark. The dream, the memory, lingered. He suddenly felt like a boy again, scared of the dark, scared of the unknown, and lonely. It was strange how a dream could make itself real. It could take control of one's mind and invoke sentiment, so much so it affected the body. Caleb felt a lump in his throat. It shouldn't be there – he was far removed from the scared boy he had been – and yet there it was. His heart hammered strongly in his chest and his palms were sweaty.

He told himself over and over it had been a dream, but the emotions clung to him like thick molasses. No matter how he tried to wipe them from his thoughts, they remained, shifting from one side of his psyche to the other, vacillating between the joys he had felt in experiencing his first moment of acceptance and the grief of knowing the future.

RezA had died. Rafiq had burned Narweh's body where Caleb had left it – inside the house. He had not looked for survivors; he had not warned anyone in the house. Rafiq had imparted the information to Caleb one morning after breakfast, when he'd finally found the courage to ask about what had happened.

114

He had wept for RezA and the other boys in private after scalding himself with a hot spoon he'd been using to stir beans. As his flesh burned, he tried to envision what RezA had felt in the last horrifying moments of his life. Caleb had killed his only friend, and in the end the only scar he had to show for it was on the inside, after his burned skin was cut away and new skin took its place.

Caleb wanted another shower, one so hot he wouldn't be able to think about anything else, but he knew the behavior was stupid and would likely cause more damage than could heal in time for him to continue with his mission. It had been some time since Caleb had had this many compulsive episodes. Yes, he sometimes needed the pain, but such needs were usually spread out over long periods of time. In the last few weeks, he'd struggled not to give in to his impulses many times. It couldn't continue.

Rafiq had done what he needed to do. For Caleb to become the man Rafiq needed him to be, to become the man *he* wanted to be, there could be no witnesses that knew him as Narweh's dog. It was a harsh and debilitating truth at the time, but Caleb understood it as a man in a way he never could as a boy. RezA would have done the same.

Caleb rolled over on the floor and sat up to stare at the shape of Kitten's body sleeping on the bed above him. She moved around a lot, her legs jumping beneath the blankets occasionally. It appeared to Caleb she wanted to roll onto her side or her stomach, but even in sleep, the pain kept her in a slightly upright position.

Her words from earlier drifted toward him:
"You could not sell me… I could stay with you… be with you?"

He sighed, wishing things could be so simple. What would Rafiq say to such a request? Did it even have to be a request? Caleb was a man after all, and a dangerous one at that. Perhaps Caleb need only inform Rafiq of the way it was to be and move on from there. The girl was beaten and bruised, her virginity in question as far as Rafiq would be concerned. How difficult would it be to simply call it a lost cause with Kitten? But honestly, it wouldn't repair anything. He would forever be her captor and she would forever be his prisoner. He had to stop going back and forth. He'd made a decision, and he would stick to it. End of story.

Kitten shifted some more on the bed and whimpered for a few seconds before her eyes finally opened. Her lungs rose and fell deeply and harshly. Apparently, Caleb wasn't the only one suffering from nightmares. To her credit, she hadn't cried out or asked for him. She looked around the room and caught sight of him, then looked away and sat up slowly.

"Morning," he said wryly.

She nodded, but otherwise didn't respond. She tossed her blanket off of her legs in a slow, taxing motion and stiffly stood before walking into the bathroom and shutting the door. Within seconds he could hear the water from the sink running. Caleb wondered how she was planning to use the facilities, because the toilet was set into the ground and

116

required the user to squat above it to do their business. It would be difficult for her to maintain her balance given her injuries, but he decided her need for privacy was perhaps greater than her need for help at the moment.

Caleb went about setting the room to rights and collecting the things he'd need to get ready for the day ahead. Neither of them had much in the way of clothing, but they only had one more day to travel, so the point was moot. He looked through the groceries he had purchased and found the bananas, as well as some raspberry pastries. That would do nicely for breakfast. There were plenty of bottles of water left as well. He checked his watch and noted it was only five-thirty in the morning. The sooner they were out and on the road, the better. They could make it to Tuxtepec by dinner time, even if they took another twelve hours to get there. He would have to make a stop in town before they left.

Caleb reached for his cell phone and dialed Rafiq.

"*Salaam.*"

"Why haven't you been answering your phone?"

"Am I to answer to you, then?"

"Why the fuck not? We're partners, or has Jair usurped my position in the last two days?"

Rafiq laughed. It was the kind of laugh Caleb had suffered through for years – a dismissive, derisive laugh, meant to put Caleb in his place, below his master. "Don't be childish, Caleb. You're the one who made our last conversation so hostile. Jair is hardly in a position to incite your jealousy."

"I'm not jealous, I'm irritated and you're only making it worse. Where are you?"

"Where are you, Caleb? Where is the girl?"

Caleb took a deep breath and exhaled away from the phone. It was the moment of truth. "We're in Zacatecas. We should be in Tuxtepec by morning at the latest."

"The morning?" Rafiq admonished. "You're less than a day's drive from Jair and your hostages, why would you be gone any longer?"

"It's the girl – her injuries slow us down. I keep having to stop for her."

"You're going to arouse suspicion by driving around with her like that." Rafiq paused, his breathing as grating as his voice. Caleb braced for it. "She is the final part of this, Caleb. She must be ready. She must be perfect. If you can't do this, I would be more than willing to take over."

Caleb clenched his jaw with so much force he could hear it popping. "It'll be fine, Rafiq. I can do it," he bit out. "Stop questioning me. I know what I need to do. That's all I think about."

"What about the hostages you've taken? What are your plans for them?"

"Revenge. Naturally."

Rafiq laughed. "There you are, *Khoya*. I'd begun to worry. Do try to keep your head this time; from what I hear, the pair might prove useful to us."

A strange feeling bloomed in Caleb's chest. "Where are you?"

"Close."

"Fine. I assume I'll see you soon." He hung up, annoyed.

Kitten stepped out of the bathroom, looking a bit lost. Last night had put them on different footing, and now it was up to Caleb to maintain the status quo he had created between them. He set his phone on the table and walked toward his captive. She stilled as he approached, her eyes set upon the floor and her hands clasped in front of her. Her nervousness was obvious, but alluring nonetheless.

Caleb swept his hand down her face, careful not to press on her bruises, and swept her hair back over her shoulder. "Whenever you enter a room and your purpose is unclear, always kneel next to your master." Kitten did not hesitate to comply, though her movements were slow as she struggled toward the ground.

"Good," Caleb whispered. "Now spread your knees and sit back on your ankles with your hands on your thighs and your head bowed. Your master should be able to see every part of you and know you will not move until you're told. Do you understand?"

"Yes," Kitten whispered with some hesitation, "Master." Tentatively, she moved her limbs into position. She wore a nightgown and her body was not visible to Caleb, but he knew her body well enough to know what he was missing and his body unwittingly responded.

"*Leet sawm k'leet sue* is Russian. When you hear the command, you will lie on your back with your knees spread and lifted toward your chest. Hold your

119

legs behind your knees." Kitten broke position and stared up at him with a pleading expression.

Caleb's breath stuttered into his lungs from his excitement. At last, she was compliant and his to command. The feeling was heady, but made somewhat hollow because he was teaching her the commands in Russian. "*Leet sawm k'leet sue,*" he repeated. His expression was hard, his eyes serious.

Kitten's mouth tilted downward at the corners in a slight grimace, her chin trembling with her effort not to cry, but she nodded. In achingly slow degrees, she put herself flat on the ground. She looked up at the ceiling and the tears she had been holding fell down the sides of her face into her hair.

This was hard for her. Caleb knew it would be, but it was the easiest thing she could do compared to the journey ahead. There was guilt on his part, but also desire, intense desire that thrummed in his veins. The guilt was nothing when pitted against his desire to have Kitten at his mercy. If that made him sick and depraved, he'd accepted it a long time ago. "Your legs, Kitten. Let's have it."

He watched as her knees began to bend, and he nearly doubled over with want as her hands pulled at the nightgown, raising it over her knees and up her thighs. He hadn't expected her to bare herself to him, but she was. His cock began to stir to the beat of his speeding heart, filling, lengthening, and begging to show itself. Kitten raised her knees toward her chest, her hands fisting the nightgown at her waist. Her pussy was clearly visible, the pink lips spread and flushed, her tiny clit peeking out from beneath its hood. Caleb drew a sharp breath and swallowed.

He could stare at her forever, but his desire was not the purpose of this exercise. It was the most concise manner of re-establishing their roles. There would be no outbursts today, no arguments on the road, no confusion about whether or not he would spare her. "You really are beautiful there, Kitten."

She whimpered.

"Excuse me?" he snapped.

"Thank you, Master," she corrected.

"Very good, Kitten. You can put your legs down now." Her movements were quicker than he thought possible with her injuries, but he declined to comment. He also ignored her sniffling. "*Lye zhaash chee* means *prone*. Do you understand the word?"

Kitten sobbed as she nodded. "Yes, Master."

"Over on your stomach, then."

"It'll hurt," she said.

"Attempt it at the very least. Always try to obey. Let me worry about what you can and cannot handle. Return to the rest position, with your back to me," Caleb said. His words were clipped and brooked no argument. "*Lye zhaash chee.*"

A mewling sound burst past Kitten's lips, but she quickly pressed her lips together and held her breath as she struggled, like a turtle flipped on its shell, to roll over. Caleb pushed away the urge to help her. The situation reminded him of the first time she had disobeyed him. He had slapped her breasts a rosy pink until she'd obeyed. It seemed like ages ago.

It took a minute or two, but finally she was in the rest position. Caleb admired the way her ass rested on her bare feet. "Now lean your body forward with your ass in the air. Normally, you have your arms stretched out in front of you, but for now, keep them wherever it's most comfortable."

Kitten was stoic as she did what she was told. She chose to keep her arms crossed over her chest, letting the side of her face rest against the ground. The nightgown obstructed Caleb's view. He stepped forward and gathered the fabric up over the soft cheeks of her ass.

"Oh, Kitten. I *do* like you like this. So much." His words held nothing but truth. He couldn't resist palming her lightly splayed cheeks and opening them slowly. Kitten trembled, but remained otherwise still beneath his questing fingers. "Can I touch you?" he asked, with a hint of challenge.

There was silence for a few seconds and then she answered, "Yes, Master." Caleb smiled. It was exactly the answer he wanted and exactly the one she should give. She was learning.

"That's good, Kitten. I'm proud of you," he said. He stroked the soft flesh of her inner thighs. Kitten let out a gust of breath that Caleb interpreted as desperation. This was a lot for her to handle so soon after the trauma of the last few days. She'd done well, and he really was proud of her. It was enough.

He pulled the nightgown back into place and urged her back into her rest position. Tears tracked down her cheeks and her face was most definitely

122

worse for wear, but Caleb kissed her wet cheeks anyway as he helped her regain her calm.

After he gave her more medicine for her pain, he calmly fed her breakfast while she sat quietly between his knees, accepting all he had to give her.

8

Day 9:

Dr. Sloan doesn't ask me why I'm crying, and I assume it's because she figures she knows. I would rather she ask me. "I know what you're thinking," I say, but it sounds like an accusation.

Dr. Sloan clears her throat. "What am I thinking?"

"That Caleb is awful, that he's cruel, and I'm stupid for loving him."

She shakes her head, somewhat wryly, and responds in a way I perceive as clinical. "I don't think you're stupid at all. If anything, I think you're extraordinarily brave."

I scoff. "Right. I'm brave. Reed said the same thing."

I hear the scratching of her pen as she makes more notes. "Well then, you have a second opinion now. You don't think your actions were brave?"

"Not especially. I think I just did what I had to do. Caleb's always saying a person has to do what they must in order to survive. Survival is the only thing that matters."

"You don't think surviving is brave?"

"I don't know. Do you think that guy who cut off his arm because he was trapped by a boulder was brave? It's just instinct."

"It's called fight or flight, and one is certainly braver than the other, depending on the circumstances. Under your circumstances, what you did was very brave. You're here, Olivia. You survived."

"I wish you wouldn't call me that. I don't like it."

"Would you prefer Miss Ruiz? Agent Reed says you don't mind that as much."

"Yeah? What else did he say about me?"

She smiles coyly and suddenly I find myself suspicious of their relationship. I don't like the fact they talk about me. "We're required to discuss the case, Miss Ruiz. We exchange all notes and information, as well as any insights we might have. I did tell you all of this."

"I know. What did he say about me?" I have a strange curiosity about Reed that hasn't abated. I don't know what it is about him, but there's definitely something.

"He said you're a brat," she says, but her eyes smile. I smile a little too. Reed didn't say that at all.

"Back to the subject. Why don't you think you're brave?"

I sigh. "I don't know. I guess…I'm here, and that's what Caleb wants." An uncomfortable silence settles between us. I'm lost in my thoughts. *What Caleb wants.* I thought I did everything he wanted, I tried my very best to make him happy, but in the end…I guess it doesn't matter.

"You keep referring to him in the present tense…. Why?"

125

I can see his face in my mind's eye, so beautiful, so sad. There's blood smudged across his cheek, but I don't care. I'm not squeamish any more. It's the face of the man I love, the only one I've ever loved, and it's difficult to imagine there will ever be another. I wipe more tears away. *That bastard.* "It's easier," I finally answer. "I don't like the idea he's gone."

Sloan nods. "Go ahead, tell me what happened next."

"Nothing much really, after breakfast he helped me get dressed. Then he tied me to the bed, gagged me, and left for a few hours." I know where he went now – he went to the bank, but I don't know if I should tell Sloan or not. Then again, Reed already knows about the money. "He went to the bank," I add. Sloan flips through her paperwork and writes something down.

"Why isn't Reed here? Why the both of you at different times?"

"Agent Reed and I have different job descriptions. He's interested in the case; I'm interested in your well-being as well as the case."

"So he doesn't give a shit about what happens to me is what you're saying." I'm not shocked by the information; it's something I already knew to be true, but still, it stings to hear it from someone else.

"I didn't say that. Please don't put words in my mouth," Sloan says. I think I've made her uncomfortable, but I can't say for what reason. "Agent Reed says you kissed him?"

My eyes open wide and my mouth is slightly agape. I can't believe he told her! Why would he do that?

"So!?!" My face is heating up, and I'm positive it stems in equal parts from anger and embarrassment.

This is a side of Sloan I haven't seen yet. Her brow is arched, and her mouth is a little tight at the corners. "I'm not your enemy. Please stop acting like I am. He told me because he's concerned for you, and the only reason I bring it up is because you were just telling me he doesn't care about you."

"Fine! I kissed him." I look away from Sloan and toward the windows. Only Reed uses the kindergarten interrogation room to talk to me. I probably make him nervous. Good.

"Why?"

"Because he had something I wanted." The words fall right out of my mouth, and although I know the picture they paint of me, I can't say I care. I'm fixated on the pigeon walking back and forth outside my window. I'm envious of the pigeon. It doesn't have a care in the world beyond eating, sleeping, and defecating on park statues. That's the life.

"Is that the only reason?" She's trying to keep her words innocent, but I know nothing she says is innocent, not even her stories about interpretive taxidermy. It would be easy to forget Sloan is a member of the FBI and she's trained to handle cases like mine. She comes off as very empathetic, and even a little vulnerable herself, but she wouldn't be where she is today if she weren't a wolf under that wool suit.

My head swivels toward her and away from the window. I make myself smile brazenly. "Are you jealous, Janice?"

She doesn't miss a beat. "Of what, Olivia?" I smile again, and this time there's an answering smile on her face. Yeah, Sloan has teeth. I like teeth.

We go back and forth for several minutes. She asks me a question, and I turn it around to pose the same question of her, and she turns it back on me again. It would seem like useless conversation, but I think we're both learning little things about one another with each exchange. Still, I'd rather be talking to Reed. I tell Sloan as much.

"That isn't unusual, you know. Some victims of abuse tend to gravitate toward strong, authoritative men...like Agent Reed. They also tend to mimic the behavior expected of them by their abusers, especially when that behavior is of a sexual nature."

I feel like she's just doused me in hot oil. "Don't. Don't do that bullshit psychotherapy crap on me. It was a fucking kiss, not a pledge of my undying devotion. And for the record, I'm not some broken rape victim you have to put back together. I'm fine." I'm crying again and I hate myself for it. Why won't my face stop leaking!

"I'm sorry, Livvie. I didn't mean to upset you," Sloan says. She sounds sincere, and that almost pisses me off more than her suggestion I'm some basket case.

Aren't you? You don't know who you are anymore. You have no place to go from here.

"I think we're good for today. Do you want to stop? We can go have some lunch in the cafeteria. Maybe play some cards in the rec room, or maybe checkers? I love checkers."

"Sloan?"

"Yes?"

"You're doing it again." I wipe the tears off of my face and blow my nose with some tissues – funny how they're ready and waiting by my bed.

Sloan lets out a deep sigh and leans back in her chair. Her expression is inscrutable, as though not even she knows what she is feeling, or thinking, or wanting to say. Finally, though, she nods slightly to herself and opens her mouth. "I don't think you're broken. I don't mean to 'psychoanalyze' you. Well…" she laughs without humor, "at least, not out loud. But I do think there are some cracks to be filled in. You've been through so much in the last few months, and I'm incredibly impressed all you have are cracks. You should be broken, but you're not. Cracks can be mended and believe it or not, you have a lot of people who want to help you mend."

I swallow really hard. I don't want to cry any more. I don't know what I want, except for Caleb. I think I would gladly go back to the mansion if it meant I could be with Caleb again. I would live it all over again. I know it isn't healthy, and I worry that maybe, just maybe, Sloan and Reed are right. I'm fucked in the head and nothing I feel is real.

"You don't know what you want, Livvie, and what you think you want, you've been brainwashed into wanting."

Even Caleb said my love isn't real, but...I feel it. I feel my love for him more strongly and deeply than anything I have ever felt in my life. I think if it turns out they're right and I am wrong...*that* will break me. Survival...it's the most important thing.

***

It's been an okay morning, I guess. I didn't care for talking with Sloan, but playing checkers with her was slightly amusing. I could tell she was still analyzing me as we played, asking loaded questions beneath the guise of conversation, but for the most part we just talked about life outside the walls of the hospital. I missed a lot of things over the summer.

For starters, I missed graduation. I'm not sure how I feel about that. I suppose I don't really care, but it's strange not to. It had seemed so important four months ago. I guess I'm still a graduate. My grades were exemplary before I left.

Left. That's funny.

Nicole started college. She's called the hospital a few times and we've chatted a little – not about anything important. I avoid that. She's offered to leave school for a few weeks and visit me, but I asked her not to bother. I'm fine and I have a lot of stuff going on anyway. It was shockingly easy to get her to agree not to come. Life goes on. Even if yours is over.

Sloan has left the building, but she says she'll be back later today. As if I'd asked or even wanted her here; the woman is daft. *I'll take "Answers to questions no one has asked" for $100, Alex.* Still, I wish I had something to do besides lie in bed and watch TV. I've raided the library, but it's all so unimpressive.

Reed is supposed to come interview (more like interrogate) me soon, and I can't help but feel a little excited about seeing him and talking to him. When he gets angry with me I can almost see Caleb in his brown eyes. It's silly, but I almost live for those little glimpses.

I'm not sore anymore – haven't been in days. My bruises are gone and my scrapes are scabbed over. When they heal, it will be as if all evidence of my time with Caleb has been erased. I wrap my arms around my stomach and squeeze until the thought passes. If you had told me a month ago I'd be sad to have unmarked skin, I'd have called you stupid and smacked you around for good measure. But here I am – a girl without a mark and without a reason to keep moving forward.

"That's not true, Pet. You have every reason," Caleb's specter whispers in my ear. I don't know if hearing his voice in my head makes me crazy, but I don't care either way. It's what I have left after the scrapes heal. I can't give him up. Besides, I know the voice isn't real, no matter how much I wish it were.

I like to play his voice in my head at night, when the hospital is quieter and I can concentrate on making him as real as I can. I spread my legs and finger myself to the memory of his mouth sucking on my tits and his fingers flicking back and forth over my clit. If I try really, really hard, I can hear him, feel him, even fabricate the smell of him – but I can never get him to kiss me. I usually cry after I come. That's exactly the kind of thing I don't tell Sloan. I'm fairly certain she'd have a field day with that information.

I make use of my time waiting for Reed; I take a shower and put on the oh-so-sexy hospital lunatic outfit they give me to wear: gray pants and shirt. You would think they'd have something more cheerful given the scenery, but then I think of the crafts room and decide it's just as well. My skin tone does not do yellow. My lunch arrives and I pick through the soggy carrots, eat the gravy-covered, yet still tasteless beef, and drink my milk. I eat the green Jell-O too. Caleb fed me better food during my kidnapping than these people. I laugh at my own joke.

"Something funny, Miss Ruiz?" I look up from my tray and see Reed.

"Yes," I say, "something is very funny, Reed." He smiles, no teeth, but it's still pretty nice just the same. I wonder if Reed has a girlfriend. He's not wearing a wedding ring. What would Reed's girlfriend be like?

"Care to share, or do you have to extort more concessions out of me first?" He casually walks into my room and stands at the foot of my bed.

"You're funny, Reed. *Me* extort *you*, that's rich." He smiles again and shrugs. I mimic him. "I was laughing because the food here is awful and Caleb fed me way better stuff. Seems like *this* place is real captivity."

"Say the word and I'll have you transferred to The Pentagon; I hear they serve amazing spaghetti every Thursday." He sets his briefcase on the chair and leans against the wall.

"Gee, thanks. But I think I'll just put up with the horrible food. If I'm going anywhere from this place, it'll be to my new digs in whatever Midwestern town you've decided to hide me in." I give him my sweetest condescending smile. "How's that going, by the way?"

Reed shakes his head, unfazed. Not that I really expected to get a reaction from him. This guy just doesn't lose his cool...unless you make out with him. I smile again, wider, all teeth, and my smile isn't remotely sweet. The idea has promise, as it seems to be the only thing we have in common.

"Let's get right down to it then, Miss Ruiz. I've been doing some more research on your boyfriend and his terrorist friends and I have a few questions for you, starting with: When did you meet Muhammad Rafiq?"

Leave it to Reed to ruin any semblance of a pleasant moment. The man is an automaton and his programming is set to one objective: get the bad guys by any means necessary. I would respect him if he weren't trying to ruin my whole life. Just another way he reminds me of Caleb. "That's not where we left off, Reed. You said I could tell you the whole story."

He sighs. "Dr. Sloan called me after she left the hospital. I'll get all of her notes later, but for now, she said the only thing to come out of your time with her today was an acknowledgment it was Caleb who left you the money in Zacatecas. Two hundred fifty thousand dollars is a lot of money to transfer and deposit for a girl he planned on selling. I definitely want to talk about that, but for now the important thing is to find out more about Rafiq. When did you meet him?"

Reed has been here for less than ten minutes and he's already managed to royally piss me off. "I didn't know that's what he was doing. I didn't know until later he'd left me the money." It takes me a second, but then the rest of his words sink in and then I'm angry with Sloan as well. The *only* thing to come out of our three hour talk is that Caleb went to the bank? That's pretty cold. Everyone around me is just full of surprises lately.

"Rafiq, Miss Ruiz. When did you meet him?" Reed has apparently decided to forgo the imposing environment of the craft room and interrogate me in my room. Fine with me.

"He was there when we got to Tuxtepec," I whisper. This isn't a part of the story I want to tell, but I know it's what I have to do. The truth is, I want Reed to make it to that auction. I want him to round up those bastards and free those slaves. I owe it to them. I owe it to myself. I owe it to Caleb. "He'd been waiting for us."

Reed and I are silent for a moment. He pulls a recorder out of his jacket pocket, presses the record button, and puts it down on the bed. "It'll help me go through your statement later. I know this is hard, Miss Ruiz. I also know you think I want to make it that way, but I don't. I just want to do my job and make these people pay for what they've done to you, and to so many other women and children. There are children there too…did you know that?" I shake my head. I hate him for putting that thought in my head. I can't stand the thought of a child suffering. No more jokes or banter. Reed quietly lifts his briefcase and sets it on the ground before he sits down.

I clear my throat and lick my lips. This is where the real story begins.

***

I don't know exactly what time it was when we arrived, but the sun had set not too long before. Caleb and I hadn't done much talking on the way. I didn't really have anything to say to him that wouldn't result in him punishing me.

My heart pounded a sharp tattoo in my chest as we made our way down the seemingly-endless driveway. The person who owned this house definitely had a lot of money and demanded a lot of privacy. Large trees hid our destination, but I could

135

see the glow of lights in the distance. Soon. Soon I would lose everything that was ever important to me.

I berated myself for not making more attempts to escape, even if I could barely walk, let alone run. Still, even if I died in the process, I felt like I should have tried again. Death had to be better than what I had coming. I knew once he got me inside that house I would be a sex slave for the rest of my life. I know Caleb said two years, but I just didn't have any faith in that. How could I?

"Don't cry, Kitten. I won't let anyone hurt you. Obey and you'll be fine." Caleb's words were supposed to soothe me, but his tone was somewhat deadpan. It seemed not even he believed what he said.

I wrapped my arms tighter around myself and closed my eyes to try and find my bearing. I could do this, I kept telling myself. I could survive. I could get well enough to escape. I couldn't lose hope. Someone would come for me.

Abruptly, the truck stopped and a man wearing a tuxedo asked Caleb for his invitation. I was tempted to shout for help, but something told me the man knew exactly why I was being brought here and the last thing I needed was to prove to Caleb he'd been right about me. I would try to escape at the first opportunity. It was true, but he didn't need to have that kind of certainty.

"I don't have an invitation, but I was invited: Caleb."

His name – that's all it took. The man waved us on, and a little further up the driveway Caleb

136

stopped the vehicle, came around to my door and, gripping me by the arm, pulled me slowly up the walkway while someone else took the truck.

"I can walk!" I shrugged out of Caleb's grasp, ignoring the pain in my shoulder. I was sobbing, completely unable to stop. I couldn't believe this was happening.

You're going to die in there. Stop marching to your own fucking doom!

I stopped walking. "Caleb. Please, please don't make me go in there. Please. Please!" I turned to run, but Caleb's arms surrounded me before I managed to take my first step. I struggled and pain radiated from every part of my body, but especially my shoulder.

Caleb's hand covered my mouth as he pressed his body against my back and held me immobile. "Kitten, don't you dare!" he half whispered, half growled into my ear. "I warned you not to use my name. I warned you not to run from me. You are going inside one way or another, and there is nothing you can do about it. Accept it. Breathe and accept it."

I whimpered and sobbed behind his hand, but I had to admit being held by him was slowly bringing me back toward center. My panic was palpable, literally thrumming and pulsing in my veins, but Caleb's arms were strong. Caleb was solid. My muscles strained and the pain was approaching unbearable. I willed myself to relax my body in degrees and I noticed Caleb's fingers also relaxed.

He slowly withdrew his hand from my mouth. I gasped for breath and sobbed. "Shh." He stroked my hair as he continued to hold me up. "I know it's terrifying. I know you're scared. I'm trying to make this as simple as I can, but you cannot disobey me. If anyone believes I am not your master.... It will be bad, Kitten. Do you understand?"

I gripped Caleb's arm, wrapped around my midsection. *Don't leave me*, I silently screamed. *Don't leave me.* I nodded slowly and let Caleb's touch comfort me and reassure me he wouldn't let anyone hurt me. So long as I obeyed Caleb, I was his and no one could hurt me. No one but Caleb.

We walked the rest of the way in silence, but Caleb let me hold his hand. I knew he'd eventually punish me for my outburst, but that was later. At the moment, his anger was tempered and his hand was warm and strong against mine. Caleb was finished comforting me the moment we reached the large wooden door of the enormous estate. My entire body trembled, but I kept my head down and tried to breathe. My safety was assured, so long as my obedience could be expected. It could be a lie, but doubt was something my fragile psyche could ill afford.

Caleb rang the bell, and after a few seconds, there was a metal clang and the door creaked open. *"Buenas tardes, Señor...."*

I tuned out while Caleb and the man who answered the door talked. In the place of their conversation, I heard a high-pitched screech. I felt dizzy, too, but somewhere in my head, I knew it was only my panic and adrenaline doing this to me. I forced air in and out of my lungs at a steady pace, willing myself not to hyperventilate.

Caleb's hand at the small of my back urged me forward and somehow I did it – I took that first step toward my own annihilation. Then I took another and another, my eyes watching my feet as they continued to carry me.

Music played in the background as we walked, and soon I couldn't help but notice the place looked like a lavish hotel. The floors were made of marble, and the use of rich, wine-colored carpets was also prevalent. I kept close to Caleb, especially since he didn't discourage it. Suddenly, I heard a loud slap, followed by a woman's whimper of distress from the left. My eyes followed the sound past the man in front of us and landed on the scene in the adjoining room.

A crowd of finely-dressed men, and even some women, was loosely gathered to watch as another man in a white tuxedo held a naked woman over his lap. Her black hair was swept to the side, her pain-stricken face clearly visible. Her body seemed graceful, even in its debased position. A glaring red hand print stood out prominently against her pale white skin. The man stroked her spine and she undulated, lifting her behind higher into the air as if begging the man to strike her again. I looked away when he did, and the woman once again whimpered but did not scream.

Is that the kind of thing Caleb expects from me? I knew the answer. I also knew I would fail at the task miserably. No matter how many times Caleb had spanked me, I always screamed and begged for him to stop, even as I surrendered to the orgasms he gave me.

"There is someone here to see you. I am taking you to him now," said our chaperone.

Caleb's fingers twitched against my spine and I felt a corresponding shock of pure panic. "Is it the master of the house? I've been eager to meet him."

The chaperone kept walking as he answered. "No, Sir. The master of the house is Felipe Villanueva. We passed him in the den with his slave, Celia. The señor often has guests; he enjoys the attention."

Another slave. Another woman being held against her will in this same house. It makes me sick. That poor woman, being humiliated in front of all those strangers and knowing none of them will help her.

Caleb stopped and I jumped when his hand pushed me forward. Our eyes met. His blue eyes were cold and they hid something very dark. I did not want to know what he was thinking. I forced myself to keep going.

The music and the sound of the other guests slowly drifted away with each twist and turn we took into the labyrinth. Unfortunately, they were drowned out by the sound of a woman screaming. I couldn't help but start crying then. I found Caleb's arm and gripped it with both arms, wrapping my body around it. I looked up to see the chaperone slide two doors apart and the screaming only got louder. The man and Caleb exchanged a short nod, and then the man left. Caleb dragged me inside as he walked.

Caleb stopped after a few steps and I could feel the way his body tensed. Something had startled him. The woman was still screaming.

I looked up, and the sight in front of me finally forced me to faint. Nancy, the girl who had assisted in my attempted rape, the one who had watched while those men held me down and tried to go at me from both ends. The one who had stood by while they punched, slapped, and kicked me! She was the one doing all the screaming. She was naked and tied face-down onto some kind of wooden horse while an Arab-looking man rammed himself into her over and over.

When I regained consciousness, I realized Nancy wasn't screaming any more. I was lying on a burgundy leather sofa and Caleb's angry face was looking down on me. He said nothing as he lifted a glass of water to my lips. I didn't even think of speaking. I'd seen what could happen if Caleb left my side, and I was determined to endear myself to him.

Suddenly, a man's voice broke the silence. He spoke a language I didn't understand. It was the same fast, clipped speech I recognized as being similar to Jair's. He and Caleb's exchange was heated and forceful. The other man *laughed* at Caleb. I dared not look in the direction of that voice.

Caleb's brow furrowed, and his eyes focused above and behind me. "She's scared. I hardly see how terrifying her further will serve anyone's purpose."

The man let out an eerie chuckle. "English, *Khoya*? Do you want her to understand our conversation?" His words were thickly accented, but understandable. "She should be afraid. After the chase she led you on and the trouble she has caused, she obviously wasn't terrified enough to begin with. Jair mentioned you've been soft with her," said the man.

I could tell the man had to be someone with a lot of power. I couldn't imagine Caleb would let anyone speak to him that way.

Caleb's voice rose and he rattled off a bunch of words in another language I didn't understand – Arabic, I thought. If I had to guess, I would say he was giving the other man a piece of his mind. I sank into the couch and tried to become invisible as the two of them went back and forth.

Finally, Caleb said, "Enough! Kitten, get down on the floor in your rest position." Though terrified, I didn't think twice about obeying and quickly found myself on the floor at Caleb's feet with my legs open and my hands on my thighs, head bowed, just as asked.

"I want to look at her. Come here…" he chuckled again, "Kitten."

I whimpered and shook, but I couldn't make myself move. I inclined toward Caleb's leg, cowering and begging as much as I could without speaking or breaking my position. He had promised to protect me. I hoped he would now.

The man tsked, and I could almost feel Caleb's anger radiating off of him, but I didn't know whom the anger was directed toward. It didn't take long to figure out. Caleb's hand pushed my head away and he left my side.

"Look at me," Caleb said.

He stood next to the Arab-looking man. The man had put his clothes back on, and I was somewhat surprised to see him in a dark, finely-cut suit. His shirt was unbuttoned some of the way, exposing some of his deeply brown and slightly sweaty skin. He was a few inches shorter than Caleb, but still tall by my standard. He was older than Caleb as well, perhaps in his forties. His eyes were dead and dark. They seemed to be rimmed in kohl, but I could tell they weren't. It was an attribute associated with Middle Eastern men to have such long, thick, and dark lashes. However, I was not attracted to him in the least. He was a monster.

"Come here," said Caleb and I knew exactly what he wanted. It took quite a bit of effort on my part, but somehow I managed to crawl toward him without using my injured shoulder. In the process, I saw Nancy was out cold in the corner, still strapped down but with a gag in her mouth. I shuddered. I obviously didn't give two fucks about Nancy, but no one deserved that.

More words were exchanged in Arabic before the strange man in front of me addressed me. "*Leet sawm k'leet sue*," he said.

I looked toward Caleb, who repeated the command with some exasperation. With tears

143

flooding my eyes, I lied back and opened my legs toward the pair, relieved I was wearing clothing. That was, until the man reached down and flipped my skirt up over my knees. Losing all composure, I flipped the skirt back down and struggled to move away.

"Stay where you are!" yelled Caleb, and I was helpless against accepting the command. He approached me at a fast clip and pushed me to the ground. Within seconds, I lay in the appropriate position with my most intimate parts displayed for this stranger. Betrayal burned hotly in my chest, but a voice in my head bade me to be smart and avoid confrontation. No one had hurt me, not yet – and until then, Caleb still kept his promise.

"She's hardly been broken. I've had more obedient hounds!"

Caleb's eyes narrowed in my direction. He was embarrassed in front of this man on my account. I knew that now. I knew who the man must be. *Rafiq*, my mind offered. This was the man Caleb owed, and he was the reason Caleb planned to sell me.

"*Lye zhaash chee!*" ordered Caleb, and once again I did as he asked. I rolled over and lifted my ass into the air, sobbing into the carpet as I struggled to demean myself fast enough.

Caleb and Rafiq spoke more Arabic as they ignored my sobbing and took stock of me. Caleb's hand traveled my body, exposing parts of me along the way. One of his hands played along my spine, trying to soothe me as the other trailed up the back of my thighs and palmed each of my ass cheeks in

144

turn. It was almost as though Caleb were trying to convince Rafiq of something. I hoped it would end in my favor, but I had my doubts.

Finally, Rafiq let out a resigned sigh. "Fine, *Khoya*. Perhaps when she is healed and trained properly, I will see her as you do. For the moment, I am not so impressed."

Caleb urged me back into my rest position and put my clothing to rights with clipped and jerky movements that made me want to cringe. Despite my relief, I knew I'd be paying for Caleb's embarrassment one way or another, and soon.

A groan from the corner brought our collective attention back to Nancy. Rafiq laughed. "Now this one, *Khoya*. This one is a whore. She's been had by almost everyone, but she continues to come no matter how brutally she is taken, or how many times. It would be a pity to kill her, but of course, the choice is yours. I would never deprive you of your blessed revenge." He walked over to Nancy and cut her loose.

She screamed as he lifted her, and I cringed when I saw blood and semen run down both of her legs as he forced her to walk toward us while he led her by her hair. It was my fault she was here. Ironically, I was glad she had been so cruel to me and had participated in my torture. Otherwise, I would be beside myself for what had been done to her. It was difficult to stomach as it was. I couldn't imagine if this had been her penance for trying to help me.

Nancy collapsed when Rafiq threw her in front of me. She cried and whimpered, but what terrified me most was the way her hands reached out for me. "Help me," she sobbed. "Please, help me."

I was frozen for a few seconds, but then I grabbed her hands and bent her fingers until she let me go. I didn't want any part in this. I scooted back and dared a glance up at Caleb.

"It's your decision, Kitten. I don't know what happened between you. I don't know what role she played, but if you want her punished, if you want her dead, say the words and I'll see to it," Caleb said. He was deadly serious. I could see it in his eyes, and I knew what he wanted me to say. He wanted me to order her death.

Broken sobs erupted from Nancy and surprisingly...from me. "I can't!" I wailed over Nancy. "I can't do that! She's awful. She helped them. She held me down," I sobbed. "But I can't kill her. I'm not a fucking murderer!"

Caleb's face was grave as I yelled the word murderer. He lunged forward and I flinched, but Nancy was his target. He lifted her head roughly, craning it in my direction. With his eyes fixed on me, he whispered in Nancy's ear.

"Yes!" she yelled. "Anything...just don't kill me," she sobbed.

Caleb let go of Nancy's head like he'd just touched a piece of shit with his bare hand. "You hear that?" He pointed his finger at me. "She just said she'd kill you herself if we let her live instead. Is that the kind of person you want to spare?!?"

146

My head literally vibrated from the strength in his voice.

"No!" I sobbed. "I can't, Caleb. I won't. Please, please don't do this. Not for me."

"Caleb?" said Rafiq softly, his face twisting, and another torrent of clipped Arabic followed.

Horrified, I realized what I'd done. "Master—I didn't mean to!" I pleaded. "I know you're my master. Please forgive me. Forgive me. Forgive me." I repeated the words as I rocked back and forth.

Without warning, Caleb hoisted me to my feet, completely unconcerned with the pain it caused me. More Arabic was spoken, and then he led me out of the room and away from Nancy and her belligerent screams.

At Rafiq's request, Caleb led Kitten back to the party. It was not something he wanted to do, but in the unfamiliar space of the grandiose home of Rafiq's "friend," he had no choice but to follow the butler in the direction of the other guests. Anger toward Rafiq ran rife through his thoughts and he needed time to process everything he was feeling. Why was Rafiq at the mansion, and why would he deliberately ambush Caleb? It didn't make sense, except when Caleb considered the way Rafiq and Jair had been conspiring behind his back. He was tempted to count the incident as a betrayal, but the word was perhaps too strong given all Rafiq had done for him in the past.

Kitten, also, had disappointed him. He had warned her about being disobedient, warned her about what it might mean if she were found lacking in front Rafiq and the others, and still, she had humiliated him. Even now, her hand continued to search out his, seeking comfort in the most pedestrian fashion. She refused to stop weeping since she'd seen the blonde woman.

Internally, Caleb flinched, but he wasn't sure why. The blonde had surely deserved everything that had happened to her. He was certain now she had played a role in what happened to Kitten. She deserved no less than the fate she wished to impose.

148

The woman had been beaten severely. Her body was littered with whip marks and bites, her throat was bruised, and her eyes were bloodshot from the oxygen she had obviously been deprived. Rafiq mentioned she had been raped, roughly and repeatedly. Tortured. Yet, despite feeling that she had had it coming, Caleb took issue with violent rape. He could not get the image of blood and semen running down her thighs out of his mind fast enough to suit him. Finally, that his mentor had participated was difficult to accept.

He'd meant to give Kitten a gift, one that meant everything to Caleb: vengeance. Caleb would have done anything to go back in time and see to Narweh's end in the slowest, most painfully-degrading way possible, but the time had passed. Narweh was dead, and Caleb had to live with the knowledge that, even in the end, Narweh had never begged for his life or offered penance for what he'd done to Caleb. It was a slap in the face that Kitten would not only forgo such an opportunity to get back at her tormentor, but also look on Caleb as some sort of monster for suggesting it. It wasn't as though he expected her to watch!

But here, now, especially so close to his objective, he could not allow himself to show weakness, especially where Kitten was involved. Time was very critical and Rafiq would be watching his every move, as expected. They had been partners for twelve years, working toward the singular goal of ruining Vladek Rostrovich's life in every conceivable way. It was a goal that had, long ago, cost both of them their proverbial souls. Men had died. Women had died. And Caleb had killed. All to ensure their revenge would be carried out one day. Finally, their sights were set on their target, and Caleb seemed to be suffering from some absurd crisis of conscience. One silly girl was trying to make him question everything he and Rafiq had worked so hard to achieve. It was absolutely asinine when Caleb put it in perspective. Kitten might not be one for vengeance, but Caleb most certainly was.

Caleb kept an eye on the butler's back as they took the seemingly-endless number of twists and turns that would lead them to the others. He had no idea what the evening would entail, but his hackles were already up and he would have no pity for the next person who decided to trifle with him – even the sniveling girl next to him. Caleb could scarcely repress a snort of derision as he recalled the way Kitten had spat the word *murderer* in his direction. Yes, he was a murderer. He reminded himself he could no longer afford to be soft with her. No more leniency or favors. She would have to learn, right now, that mercy ended with him.

The murmur of loud voices finally reached Caleb's ears, and he was relieved to know he wouldn't have to listen to Kitten's sobs echo around him much longer. At last, they reached the other guests and the butler asked Caleb to wait while he let the master of the house know they were joining the festivities.

Caleb didn't know a lot about Felipe Villanueva, other than the fact Rafiq obviously trusted him.

Rafiq had told him they had come to know each other in the years after the coup in Pakistan, when Rafiq's general had taken power. They were not, by Rafiq's own admission, very close, but his mentor was meticulous when it came to whom he decided to trust. Caleb didn't need any higher recommendation. He also had no other choice, either.

Kitten, once again losing her composure, pressed herself to Caleb's back and wrapped her arms around him from behind. Annoyed, he pressed his fingers into the insides of her wrists until she released him. "Do not embarrass me in front of these people again or I will be forced to make an example of you. What did I ask you to do when you're unsure of what is expected?"

Kitten sobbed, rubbing her wrists, but had enough sense to get into her rest position. Caleb was momentarily satisfied when she was able to take slow breaths without drawing attention to herself.

He stroked the top of her head and spoke in a whisper only the two of them would be able to hear. "Good girl, Kitten. Obey me and I'll continue to see to your safety." He felt her nod beneath his hand. He couldn't wait to be done with this day, even as he dreaded what the next might bring.

A Mexican man in his late forties, with dark hair, green eyes, and an impressive beard, made his way toward Caleb and Kitten. He was dressed in an outlandish white suit and his demeanor was vastly different from those around them. From the general description Rafiq had given him, Caleb knew it had to be Felipe. Only the owner of an estate such as the

151

one they were currently occupying would dare wear such an ostentatious suit to an extravagant party. Caleb, in ill-fitting jeans and a t-shirt, was vastly underdressed and he was slightly self-conscious at his disheveled appearance. He would have liked to meet the man on equal footing.

"*Bueno!* You must be Mister C," the man said, his tone formal but light. "Mister R has told me very good things about you. I am Felipe. Welcome to my home."

Felipe's accent was thick, but his words remained clear enough to understand. Caleb extended his right hand only after Felipe had offered his right hand first. They shook hands firmly. Rafiq had long ago taught Caleb the importance of never offering to shake hands first, nor being the first man to enter a room. It established a subtle but important power dynamic between two people meeting for the first time.

"*Buenas noches*," Caleb offered in greeting. He slowly drew his hand away.

"*Buenas noches*," Felipe replied. His face was strangely jovial and kind. Something Caleb would not expect from a friend of Rafiq's. However, appearances could be deceiving as Caleb well knew, and he was in no rush to make judgments. Felipe's eyes darted down to Kitten and his smile became lecherous. "Please, use English. I like to practice whenever it is possible. You must like to practice as well. Where is your accent from? I cannot place it."

Caleb tensed. "I've no idea what you're talking about."

152

Felipe laughed and continued. "Is this her? The girl you have been chasing all over Mexico?" He laughed. "She doesn't look like so much trouble. Then again, neither did my little Celia – and she is a handful, that one." He laughed again, but there was a certain twinkle in his eye.

Caleb knew Felipe was very happy with his *little Celia*. Caleb could only hope *little* did not translate into *young*. Even he had his limits, and Rafiq damn well knew them. Then again, he had just walked in on Rafiq committing a rape.

Caleb forced himself to smile. "Yes, this is Kitten. I apologize for the way we are dressed. It was not by choice."

Felipe's expression was inquisitive, but Caleb offered no more information. After a few seconds, Felipe continued the conversation. "Her face...your doing?"

Caleb was realizing that Felipe's sense of etiquette was less than conservative, even familiar, which he didn't approve of at all. He was rather insulted at the man's insinuation, but also at the audacity of this stranger to ask him such a question. Even if the house belonged to Felipe, as guests, Caleb expected a little more. "No," he answered coldly. "But I dealt with them."

Felipe smiled surreptitiously and nodded his approval. "The other slaves are appropriately undressed according to their owners' wishes." Caleb smiled stiffly, finding Felipe's unchecked mirth, and this conversation, somewhat grating. "One of them has a tail! Poor girl has been begging to have it

153

removed, but Mr. B thinks it is too much fun. I have to agree." He laughed again. "It is not my place, even if I am the host, to tell you how your Kitten should be dressed, but perhaps it would help you both settle in if she were out of those clothes?" His eyes once again landed on Kitten, surprisingly subdued.

Caleb's ire was high, but he tried to remain respectful in his dissenting opinion. "We are tired. Also, the girl has been beaten very badly, as you can see. She isn't ready yet – perhaps another time."

Felipe's disappointment was obvious. "As you say. Please join us and have some appetizers with wine. I am not sure if Mr. R mentioned it, but I have been making use of the boy that was brought here. I hope you do not mind, but he seemed more… sensitive than the woman he was brought with. You don't mind, do you?"

Caleb felt heat rush down his spine. Of course he fucking minded. They were supposed to be *his* hostages, not a damn party favor for Rafiq, Felipe, or anyone else who wanted to have a go at them. However, Kitten seemed lacking in her thirst for revenge and he'd shed enough blood to last him a while, so why the hell should he care?

"Consider him a gift. I only hope he's worthy of being kept in such luxury." Caleb tried to keep the sarcasm from his voice and only marginally succeeded.

Felipe smirked. The man was no one's fool. "You are very kind, Mr. C. Please consider me your friend."

Caleb nodded once as he followed Felipe past his curious guests and toward a set of red, velvet chairs in the corner.

"So you can see, but keep your privacy." Felipe gestured toward the chairs.

"Thank you," Caleb offered as humbly as possible. "I'm Caleb. Kitten is painfully aware of my name, so the formality is not necessary on my account." Caleb had no desire to be called *mister* all night.

Felipe looked down at Kitten and smiled. "As you wish, Mr. Caleb," he said and then stepped away to attend to his other guests.

Caleb took a seat in one of the velvet chairs and stroked Kitten's hair when she quietly took her place next to him on the floor. She had followed him through the crowd on her good hand and knees, carefully guarding her shoulder. Caleb sighed deeply as he stroked her hair, comforting them both. He didn't want things to be so complicated, but the time for wants had passed.

Abruptly, Caleb heard the tinkling of a bell and a petite Asian girl with raven hair and almond-shaped eyes commanded his attention. She crawled very slowly on her hands and knees, but a cursory examination revealed the need for her hesitant movements. The tinkling sound came from the tiny bell attached to the leather collar she wore. In addition to the collar, she wore a silver serving tray on her back, strapped across her midsection but allowing access to her otherwise-naked body. On the tray, tall, thin wine glasses were half-filled with white wine.

Caleb knew the game. If she spilled her tray of drinks, she would draw the collective attention of the guests and her master would punish her for their amusement. It was wicked, but relatively benign as far as games went. The young woman's master didn't appear to be predisposed to violence. The girl's tawny skin was pristine.

Caleb looked at Kitten, who seemed transfixed by the sight of the woman. Her slender hands were balled into tight fists and her face appeared flushed.

"What are you thinking, Pet?" Caleb asked. It was the first moment they had to themselves, and he was somewhat surprised at how much he enjoyed being in Kitten's sole company. He smiled gently when her big, puffy eyes shyly met his.

Her lips trembled from her effort to keep fresh sobs from escaping. Caleb sighed. *So much for a moment of peace.* He pulled his fingers away from Kitten and stood up to get a glass of wine from the tray.

The girl was deathly still as he reached for the glass. Her lips were slightly open, allowing for slow and shallow breaths. Caleb did the girl a favor and carefully selected a glass that wouldn't disrupt her balance and returned to Kitten, who immediately rubbed her head in supplication against his knee.

"Scared I would leave you?" he taunted.

Kitten nodded against his knee.

He was still angry from their showing with Rafiq earlier, but it was directed mostly inward. He shouldn't let Kitten get to him. "It would be no less than you deserve."

She whimpered and pressed even closer.

Caleb knew he should correct her behavior, but he opted to reward the fact she wasn't crying. He was also oddly pleased that while she did not respond to Rafiq, or his orders, she had attempted to follow all of Caleb's. *To varying degrees of success*, he mused. He reached into his pocket and took two Vicodin from the bottle he kept there. He was out of morphine, and Kitten still had a lot of pain.

"Open your mouth," he said. He offered her a smile when she immediately complied. He knew she was scared. He had no doubts it was the only reason she obeyed him, but having her yield was still incredibly arousing. He put the pills in her mouth and lifted the wine glass for her to drink. He watched the long, graceful slope of her throat as she lifted her head to swallow greedily until the glass was empty. His cock stirred.

Kitten's chocolate-colored eyes looked on him in gratitude and supplication. She could say so many things with her eyes. All of her emotions were there for him to see. If she was an actress, she was a very good one.

Or perhaps you only see what you'd like to see. Caleb's brow furrowed slightly and he noticed Kitten instantly returned her stare to her thighs. Perhaps Caleb *also* said things with his eyes. He needed to stop that. Caleb looked up just as Rafiq made his way over and sat in the seat next to him.

"I put the whore down," Rafiq said in Arabic.

"Here?" Caleb was careful not to telegraph his mild surprise.

"Caleb, please. We are guests here. I put her down in the cellar... to sleep." Rafiq's tone was meant to poke fun at Caleb.

Caleb didn't see the humor. He nodded and let the subject drop. "How much longer is this going to last? I want to get out of these ridiculous clothes. You deliberately didn't tell me you were here. Furthermore, you didn't mention there would be so many people bearing witness to our crimes. Yet, *I'm* the sloppy one."

Rafiq laughed and smacked Caleb on the back of the shoulder. "Ah, *Khoya*. It's always betrayal with you. Even as a boy, you had to have things on your own terms. Do you remember the first time I took you to a brothel? You'd never been with a woman, but you would not be content with just any woman. It had to be the 'perfect' woman! Then what happened, *Khoya*? I'll tell you – you lost control and finished in less than a minute!" Rafiq laughed so hard he shook Caleb's shoulder as he laughed.

He *loathed* that story and the way Rafiq took such enjoyment in its telling. He did not like being made fun of, even by someone he considered a friend, a brother, and most importantly, an ally. Caleb felt his face warming in equal parts anger and embarrassment. "Damn you, Rafiq! If you want to reminisce with someone, why don't you find your friend Jair? I'm sure you'd enjoy his company much better." Caleb shrugged off Rafiq's hand.

158

Rafiq wiped tears from the corners of his eyes as he slowly brought his laughter to a winding halt. "Such a child, Caleb. Jair is a source of information when you are less forthcoming. I know you well, *Khoya*, and I would be a fool to think you tell me everything. Besides, I wanted to see this girl you've selected for Vladek. I want to be sure she's *perfect* for the task. Frankly, as of this moment, I am unconvinced."

Caleb drove his anger inward; absently, he reached out to stroke Kitten's hair. "I take offense, Rafiq. I chose Kitten myself and, just as in your story, I'm content with my choice. Did it ever occur to you that a minute in that whore's arms was all I needed?" Caleb finally relented and smiled. "She said it was perfect."

Rafiq chuckled, and Caleb couldn't help but laugh with him. They'd known each other for a very long time. Rafiq was the only person who really knew Caleb, and despite their odd and often tense relationship, Caleb had to admit it was good to laugh with him again. It had been a long time since they'd seen one another and their phone calls had been mainly business.

Caleb relaxed.

"I'm sure it was the best minute of her life, *Khoya*."

"I agree." Caleb smirked. He was sure Rafiq was about to offer another witticism when their host for the evening called the room to attention.

"Ladies and gentlemen. Tonight, I have a special treat for all of you. Thanks to some dear friends, I have recently come into possession of a glorious new slave. He is raw and unbroken, but I am sure you can appreciate the novelty of seeing one so inexperienced." He chuckled. "Alas, I have given the pleasure of mastering him to my long-time slave, Celia."

A soft murmur of approval and applause rippled through the room. Caleb glanced at Rafiq, who seemed amused by Felipe's antics. For Caleb's part, he was somewhat reticent given Kitten's reaction to seeing the blonde girl. He braced himself for whatever might come next. It was too late to leave the room.

"My Celia hails from Spain, and her English is very poor. I will be translating on her behalf and assisting. I hope you enjoy." Felipe waived his hand and a door opened, revealing Celia, dressed in a tight, white leather corset, with matching stockings and shoes.

Caleb's pants seemed tighter. Celia was a quintessential Spanish beauty. Her hair was jet black and her eyes were so dark, it would be easy for anyone to get lost in them. Her mouth had been painted a deep red to match the flower in her hair. Her skin was a milky expanse that would surely show every mark laid on it. Celia's breasts were bare in the corset, and her tiny breasts were pale white against the deep raspberry color of her pebbled nipples. Beneath the corset she wore no panties, leaving her bare, pink flesh open to the scrutiny of prying eyes. She had been spanked earlier and the rounded globes of her ass showed it. Her stockings were white fishnet and created an alluring pattern as they hugged her thighs and legs. Her leather half-boots were small and dainty, with a tiny bit of lace at the top. Caleb had to give credit where it was due – Felipe's slave was glorious. He was suddenly aching to see what she could do with her whip hand.

Next to his chair, Caleb noticed Kitten was also transfixed by Celia. He stroked her hair, silently content when she inclined toward him and rested her head against his knee. He did not neglect to notice she kept her hands dutifully in her lap.

There was a slight commotion as two men escorted the boy Caleb knew as *Kid* through the same door a few seconds later. Kid was obviously a man, no younger than eighteen, no older than twenty-three, but his face lent itself to a certain boyish quality that had obviously led to his nickname. Caleb had to agree it had been well chosen.

Kid entered the room blindfolded, bound, and gagged, but otherwise naked. A cursory evaluation showed he'd been beaten, but it wasn't as bad as Caleb would have thought. Almost as if someone had intervened on his behalf before the boy ended up like his girlfriend. Caleb shifted uncomfortably in his seat. Something about the boy was off-putting to Caleb.

"He looks like you a bit," said Rafiq.

"Fuck you," Caleb said in English. Kitten's head snapped up, but came back down to Caleb's knee when he gently pressed.

Rafiq laughed, but offered no further comment.

161

Celia spoke her words with authority. "Put him on his knees and lock his wrists to his ankles." As the men did as she asked, Felipe translated and the crowd clapped softly.

Kid noticeably trembled, but surprisingly, he did not struggle against the two men. Caleb wondered if he was naturally submissive, or if he'd been brutally reminded of the punishment for disobedience. He hoped it was the former. If the boy had anything to do with Kitten's condition, Caleb would see to it he suffered – compliant or not.

"Take the gag out of his mouth," Celia ordered. She sauntered over to Kid and ran her fingers through the boy's shoulder-length hair, easing him into a false sense of security before she fisted the gold strands and snapped his head back.

"Fuck!" the boy yelled. He tried to pull out of Celia's grasp, but she held him easily in her tight little fist. Caleb was impressed.

"Does it hurt, Slave?" she crooned. Laughter could be heard in the room.

The boy was silent. Behind his back, his fists clenched and his arms strained against the restraints he wore. Celia pulled harder, wrenching his head back in such a way his throat was completely exposed. "Yes…Celia," he finally whispered.

Slowly, the soft music that had been playing began to fade until the room was stark in its silence. It drew the moment into sharper focus, each sound lending itself to an action. The room itself seemed to become a living thing, breathing, vibrating, and

162

hungry. Even Caleb was not immune to the charm of one petite girl mastering someone twice her size.

"Very good, Slave." Felipe's voice was scarcely above a whisper when he translated Celia's words. Caleb did not require the translation, but he could appreciate the way Felipe's voice – low, but full of authority – drew the others in as they strained to hear every word.

Celia released Kid's hair and he audibly sighed in relief. She stroked the gold strands for a few seconds. Her audience sighed in approval as they listened to Kid's ragged breaths.

Caleb had always marveled at the way a person's inability to see lowered their inhibitions sharply. Surely, Kid would be humiliated to know the sounds he was making were being heard and interpreted by a room full of people who lived for such things. Caleb was almost embarrassed for him, or perhaps he was only uncomfortable watching.

Slowly, seductively, Celia caressed the boy's face, his neck, and his shoulders. She let herself take the time to coax him into desiring her. Kid could probably smell her perfume, nearly feel her nipple make contact with his face as she stood in front of him, touching him like a lover in a room full of strangers. When Celia pulled away, the boy nearly fell on his face chasing after the smell of her.

"She's very good," Rafiq suddenly whispered in a hushed tone. Caleb nodded in assent.

Celia quietly circled the room, finally coming upon a squat, round man wearing a cowboy hat and a bolero tie. She inclined her body toward him, rubbing her pert nipples across his chest sinuously. The man chuckled and leaned forward in an attempt to kiss Celia, but at the last second, she reached for the flogger in the man's hand and sharply turned on her heel, slapping the man in the face with her hair.

The room erupted in laughter. "Damn it, Felipe," said the man in a thick Texas drawl, "you are a lucky bastard. Go on, honey – you teach that boy a lesson."

Celia smiled for the crowd and cheekily waved her flogger. "Put your face on the ground and lift your ass in the air," she said.

Kid flinched and didn't move to obey, even after Felipe translated. The crowd hissed in disapproval.

"No?" inquired Celia.

"Please," Kid said with a whimper. And it was most definitely a whimper. "I've had enough. No more."

Caleb shifted in his seat. He stroked Kitten's hair again, and abruptly she shifted to sit between Caleb's knees. Her head landed on his upper thigh and she pressed his hand to her ear.

"She's quite bold, Caleb. I'm surprised you let her get away with things like that," Rafiq quietly scolded.

"I told you, Rafiq, she is not herself. Stop acting as though you've never been lenient. I've seen you train. Even you have your moments." With that, the subject was momentarily dropped.

"Enough? I've barely started," simpered Celia. "And of course..." she said as she raised the flogger. She waited a moment, letting her audience share in Kid's anticipation before she brought the flogger

164

down across his chest. "You forgot to say, 'please, *Celia*'."

Kid groaned, biting hard on his lip as he attempted to rub his chest against his knees by doubling over.

Celia swished the flogger in the air and brought it back down across Kid's back, and this time his groan was loud and open-mouthed. "Will you obey me?"

"Yes, Celia," the boy said through gritted teeth. The crowd applauded.

Caleb chuckled to himself. Yes, it was good to be surrounded by his peers. The debilitating guilt he had been feeling lately was practically non-existent. It had evaporated and was replaced with a more familiar sentiment: lust.

Kitten's head, resting on his thigh, was so close to his dick he could almost feel her breath on it. He was tempted to take it out and make her suck it. He had yet to demand that particular act from her, but he knew he wouldn't be able to resist forever. He'd fucked her ass, why not her mouth?

"Prove it, Slave, and lift that sexy ass in the air," Celia purred.

Caleb heard the catch in the boy's throat as he struggled to lower his head to the floor. He teetered on his knees before he finally managed the head-down-ass-up position Celia demanded. The crowd murmured, their excitement palpable.

Celia dragged the long, leather strands across the bare expanse of Kid's flesh. Naked and tightly bound, Kid had no control over what was about to happen to him. His breathing was quick and ragged, and each breath moved his entire body. Celia gently flicked the tips of the flogger against Kid's balls, which could be seen by those standing or sitting behind him. He hissed, writhing against the carpet as much as he could.

"Do you like that, Slave?"

"No, Celia."

Another tap. "That's not nice. Shall I hit you harder? Like a man?" The audience was positively giddy over that idea.

"No! No, Celia. I'm sorry. I'm sorry," Kid pleaded.

Celia raised the flogger and whipped the boy harder, until he lost all control and sobbed into the carpet. "How was that, Slave? Hard enough?"

Kid could hardly breathe, let alone speak, but he struggled to get the words out anyway. "Yes... Celia."

Caleb didn't believe he was gay, or even bisexual. It was a subject he spent time exploring after he left his life as a whore behind, but he had to admit, Kid's submission was compelling. Celia, also, was impressive in her approach.

"You're doing so well, Slave. Just a little more and I'll reward you," Celia crooned.

Caleb listened, as did everyone else in the room, to Kid's sobs catching in his chest. What Caleb didn't expect was the answering sob coming from Kitten in his lap. "What's wrong, Pet?" Caleb whispered. He traced the delicate shell of Kitten's ear with his finger; she shivered.

"All of these people…." She trailed off.

The sound of the flogger slapping against naked flesh echoed through the room and was punctuated by Kid's pained growl. Again and again the flogger fell against Kid's increasingly-warming skin. With each stroke, he lost more and more of his bearing, until at last his muscles stopped bracing for the blows and he ceased to temper the sounds pouring out of him.

Caleb should abhor the spectacle. Somewhere in his mind he knew that watching someone essentially getting whipped should disgust him, but nothing could be further from the truth. Whippings excited him in a way not much else could. His mind replayed the evening he had whipped Kitten. She had struggled, cursed at him, lashed out at him physically, but in the end she had come apart at his hands. He hadn't worried about her feelings then, and he felt he shouldn't worry about her feelings now.

He leaned down and spoke to her. "You embarrassed me earlier. Should I strip you and return the favor in front of all these people?"

Kitten muffled a cry by pressing her mouth against his leg. She shook her head fervently. "No, Master," she managed to say.

"I would certainly like to see that," Rafiq interjected. "At the very least it would prove you haven't gone completely soft." Caleb spared a glance for his mentor and raised an eyebrow. "At least she's addressing you properly."

167

Caleb laughed, ignoring the way some of the other guests glared at him. He wasn't interrupting Celia. She was much too focused to notice him, or anyone else who wasn't the slave at her feet for that matter. "I would, but I know she isn't ready. She'd only cause me more embarrassment."

"Well then, perhaps you should allow me," he said, in English.

Suddenly, uproar spread throughout the room and both Caleb and Rafiq craned their necks to see beyond the other guests blocking their view. Caleb gasped, and unwittingly, his lengthening cock brushed against Kitten's cheek.

Celia, the exotic little vixen, had stepped into a harness, and jutting out from her bare pussy stood one of the largest dildos Caleb had ever seen. She let the crowd admire it, waiting for the noise to die down before she went any further.

Kid, still blindfolded, was rigid with apprehension. He was trying, unsuccessfully, to ball himself up tighter – as if he could crawl so deep inside himself he would disappear. All he succeeded in doing was building the collective lust of his voyeuristic audience.

"Push him back. I want him sitting on his heels," Celia said, and the men eased the boy back.

Kid's face was bright red and wet with tears. His chest, unlike his back, bore only one raised, red stripe from the flogger.

"Open your legs, Slave," said Celia.

Kid sobbed harshly, his chest shaking with the effort, but he complied.

168

"You've been such a good boy, Slave. I think you've earned a gift." Celia trailed the flogger slowly across Kid's cock and balls. Kid's breath stopped all together and didn't return until after Celia had made a few passes with the soft leather.

Slowly, his cock began to stir, growing despite his shame and humiliation. Despite the fact his audience watched with bated breath for the moment Celia would unleash her dildo on him. Despite the fact he couldn't possibly know what was going to happen next.

Celia continued to coax Kid's erection, going so far as to lower herself to her knees and stroke him with her bare hand. Kid groaned as his sensitive flesh was expertly caressed. He'd seemingly forgotten about the flogger, didn't know about Celia's cock, and his body swayed toward her slowly. Forward and back, following her fingers and whimpering when they didn't come back fast enough to suit him.

"Greedy slave," Celia said. "I'm greedy too, and I don't think you've earned your present yet." She stood and Kid held his breath again. Slowly, Celia put her plump nipple to Kid's lips. It was brave, considering the boy could bite her, but Celia seemed unconcerned with such things. "Suck."

Kid opened his mouth and accepted Celia's nipple. He groaned, loud and unabashed. His cock jerked in midair. The pain seemed to be a memory to him as he latched on and suckled Celia in long, hungry pulls that had her gasping and pulling his mouth closer.

"Yes!" Celia yelled, and it required no translation on Felipe's part. "Suck harder."

Kid obliged, only pulling his mouth away to breathe and occasionally switch breasts, which Celia took great relish in.

Finally, the moment had arrived, and she forced Kid's head away with a loud pop. Her nipples were bright red and fat from having been sucked so hard, but she didn't seem to take notice or care. She grabbed her rubber cock and brought it to Kid's mouth. "Now, suck this."

Kid, obviously sensing something foreign, reared back and turned his head. "No, Celia. Please, no."

Celia didn't bother to respond. She raised the flogger and struck him across the chest with so much force, there was a collective wince in the room. Kid tried to double over, but the men held him up.

Caleb wondered what it would be like to let a woman whip him. Aside from Rafiq, no one had dared strike him and lived after Tehran. Yes, Rafiq had punished him in the very early years, when Caleb still needed it to remind him he had survived. It had been well over a decade since Caleb had been on the submissive end of any encounter.

"Suck it!" Celia repeated. This time, Kid opened his mouth and let Celia fuck his mouth with the enormous phallus.

The room was filled with the occasional chuckle whenever Kid choked, but even then, they were apparent in their lust. A look around the room would reveal some of the masters had decided to make use of their slaves' mouths, mimicking Celia's movements and thrusting their very real cocks into the ravenous mouths of the slaves at their feet.

Caleb looked down at Kitten. She had abandoned her quest to not see or hear what was happening around her and was openly watching as others fornicated around her. Caleb reached for her hand and gently pressed it against his erection. His cock leapt when her wide eyes darted to his. He expected her to try and snatch her hand away, but he felt her fingers tighten around him through the fabric of his pants.

"She seems to like you just fine. It must be me she doesn't care for," said Rafiq, rather wryly.

"Unlike some, she has taste," Caleb countered. He slowly lifted his hips and pressed deeper into Kitten's hand. He remembered the shower, the way she had eagerly wanted to please him. He wanted that again. He wanted Livvie. The thought jolted him back into the moment, and he stilled Kitten's hand on his erection. She looked up at him.

Did I do something wrong? Her eyes asked. Caleb shook his head, but drew her hand away.

"Shy, Caleb? Really? You of all people," said Rafiq, mocking.

"Fuck you," Caleb said, his tone pleasant.

"Let him loose," Celia said, once again drawing both him and Rafiq back to the scene in before them. As the men worked to unbind Kid, Celia shimmied out of her strap-on and seemed to brace herself.

The room was tense as Kid eagerly tried to get loose even faster. Still, once he was free of the locks, he remained on his knees and blindfolded in front of

Celia. His cock was still hard, which was impressive given the circumstances.

"Do you think you were good, Slave?" Celia's voice had dropped to a whisper that Felipe mimicked as well as he could.

"Yes, Celia?" replied Kid.

"I agree. You were very good, for your first time. Would you like to fuck me?" Kid jolted when Felipe repeated the words for him to understand, and though he didn't seem capable of rendering a verbal response, the crowd witnessed his cock bobbing up and down as it filled completely. Precome wept copiously from the tip. "Well, Slave. Do you want to fuck me or not?"

Kid nodded and stammered through his reply. "Y-y-yes, Celia."

Celia stepped in front of Kid and lifted his arms to put them around her. Kid let out a needy sound and greedily mauled the flesh offered to him. "Then fuck me," Celia said.

Without further ado, Kid leapt on top of Celia, tossing her to the ground with brutish force. Celia cried out in abandon but made no attempt to stop Kid from doing what he wanted. His hips tilted back for only a moment, and then he thrust forward, savagely, into Celia's pussy. He whimpered as he rutted against her.

Celia moaned, arching her back and spreading her legs as wide as she could, surrendering to the man pounding away on top of her. *"¡Sí, mi amor! Es todo para ti."*

Yes, my love. It's all for you.

Kid sought Celia's nipple blindly and finally pulled one into his mouth. He suckled Celia in rough, bruising pulls. His hips moved like a piston. Indeed, the boy seemed violent in his need to come, and by the way he gripped Celia, it was obvious he would fight anyone who attempted to stop him.

Finally, Kid let out a sound best reserved for a dying animal and thrust into Celia one final time. As the crowd applauded and cheered, the boy shuddered and collapsed on top of Celia.

Caleb quickly made his excuses, helped Kitten to her feet, and left the room in desperate search of the butler and his room.

10

Matthew swallowed past the dryness in his throat. If he didn't know better, he would suspect Olivia of having some sort of telepathic ability. He sat still in the uncomfortable chair and tried not to draw attention to the raging erection he was sporting.

Olivia's eyes were fixed on him, but her stare seemed to move through him and beyond, to some place he couldn't see. Her eyes were brimmed with tears, but for whatever reason, Matthew doubted they had much to do with the story. In fact, she had told it with some fondness, which he found disturbing given the situation.

Unbidden, the image of a young woman dressed in white leather and wearing an enormous dildo flashed into his mind, and right on its heels he wondered what it might be like to be forced to suck it in front of a room full of strangers. Matthew's erection throbbed angrily and, not for the first time, he was ashamed. He sighed, disappointed with himself, and crossed his ankle over his knee to better hide himself.

He clicked his pen a few times, because his fingers were anxious for something to do and then he wrote down the names: *'Kid', Nancy, and Celia (No known last name)*. "So, that was the night you met Rafiq and Felipe. Do you know what happened to Kid or Nancy? How did they end up at the house? Did Caleb kidnap them, too?"

Olivia glowered, but seemed unable to stop staring off into space long enough to direct it at him. He couldn't make sense of her feelings toward her captor, despite knowing how common it was. There just didn't seem to be anything there worth caring about, as far as Matthew was concerned. However, he did acknowledge there was a lot about Olivia worth admiring. She had spent the last four months in the company of kidnappers, rapists, murderers, drug dealers, and human traffickers, but she'd somehow maintained a certain naivety and triumphant strength that apparently could not be stripped away from her.

"I don't know what happened to them. The last time I saw them, they were both alive. Kid is probably fine; Felipe really liked him. Nancy...I don't know. Maybe she's still with Rafiq," she whispered without blinking.

"Are you alright, Miss Ruiz?" Matthew asked. His erection was finally starting to wane and he could focus on his questions.

The girl finally blinked and swiped at the fat tears sliding down her cheeks as a result. "I'm fine, Reed. It's just...never mind." She looked up at him and tried to smile, but it was a weak effort and they both knew it.

"Tell me. I know I'm not Sloan, but I have been around, Miss Ruiz." Matthew smiled when she finally let her smile reach her eyes.

"Sloan. I don't know what her deal is. She's always so nice to me, but it annoys me for some reason. I don't think she's disingenuous, but I just know there's more to her than she lets on. I mean, she works for the FBI, like you. Only she's not like *you* at all."

"Oh? And what am I like?" Matthew raised a dark brow.

She rolled her eyes. "You're a jerk, Agent Reed."

"You're kind of a jerk, too, Miss Ruiz," Matthew said dryly. She laughed.

"Aww, that's so sweet," Olivia said, slightly mockingly, but she laughed again, unrestrained – almost like a girl without any problems.

"So, you don't like Sloan," he rephrased. "Why?"

"I didn't say I didn't like her, Reed. You're always putting words in my mouth," she admonished. "Don't think I didn't notice you implied Caleb kidnapped Kid and Nancy. He couldn't have – he was with me, remember?"

Matthew smiled wryly and shook his head. "I didn't imply it, Miss Ruiz. I asked the question. That's my job. Also, we both know he did. Maybe he didn't do it himself, but he was there and he ordered it. Regardless, adding more kidnapping to the list of charges against him is hardly going to make a difference." Olivia was quiet for a long time after that – thinking, Matthew assumed.

"You keep talking about him like he's alive, Reed, and I told you…he's not." Her eyes were filled with unshed tears again, and it was difficult for Matthew to remain unaffected by them. No matter what he thought of Caleb, Olivia obviously felt very deeply for him.

"Why do you care about him so much, Miss Ruiz?" he demanded. He just didn't get it, and it pissed him off – more than it should. "He was terrible to you. The things he *did to you*. Don't tell me you wanted those things. I can't believe you could have."

Olivia was staring off into space again, but she spoke through her tears. "A lot of bad things happened to him too, Reed. His back was covered in whip marks, and he told me he was very young when someone did that to him." Matthew couldn't hold back a scoff, and Olivia blinked and scowled at him. "I'm not stupid, Reed. I know the shit he did to me was awful – I fucking lived it. But I'm telling you, monsters aren't born – they're made. And someone made Caleb. Someone beat him, someone did horrible things to him, and the only person who helped him, Rafiq, made him into a killer. He didn't have someone like you, or Sloan, or the goddamn FBI to help him. He had to survive all by himself, and even though I can't forgive him, I understand him."

"Are you trying to tell me he's the monster with a heart of gold?" he said, disbelieving. "Come on, Miss Ruiz. Really?"

Anger flashed on her face. "There isn't a permanent mark on me, Reed, not one. And you don't know how many times he was there to hold me together when I was sure I was going to fall apart.

He's a monster," she sobbed, "I know he is. I know, and…it doesn't matter to me anymore."

Crying women left him bereft of action. They reminded him too much of his birth mother lying on the couch, shaking and begging him to find a way to score more drugs for her. He'd panic at times like that, knowing if Greg came home and found her, he'd beat her and then turn his rage on him. He'd only been seven, but he knew how to get lost for a while. He would grab his coat, kiss his mother, promise her he'd be back with her medicine, and then he'd leave. There was an older lady, Mrs. Kavanaugh, who lived a few blocks away. When things got bad, he would stay at her house, eating cookies and watching game shows until his mom, or Greg, came looking for him.

His mother had been a weak woman, a drug addict who cared more about being loved by an abusive man than she did her own son. Matthew had tried for years to help his mother get clean, but in the end, she couldn't stop using. One night, she was too high to defend herself, and Greg beat her to death. Matthew hadn't been home. He'd been out with his friends.

When he'd arrived at home, he'd found her – cold and still.

Matthew was thirteen and he went to live with Mrs. Kavanaugh's daughter, Margaret, and her husband, Richard Reed. Greg committed suicide in lieu of going to jail for murder, and Matthew had never gotten over the injustice of it, despite the fact his life had improved drastically after that. Margaret and Richard were his real mother and father as far as he was concerned. He tried not to think of those other people.

"Horrible things happen to a lot of people, Miss Ruiz. Not everyone becomes a monster," he said.

"No, but the world is full of people who do. It's like those kids in Africa who get taught how to use machine guns and kill. Some of them can barely lift the guns, but they're killers. What about them, Reed? Do you hold them responsible? Would you lock them away or put them down?" She wiped her eyes.

"That's different, and you know it. The entire continent is rife with civil unrest and it's people like Muhammad Rafiq, Felipe Villanueva, and yes, even Caleb, who get those kids hooked on cocaine and then teach them how to kill. I hold those people responsible."

"What about the ones who grow up? What about the ones who survive long enough to become adults? Can you blame them for doing the only thing they know how?" She had to stop and breathe, her anger making her shake. He could see it on her face. She wanted to hit him. "Do you think that ten or twenty years from now, I'm going to feel normal or be normal or have a normal life, *like you*?"

Matthew let out an exasperated sigh. "I don't know, Miss Ruiz. I don't have those kinds of answers for you. It's wrong, what happens to those kids, but it doesn't give them free license as adults to rape and murder just because they've been doing it

179

since they were young. Nor does it justify their actions because they had a fucked up childhood."

"So…what? Fuck 'em?" she challenged, her eyes wild. "Is that the best you can do?"

Matthew shrugged. "I don't see the comparison, Miss Ruiz. Even if I did, are you telling me if one of those kids pointed a gun at you, if one of them raped you, you'd be willing to forgive them? Because I don't think I have that much compassion. Anyone who points a weapon at me is going to get brought down. I don't care if it's a fucking Girl Scout."

Olivia laughed without humor. "You're fucking wrong, Reed. That's exactly what Caleb would say." She regarded him for a moment. "You are different from Sloan; she would never say anything like that."

Matthew shrugged, trying to find his calm. The conversation had gotten out of control, and really, it just wasn't necessary. "I tell it like it is and believe me, you're not the first person to find it annoying."

"Speaking of…why would you tell Sloan I kissed you?"

"Because you did. Dr. Sloan would have asked, and it's irrelevant to me but important for her to know."

She rolled her eyes again. "I just wanted to distract you. You wouldn't give me Caleb's fucking picture and I wanted it. Now Sloan thinks I'm some kind of sexual deviant who tries to seduce asshole FBI agents who want to shoot Girl Scouts."

Matthew smiled in spite of himself. "Well, aren't you?"

"*Tell me* you're joking." She stared at him, a startled, even comical, expression on her face. "No one is that self-absorbed."

"I'm joking. And I *am* that self-absorbed." They both laughed amiably, but the conversation was far from over. It was up to Matthew to bring it back around, but he wanted to give Livvie the time to get there. "You still haven't answered the question. Why do you care so much about Caleb?"

She sighed at that, her focus seemingly far away. When she spoke, her tone was soft and somewhat wistful. "He used to talk to me at night. It was almost like the dark gave us permission to be ourselves, to put aside the fact he was my kidnapper and the man responsible for all the terrible things that happened to me during the day. But you have to understand, for all the bad Caleb did, he protected me too – in his own ways. It could have been so much worse for me without Caleb.

"That night, after Celia had whipped Kid in front of everyone, Rafiq had tried to separate us. He wanted me to stay in his room, and I was terrified Caleb would let it happen. I'd seen what Rafiq had done to Nancy. I could still hear her screams in my ears and feel her hands grabbing for me. I didn't want to end up like her.

"Caleb refused. He said I would scream for hours on end if I were separated from him. He said I was a danger to myself, and Rafiq didn't know me well enough to know what I needed. He'd said it all in English, and the moment Rafiq reached for me I started screaming bloody murder until Caleb lifted me into his arms. I even threw in some feverish gibberish, clutching at him and begging him not to let me go. I didn't have to work hard to be panicked. I *was* panicked.

"Caleb stroked my hair and I slowly relaxed into his arms, going so far as to 'faint'. Maybe it was a little over the top, but it worked. Felipe had begged Caleb's forgiveness for not offering to have him shown to his room sooner and called the butler over to take us to Caleb's room." Livvie chuckled softly as she recounted the story, and Matthew had to wonder if her sense of humor had always been so dark or if it was an aftereffect of her time spent in ruthless company.

"Oh!" Olivia suddenly exclaimed, "I remember something. Felipe told Rafiq the boat would be arriving in four days, and he asked if Rafiq would be leaving to meet it or if he planned to stay and have someone else handle it."

Matthew leaned forward, pen poised over his notepad. "He said this in front of you?"

"He thought I was passed out. I don't know if it's important. It was months ago, so the boat has obviously already come and gone, but I do remember it because I wondered if we were near water and if I was going to be on that fucking boat."

"Obviously, that didn't happen," Matthew said, stating the obvious.

"No, but you didn't ask me if it happened. You told me to tell you everything I remember," she said.

"So what happened?"

182

"I don't know, but Rafiq was gone a few days later, so I assume he went to meet the boat and whoever or whatever was on it."

Probably drugs, Matthew thought, and he made a note to look into locations near water and cross-reference them with his list of military installations in Pakistan. He would also have to call the Federal Investigation Agency in Pakistan. The FIA likely knew something. The difficulty came in getting them to admit it. "Anything else that might be useful?" he asked.

"Not that I can think of right now. Besides, I was telling you about me and Caleb."

Matthew rolled his eyes. "Fine. It seems to be helping you remember things, but please, try to keep the sex stuff to a minimum. I really don't need to hear the blow-by-blow."

Olivia smiled. "Was that a pun, Reed?"

"Hardly. Just a poor choice of words," he acknowledged. The image he'd manufactured of Celia thrusting that dildo into Kid's mouth once again assaulted him. He shook his head and it dissipated. He wished he'd never heard that story. It wasn't the act he guiltily found intriguing, but the authority behind it. Matthew didn't care for weak women, but he certainly had a thing for domineering ones. And in the darkest recesses of Matthew's mind, he knew why.

"Are you really going to listen? Will you at least try to see things the way I do?" she requested earnestly.

Matthew's stomach did a strange flip-like thing at the sound of her begging tone. This was always the part of the job he hated. He liked solving the puzzle, putting the case facts together and tracking down the criminals – but this part, dealing with the victims and their myriad personalities and experiences, most of them tragic, he couldn't stand. He could stand Olivia more than some other people he'd interviewed. Now that she wasn't so much of a basket case, she seemed made of much stronger stuff, but she was still in a strange limbo between victim and suspect.

"I don't know if that's a promise I can make, Miss Ruiz. I can promise I'll listen. I can promise I'll do my job. I can even promise to help you as much as I am able. But I can't promise you I'll ever see things the way you do."

His refusal really seemed to upset her. Olivia's shoulders slumped, but she nodded for far longer than she needed to, lost in space again. When she spoke, she seemed to be talking to the room with Matthew as a set piece. Her words weren't for him and they both knew that. "I figured you might say that. It makes sense, I guess. It's just…. I don't think anyone is ever going to see it the way I do, Reed. No one is ever going to understand. If it ever comes out, everyone's just going to think I'm crazy. That I'm young and I don't know what I'm talking about. That I'm a victim and my feelings are all a result of my trauma. I think that's what hurts the most.

"I lived through all of it. I saw and felt and experienced more in one summer than I think most people experience their entire lives, but in the end? I'm just a girl who no one will ever understand. There's so much about me that will never be the same.

"You don't want to hear about the sex stuff. I know that. I know how inappropriate it is to sit here and tell a complete stranger about people getting tied up and whipped, even fucked in front of me. But...I have to tell someone. Someone who won't make me feel like a freak. Someone who won't analyze me like Sloan does.

"She doesn't mean to make me feel like a freak, not on purpose. It's when she says I'm drawn to you because you're a strong man, like Caleb. When she says I kissed you because sex is the way I've been conditioned to get my way, that it's all psychological, and it's all because Caleb fucked with my head. I can't stand it. I can't have everything I feel reduced to a textbook description that fits me and millions of other broken idiots. More than that, I can't stand thinking that maybe...she's right.

"Maybe I don't really love Caleb; maybe my brain made it up so I wouldn't kill myself or feel so scared and alone. Maybe I'll accept that one day and I won't be able to stop having nightmares. Maybe I'll never trust another emotion I ever have again. Who's going to love a girl like that, Reed? Who's ever going to love a freak like me?" She collapsed onto her bed and rolled into a ball, crying and rocking.

Matthew's heart beat a frantic tattoo in his chest. He didn't know what to do to make her stop crying.

He didn't want to touch her – that felt like the wrong thing. A hug? Not him either. He wished Sloan were here. She was the social worker. It was her job to deal with all the mushy shit. He remembered Olivia didn't care for mushy.

"Someone will love you, Miss Ruiz. Even if you're a jerk."

"Fuck you, Reed," she sobbed.

He laughed. "And you're so charming, too."

"You're an asshole, you know that?"

"Yes," he said as a matter of fact.

"God! Why are you so messed up?!?" She sat up and glared.

"Everybody is fucked up, and we're all freaks in our own ways."

"How would you know?" she shot back, sniffling and glaring at him. "You probably had a charmed life in suburbia. No cares. No worries. A perfect life."

He gave her a deadpan look. "I was abused as a child. African militants forced me to snort gun powder and cocaine and plow villages with my Uzi. Feel sorry for me and stop whining about how no one will love you," he suggested calmly. Her shocked expression was priceless. He gave her a leveling look and softened his voice. "You're young, strong, and you're an asshole to boot. With your smarts, you're going to be just fine. Don't let anyone ever tell you different. Not even you."

Olivia's expression softened, and after a while she gave a little smile. "You're okay, I guess, Reed. No one's ever going to love you, but you're okay."

He gave her a wry smile. "Thank you, Miss Ruiz. I'll remember that when you're begging for sympathy."

She sighed. "Can we be done for today? I'm really tired. Talking to you takes a year off my life."

"Want me to turn off the lights? Would the dark help you confess?" he said, and he was only half joking.

"Funny."

"I try," he said. "I'll be back tomorrow." He paused and leveled with her. "Look. We're running out of time, Miss Ruiz. We need to get to that auction and you're our best hope to rescue the others like yourself – Nancy, Kid, Celia. All of them. I don't want you to lose sight of that. I'll listen to you, I'll even try to see things from your perspective, but at the end of the day...you're safe. Others aren't so lucky."

She nodded solemnly. "I know, Reed. Trust me, I *know*. I don't want those evil bastards to get away with it either. I really don't."

"I hope so, Miss Ruiz. Get some sleep." Matthew stood and gathered his things, remembering to shut off the recorder and tuck it into his jacket where it couldn't get lost.

He left the hospital and decided to go back to the office for a few hours. It was still relatively early and the offices in Pakistan would be open. He had to make a few calls.

Back at the office, he got on the phone with the FIA and asked if they had any information about a slave auction happening in the next few days. As predicted, the FIA agents weren't pleased to be getting a call from the FBI, but after interweaving the standard threat-coax key words in his most polite voice, they begrudgingly said they'd look into it and pass along any information.

"Please keep an eye on the private airports for any high-profile people entering the country – billionaires, sheiks, anyone with a lot of money and power. Especially if they have any ties you know of to organized crime, including guns, drugs, and human labor."

"You don't have to tell us how to do our job, Agent Reed," said the agent on the other end. His accent was South African. "We're quite capable of gathering intelligence without the U.S. Government."

"Then I'll expect a call from you boys in a couple of days?" Matthew baited.

"A pleasure, Agent Reed. We'll keep an eye out for Demitri Balk or anyone traveling under the name Vladek Rostrovich." The line went dead.

"Dickface," Matthew grumbled. He pressed down on his phone to make another call. He looked down a listing of government agencies in Pakistan and also put a call in to the office in charge of PACHTO. The Prevention and Control of Human Trafficking Ordinance had only been in place since 2002, but it was gaining steam. It was difficult to get a hold of someone who spoke English, but after a few redials he finally got in touch with a linguist who worked there.

It was a little after eight when Matthew decided he'd done all he could for the night. He gathered his belongings, including his recorder, and headed for his hotel. He couldn't stop thinking about Olivia's story. He couldn't stop thinking about Celia.

By the time he'd arrived at his room, set his briefcase down on the table, emptied his pockets, carefully stacked any loose change by denomination and placed them in a row by size, placed his keys, wallet, and watch on the table, and hung up his suit jacket, he'd made up his mind to listen to the damn tape he couldn't stop thinking about. He was already so hard; he could barely sit down to remove his shoes and socks. He rushed through his process, eager to get his clothes off and touch himself.

Finally, he finished hanging his clothes, and all that remained was his underwear, tented with his shameful arousal. Ordinarily, he had no problem with jerking off. However, it was the circumstances surrounding his hard-on that left him feeling guilty.

"You're a sick motherfucker," Matthew whispered, but he gave in and pushed his underwear down his legs and put them in the laundry bag. He didn't bother showering – he was too needy. Instead, he pulled the bedspread down and flung himself onto the crisp, cold sheets of the bed. He reached for the recorder on the nightstand and rewound it to Celia's entrance. His cock leapt. He shut his eyes and put his hand on his hot flesh as Livvie's voice filled the room.

Matthew wasn't gentle with himself. He didn't like gentle. He grabbed his dick like it was some sort of enemy and squeezed it until it hurt. Margaret and Richard were great parents: kind, loving, and warm. They took a damaged kid whose mother had been murdered and gave him a great life, but they couldn't wipe his memories. They couldn't strip away the darkness in him. They couldn't make him stop liking this.

Matthew dragged his fingernails across his chest, sure to scratch his nipple hard enough to make him wince and buck his hips up into his fist.

"She raised the flogger over her head and brought it down hard across Kid's chest. He cried out, doubling over, and when those men held him up, there was an angry red stripe across his chest. Kid sobbed..."

Matthew imagined himself in Kid's place, ashamed the image was so arousing, so crushingly right, but Matthew had tears in his eyes because he knew it was wrong. It was wrong to listen to Olivia's voice. It was wrong to listen to Kid's misery. It was wrong. Wrong. Wrong!

Matthew came. Hard. His come spraying him across his chest, burning against the scored skin, was glorious. He panted loudly, alone in the dark, listening to Olivia's voice. His other hand, the one not covered in come, reached for the recorder and switched it off.

In the end, it didn't even matter. He was getting hard again. It had been a while since he'd allowed himself to come, and his dick wasn't going to be happy with a quick jerk-off session. He refused to listen to the tape again, though. He refused.

He jolted out of bed and into the shower to rinse off. There was a club. There was always a club. And no matter how Matthew tried not to seek them out, he always did. He was constantly aware of where he could go to find what his subconscious demanded of him.

Out of the shower, he quickly dressed in a pair of jeans and a button-up shirt. Nothing black – nothing that would suggest he was dominant. He hated when eager subs sat down next to him, thinking he'd love nothing better than to put them over his knee. He always sent them away in tears, ashamed he couldn't give them what they wanted. He'd tried. He'd tried to be that guy. It always ended badly.

11

Day 10:

Matthew woke up sore. Everything hurt. Slowly, he bent his head forward and grunted when pain shot down the back of his neck and settled in between his shoulders. He went limp and fell onto the mattress again. This was going to be more difficult than he thought.

With each passing second, more of his consciousness was regained and soon his heart picked up a frantic rhythm. He'd gone out last night.

"Matthew? Is that you?"

Matthew groaned. *No. No, no, no, nooooo.* He pressed his face hard into the bed beneath him. He noticed his dick was hard. It wasn't just morning wood, either. He was remembering.

He was startled to hear a familiar voice. Her voice. "Fuck!" he grumbled under his breath. How could he handle this? How could he explain?

Anyone else! Anyone else would have been fine. No, it'd been *her* sitting next to him when he finally had the courage to turn on his barstool.

Her red hair was worn loose; soft waves cascaded down her back. She wore a white shirt wrapped around her waist and tied at the back. Her cleavage peeked out a little, just enough to make a man curious, but not enough to expose what she was hiding beneath her tight shirt. A black leather skirt at mid-thigh and metal-studded heels completed the ensemble.

Matthew's face was hot all over again, his cheeks colored with his embarrassment. Especially when he recalled the way he'd tried to explain his presence.

"I needed a drink."
"Oh, I understand that, believe me. I don't drink when I play, though," she said casually.

Matthew had wondered how the fuck she could be so casual. He'd wondered all night, actually. He knew most people thought he was cold, efficient, and detached, but he had nothing on her. She'd wrecked all of his carefully-constructed control, and she'd done it without losing any of her cool.

"I'm not here to play. I just needed a drink," he said. His ears felt hot and he knew it would be spreading to his face and neck any minute. He wanted to leave, but she blocked his exit and stayed there, eyeing him with suspicion.

"And you just ended up here? Forgive me, Matthew, but that's doubtful." She arched a red brow.

"I'm.... I'm..." he started to say.

"No need to be shy, Matthew. I mean, I'm here too, right? The only real question is... who are you looking for?"

Matthew's hips rolled and he felt the burn of his muscles protesting against the action. He'd be surprised if he could sit today.

"I'm not looking for anyone. I just –"

"Lying? Really? Of all the things I thought you might be, a liar didn't really cross my mind," she said.

"Fuck what you thought," he countered and slammed his whiskey neat. He stood to leave, but Sloan blocked his path, trapping him between her body and the stool. She smelled sweet, like green apples. It certainly wasn't the kind of thing one expected. Not in a fetish club.

Knowing it would hurt, he braced himself and reached back to touch his ass with his fingers. Yes – there were raised welts all over his butt. He traced them with the tip of his finger, marveling at the fact there was a perfect handprint where her slender, whip-like fingers had landed. He'd always wondered if the brilliant Dr. Janice Sloan would psychoanalyze during sex. Now he knew the answer.

"That's rude, Matthew. You're trying to hurt my feelings. But I forgive you because I know you're embarrassed." She stepped closer, a hand on his chest urging him back onto his seat. Her hand felt hot, really hot, like it could burn a hole in his chest. Matthew relented and allowed himself to be pushed back onto the barstool.

Sloan rose up on her tip-toes and leaned over Matthew to whisper in his ear. "Your cheeks are red and your heart is beating really fast."

Matthew moaned and rubbed his ass cheek again. Yes, he'd been embarrassed. He'd never expected to see Sloan, dressed like a cross between the Madonna and the whore, smelling like apples and at the same time rubbing her tits against his chest. She'd known what she was doing, that much was even more obvious now.

"Look, Sloan..."

"Leave Sloan for the office, Matthew," she said with a smile.

"Fine. What the hell do you want, Janice? You want to tell everyone you saw me here? That I'm a freak? Go ahead. I don't give a fuck," he said. He whispered the words, half angry, half nervous. He didn't know what he'd do if she decided to tell people about him.

He was still worried about that. The things he'd let her do! The way he'd begged her not to stop. He shook his head, trying to clear the memories, but it

195

wasn't working – not when he was still so sore and her smell still lingered in his sheets.

"You're not a Dom." Janice shook her head. "I didn't think so. I mean, you could be, you're so strong, so masculine and in control. But that's the problem, isn't it, Matthew? It's a lot of work to be in control all the time." She raised her delicate hand and twirled her fingers in the hair at Matthew's nape. It was an intimate act, full of implications.

Ah, yes. The fucking psychobabble. Olivia had had it right – Sloan couldn't help herself. She looked right into people and started tearing them apart. No matter that it hurt. No matter that she wasn't invited to do it. All night, she'd done it to him – poked and poked and poked, until he'd given it up.

Janice's other hand grabbed Matthew's thigh and gently prodded. Matthew swallowed hesitantly, but then he let Janice in and she stepped between his spread thighs as if she just belonged there. "I wouldn't tell anyone your secrets, Matthew. I keep a lot of secrets; it's my job. If you tell me to leave you alone, I will. It's just...I want you."
"Why?" Matthew croaked.
Janice smiled against his ear and chuckled softly. "Because I couldn't possibly think of anything I'd enjoy more than your sexy ass over my knee."

It was definitely sexy. Matthew had never come so hard, never begged so much. He'd tried to be defiant, not caring for Sloan's invasive questions. But in the end, he wanted to come so badly, he'd have done anything, said anything. Sloan made sure to take advantage. She'd pulled confessions out of him that made him so ashamed he could barely breathe. She'd been ruthless.

Her hand followed along the path of his thigh and turned inward to cup his balls. Matthew jumped, startled, but his hands stayed gripped to the barstool. Janice's fingernails scratched him through his jeans, and he couldn't suppress the helpless sound that came out of him.

He couldn't face her – not today, not ever. She knew him too well now. He'd told her things he'd never told anyone.

"Okay," he whispered.
"Okay?" she purred against his ear, her fingers alternately caressing and scratching.

She'd been so reassuring, stroking his hair and telling him it was okay, that there was nothing wrong with him.

Matthew nodded, his eyes closed. Already, it was difficult not to come right there in his jeans, like a school kid having his dick touched by the head cheerleader.

"You won't tell?" he pleaded softly.

Janice gripped the hair at the nape of his neck with enough force to make his eyes sting. "No, Matthew. I won't tell anyone. Now get the fuck off this barstool and let's get out of here."

Last night it had been glorious and liberating. It had been a light to the darkness in his soul, but today...today it was all he could do not to call in sick and lie in bed and hide.

Matthew finally rolled over and let the pain have him. He closed his eyes and moved his body along the sheets, testing all of his muscles. His shoulders hurt quite a bit and his neck was stiff, but mostly it was his ass. His ass felt bruised all the way to the bone, and he knew even after his hot shower the pain would remain. He'd think about Sloan all day, all night, and every time he sat down until the pain went away. And suddenly, it was his pride that hurt the most.

He slowly opened his eyes. He was supposed to go back to the hospital first thing this morning and get the rest of Olivia's statement. He wondered if Sloan would be there and his stomach hurt. No. He couldn't see Sloan. Ever. He couldn't stand the idea of facing her and encountering her smug face. And really, who wouldn't be smug?

Matthew was a notorious jerk. He knew plenty of people who would pay to hear about him being brought so low. Well, he wouldn't give Sloan the satisfaction of getting to him again. All he had to do was avoid her. It was the coward's way out, but

Matthew figured he could be a coward every now and again. He wouldn't let it affect his case.

With a loud sigh of resignation, Matthew rolled out of bed on unsteady legs and fumbled toward the table for balance and his phone. There was a note:

> *Dear Matthew,*
> *Thank you. You were better than I dreamed. Difficult to leave you, but I know you need your space. I'll be at the hospital in the morning. Stop by if you want – otherwise, I'll be sure to give you time in the afternoon to do your job. Of course, I hope I'll see you.*
> *Agreement stands, my lips are sealed.*
>
> *Jani*

"Fuck," Matthew sighed. Even in a note, he could sense how obviously smug she was about last night. If he didn't show up, then he was a coward. If he did, then he was trying to prove something. It was a catch-22. Angrily, he reached for his phone and fired off a text:

> *Reed: Intel @ office. Busy til lunch. Pls rcrd interview.*

He figured his text was vague and yet succinct enough. He hoped she would get the hint and not discuss last night. It was better if they stuck to the work. The case would be over soon and both of them would be reassigned. With any luck, he'd have no reason to see her again. All he had to do was make it through the next few days. Less, if he could get Livvie to talk. It was all the motivation he needed.

Matthew took a long, hot shower. It helped loosen his aching muscles. The damage was fairly miniscule – only a few bruises and welts on his ass. It was a relief to know he had no marks on him that would be visible when he was dressed.

He stopped for coffee on the way to work. He didn't want to stand around the pot at the office. The officers sometimes tried to engage him in conversation, and Matthew just wasn't in the mood. He walked in quietly, nodding in greeting to the desk sergeant and taking the elevator in silence to the chagrin of the building janitor who rode with him.

"This is Agent Reed." Matthew set his briefcase next to his desk and his coffee next to his keyboard before he turned to acknowledge the officer's presence.

"Yes?"

"Message came for you late last night. The desk sergeant brought it up this morning." The young man handed the message to Matthew and walked away.

"Thanks," Matthew muttered toward the man's back and looked down at the message. The agent from the FIA had called. Matthew looked at his watch and hoped their offices were still open. He was cutting it close.

He rolled out his chair and picked up his phone to dial the long number. "Hello? Staff Sergeant

Patel, please." He waited for a few minutes while they tracked the man down, relieved he'd called in time.

"Staff Sergeant Patel speaking."

"Matthew Reed, FBI," he said quickly. "You left a message for me. What did you find out?"

There was a deep sigh on the other end of the phone. "We looked into private planes with scheduled arrivals in the next three days." He hesitated. "You were right. There seems to be a lot more activity than usual. No information yet on Demitri Balk or Vladek Rostrovich, but we don't have all the passenger manifests yet."

"Can you send me a list of all the information you have available? I'd like to look through it if you don't mind."

"We do mind, Agent Reed. If there is something going on, then it falls within our purview and our office can handle it. Is there any other information you would like to share with us?"

Matthew ground his teeth hard enough to make his head hurt. He wasn't in the mood for the bureaucratic games. "I'm willing to share information so long as we are coordinating. For that to be the case, information has to flow both ways. Time is limited, Staff Sergeant. Neither of us has time for a pissing contest."

"You Americans and your colorful slang," Patel said. "No one is 'pissing' on anything, Agent Reed, but I'm sure you can see the political implications of this. The world's eyes are on Pakistan right now, and we need to know the situation can be handled discreetly and without embarrassing either country."

"If you won't share information, I'll have to contact my superiors and have them reach out to your government. It could take days, and by then the slave auction could be over," Matthew said.

"I understand you have a job to do, Agent Reed. I do as well. I will continue to gather information on the private aircraft, passenger lists, arrival times and scheduled departures, etcetera. In the meantime, I suggest you get in contact with your superiors. I will do the same and perhaps we can come to a mutually beneficial agreement?"

"Fine," Matthew growled into the receiver.

"Until tomorrow," SSgt Patel replied coolly.

"You can bet on it," Matthew repeated and waited until the line went dead before he placed the handset back onto its cradle. He was careful not to slam it. He didn't need the attention.

He had a few hours before Sloan finished with Olivia, so he decided to dig out his research on Demitri Balk. If Rafiq and Caleb were set on getting to the elusive billionaire, then Matthew would have to do the same. He was hesitant to get too close to the man through traditional channels. He didn't want him spooked. He might decide to stay clear of the auction, and then Matthew wouldn't be able to use him as bait.

Demitri Balk didn't have much of an identity until the mid-90s. Balk Diamonds had appeared seemingly overnight with a long list of prominent investors that catapulted the price of the stock within minutes of it becoming public. Demitri Balk had been the primary share holder and was listed as the CEO of the company.

The large conglomerate was primarily billeted as a jewelry company but was also supported by a myriad of other businesses. The company had its share of controversy surrounding it. More than one story claiming Balk Diamonds did their mining in Africa could be found by doing a cursory search, but ultimately no formal investigation by any government had been conducted.

Blood diamonds were highly contentious, but no one had been able to directly link Balk Diamonds to any of the mines in Africa – probably due to the web of companies and subsidiaries associated with them. One of the subsidiaries caught Matthew's attention. AKRAAN was established in Russia and dealt in weapons manufacturing and sales. More research revealed AKRAAN had been part of Balk Diamonds when it first went public, meaning the CEO would have direct knowledge of it.

Matthew wasn't surprised to see a diamond company involved in weapons. However, what was surprising was the weapons company existed first, as early as the 1960s. The manufacturer, run by the government, sold weapons to several countries – most notably, Iraq and Pakistan.

How did Demitri Balk come to run both companies? As CEO, no less?

Demitri was described by *Forbes Magazine* as a "self-made billionaire with humble roots in soviet Russia."

Matthew scoffed. "Humble, my ass." He winced at his own words, remembering the very real way his ass had been humbled the night before. Sitting was definitely a chore. He tried not to fidget.

Finally, inspiration struck and Matthew made a call to his home office. After a brief conversation with his boss, the man had finally relented and agreed to give Matthew all the resources he would need to put his case together. He also agreed to start cutting away at the red tape between Matthew and the FIA.

Within the hour, two techs were running every picture and story associated with Balk Diamonds, AKRAAN, Demitri Balk, Vladek Rostrovich, and Muhammad Rafiq through facial recognition software and the National Security Database. Matthew predicted something would show up sooner rather than later.

He looked at his watch. He should probably get to the hospital. He called the nurse's desk on Olivia's floor to make sure Sloan had left for the day and then he gathered his belongings and headed for the door.

**

Olivia was furiously writing when Matthew walked in. She seemed in better spirits than the night before. Matthew gave Sloan credit.

"What are you writing?" Matthew asked. He put down his briefcase and took a seat. The chair was far more comfortable than the one in the recreation room. Also, sitting in her hospital room had the added benefit of making her more talkative.

"Dr. Sloan gave me a journal. Pretty sweet, huh? It's been so long since I've written anything, I almost forgot how much I love it," Olivia said. She smiled.

"Not what I asked, Miss Ruiz," Matthew replied, but there was no bite in his words.

She sighed. "I'm...you know. I just want to preserve my memories before I stop trusting them."

Matthew really didn't know what to say, except, "That could get subpoenaed, you know?"

She looked stricken, dropping her pen with a rattle. "Seriously? Why would you do that?"

"Never mind," he said easily, "forget I said anything."

She looked at him, then down at her notebook and up at him again before she raised a suspicious brow and snapped the journal shut. "I don't forget anything you say, Reed. Only an idiot would."

Matthew inclined his head and winced. "Thanks for the compliment."

"What's wrong with your neck?"

Matthew focused on not letting his embarrassment show and did a fairly good job of it in his estimation. "Hotel bed. Hurts my neck."

"Aww, poor Agent Reed," she teased gently.

"Funny girl, but let's get this over with so I can go home and sleep in my own bed," said Matthew.

She sighed. "Always business with you. Is that why Sloan's mad at you?"

"What?" Matthew snapped. "She talked about me?"

Olivia gave him a confused look. "She asked if you were here this morning and when I said no, she seemed a little annoyed is all. You seem to bring that out in people... or just women. She didn't want to talk about it. What's going on with you two?" Getting even more curious, Olivia raised her eyebrows. "Did something happen between you two? Was there an FBI showdown?"

Matthew let out a breath he hadn't realized he held. He was relieved and felt foolish for overreacting. "A showdown? No. Has anyone ever told you you're overdramatic?" he dismissed her coolly. "Dr. Sloan's usually more professional in keeping her focus on the case, not external distractions – whatever they may be."

"Jeez, Reed. What the hell got up in your ass this morning?"

Matthew's cheeks felt hot, but he forced himself to calm down before it could show. The things that could make him blush were limited, but damn it if the last few days weren't designed to expose his weaknesses to the world.

"Just go on with your story. Please. I'm exhausted, my neck hurts, and I feel a headache coming on – so can we just get on with it?"

Olivia's face was suddenly devoid of its light and humor. "*Fine*, Reed. Ask your fucking questions."

He took a deep breath. "What did you and Sloan talk about? I'll get her notes later, but just bring me up to speed."

"We talked about Caleb. Nothing that would interest you, I'm sure."

"Tell me anyway," Matthew insisted. He tried to work up a smile to re-establish their otherwise good rapport, but by the look on Olivia's face, it would take more than a smile.

"I had a lot of nightmares when I first got to the mansion. Sometimes about Rafiq raping Nancy. Sometimes I dreamt about Caleb selling me. Mostly, though, I had nightmares about the night the bikers almost raped me. I dreamt about them beating me, stepping on my stomach, and slapping my face." She swallowed.

"I could almost feel blood pouring into my mouth. I would wake up gasping. When Caleb was there..." Livvie sighed. "He would just hold me. Caleb liked sleeping next to me, I think.

"Morning was our problem. I would lie in bed next to Caleb, watching him sleep and thinking he was so child-like when he wasn't so obsessed with training me or proving how much control he had over me—"

Matthew interrupted. "Was Rafiq still there?"

"No. He left a few days after I met him. He and Caleb had breakfast on the balcony. Rafiq used Nancy as a table, and I don't know how many times I had to shut my eyes because I thought Rafiq's knife was going to go right through his steak and into Nancy. It never happened though."

"What happened to Nancy?" Matthew asked.

"I didn't know it until later, but Rafiq took her with him when he left. And before you ask – no, I don't know where he went."

"To meet the boat. Remember?"

"Right, to meet the boat," she said.

"So where did you eat?"

"On the floor, next to Caleb. He cut things up for me and fed them to me as he ate. That's what I'm telling you, Reed – he was good to me. I didn't really appreciate it until I saw the way Nancy was treated. Even Kid. Celia was treated better than anyone, though. Toward the end I'd sort of hoped…" She was starting to drift off.

"Hoped, what?" Matthew asked in an attempt to regain her focus.

"That Caleb and I could have what they did. Felipe isn't a great guy. He wouldn't be involved with Rafiq if he were, but…. I don't know. Celia loves him, and Felipe seems to feel the same way. He's pretty protective."

"You want me to call Sloan?" Matthew asked patiently.

Her eyes drifted toward him, narrowing suspiciously. "Why?"

"Because you need a lot of therapy, Miss Ruiz. A lot."

She shook her head at him, clearly amused by his bluntness. "Fuck you, Reed," she said through a smile.

"Please. Continue your story…"

208

12

When I opened my eyes and realized it was morning, it took me a few minutes to orient myself. The trepidation I felt during the night was slow to fade. I didn't remember falling asleep – only lying in bed for hours trying to think of a way out of my situation that wouldn't later involve Caleb having to rescue me.

The room I slept in was beautiful and immaculate. Every morning, the sun came spilling into the room when Celia came in to draw back the heavy curtains. I had told her I was more than capable of drawing back the curtains myself, but she simply ignored me as she went about her business of preparing the room for the day.

"She's not allowed to speak to you," Caleb said as he sat on the edge of the bed. It was only our second week at the mansion and he looked so tired, like he wasn't able to rest at all. He complained he couldn't go on sleeping in all his clothes forever. Yet every night, he did.

Caleb was more erratic than usual during those first few weeks. Yes, he was cruel. He put me through my paces, teaching me certain phrases in Russian and what actions to take when I heard them. He insisted I crawl, call him master, and that I go through a series of humiliations meant to make me get over my shyness.

For all that, he didn't really touch me. He kept

me clothed. He protected me by not letting others near me. I knew he stayed with me at night because I had nightmares when he didn't. He slept in his t-shirt and shorts, seemingly content to just sleep next to me and not touch me unless I woke from some horrible nightmare and huddled close to him. He soothed me.

"Why isn't she allowed to talk to me?" I asked in a sardonic tone.

Caleb glared at me for several moments before he replied. "Kitten, you should really watch the way you speak to me. Just because you're hurt doesn't mean I'm not keeping score." He stared at me, squarely in the eyes, until I finally looked down.

"Sorry, Master." He eyed me strangely. "Can I *please* know why she's not allowed to speak to me?"

"Celia isn't just her master's lover – she's also his servant. It's not so unusual, I guess. I've never been involved with someone long enough to know the idiosyncrasies that go along with being in a relationship, but I know enough to say it makes sense. It's not like he can use her for sex all the time." My face must have shown my indignant shock because Caleb pressed his finger to my lips to keep me from speaking.

Even though I shouldn't have and it might've pissed Caleb off, I spoke anyway. "Don't you think that's a silly rule? It sounds pretty mean to me."

"Well trust me – sometimes talking to *you* is what is mean," he commented, but smiled.

I smiled back. *Asshole*. Perversely, I thought about how much I would miss him after he sold me, and I wondered if he would miss me too – perhaps even enough to come for me. *You're not a princess and he isn't the handsome prince come to save you. Or don't you remember?* I sighed at my inner voice. I was talking to myself more and more. Not only was I going crazy, but I was bitchy company.

Some days I could almost forget I was being held against my will. I never did, but I flirted with the idea every now and then. Caleb would have Celia bring us breakfast and we'd eat it outside, just the two of us. Out in the sunshine, eating fresh pastries from Caleb's hand and sipping hand-squeezed orange juice, I thought: This isn't so bad.

Of course, some days it was nearly impossible to forget I was Caleb's prisoner. I was still moving slowly from my injuries. The bruises had nearly faded away, but the pain in my ribs and shoulder was always there to remind me about a lot of things. It was a deterrent against running away again. It was also a reminder I had gotten off easy with Caleb. Still, leave it to Caleb to think of a way to use the pain toward his own ends.

One morning in particular, he'd left me alone in the room with Celia and, against my better judgment, I decided to talk to her.

Celia's eyes avoided mine as she went about my room straightening things that didn't need to be straightened and dusting. I really pitied her. She was beautiful and her demeanor hinted at her immense inner strength, and yet...she was a slave. I wondered if I would be half as graceful as she when my time finally came. I did note, with some hope, she didn't appear to be abused. There were no bruises on her, no outward signs to suggest she was suffering. Yes. There was definitely hope in that.

"Celia?" I spoke her name haltingly, scared she would answer me and scared she wouldn't. Her gaze fell upon me kindly, with only a quirked eyebrow in question. It wasn't really a response, but it was more than I'd gotten from her before. I figured since Caleb wasn't present she would speak to me. "How long have you been here?"

She stared at me for a long while, until I grew uncomfortable and squirmed. I didn't think it was a complicated question, though at some point I wanted to ask her those, too. Finally, her mouth quirked to the side and she nodded briefly; neither was for my benefit. She looked at me with a smile in her eyes and held up six fingers.

I wanted to yell at her for not using her words, but I was sure it wouldn't get me anywhere good. "Siiiiiix…months?"

She shook her head.

I took a deep, fortifying breath for my next question. "Years?"

She nodded and smiled.

Fuck. *Years?* She'd been Felipe's slave for six years. I couldn't imagine. "Did you never try to escape?!" My voice was apparently too loud. Her eyes were suddenly frantic, and she looked at the door as if it would burst open and something horrible would happen. She scurried toward me and held her fingers to my lips.

I was stunned and still, waiting for the moment

to settle. Her eyes scolded me and continued to scold me as she backed away from me, shaking her head.

She left the room before I could apologize or ask another question.

Nice going!

"Fuck you," I whispered to no one at all.

I had expected to face Caleb's wrath within minutes of Celia's exit, but no one came. I wasn't allowed to leave my new room – Caleb had made that clear. So I waited…and waited…and waited. Hours later, I was starving and the pain in my ribs and shoulder was becoming less bearable with each passing minute. Finally, I risked trying the door, but it was locked.

Eventually, I resorted to screaming and begging Caleb through the door to forgive me and give me my medicine. I wondered if I might be an addict, but given the level of pain I was in, I doubted it. I needed those fucking pills. I also needed to eat! Of course, Caleb knew it as well, and his punishment, free of violence, was still cruel.

Gradually, it became dark outside. As I lay crying on my bed, I heard the sound of someone unlocking my door. I cried in stark relief when Caleb entered the room.

"Are you ready?"

I whimpered and nodded. "Yes, Master. I'm so sorry. I won't do it again."

"You always say that, Kitten, but then you refuse to follow the rules and I have to punish you all over again. Didn't I tell you Celia isn't allowed to speak to you?" he chided.

"Yes, Master. I know you did. I'm sorry."

"Well, if you weren't before, at the very least I know you are now." He sat on the bed and held out a glass of water and some pills. "Sit up and take these."

I sat up slowly, sobbing. Part of it was the pain, but there was also a sense of shame involved. Caleb was disappointed with me. He'd told me the rules; he'd explained. I hadn't listened. "I can't believe you left me this long. It fucking hurts," I cried.

"I didn't choose to leave you, Kitten. You made that choice yourself," Caleb said. It came as a surprise he wasn't yelling at me or promising me more pain. He was very matter-of-fact about the whole thing. I wondered if it was just another way to mess with my head.

"Where were you?" I asked before I could stop myself.

"Just now? Bed. Earlier, I went out. Felipe has horses and I'd never ridden one," he smiled.

"Me neither," I whispered. Now that Caleb was near, I felt calmer. I was angry with him, of course, but I'd come to live for these moments with Caleb. I felt protected. I felt kept. Without him, my life was a giant question mark.

He smiled a little and pushed an errant lock of hair behind my ear. "Maybe when you're better, I can take you."

My heart seemed to swell in my chest. "Will I be here long enough? With you?" I met Caleb's clear blue eyes and they appeared wistful. I would have given anything to know what he was thinking, but I

214

knew better than to ask.

"Maybe, Kitten. Sometimes…" he paused.

"Sometimes?" I tried to urge him along.

"Sometimes." He smiled and stroked my hair with so much silent affection I felt like crying again. "Are you hungry, Kitten?" he whispered.

I inclined my face into his hand and closed my eyes, trying to hold on to him and knowing there was no way I possibly could. "Yes, Master."

Then we ate, Caleb feeding me pieces off his plate. It was strangely…comfortable. Afterward, he rubbed my sore body until I fell asleep.

***

I slept, but I was having that horrible dream again. My stomach felt like a tight, hot knot of pressure weighing me down from the inside. I turned and turned, the knot only getting tighter and hotter and heavier.

They held me down, and the smell of beer and cigarettes came off of them in waves. Their rough hands blazed a trail along my skin as they pulled at my clothes, and the sound of my protests fell upon deaf ears. The horror played in slow motion, coming in random flashes of what I remembered and what I still felt. Then the nightmare took on a life of its own, no longer bound by the facts.

I couldn't fight them. My fists moved in slow motion, unable to land solidly. My voice wouldn't rise above a whisper. One of them held me down as the other kissed me. I yelled for someone, but I wasn't sure who – all I knew was this person could only help me if I made a loud enough sound. I fought with every ounce of my strength. My wrists were limp and my voice was small, but I fought. I started crying.

The worst was about to happen when the dream unexpectedly changed again. It was faster now, faster even than real time. Caleb opened the door and asked what the hell was going on, and the arms holding me let go. They backed into the corner behind me. Free, I stood and ran into his arms. I wrapped my arms around him and I told him what they had meant to do.

They tried to deny it. Caleb told them to shut their mouths. He lifted me into his arms, telling them to stay put, and carried me past the decrepit room filled with air-mattresses and clothes – into a room I recognized as his.

He set me down beside the door as he looked me over. "Are you okay?" he asked. I nodded, only slightly aware he ran his hands over my nakedness as he searched for injuries. He seemed satisfied I wasn't hurt and hugged me again.

"What do you want me to do?" he asked. The moment slowed and I looked him in the eyes.

"Hurt them for me," I whispered.

"I'll make them pay," he said. His hands continued to move over me, and my hands held on to his shirt tightly. The tension in my belly transformed from solid to liquid, and it ran down toward my thighs. The knot came undone and now felt like a cord stretched taut from my nipples to my sex. When

216

he touched me, the cord tugged, and the feeling was overwhelming, savage, and strangely welcome.

I took my hands off of his chest and shrugged off the open top I wore. "I could've been really hurt if you hadn't helped me," I said. His eyes fixed on me, mixed with shock and lust. He pinned me against the wall with his body, and the heat of his breath warmed and moistened my neck. I wanted to say something, but his right hand cupped me, down low, and my body felt paralyzed. The invisible cord inside me pulled taut. A lascivious yelp escaped my throat.

He pressed his lips close to my ear. "Don't fuck with me," he growled.

"Fuck me," was my only response.

He reached his arms between my thighs and lifted me against the wall. He fumbled with his pants for a second before he pressed his way inside me. I groped for his mouth to distract myself from his size, and when our tongues connected, a rush of heat flowed out of me.

***

A loud grunt escaped my lips as I jerked awake, panting, my heart pounding, and the now-familiar feeling of my entire body contracting and expanding for several seconds cascade through me for several seconds. I was definitely coming. Beside me, Caleb sat up swiftly and turned on the light on the nightstand.

"What's wrong?" he asked.

I was sweating and still taking in deep gulps of air.

"Are you okay?" His voice sounded more

annoyed and tired than anything else.

I nodded. "Bad...bad dream," I stammered. He looked at me for a few seconds, and just seeing his eyes wouldn't let me shake the dream. I looked down, and my breathing finally started returning to normal.

"You're blushing. Why?" he asked softly and smoothed back my hair.

"I'm fine...I...I was just having that dream again." My breathing evened out and the unexpected pulsing between my legs subsided. Finally able to, I looked in Caleb's direction. He was staring at me.

"Why are you looking at me like that?" I asked. His eyebrows knit together and a smile played on his lips.

"Why are you looking at me like that – *Master*," he replied.

I bit my lip and looked away.

"Oh, Kitten," he whispered, his hand still stroking my hair away from my sweat-slick forehead. "If only you were well enough to play – the things I would do. But if you must know...." He leaned toward me and kissed my shoulder. "I'm looking at you because I think you're sexy." He kissed me up higher toward my neck. "Your face is all flushed and your hair is a mess." He kissed me higher. I closed my eyes and held my breath.

"Why are you touching me? You haven't...." I said in a rush.

"I'm not touching, I'm kissing. There's a difference."

"Not to me," I sighed, my voice a little too airy

to suit me; I'd much rather have sounded firm and resolved.

"So…if I do this," he said against the nape of my neck and cupped my right breast, rubbing it lightly through my nightgown. "It's just the same as this?" He kissed my neck. I could barely move or breathe. He sucked up all the oxygen around me.

"Stop," I said, and this time I made it sound convincing. He rolled my nipple between his thumb and forefinger with just enough pressure to make me feel it in my belly. "Please stop…Master," I said through gently gritted teeth. To my surprise, he did actually stop.

He sat back and stared at me for what seemed like an eternity, but couldn't have been more than a few moments. Heat radiated from every part of my body, and my face must've been a deep, deep shade of red. He rubbed his hands over his face and groaned. I was really nervous, and I wanted to say something, but I couldn't think of what it was. Abruptly, he threw his side of the sheet off to one side and stood up. My eyes were immediately drawn to the enormous erection straining against the fabric of his boxer shorts.

"Go back to sleep," he said. He picked up his pants and shoved his legs into them.

"Where are you going?" I asked, nervous.

"Don't fucking worry about it," he said and walked out the door.

Shocked, I watched him leave and gruffly shut the door behind him – but the shock stemmed from my desire to say something that would make him

219

stop. Anxiety built up inside my stomach as I sat
alone. All I could think about was my dream and
how good it had felt to have him kiss me. *What's
wrong with me!*

 I didn't have too long to ponder my questions,
or my body's response to them. My door abruptly
opened and Caleb walked in. Celia came in behind
him, wearing nothing but a pair of black lace panties.

 Caleb closed the door behind them gently, not in
any hurry to address the question written all over my
face: *What the fuck is* she *doing here?*

 Celia had obviously been sleeping. Her hair was
loose and gently disheveled. She stood silently, her
hands covering her small breasts. She didn't seem
distressed – only a little shy and curious. It was a
stark contrast from the night I'd seen her dominate
Kid in front of a room full of strangers. I looked at
her eyes, and when hers met mine I thought she gave
just the slightest hint of a mischievous grin.

 "Drop your arms," Caleb said in Spanish. He
didn't speak it as well as English, but I was
begrudgingly intrigued nonetheless. Celia
immediately dropped her arms to her sides. Her
nipples were already hard.

 Caleb turned his attention to me. "You remember
Celia, don't you, Kitten?" When I said nothing, he
snapped, "Answer me!" Celia and I both jumped a
little at the sharp sound of his voice.

 "Yes, Master," I replied.

 "Good." He smiled. "Because she's going to help
you understand something. I'm not yours to taunt.
Don't think I haven't noticed the way you try to

manipulate me. I invented that game."

My mouth was agape. *What the hell is he talking about?* "Manipulate? I don't—"

"You do!" he barked low. "One minute you're pressing yourself against me, trying to…I don't know. The next, you're telling me – *telling* me, not to touch you."

I wanted to tell him he was being ridiculous. How could I possibly be the one manipulating him when he was so thoroughly the master of my fate?

"Caleb, I—"

"Stop. Just watch," he said.

My mouth went completely dry and anxiety coursed through me, burning inside my stomach. I looked into Celia's eyes again. She smiled – just the tiniest quirk of her lips. A smile meant only for me. It shocked me.

Caleb stood behind Celia, and she shivered as he swept her hair over her left shoulder. "Don't look away, or I promise I'll find a way to punish you – injured or not," he said to me. I swallowed hard. Caleb turned his attention to Celia, who seemed to be swaying gently in anticipation of his touch. He kissed up along her shoulder and her neck, just as he'd done to me. She let out a deep groan and tipped her head back against him. I couldn't believe I was watching this.

"Do you like that?" he whispered into the dead silence of the room.

"Sí, Señor," Celia whispered in her breathy, accented voice.

My stomach knotted and I wanted to double

over, yet I couldn't tear my eyes away as he reached
his arm around her and cupped her breast. She cried
out as he massaged it, pulling her nipple between his
fingers. Her nipples were a deep apricot and looked
like hard raspberries perched on the gentle upward
slope of her bosom. My face burned, and something
vaguely familiar and unsolicited took up residence
inside me. Celia's moans grew a little louder. She
made fists in the fabric of Caleb's pants and pressed
her backside into him.

I wasn't quite ready when Caleb dipped his free
hand into her panties and her knees buckled. My
body moved all at once to stop her from falling and
recoiled in pain. It turned out my efforts were
wasted. Caleb held her firmly in his grasp. He
looked into my eyes, which were now misted over,
and kept his hand busy inside Celia's panties. I felt
angry...and scared...and physically hurt...and...
and...hot.

I wanted to curse at him, but why, I wasn't
entirely sure. His chest rose and fell faster than
usual, and I knew he was all worked up. Suddenly,
he pushed Celia forward onto the bed and her arms
reached out to catch her, landing on my knees. I
heard her panties rip as Caleb pulled the delicate
material in one swift jerking motion and discarded
them.

"Turn around and spread your legs," he said,
huskily. Celia scrambled to obey, and I sat in
unabashed horror as her head rested on my knees.

Caleb undid his pants and slid everything down,
his thick cock springing upward like something that

shouldn't be there, and I couldn't help but close my eyes.

"Do not fucking look away," he sneered. I opened my eyes. My tears fell.

Caleb dipped his head between Celia's legs and said something about loving a bald pussy before he buried his face between her thighs. Celia was somewhere else after that. She moaned and her head went from side to side. Her hands reached up toward me, and she made fists into the hips of my nightgown. I tried to pry her hands off of me to back away, but the bitch held on tight.

"Please," she said on a sigh. "Please. Let me come." She repeated the word *please* like a mantra. My heart raced.

Caleb emerged from Celia's thighs and took absolutely no notice of me as he sucked and kissed his way to her nipple. He reached down and must have put himself inside her, because Celia all of a sudden went perfectly still. Her face turned a ridiculous shade of red and an ungodly groan came out of her. Caleb looked at me, fire and hunger in his eyes.

He whispered, "I could have made you come like that. If it were really what you wanted. If you weren't such a liar." Before I could grasp the words he'd spoken, he grabbed the back of my head and kissed me. The taste of Celia saturated my mouth, and something in me snapped. I shook loose from the kiss and slapped Caleb across the face with so much force my hand stung.

I ran into the bathroom before he could recover. I

was breathless. I pressed my back against the door,
terrified of him bursting through it and some horrible
scenario playing out between us. I cried pitifully and
wiped at my mouth with my free hand to get the
taste of Celia out of my mouth. It wasn't that the
taste of her was altogether unpleasant – it had more
to do with the fact it came from Caleb's mouth. Of
all the emotions running through me, why was the
nagging sense of betrayal one of them? I couldn't
deny it – I was hurt, and I couldn't put my finger on
exactly why.

Nearly fifteen minutes went by, and Caleb still
hadn't come to confront me. I pressed my ear to the
door and I could hear them. They were still fucking.
I could hear her moaning and the rough timbre of his
voice. He was saying things, but I couldn't make
them out. I should've been happy he wasn't
interested in making me pay for what I'd done, but I
wasn't. That familiar and unsolicited feeling I had
earlier was still present, growing inside my chest,
and keeping the flow of tears coming to my eyes –
jealousy.

The idea I was jealous consumed me for several
hours as I lay on the tile. Why was I jealous? Of
whom? I don't think I was jealous of what Caleb
was doing. I had no reason to care. No reason,
except for more than a month he'd been trying to
seduce me and draw me in and make me feel
something I didn't feel – for what? So he could turn
around and fuck someone else? And her! Walking
around my room as if she were some sort of victim. I
actually felt sorry for her, up until I saw that smile of

hers – up until she made it obvious she was better than me in some way. Tears of frustration rolled down my cheeks, and no matter how I thought about it, I still hurt.

Later still, after the tears faded, I finally decided to leave my self-imposed prison and face whatever sick punishment Caleb undoubtedly had in store for me. I opened the bathroom door. Light from the bathroom spilled into the dark room, and there was a deep pinch in the middle of my chest when I saw they were both cuddled up together in what I'd come to think of as my bed. I stepped closer. They were both obviously naked, and the sheet only covered them from the waist down. Celia's face was still flush, and her lips looked swollen from kissing. She looked content. Caleb held her in his possessive way, as if he didn't want her to get away, though I doubted she would try. I swallowed past the lump in my throat and looked around. *Where am I supposed to sleep?*

I paced around the room, knowing I'd probably end up on the floor but not able to accept it yet. I walked past the door to the bedroom, and my heart skipped at the thought the door might actually be open. I looked back toward the bed and saw Caleb's face within the sliver of light coming from the bathroom. He slept peacefully. I put my hand on the latch and pressed down, and I held my breath as I pulled back gently. The door opened.

Soft light gave the long hallway an eerie glow and I almost had the feeling of being in a hotel, but my door seemed to be the only one down this

225

hallway. At the end of the hall, I could make out a railing, and just beyond it, a large chandelier hung from the ceiling. I took a step forward onto the soft carpeting and I was suddenly overwhelmed by the urge to pee. *What the hell are you doing?* I crept further out into the hall, not knowing what I intended to do once I reached the end. As I reached the middle of the hallway, I looked back toward the bedroom door and was suddenly overwhelmed with the memory of the bikers. Immediately I knew I wouldn't be running away. More than anything, I just wanted to look around – but I didn't want to risk Caleb's temper any more than I already had. I turned back. I closed the door behind me, as gently as I had opened it.

"Did you find what you were looking for?" inquired a husky male voice.

"I wasn't looking for anything," I replied. My anger gave my words a harder edge than I intended, and it belied my surge of fear at being caught. Caleb sighed. I watched as he disentangled himself from Celia and rolled over on his side to face me. Celia groaned and wrapped herself around my pillow and continued to sleep.

"Come here," he said softly, but I knew it wasn't a request. Conveying a confidence I didn't have, I crossed the short distance between us and stood next to the bed.

As I stood there, trying not to let my knees knock together, he looked me up and down, and from that alone my entire body grew uncomfortably warmer. He reached out with one hand and ran his fingers from my elbow to my wrist. He pressed his lips to the inside of my wrist.

"You slapped me," he said. He looked up into my eyes and I swallowed.

"Yes, Master," I whispered. I hoped addressing him properly would please him. He intertwined his fingers with mine and pressed firmly. I winced.

"Before you, I've never known a woman to get away with that." Tears fell from my eyes. I couldn't pretend to be brave.

"Please, don't hurt me," I sputtered.

He looked at me calmly, with a smile playing across his lips. "Well, it wouldn't take much would it? You're already broken as it is. It wouldn't be any fun for me." I let out a deep breath I didn't know I was holding and took another. "Still, I can't exactly let it go." Without thinking about it, I squeezed his hand when he spoke. "What are you bracing for?" he asked. "I already told you I'm not going to hurt you."

Inexplicably, sobs caught in my chest, but I managed to respond. "You've already hurt me, Caleb. Why would you do that? Why?"

He was silent for a long moment before he responded. "This thing between us…it has to stop. I don't like it. I've tried to make this easier for you, as ridiculous as it sounds. I can't keep you, Livvie. Stop trying to make me."

My heart clenched in my chest at the sound of my name. He remembered. I hadn't imagined those moments with him. They were as real to him as they had been to me, and it was almost more than I could

227

bear. Everything he had said was true. I'd been trying to manipulate him since the night he'd told me the truth. The night I realized I was nothing more than an object, a thing to be bought and traded.

I had no guilt over it, either. Caleb wanted me to survive, and I was trying my fucking best. I'd chosen my path and carefully placed my moments. Caleb was my way out of this whole thing, and I was set on doing all I could to bend him to my side. What I had never anticipated was the way my feelings would develop.

"I don't know what to say," I finally replied.

He smiled sadly. "Don't say anything. I shouldn't have. Just get in the bed."

A look of shock crossed over my face. "I'm not getting in there with the both of you," I said matter-of-factly. "Besides, you're naked."

His laugh was a low rumble that made me feel like a petulant child, but I didn't care. He sat up, and the sheet did a bad job of covering his thickening penis. He put his hands on my hips and gently urged me forward. Heat spread through my belly and I looked up past his head, my eyes landing on Celia's sleeping form.

His breath touched my belly through the thin fabric of my nightgown as he spoke. "I'm not asking, Kitten." I was about to say I didn't feel right sleeping next to Celia when his hot mouth closed over my puckered nipple, and an unbelievably hard tug inside me quickened my pulse and made the lips of my sex swell.

He let go quickly, but the damage was already

done. The residual wetness left by his mouth continued hardening my nipple as the air touched it. My breath was seemingly harder to come by, but Caleb seemed calm and in control.

"Now," he said over the roar in my ears, "are you going to get in this bed and go to sleep, or are you going to give me a reason to torture you in a thousand different ways that don't hurt?" A whine escaped my throat.

He coaxed me toward the bed, but I dug in my heels and gently refused to move. Caleb sighed deeply.

I knew I was testing his patience, but I wouldn't relent. "Please make her go," I whispered.

"Wouldn't that be mean?" He teased me from previous conversation, and I smiled in spite of myself. He regarded me for a few moments, then rolled his eyes playfully and yelled, "Celia!" I jumped. Celia woke with a start and rubbed the sleep from her eyes.

"Sí, Señor?" she said, alarmed and groggy.

"Go back to your room."

13

Matthew sat in silence for a few minutes, trying to soak in the story. What could he say? There wasn't necessarily any relevant information to be gleaned, but he was beginning to become curious about Caleb and the kind of man he was.

Caleb seemed like a very conflicted person. To Matthew's thinking, the conflict didn't excuse Caleb's actions, but as he sat in Olivia's hospital room struggling not to notice the throb of arousal he experienced every time he shifted in his seat and thought of Sloan, he wondered if he didn't share something in common with the man. It wasn't a comforting thought by any stretch, but there it was. He was curious.

As Olivia spoke, he recalled their earlier conversation about whether or not monsters were born or made. He believed they were made, as did Olivia, but Matthew had trouble with the notion that cruelty justified further cruelty. Or a lust for it.

In Matthew's case, he felt he should be able to subjugate his need to be humiliated and dominated sexually. His desires were a remnant from a childhood spent taking care of a weak woman and getting verbally and physically abused by an even weaker man. That Matthew had become a strong-willed and self-assured person was a blessing, but his need to be abused from time to time was a curse he struggled with in every romantic relationship he had.

Matthew wondered if the situation were reversed between him and Caleb, if it would have made any difference in how either of them turned out. Would Matthew have been a kidnapper? Would Caleb feel the need to submit instead of dominate? Or were certain aspects of a person's personality ingrained in them from birth?

A loud ping from his laptop snapped Matthew out of his thoughts. He received an email from Agent Williams. It was probably rude to open it, but he was glad for the distraction and the information could be important.

"Sorry. I have to read this email," Matthew said.

"Can you tell me what it says?" Olivia asked. She seemed to also need a distraction.

Matthew's finger scrolled through the email. His brows furrowed as he went over bits of information, his mouth quirking in different expressions depending on what he read. "I suppose. It might be helpful if you can tell me anything new."

"I can try," she said and Matthew realized he believed her. He still strongly believed Olivia was suffering from Stockholm Syndrome, but it didn't mean she was trying to stop him from doing his job.

"Demitri Balk has gone through a lot of trouble to cover up his past. According to this, prior to 1988 he was known as Vladek Rostrovich. Allegedly, he was a small-time arms dealer out of Russia," said Matthew.

"He disappears after '88, and then reappears as Balk in '98. In 2002, his company goes public and he becomes a billionaire seemingly overnight."

"What does that mean?" asked Olivia.

"I'm not sure," Matthew said. He obviously couldn't give Olivia all the details. She didn't have a need to know. However, he hoped giving her some of the information might lead her toward divulging information she was either keeping or didn't know she had.

Given the information, Matthew surmised that Pakistan, like many of its neighbors, bought weapons from Russian arms dealers in the 1980s. It was the most plausible explanation for Rafiq and Vladek crossing paths. For a moment, Matthew wondered if the bad blood between Rafiq and Vladek revolved around the sale of weapons to enemies of Pakistan, but that didn't seem like the kind of thing that would justify a vendetta spanning twenty years. It had to be personal.

At least now, Matthew had a timeframe for when it might have occurred. Also, given the fact Olivia had been kidnapped for the purpose of human trafficking and not drugs or guns, there was a large piece missing from the puzzle.

"Did Caleb ever mention why he and Rafiq want Balk dead?"

Olivia cocked her head slightly to one side and looked up toward the ceiling, as if answers were written there. Matthew recognized the behavior of someone trying to remember something. He found it interesting how people, with all their differences, were still inherently the same. Olivia finally responded. "Yes and no. The night Caleb told me he was…" She suddenly looked sad.

"What is it?" Matthew asked.

"I think you're right, Reed," she said, her voice rough at the edges. "I'm going to need a lot of therapy."

"I'm sorry," he said and meant it.

"Me too," she whispered and took a deep breath. "Anyway, the night he told me he planned on selling me, he said something about Balk needing to pay for what he did to Rafiq's mother and sister. Apparently, he did something to Caleb, too. I remember because later I wondered if that's where Caleb got the scars on his back."

"Is it?" Matthew asked.

She looked away, getting choked up again. "No. He said it was some guy named Narweh. He wouldn't tell me much – just that he was the one who whipped him when he was younger. Caleb said his life was hell until…Rafiq rescued him."

Matthew wrote everything down, hoping all the pieces would fall into place for him soon. Every piece was valuable because he knew alone they meant nothing, but together, they would lead him toward realizing the whole picture. That's what he loved. It was all he lived for: solving the puzzle.

"Did he say anything else about this 'Narweh' person? Do you have a timeframe?"

Olivia shook her head. "Sorry, no. I know Caleb was younger than me when it happened."

"How do you know?"

"He told me. We…we became very close by the end, Reed. Last time you were here and Sloan had just left, I was scared that maybe I made it up. I was scared that what I feel for Caleb was my way of surviving. Then I think about all the things he told me. I think about the way everyone gave him shit for being soft with me, and I…. I just don't think I made it up. It's real. The way I feel for him is real," Olivia said.

"I couldn't tell you one way or the other." Matthew shrugged. "My job is the case, not to determine if your feelings are real. Not to say your feelings are irrelevant – it's just no one can answer that question but you."

"I know, Reed. I just…."

"I know, Miss Ruiz," said Matthew. "When this whole thing started, my job was to get your statement and bring someone to justice. It's become something much larger than I, or my superiors, had anticipated. I don't want to hurt your feelings, or discount them, but the bottom-line is: Someone has to stop that auction. Everything else? I'm not sure," Matthew said. He had done a lot of talking with Olivia over the last week. He'd learned a few things, but whether or not it would lead him to the auction was still unclear.

Luckily, he had a team working on it now.

"Why don't you tell me the rest?"

Olivia was staring off again, but she nodded. "Yeah, why not."

***

My attachment to Caleb was evolving, but it

234

wasn't just that. I found myself anticipating his needs and learning the meanings behind his many silences. Some days he was brutal, and I scrambled to obey his every whim as flawlessly as I was capable. Other days, he seemed content just having me near while he attended to mundane things.

Caleb liked to read, but when I asked, he never let me know what it was he was reading. When I mentioned how much *I* liked to read, he gifted me a copy of Shakespeare's *Hamlet*. I thought it was ironic he gave me a story about one man's obsession with revenge and how it literally poisoned everyone around him. He didn't seem to find it amusing but let me keep the book anyway. I wasn't sure what to make of the gesture.

I thought a lot about the night he had sex with Celia in front of me. It was a painful memory for many reasons, but the worst seemed to be my nagging sense of jealousy. No matter the circumstance, I found having Caleb near was always better than not having him around. It wasn't only his presence I came to crave, but also the man himself.

Several weeks after the night with Celia, I was finally free of all tape and bandages. My ribs still hurt from time to time, but it wasn't the horrible kind of pain that stole my breath. I opened my eyes and it was still dark in the room, but light enough to suggest it was morning. Celia hadn't been in to open the curtains yet. I yawned and stretched out. I was careful not to hit Caleb as he slept beside me.

I didn't have the nightmares as often anymore, but whenever Caleb opted not to sleep in my room I found myself terrified of the dark and unable to sleep. Such had been the case the night before, and I'd ended up yelling his name loudly over and over until he angrily opened my door in his boxer shorts and asked me what the hell I was screaming about.

As soon as I had seen him, I relaxed. I ran toward him and put my arms around him. With my face buried against his chest, I immediately breathed in comfort and security. He had seemed annoyed, but he'd wiped my face and told me to get in bed – he'd stay.

I knew morning would bring about a change in him, in the way he behaved toward me, and I wasn't ready to accept it yet. It was ironic because at first, I hated the dark. I had spent so much time those first few weeks of my captivity craving the sun and the light on my face. Suddenly, it seemed the opposite. In the dark, my master let down his guard and he was Caleb again. He didn't correct me. He didn't punish me. He didn't push me away emotionally. Caleb was there to hold me until the nightmares passed. He was there to tell me I was beautiful. He was there to tell me I was going to be okay. In the dark, he seduced me. I didn't want the seduction to end.

I turned toward Caleb slowly, staring at his back. I'd seen his scars before, kissed them, but Caleb had never let me study them. With his eyes so firmly shut and him taking deep, even breaths, I took advantage of the situation to satisfy my growing curiosity. Even in the dim light, I made out the thick lines crisscrossing his tanned skin. They almost looked like welts, but I could tell they'd been healed for a long time.

Unable to resist, I reached out with my fingertip and traced one from his shoulder to about the middle of his back. He groaned and shifted a little, and I withdrew my hand. I waited a few impatient seconds to see if he woke up, and when he didn't, I went over the same spot again. The skin was raised by the slightest of degrees, and I marveled over how many there were. *How did you get these?* My curiosity made me bolder and I pressed my palm to his skin, letting it travel the length and breadth of his back. There were dozens of the tiny welts. *Who did this to you? Is this why you're the way you are?*

Without thinking, I drew closer and pressed my lips to the ill-treated flesh. Caleb was soft, softer than I'd expected him to be given the firmness of him. Tiny, invisible blond hair met my lips and I smiled against his flesh. I'd never been so close to a man as I was to Caleb. Everything with him was a new discovery. Granted, most things I discovered about Caleb were horrible, but sometimes... sometimes I discovered he was soft.

I lingered over his bare skin, scooting closer and enjoying him. He never asked me to touch him anymore. I thought about the time he asked me to touch him. I'd been hesitant at the time. I'd hated him. I was surprised to realize I didn't hate him so much anymore. I felt so many things toward him, and yes, hate was perhaps among them – but there were other feelings too, far more complex than simple hate.

Caleb planned to sell me. I hated him for that. Everything else? I was shocked to realize I could, perhaps, forgive him. I struggled against the idea every day, at every opportunity, telling myself it would only leave me in ruins…but my heart. My heart, independent of my logic, had reserved a place for my tormentor and my solace.

I was lost in my thoughts, stroking Caleb's back, when he let out a gruff sigh and swatted at his shoulder, almost hitting me. I flinched and made a startled sound. Abruptly, he turned and grabbed the hand I had used to touch him. We stared at each other for a bit, my eyes wide and nervous, and his presumably confused and a little angry.

"What are you doing?" he asked suspiciously. He held my hand as if he'd just pulled it from the proverbial cookie jar, and what could I say – I looked the part.

Brazenly, I pulled my hand free and asked, "What happened to your back?" He looked at me as if I'd said something distasteful, and then fell back against his pillow as he expelled a big yawn.

"You know, Kitten, when I first decided to call you that, I didn't realize how aptly I'd chosen." He read my perplexed expression and proceeded. "Curiosity killed the cat." He smiled, but I didn't think it was too funny.

Jokes about killing me. Yeah – not funny.

"Will you stop asking if I tell you?" He stretched. I tried not to be distracted by his nearly-naked body and the serious case of morning wood he had going.

"Why would I keep asking you if I had the answer?" I retorted and boldly smiled when he glared at me.

"The better question would be: why do I put up with you?" I knew he meant it to be banter, but all he'd done was thrust our situation into awkward focus. We both knew why he put up with me, and the answer was shitty.

I was just about to lie and tell him I wasn't really curious, but Celia finally came into the room with breakfast. Celia – things were surprisingly not strained between us. She hadn't been happy Caleb had used her and sent her packing, but the following morning she'd come in, business as usual.

Once, when Caleb hadn't spent the night and therefore had not been in my room the next morning, I spoke to her again. She'd actually seemed a little frightened when I grabbed her arm and asked her just what that smile she'd given me had been about.

"Please don't be upset with me," she'd said, and I felt a little snotty and let her go. "He brought me here for you," she continued. Her expression suggested I was stupid for not knowing – which apparently, I was.

"What do you mean, for me?"

"He cares for you. He cares for you the way I wish my master would care for me," she said in an almost sad and thoughtful tone. "In a way, I was glad you were jealous – I could see it on your face. It was a nice change from being jealous of you."

239

She had stunned me; I'd never considered she was jealous. I'd never considered my position to be an enviable one.

After Celia concluded her morning business, Caleb and I still lay in bed, just the two of us. The feeling grew more and more comfortable as the days and weeks progressed. I still hadn't been able to convince him to let me roam the mansion, but I could go out onto the balcony if he accompanied me. The view was breathtaking. It appeared to be the quintessential Spanish villa, surrounded by lush fields below and cactus in bloom in large ceramic pots, set on Spanish tile on an extravagant balcony. I'd only dreamed of living places like this. Though, in my dreams, I was never living there as a captive. *Semantics.*

"Breakfast on the balcony?" I asked with more enthusiasm than necessary.

He smiled. "What do you think this is, a vacation?" I felt a tight pinch in the center of my chest when he teased me. I think I'd rather come to like it. Not the teasing, but the way he smiled when he did.

"Hardly," I said, coyly.

He stretched out again and put his hands behind his head, then looked at me disbelievingly. He had a grin playing across his lips.

"Did you...*kiss me* this morning?" Instant heat rose to my face, turning me what had to be at least eight different shades of red. I worked hard to resist the urge to bury my face in my pillow.

Kill me. Kill me, now!

I couldn't even speak; I just shook my head emphatically, but the look in his eyes told me he knew I was lying.

"Yes. You did." This time his teasing was a little painful. I was really embarrassed, and I knew he just wouldn't let it go. Tears started to well up in my eyes.

"No, I didn't!" I said on a rush of breath, and I felt the heat of my tears cutting across my cheek.

He rolled his eyes as he sat up. He put his finger under my chin and tilted my head upward. "Really? Tears, Kitten? *You* kissed *me*. Against my will, I might add. Shouldn't I be the one to cry?" he asked. He laughed uproariously as I buried my face in my pillow again.

"Oh, come on!" he said in an annoyed tone and laid his face next to mine. "I'll drop it, okay?"

Bringing my head up slowly and wiping away my tears, I whispered, "You promise?" He put his hand around my waist, pulled me close, and rolled me onto my back. Stunned, I simply looked up at him. "Absolutely not," he said. Carefully, I tried to move, but his weight pinned me to the mattress. "By now you should know I always get what I want."

As I stared up into his enigmatic blue eyes, it was hard to ignore the sensual line of his jaw. It showed the barest trace of his morning stubble. His hair was ruffled from sleep, and while I thought it should make him look ridiculous, it only made him more handsome. Caleb was a person, bed head and all. But of all the things difficult to ignore about the man on top of me, there was one that stood out...

quite literally. He was incredibly hard between my thighs.

"And what *do* you want?" I asked, softly.

We stared at one another for what felt like an eternity. He looked at me in a way I'd never seen before. I didn't want to give it a name or classification. I was more than content to just have him look at me with that expression on his face.

Slowly, I brought my hands up to his face. I couldn't help myself. Knowing how soft he could be, the urge to touch him was something I didn't want to fight off.

He seemed taken aback by my touch, and the playful smile he held fell from his face. Our eyes met for the briefest of moments, and my fingers sensed the gentle shake of his head just before I kissed him so hard we both made a hurt sound. My brain fired synapses to every part of my body, and heat flooded my skin and pooled between my thighs. His tongue begged to be allowed into my mouth and I opened up to him. My hands weaved through his hair. He moaned into my mouth, and my hunger for him exploded from a place I had begun to suspect was there for quite some time.

I started to get a little frightened when he reached down and pulled up my nightgown. *I don't think I'm ready for this.* He spread my legs with his body, cradling himself between my thighs. His cock was incredibly hard. I wanted to say something, protest in some way, but then I felt the heat of him against the wetness I'd created, and I could've sworn I heard us sizzle. He withdrew his lips from mine and latched his hot, sucking mouth onto my neck. I threw my head back, surprised by the sensation of both pleasure and pain, a sensation that only became more powerful as the son of a bitch bit me.

I gasped loudly. My hands instinctively flexed into fists in his hair and I pulled him backward. "That hurt!" I said through gritted teeth.

He pulled my hands free from his hair and held them above my head with his left hand. "You think I don't know?" The unmistakable look of lust had taken over his features, and he appeared almost feral in his intensity.

I was a little frightened, but my desire for him wouldn't let me care. I pulled his mouth down toward mine. My heart slammed around in my chest as the liquid fire in my veins seemed to burn me from the inside out.

Abruptly, his touch turned soft and he kissed me so gently I wanted to cry again. "You're so wet; my cock is covered in you," he whispered against my mouth. I moaned loudly at his words, and I knew my mind was made up.

"Make love to me," I replied. My voice sounded alien to my own ears. His heart beat hard against me, and his cock twitched against my pussy. He took a deep, ragged breath and placed his forehead against my shoulder. In the silence, my hunger feuded with my growing shame over the idea he would say something cruel or make some silly joke. I would be undone.

He finally picked his head back up and looked at me. I couldn't decipher the message in his eyes. He conveyed so many things at once: need, anger, confusion, and something else. "Fuck," he said.

His shoulders slumped subtly, and I worried this was the part where he was going to say something to make me wish I could crawl inside myself and die. I wanted to say something, perhaps offer some preemptive strike, like 'I was just kidding,' but I couldn't say anything. Then, to my relief, he let my hands go and slipped the straps of my nightgown down my shoulders, exposing my breasts.

"You have the most beautiful tits." Heat crawled over my flesh and my nipples tightened.

"Thanks?" I said, unsure.

"You're welcome," he said through a smile and put his mouth around my aching nipple.

I attempted to wrap my arms around him, but they were trapped in the straps of my nightgown. Overcome by a rush of sensation, I pressed my thighs tightly in an effort to close them and crushed Caleb closer to my body as I writhed under his consuming touch. He sucked and bit at one nipple and then the other, and did not neglect any part in between. I closed my eyes and swam in a sea of pleasure, pain, and longing.

I think I love you.

The thought swirled in my brain like an angry tornado begging me to say the words out loud, but I couldn't – I couldn't possibly. I felt like I might have an orgasm just then, before he was even inside me, before he'd even touched me down there. I teetered on the edge, which felt both delicious and annoying.

Say it! I think I love you.

He reached down between our bodies and slid his underwear past his erection.

Oh my god! Oh my god!

"Wait," I said, breathless. Caleb paused.

"What?" he asked. He sounded genuine in his concern.

"Be gentle, okay?" I whispered and resigned myself. The look in his eyes turned devastating. It was as if he wanted to tear me apart with his teeth, and I probably would have let him.

"Don't worry, Kitten. I'm not going to fuck you," he said through a rueful grin.

Before I could ask him why the hell not, the hot pulse of his thick shaft splayed the lips of my sex. He rubbed the hard, yet pliant, flesh of his cock against the swollen bud of my clit, and I was paralyzed. Desperate, mewling sounds came out of my throat, and my hips instinctively rocked back and forth against the heat of him. I was going to come, and it was going to be incredible. Up and down he moved his cock against my sensitive flesh, and all I could do was pine as I tried to get my stupid arms out of my nightgown so I could touch him.

His mouth traveled up my body and nestled at the nape of my neck. He bit me again, but this time I inclined toward him. "Does it feel good, Pet?" he asked in a voice dripping with arrogance. I didn't care. I nodded fervently and looked for his mouth. He let his lips dance just above mine, all the while keeping his rhythm against my clit.

"I want to hear you say it. Tell me it feels good.

Tell me how much you want me to make that little pussy of yours come."

Oh. My. God!

Every muscle in my body tightened all at once. The opening of my pussy contracted and grasped at what wasn't there. My heart pounded and my hands grabbed at the sheets while my legs pressed against Caleb as hard as they could. Orgasm ripped through my body indiscriminately, engulfing everything in its path, and I was so overwhelmed, tears ran down my face.

"I love you!" I screamed. I couldn't help myself and I kept crying, even as Caleb's hot semen splashed against my sex and belly.

He panted hard and grabbed at his cock, expelling everything he had onto me. Then he grabbed my ass tightly and squeezed me as his mouth once again found mine. He kissed me until we both settled some and then gently collapsed against me.

14

Caleb knew his weight was probably crushing Livvie, but he wasn't quite ready to address this new and provocative situation. He supposed it was common for a person, especially a female person, to say incredulous things in the throes of passion, but he couldn't actually say it had ever happened to him before. She had said she loved him. She'd said it during a very intense orgasm, but she'd said it just the same. Even now, he felt the heat and wetness of her tears against his shoulder. She wasn't sobbing, or blubbering. In fact, the way she was caressing his thigh with her fingertips suggested she was quite content, if not sated.

Wanting suddenly to put an end to his discomfort, stemming both from his own thoughts as well as the feeling of heat and stickiness, he moved to disengage himself from Livvie. She made a series of adjusting sounds as he peeled off of her and watched as Caleb wiped the semen off of his lower abdomen with the edge of her nightgown. She scrunched her nose, as if it were the most disgusting thing she'd ever seen; he didn't respond.

He didn't like the feelings running through him. He replayed the incident in his mind, trying to find the exact moment in which he'd lost control and fallen under the spell of the woman who was supposed to be *his* captive. She couldn't even move, yet it was impossible to ignore the hold she had over

247

him with her big, innocent eyes and pouty, trembling mouth.

He pulled his boxers up and sat on the edge of the bed, trying to think of what to say. He heard her sigh contentedly just before the warmth of her cheek pressed against his back, causing a mild tingle to spread through him. She wrapped her arms loosely around his waist.

"Please, don't," Livvie whispered softly against his back.

"Don't what?"

"Whenever something nice happens…between us…you're mean after." Livvie pressed herself against his back and held him tighter.

Caleb's confusion was turning toward anger, but he knew she was right. His instinct was to lash out in an effort to put distance between him and Livvie. He'd called her a coward, threatened her with humiliation and violence, even fucked another woman in front of her to try and stop whatever was happening between them. None of it worked. Here they were, in yet another emotionally compromising situation. It was exhausting.

"I love you!" Livvie's words echoed through Caleb's thoughts. He looked down at Livvie's arms, the way she held him there. He realized it was a silent plea: *"I could stay with you…be with you."* Caleb closed his eyes and let himself place his hand on her arm, holding her there in return.

"I can't," he replied, knowing his words were odd. Livvie had neither asked a question nor requested a response, but he just knew she would understand what he was trying to say.

"Why, Caleb? Why can't you?" she whispered. Caleb swallowed thickly. She did understand. He'd known she would, but it affected him nonetheless.

Because none of this makes any fucking sense! He wanted to yell the words, but said, "I have to go."

"No, you don't, Caleb. You don't have to go." Her arms gripped him like a vise.

Caleb wanted to correct her, yet again, for using his name, but it felt ridiculous to do so at this point. Livvie was just too fucking stubborn. It didn't matter what he said or did. Ultimately, there were simply some orders she would not obey. If there was any compromise on the issue, it was that she didn't do it in front of others.

"I need to take a shower," he said, in the hopes logic would prevail.

"I need to take one too," she countered. "We could take one together? I need your help."

Caleb laughed ruefully. "You don't need my help. You hate my help."

Livvie rubbed her cheek against Caleb's back as she laughed. "All the more reason for you to help me. You love doing things when I ask you not to – it's kinda your thing."

"It is, isn't it?" Caleb agreed.

"It is. Also…" she shifted uncomfortably, "there's something I've been thinking about." Caleb was begrudgingly intrigued by the hesitant, but excited, tone of her voice.

"And what, exactly, might that be?" Caleb asked.

Livvie shifted her body until she was on her

knees behind him and then pressed her naked breasts against his back to whisper in his ear. Caleb's eyes widened ever so slightly and his heart picked up speed.

Over the last few months, Caleb had taken advantage during their sexual encounters, and though she'd always been incredibly wet when he touched her and she'd had several orgasms, he'd always suspected her heart had not been in it – and he hadn't cared. Somehow, things were different now.

"Make love to me."

He'd intended only to play the game they'd always played, the one featuring him as The Big Bad Wolf and her as frightened Little Red Riding Hood. He hadn't been prepared for the kiss or....

"I love you!"

After she'd been injured, he'd treated her like spun glass. He'd been careful not to injure her further, or cause her unnecessary pain. Unfortunately, it had also allowed her to work herself into more than his thoughts. For the first time since his life had descended into this dark place, something akin to caring for another person found a place to thrive inside him.

It seemed a lifetime had passed since Caleb had been made to submit to the will of another. It had nearly killed him the last time. Still, her hold on him...was far more than physical. "Kitten?" he said.

"Yes?" Livvie said hesitantly.

"I came on you," Caleb said through a laugh.

Livvie laughed. "Yep." She kissed Caleb's neck.

"I'm pretty sticky, too."

"Shower?"

"Absolutely," Livvie said.

Caleb walked into the bathroom and stared first at the shower, and then at the bath. Either would serve their purpose, but each had its own appeal. The shower had a bench, and the glass enclosure trapped steam to keep them comfortable when not under the direct spray. Caleb had a vision of pressing Livvie up against the glass. It left him light headed for a moment.

"The shower or the tub?" asked Livvie.

"I was just asking myself the same. I suppose it's up to you. This is your fantasy, after all." Caleb grinned and turned to watch Livvie blush.

She playfully slapped him on the chest. "Yeah, right! I'm sure you're just gonna hate it." She smiled brightly, but then seemed to doubt herself.

"What's wrong?" Caleb asked.

"Nothing. It's just..." She bit at her bottom lip, then started picking at it with her fingernails.

Caleb pulled her hand away from her mouth. "It's just, what? Change your mind?" He was at once relieved and annoyed.

She shook her head slightly. "No, it's just...I've never done this before." She looked down at her feet, up at him, then back down.

Caleb wanted to help her out, he really did. He wanted to let her know it didn't matter. Anything she deigned to do to him, or with him, would be perfect. But frankly, watching her squirm was too much fun to pass up.

"Never done what before?" he asked and went toward the shower to turn it on. This could get messy. The shower was perfect for messy.

Livvie rolled her eyes in exasperation. "You know what."

"Kitten," he said as the sound of running water echoed around the room, "if you can't say it, how do you expect to do it?" Livvie blushed and Caleb smiled.

"Don't make fun of me, Caleb. I don't like to be made fun of," she said and covered her breasts. Caleb didn't like that so much.

He stepped closer, building his own arousal by taking Livvie in with his eyes. She was beautiful. She'd healed almost completely, and Caleb couldn't help but feel...grateful. There would be no scars for Livvie. At least, not on the outside.

The thought of Livvie's mental scars brought him up short. He'd been having dreams lately, old memories bombarding him in the middle of the night. When he'd first been rescued, they had been an almost-nightly occurrence – but after a year or two with Rafiq, they had stopped. The stronger he'd become, the more sure of himself and his destiny, the more peaceful his sleep. He hated to speculate on why the dreams would return now and why so many of them involved Rafiq.

Caleb stood in front of Livvie and pulled her head to his chest. "I wasn't making fun, but Kitten... we shouldn't do this." Caleb was surprised to have Livvie squirm out of his arms and push him back. He stumbled back a step but quickly set himself to rights.

Livvie glared at him. "No. We're doing this. You're going to take off those shorts and get in the shower," she pointed, "and I'm going to…to…."

Caleb crossed his arms and watched in smug amusement as Livvie struggled to get the words out and blushed something furious in the process. "To suck my dick."

"Yes! That!" Livvie said seriously.

Caleb laughed. "Not until you say it. In fact, not until you beg me."

Livvie's eyes held a spark of outrage. "You want me, to beg you, to let me suck your dick? That's… that's…you're a pig."

Caleb straightened. "No, I'm your Master." Some of the color seemed to drain from Livvie's face. "Did you forget? Does allowing you to use my name when we're alone make it any less true?"

"Of course not, Caleb. I'm sorry."

Caleb wasn't angry – a little unsettled, maybe, but not angry. He reasoned that perhaps returning to some sort of normalcy would get them past their awkwardness. "You can call me by my name when we're alone – I've come to expect it – but that doesn't mean you're allowed to forget who and what I am to you. Understand?" He pushed an errant lock of raven hair behind her ear. It had gotten so much longer. *Beautiful.*

"Yes, Caleb," she whispered and inclined her head into his hand. Slowly, her eyes focused on his, her pupils growing larger. "Please, Caleb, let me suck your dick."

Caleb was definitely light headed. Hearing her say dirty things turned him on to the point of physical ache. He cleared his throat. "Get in the shower, Kitten."

Her hand reached for him and boldly wrapped around his dick. Caleb hissed and pushed her toward the shower, pinning her against the warm glass.

"I'm not going to repeat myself," Caleb said. Livvie gripped Caleb's cock even harder and he moaned above her head, rocking his hips into her hand. This was a side of her Caleb hadn't seen – not sexually. He liked it.

"You're so hard," she groaned and writhed against him.

"Take it out," Caleb urged, and the longing in his voice was a shock. He ran his hands into her hair, loving the feel of her warm breath against his wrist. He looked into the liquid black pool of her eyes; she was so innocent, so striking. He licked his lips, hungrily preparing his assault upon his prey, bowing his head down toward her mouth. She pulled back, their eyes meeting in an awkward, sensuous moment. Her eyes continued to look at his as she slid down onto her knees.

Caleb let out a hushed moan as her shaky fingers curled along the inside of the waistband of his shorts. He tilted his head back, wanting to relish every moment of her soft fingers on his skin. He rocked forward as his shorts slid down, and finally her fingers made contact with his rigid flesh, freeing him. It seemed nothing else existed – nothing, but Livvie. She reached out carefully and wrapped her hand around his hot length. Though she squeezed him, her fingers barely touched.

Unable to resist, he rocked forward, touching it to her lips. "You're such a brat. I told you to get in the show–" He couldn't get out the rest because Livvie's tongue swept across the tip of his cock. He watched, stunned, as Livvie pulled away and his precome left a slick trail on her bottom lip. Her kitten tongue darted out to collect it.

Livvie swallowed. "You taste good."

Caleb took in a breath that rattled in his chest. "You taste better," he said and ran his thumb across her plump, pink lip. He couldn't wait to get back in her mouth and watch those sexy fucking lips sliding up and down his cock. He groaned when she opened her mouth and sucked his thumb into her mouth.

"Kitten. Get in the fucking shower. Now."

Livvie gave his thumb one last loving lick. "Yes, Caleb." She stood slowly and opened the shower door. Steam drifted out, already dusting her body with beads of moisture.

Caleb hurried her along, eager to touch her, to be touched by her. He shut the shower door behind him and a moment later snatched her up and pinned her to the wall with his body. Warm water cascaded from the showerhead above them as he lifted her legs around his waist and held her in place while they kissed.

Livvie moaned into his mouth, her hands gripping his shoulders and pulling him even closer. Her legs squeezed him, pressing her untried pussy against Caleb's stomach in a frantic plea for his attentions.

Caleb's hands roamed her slick body, cupping her ass and digging his fingers into her firm and pliable flesh. Reluctant to move on, but eager to enjoy the rest of her, he slid his hand up to her left breast, his thumb and index finger finding her pebbled nipple and rolling it as his hips gyrated. His cock, hard and leaking, bumped against her ass and Caleb curved his body, seeking the warm cleft between her cheeks.

"Oh. God," Livvie moaned. She joined in Caleb's rhythm, loosening her arms so her ass met Caleb's slippery cock.

"Fuck!" Caleb shouted, squeezing Livvie until she whimpered.

"Caleb, my ribs," she said softly and without halting her movements against him.

"Sorry." Caleb lessened his hold slightly. Only enough to stop hurting her.

"What's happening?" Livvie moaned and rocked against him. "I thought I was going to suck your dick."

Caleb's cock throbbed and leapt between Livvie's ass cheeks. If he waited any longer, he was going to demand to get in her ass. The thought was enough to get more sounds out of him, but damn it, he wanted a blowjob. Abruptly, he set Livvie on her feet and gave her a moment to gain her balance before he put his hand on her shoulder and urged her to her knees in front of him.

"You are. Right now," he said.

There was no discussion, no hesitation, and

Caleb's chest seemed to expand with pride as Livvie licked her lips and put her mouth on him. Caleb's knees buckled slightly and he could not resist thrusting into her mouth, forcing her to regain her balance. He grunted low, as if he didn't want her to hear, thrusting as much as he could without holding her head in his hands and having his way.

Her mouth was warm and caressingly tender, despite her obvious inexperience. She held him in her hands, licking the head of his cock slowly and then putting it in her mouth. Caleb fought every impulse to force himself deeper. He wanted her to do it on her own.

"Mmm," she moaned.

Caleb echoed her sounds, loving the vibration of her mouth against his dick. He wanted more. More. More. More. Her touch and her mouth were all over the place in their intention. Pain and pleasure mingled every time she accidentally grazed him with her teeth, but then caressed the spot with her tongue.

"Deeper, Livvie. Please, deeper," he found himself saying. He couldn't think straight and didn't realize what he'd said.

Livvie whimpered as she endeavored to take him deeper, her mouth stretching over his shaft. Teeth scraped him, but he didn't care – he knew it would be impossible to get even half of it into her mouth.

Caleb refused to take control. He was getting off on the fact this was her fantasy and not his own. He wondered how long she'd wanted to do suck him off and lamented the time wasted. Livvie went deep, and Caleb felt her throat contract around the head of his cock before she pulled away to take air into her lungs.

Caleb clenched his hands into fists at his sides, determined to let her breathe before he demanded to be let back into her warm, wet mouth. He sighed when she rested one hand against his thigh for balance and, with the other, held his cock in place as she took him back in.

She increased her pace, keeping her eyes closed and focusing on her rhythm. It was almost more than Caleb could stand. Unable to resist, he reached down for his cock and wrapped his hand around hers, guiding it up and down with the rhythm of her mouth.

She slowed, and Caleb fought not to thrust. *Harder. Faster. Deeper.* Caleb held her hand firmly, moving it up and down the length of him. With his other hand he caressed her face, coaxing her mouth to continue its maddening suckling, relieved when it began anew. Caleb removed his hand, letting Livvie have her way once more. His hand was covered in Livvie's saliva, much like his cock.

Livvie mewled and moaned around his cock, sucking him deeper as her lust grew and her instincts took over. Her hand pumped him, and she moved her lips with growing speed and firm pressure over the tip of his cock.

Caleb was nearing his crisis, his body tense as a drawn bow. He breathed heavily and his hands kneaded Livvie's shoulders, encouraging her. Suddenly, he grabbed fists of her hair and pulled his cock out of her wet mouth.

"Open your mouth," he demanded.

Livvie was powerless as he pushed himself almost violently back into her mouth and pumped only a few times before coming long and hard into Livvie's mouth. She moaned, but her hands pushed against his thighs.

Caleb couldn't stop himself, couldn't help the way he held her still, emptying himself. He felt her trying to swallow the salty fluid overwhelming her mouth, but there was too much. It trickled down her chin and down her neck. Caleb growled from deep in his throat and his knees gave way under him until he straddled her. He kissed her over and over, sucking on her lips and searching for her tongue. His taste in her mouth felt like a claim, a brand.

"God," he whispered to no one at all, kissing her neck.

Livvie panted hard into Caleb's ear, gripping him close and returning his fervent kisses. She grabbed Caleb's hand and pressed his fingers to her clit, whimpering for attention.

"Only fair," Caleb whispered. He circled her clit hard and fast with his fingertips, and within seconds, he felt the hot rush of Livvie's juices rushing out of her pussy as she came apart in his arms for the second time.

"Oh, oh, oh," she moaned against his ear, "I love you. Oh, god, I love you."

Caleb was too sated to care she'd said it again.

Slowly, the world began to come into focus and Caleb peeled himself away from Livvie to help her onto her shaky feet. Their eyes met briefly before

Livvie turned her face toward the spray of water over head. Caleb felt a twinge of anger as he watched her rinse her mouth out, but realized it had to be done. He tried not to take it personally.

She'd given him so much, opened herself so fully and exposed a part of her Caleb had never seen or touched in another human being. He felt he should offer something in return. He longed to offer something in return and, unable to think of anything else, he said, "I was almost beaten to death when I was a teenager." Livvie jolted to attention, her gaze fixed on Caleb. He reached for the soap and began to lather it in his hands before he turned Livvie toward the wall and started soaping her skin.

"I was younger than you. I know that much. A man named Narweh used a bullwhip on me. There was a lot of blood. The beating left scars, but I would have died if...if Rafiq hadn't saved my life." Caleb cleared his throat and focused on soaping.

Livvie tried to turn and face him, but Caleb wouldn't allow it. He simply moved her body in the direction he wanted and continued to wash her.

Her deadened voice broke the silence. "Why would someone do that to you?"

"I was...." He couldn't tell her. He couldn't tell her about the person he'd been, or the things he'd done. She was the one person who deserved to know, but he refused to say. "I was too weak to defend myself. Instead, I went back later and killed him." He chuckled, lost in thought. "With the gun you pulled on me, in fact."

Livvie was tense under his hands, her shoulders

knotted. "Is that…? Is that the reason you feel like you owe Rafiq? Because he saved your life?"

Caleb's hands inadvertently clenched, and Livvie hissed in pain. He immediately let her go and reached for more soap. "Sorry," he mumbled.

Livvie didn't face him. She simply stared at the wall. "What about me, Caleb? Don't you think you owe me anything?"

Caleb regretted having said anything at all. What had he been thinking to say anything so personal? And to Livvie of all people, whom he planned to subjugate for his own ends to repay a twelve-year debt? It was reckless and stupid beyond anything he'd done so far.

"No," he said. It felt like a lie. It was a lie. He owed her plenty. He'd been naïve to think he'd ever be free of his debt. He'd always owe someone. "But if you ever want your revenge against me, you let me know."

Livvie said nothing for several minutes before she turned to look at Caleb. "I don't want revenge, Caleb. I don't want to end up like you, letting some fucking vendetta run my life. I just want my freedom. I want to be free, Caleb. Not someone's whore…not even yours."

Caleb's throat felt like it was on fire as he acknowledged the sincerity in Livvie's words. This had been her game the entire time. He'd known it, reminded himself of it repeatedly, even begrudgingly respected her attempts – but he'd still fallen for it. He deserved every bit of what he was getting. He knew it and didn't care.

He stepped forward, prodding Kitten out of the way, and rinsed his body beneath the cooling spray of the water. He could feel Kitten's stare on his body but refused to acknowledge her. Once he was done rinsing, he opened the glass shower door, grabbed a towel, and headed for the bedroom.

"You're leaving!" Kitten cried, busting out of the shower and gripping his arm.

Caleb pushed her away, somewhat forcefully, and continued into the bedroom. "I have a lot of things to do today. You've taken up too much of my time lately as it is," he said coldly. For a moment, he looked about the room for his pants – then realized he hadn't come in wearing any because he'd come to address her late-night ranting some time after he'd gone to bed. He glanced at her face and saw the hurt in her eyes, tears standing at the ready. She swallowed hard to keep them at bay as her hands covered her breasts.

"You're going to go *now*, after everything? I thought…" Her voice trailed off, teetering somewhere between anger and hurt. Something twisted inside Caleb's stomach at the sight of her. He wanted to kiss her and tell her things that would make her stop crying – but then just the thought he'd considered such a thing solidified his anger and resolve.

"You thought what? You thought offering me a little pussy was going to make some kind of a difference? You thought you'd suck my dick and I'd just give you whatever the fuck you wanted?!"

His words cut her deeply, as he intended. He

262

wanted to make sure there was absolutely no confusion. He walked toward her and tilted her chin upward, and she instinctively recoiled, trying to get away from his hand. He gripped her harder, holding her in place.

"I did think it was really cute when you said you loved me, though." He visibly saw her shoulders slump then, and her eyes closed slowly. He let her face go, and without hysterics she walked toward the bed and put her head down onto her pillow and crawled into a ball.

For a few moments, he waited for her to retaliate, but she said nothing. He walked calmly toward the door, opened it, and walked through without a glance in her direction. He closed the door behind him gently and awkwardly wondered why he suddenly felt hollow. Wrapped in nothing but a towel, he made his way toward his room.

Once inside his room, Caleb stood for a moment, staring into nothingness as water dripped off of him. Livvie had said she loved him, and he'd made her feel stupid. Something in his gut twisted at the thought and at the memory of her tears. He often thought she looked beautiful when she cried because she was nervous, or afraid, or embarrassed, but these weren't the same; he'd really hurt her. She'd hurt him, too. Caleb couldn't change who he was.

He hadn't thought about Rafiq in a very long time. He'd been too busy playing house with Livvie. Too busy to think about the debt he owed and why he owed it. It was probably the reason Rafiq had been in his dreams as of late. It was his subconscious's way of reminding him not to lose focus. He'd ignored it. He couldn't do it anymore.

The night before, he'd had a dream about speaking with Rafiq about the murder of his mother and sister. Caleb had been in Rafiq's study, learning the English alphabet and the sound each letter made. He'd been proud to discover he could use the sounds of the letters to make sense of words. They had begun to look less like a collection of squiggly lines, and slowly, but surely, he could read some words without sounding them out.

Rafiq had been teaching him English and Spanish at the same time, because they used the same letters. It had been confusing at first, because they didn't make the same sounds, but Caleb was learning. The Arabic and Urdu were much harder to read but easier to speak because he'd grown up with them. His Russian was a mess on both counts, but Rafiq insisted he learn it.

Caleb knew he had to learn the Russian because it was Vladek's native tongue. Caleb had become hungry for information about Vladek after Narweh's death, but Rafiq often refused to give too much detail when it came to the murders of this mother and sister.

Somewhere in his mind, Caleb knew the incident was painful for Rafiq, but as Caleb didn't have a mother or any siblings he knew of, it was difficult to wrap his mind around Rafiq's emotions. With the exception of Rafiq's thirst for revenge, which Caleb understood empirically, he often wondered what Rafiq was dealing with emotionally.

Rafiq had given him a long speech about family, loyalty, duty, and honor. He'd said he had responsibilities to his father and to his country.

"I expect obedience, Caleb. I expect your loyalty. Anyone who betrays me will only do it once. Do you understand?" Rafiq had said ominously.
"Yes, Rafiq, I understand," Caleb had replied.

Caleb finally returned from his far-off thoughts and began to dry off and dress. It was going to be a shitty day. That much was obvious.

A knock on the door drew his attention. He answered, and Celia immediately cast her eyes downward and held a deep curtsy.

"¿Qué quieres?" he asked, more harshly than he intended.

Celia stood slowly, eyeing him with confusion, but then explained her master, Felipe, had requested an audience with him.

Caleb reluctantly agreed to come down stairs after he was fully dressed. He also reminded her to please feed Kitten. He wouldn't be returning to her room for the day, and he didn't want her starved. Celia nodded, gave him what he interpreted to be a judgmental look, and walked away. Caleb slammed the door behind her.

Caleb dressed quickly, but not because he was in any particular hurry. Afterward, he descended the stairs and met Celia at the bottom. He noted the stern expression and instinctively knew it had to do with the state in which he'd left Kitten. However, he had

265

better things to do than indulge the scorn of someone else's fuck toy.

"Take me to him," he said.

Celia eyed him with open disdain, but still dipped her head in acknowledgment and led the way to Felipe's library. It was the same room in which he'd first encountered Rafiq, and for a moment, he had to wonder if it was truly Felipe who would greet him when he entered. He squared his shoulders and prepared himself mentally for any eventuality.

Celia knocked on the library door and waited for Felipe's recognition before she glared at Caleb one final time and walked away in a huff.

Fuck you, too.

"Come in, Señor Caleb. Let us have a conversation," Felipe said jovially. Whatever was up Celia's ass, Felipe didn't seem to share it. "May I offer you a scotch?" Caleb entered the library and took the beverage Felipe offered.

"*Gracias*," Caleb said and took a seat in a reading chair near one of the book shelves. He refused to sit across from Felipe's desk.

"*De nada*," Felipe replied and joined Caleb by the books.

Caleb got comfortable in his seat and sipped from his scotch. It was perhaps too early to be drinking, but he reasoned it had already been a long day. He was eager to get this conversation with Felipe over with and find more interesting diversions for the day. "Forgive me, Felipe, but why am I here?" Caleb got to the point.

Felipe smiled and sipped from his glass. "I only

want to talk. You and your slave have been here for quite some time, and we have shared very few conversations."

Caleb sighed, but tried to keep it respectful. "What did you want to discuss?"

Felipe leaned back. "So serious, my friend. How are things progressing with the girl?" Felipe asked. He was too casual for Caleb's taste.

"Fine."

"Only fine?" Felipe seemed incredulous.

Caleb's face warmed with a building anger. "Felipe, I realize you're a friend of Rafiq's, but I fail to see how the girl is any of your business. As you've said, we've been here for a while – why the sudden interest?"

"Kitten," Felipe said through an obnoxiously saccharine smile. "The girl's name is 'Kitten,' is it not?"

"Yes," Caleb said through gritted teeth.

"Well, Caleb," Felipe's expression suddenly turned sinister, "Kitten is your business, but Celia is mine – and seeing as you've involved yourself in my business, I don't see my questions as an intrusion in yours."

Caleb had expected this sooner. "What do you want, Felipe?"

"Well, to be quite honest, Caleb, you've overstepped yourself and done my house a great dishonor. My purpose here is to let you make it right." Fire spread through Caleb's body and anger flashed in his eyes.

"To what dishonor are you referring?"

"You know the one," Felipe said. Malice edged his tone.

"I did nothing out of the ordinary, and I had no idea you were so enamored with your property. You obviously don't feel as strongly about your horses. I believe I rode one of them once as well." Caleb was purposely smug.

Felipe's entire body tensed with rage, but he smiled nonetheless. "You should be careful, Caleb," Felipe said calmly. "I'm a very dangerous man in some circles, and I happen to know a great many things about a great many people. Including you."

"Watch yourself," Caleb said through clenched teeth.

"I've *been* watching, Caleb. I've been watching you. And Kitten," Felipe said. Suddenly, he was the smug one. "I wonder what Rafiq would think if he saw what you've been up to."

"What the hell are you talking about?" Caleb growled.

"Cameras, Caleb. A man like me, in the business I'm in – I can trust no one. And so, I watch. Everyone," Felipe said and smiled.

Caleb's heart hammered fiercely in his chest, but he did his best to remain calm. He thought about what had happened between him and Kitten since they had arrived. He thought of all the things he'd confessed to her, believing they were alone. It was enough to have him seething with rage and thrumming with anxiety. "What do you want, Felipe?"

Felipe shook his head. "I really didn't want it to go this way, Caleb. Truthfully, I wish you no ill will. I only wanted to talk. You're the one who made this nasty."

Caleb tried his hand at feigning remorse. "My apologies. I've had a bad morning."

Felipe smiled. "Yes, I know. However, I plan to keep what I know to myself. I only wish for you to grant me a favor."

Caleb's jaw hurt from how hard he was grinding his teeth. "What favor?"

"I'm having a party tomorrow night. I would love it if you and Kitten would attend," Felipe said cordially.

"That's it? You want us to attend?" Caleb didn't buy it.

Felipe quirked an eyebrow. "Well…seeing as you've made use of my Celia, I was hoping I could borrow yours for the evening."

"She isn't mine, and you know she's a virgin," Caleb said.

"Yes, but I also know she has other talents that don't require her to be…" he pretended to struggle for a word, "compromised."

Caleb wanted nothing more than to grab Felipe by the throat and choke the life out of him in a slow and satisfying fashion, but he knew it would only make matters worse. "I want whatever you have and your assurances Rafiq will hear nothing on the matter."

Felipe smiled and nodded. "Of course, Caleb. I know you care for the girl. Rafiq won't like it, but I understand. She's quite…intriguing."

"Yes," Caleb ground out.

"She loves you," Felipe said.

Caleb side swept those words. "Will Rafiq be at the party? He's been difficult to get in touch with lately," he said instead.

"Hmm," Felipe said, "these things are always so unfortunate when they happen."

Caleb watched the other man very carefully. "What are you getting at, Felipe?"

"Rafiq's been pulling away from you." His expression was amazed when Caleb didn't respond. "Are you so involved with your plaything that you haven't you noticed?"

Caleb set his drink down. He didn't believe it. The mere implication was untenable. "The auction is in a little over two weeks – he's been preoccupied. I know he'll be here any day. I'm asking you if he'll be at the party tomorrow night."

"Yes," Felipe said ominously. "I believe he will. Don't you think it would be a perfect opportunity to showcase all the progress you've made with the girl?"

"Yes," Caleb whispered. His thoughts were upstairs with Kitten, and his chest felt simultaneously empty and too full. Their time was coming to an end.

No, it's already over. Let her go, Caleb.

Caleb stood and left the room. He'd had enough bullshit confrontations for one day.

270

15

Two in the morning. Caleb stood outside Kitten's door, absorbing the knowledge he didn't have much of a choice in what had to happen next. After his confrontation with Felipe, he'd spent the day going through his room. He'd found several cameras and still could not be certain he'd found them all. Felipe was a sick bastard, an obvious voyeur with no sense of decency or shame.

Caleb had half expected someone to try and stop him from shattering every lens he found, but no one did. In fact, everyone had stayed away from him. Caleb wasn't sure if it was a good thing. He would have loved to take his frustration out on someone.

After he was reasonably sure he'd done away with the cameras, he thought long and hard about everything Felipe could potentially know. The answers were nauseating. He'd found cameras in the shower, discreetly hidden in the vent. What he'd assumed to be a screw holding the lights above the bathroom mirror had turned out to be a camera. Felipe had them everywhere. He'd seen Caleb masturbate, fuck, and even punish himself.

Caleb decided he'd kill Felipe when the time was right. For now, Felipe held strong cards and Caleb had none to play. Rafiq would be returning tomorrow night. He would want to see Kitten and make sure she was ready. He would want Caleb and Kitten to return to Pakistan with him and prepare for

271

the auction in Karachi.

It was all coming to an end, and there was nothing Caleb could do to prevent the inevitable. There was nothing he could do unless he was prepared to surrender everything he knew – perhaps even his very life. Caleb had struggled too long and fought too hard to survive. Forfeiting now was unacceptable.

Caleb opened the door slowly and entered Kitten's room. He noticed immediately she hadn't turned on her nightlight, which was uncharacteristic of her and made the room unusually dark. He took a moment to adjust to the dark, though he didn't really need it. He'd been in her room enough times to have memorized the layout. He came close to the bed and heard Kitten breathing. For a moment he thought about leaving the room and letting her sleep in peace, but he steadied himself – it had to be now.

He opened the curtains and let the moonlight come spilling into the room and onto her sleeping form. He studied her intently and noticed her eyes were red and puffy. Her body was wrapped around one pillow and her hair lay across another, the comforter pulled up to her chin. He reached out and touched her hair. Kitten sighed fretfully and buried herself deeper in her blanket.

"Be gentle," she'd said, as he'd looked into her eyes earlier. He lifted a corner of the comforter and encountered her naked shoulder and, a little lower, her bare back and ribs.

"If only I could be," he whispered into the dark, certain she couldn't hear him. He threw back her

272

blanket and lust tugged sharp in his belly.

Kitten woke, startled and naked, before she sat up and covered herself with a pillow. "What's going on?" She rubbed her eyes.

"Come with me," he said with enough bravado to let her know he was in no mood for protests. She hesitated for only a moment, then cast the pillow aside and stood in front of him with a questioning expression. He looked into her eyes steadily and saw the questions disappear as she looked toward her feet.

"Come on," he said and walked to the door with her trailing close behind. They walked down the hallway in silence, which was both better and worse, Caleb thought. He glanced back, expecting to see her eyes wandering, but she seemed more preoccupied with her own shivering.

"Are you cold?" he asked. He stepped down the stairs.

"A little, Master," she replied smoothly. He stopped for a moment, surprised at her address, then continued walking.

"You won't be for long."

Caleb didn't relish the idea of pushing Kitten away for good. It didn't give him any satisfaction to know she would soon come to hate him with such fervor as to annihilate any warm sentiments she may or may not harbor toward him. He didn't like knowing Felipe, and possibly Celia, had been watching her, watching *them,* since they arrived. Without exception, he loathed the thought of her being sold to Vladek Rostrovich. Regardless, he had spent the day trying to make peace with each of those things.

As he descended the stairs, he could hear Kitten's naked feet slapping against the marble behind him. He glanced back and watched her breasts bounce as she took each step. If there was anything left to be excited about, it was the guilty pleasure of still having time to spend with Kitten. Even if the time would be spent torturing her with pleasure and pain…or perhaps, because of it.

Caleb's tastes, while narrowing toward a specific person, had not changed. He still liked power and control. He still liked tasting Kitten's tears and forcing her to ache for pleasure she'd first said she didn't want. In short, he was still the sick fuck he'd always been, and he was going to enjoy every minute of what he had waiting in the dungeon downstairs. He'd been sure to sweep for cameras.

As he reached the bottom of the steps, he turned and waited for Kitten. "Stop looking around and hurry up," Caleb prodded.

Kitten's gaze met his for a fleeting moment before she covered her breasts with her hands and took the last few steps at a brisk pace. As she stood in front of Caleb, he could see how much she trembled.

Caleb turned quickly and made his way toward his destination with Kitten close on his heels. Finally, he approached the heavy wooden door that would lead them down into what had previously been a wine cellar, but was now a dungeon designed for far more interesting pursuits. He begrudgingly had to give it to Felipe – the man had an impressive imagination.

"Give me your hand," he said to Kitten. It felt cold and clammy to the touch, but Caleb didn't mention it as he delved into the darkness below. He carefully placed each step and guided Kitten along. A few more steps and Caleb reached for the light switch. The light flickered as it came on and bathed the stairs in a soft yellow glow.

Kitten's trembling became intense and she gripped his hand. Though Caleb tugged gently, she wouldn't move any further down the stairs. She seemed incapable of moving, such was the nature of her apprehension. Nonetheless, there was no begging. No crying. Her fear was obvious, but her courage more so.

Without another word, Caleb turned and placed her over his shoulder. Kitten gasped, but didn't otherwise protest. She held on to him tightly as he descended the stairs backward.

"This used to be the wine cellar," he said softly against the curve of her hip. Her body shook again, but this time it had nothing to do with the cold. All around her were restraints and pain inflicting instruments. In the center of the room stood a large, leather-clad table with ominous metal parts attached.

Caleb sighed headily. Though he didn't much like the reason he was doing this at this particular moment, he knew it was something he was still going to enjoy. Even now, he grew hard as she pulled her weight up and managed to wrap herself around him tightly. He was sure she hoped he wouldn't do what he was about to do. He lifted her legs and had her wrap them around his waist as he brought her down from his shoulder and into his arms. He took a moment to revel in the clean, wet smell of her hair, the feel of her warm breasts pressed against his chest, and her pussy hugged firmly against his belly.

"The first thing you should know," he said softly into her hair, "is obedience is expected – and will be forced if necessary." He slid one of his hands down her back and over the curve of her behind until he reached the lightly-parted lips of her pussy. She gasped and froze in his arms. "And despite how I torment you, I always find a way to make you feel good." He rubbed her gently, coaxing her shy clit to swell beneath his fingers. "Don't I?" She nodded, but gripped him tighter. "Do you trust me?" She shook her head.

Caleb sighed. "I guess you'll learn to."

He walked to the table and laid her down, his body held firmly to hers as she silently refused to let go. Her eyes misted over with tears, and the fear crouched within them was unmistakable.

"Trust me," Caleb said. He reached behind his neck and gently pried her arms away to hold them in his right hand, close to her chest. "I know you think I haven't given you a reason to trust me, but I've never really hurt you if you think about it."

"Caleb...*please*," she whispered.

Caleb knew she hadn't meant to speak. He watched as she shook her head and closed her eyes. Perhaps she was waiting for his anger. Caleb knew she had a right to expect it, but he wasn't angry. He was much too excited for anger. Too surprised at how good it felt to have her call him by his name again. Even if on the heels of realization was the reminder that it couldn't last between them. Their time together was short.

"Put your legs in the stirrups – and don't use my name again," Caleb said. He ignored the hurt in Kitten's eyes. He ignored the hurt in his chest.

Abruptly he stepped back, looking on authoritatively as she sat up and crossed her arms over her nakedness. She eyed the metal attachments curiously, and then placed her legs in the stirrups without flinching. A roaring silence filled the room as he watched her studying him. She sat on the edge of the table with her thighs and legs spread apart in the stirrups and her arms set stiffly behind her for support. Caleb could just imagine what she was thinking.

"Still cold?" he asked.

"No, Master," she replied coldly.

"Lie back," he said, just as cold. Slowly, she obeyed. He came closer and secured her thighs to the stirrups by strapping a large, leather band around each one and doing the same to her calves and ankles. It would be impossible for her to move them, and already Caleb could see she knew it as well. Her chest moved up and down, rapid and deep.

Slowly, he stepped away and toward the corner, where he retrieved a folding chair. Her eyes followed his every move, and Caleb's heart picked up speed as his excitement and her trepidation grew.

277

He set the chair down between her spread legs, out of her view, and sat in it.

Caleb's arousal grew as Kitten's thighs trembled, and she tried to close her legs in vain. Her pussy lay open to his view, his touch, his every whim and will. He tried not to let it go to his head.

"Touch yourself," he gently commanded.

"Master?" Kitten fretted. She gave a start as Caleb ran a finger along the seam of her sex.

"Right here," he said. He made circles around her clit. "Touch yourself right here. I want to watch you come."

Kitten's hips tilted forward by the barest of degrees, the sharp pull of desire already making her nipples hard and her pussy wet. She hesitated, but only for a moment. Swallowing hard and biting her lip, she did as he asked and placed her right hand on her swollen sex.

"Do you touch yourself, Kitten?" he asked. He deliberately let the warmth of his breath caress her splayed flesh.

Kitten shivered. "S-s-sometimes."

"Do you make yourself come?" Caleb carefully placed his hand on top of hers and pressed her fingers deeper into her own flesh. Kitten whimpered, flexing her hips upward toward their hands.

"Sometimes!" she whined loudly.

Caleb smiled at her, though he knew she couldn't see it. Her eyes were fixed on the ceiling overhead. Caleb leaned forward and ran his jaw along her inner thigh.

"Show me," he said.

Kitten's body tightened – he could feel it beneath his cheek. He heard her take a deep, trembling breath and then her hand moved under his. He kissed the inside of her knee as he sat back and adjusted the painful erection in his pants. Every moment with her seemed both painful and sweet. He watched her small, delicate fingers find the apex of her pleasure and touch it experimentally. He smiled suddenly and brought his hand to his mouth, instantly realizing her scent saturated his fingers. He had the sudden urge to lick them, but didn't. He knew it would only lead to other things.

Kitten arched her back. She rubbed at the little bud with mounting pressure and speed as her wetness made the flesh increasingly slippery between her fingers. It wasn't long before soft but insistent moans began breaking past her lips.

Caleb could feel the beat of his heart in his cock as it worked to push blood down to his erection. He knew he shouldn't be so aroused, not when he'd already come twice – once against her pussy, and again in her mouth. However, being reminded and watching Kitten grow wetter did little to quell his desire and more to stoke it.

Kitten rocked her hips back and forth, slowly at first, and then with growing speed as her obvious desperation grew. Her fingers rubbed her little clit and it visibly became redder, more swollen, but the sounds Kitten made had gone from need to frustration.

"I can't…. I can't when you're watching me," she said.

Caleb smiled. "The second thing you should know is to take pleasure whenever you can." As he thought about what he was trying to express, his smile faded. "Know your body, Kitten. Know what turns you on. Most of the time you'll be responsible for your own pleasure. There will be times when it will seem impossible, times when it will *be* impossible. Either way, you'll have to be convincing. Convince me."

Kitten's fingers stopped, and the only sound in the room was the sound of her pulling air into her lungs. She took her hand away from her body and tried to sit up.

Caleb stood and met her watering eyes as she placed her hands behind her for balance. "Caleb," her chin trembled, "no." She seemed to be looking for more to say, more emotions to express.

Caleb didn't want to hear what she had to say. He couldn't bear to hear it. He stepped closer and reached behind her for her hand, only just avoiding her mouth as she turned to kiss him. He couldn't bear that either.

"Master," he said, "not Caleb."

"But...you said –"

"I know what I said, Kitten. It was a mistake," he said. He was confusing her, and for that, he was sorry. It had been selfish of him to allow her such intimacy when she didn't belong to him.

Kitten sobbed – once, twice – but then nodded.

Caleb took her hand as he guided her back down onto the table. Before any more tears were shed or words spoken on Kitten's end, he took her wet fingers into his mouth and tasted her pussy on them. He closed his eyes as the taste of her, both sweet and tart, burst over his tongue. He moaned low, sucking them into his mouth until he saw Kitten's eyes widen and go darker, signaling her arousal.

Slowly, he pulled her fingers out of his mouth and guided them back onto Kitten's pussy. Kitten closed her eyes for a brief second and lifted her hips to meet them. "You've been touching your clit," he whispered, making small circles against her clit with her own fingers. "Don't forget you have this delicious little hole." He guided her fingers down and pushed the tip of her slender middle finger into her pussy.

"Oh, God!" she exclaimed. Her back bowed and her body froze, but Caleb could tell she was only adjusting to new sensations and not coming.

"Is it good, Pet?" he asked.

Kitten only nodded and let her body drift back down gently before her hips began rocking against her hand. Caleb slowly took his hand away and sat back down in his chair to watch. Kitten cupped her breast absently and pressed the hard pebble of her nipple between her fingers as Caleb had done to her so many times before. She whimpered, her previous trepidation fleeting in the face of her mounting pleasure.

He watched Kitten's fingers, the middle one delving a little further with each hesitant thrust. Caleb felt like he could only handle so much, especially with the taste of her still so pervasive in his mouth. Once again, he placed his hand on hers.

He marveled at the way her body seemed to pulsate with need. She tried to keep touching herself, but his hand prevented it. Caleb inhaled sharply, dizzy with desire. He leaned forward, slipping his tongue up through her fingers.

Kitten cried out. She writhed against his all-too-gentle mouth, rattling the stirrups and filling the room with her desperation. He was too gentle. He knew there was no way she could come from the soft licking. So he kept licking, sometimes pushing the tip of his tongue into her pussy. He loved the way she whimpered, whined, and moaned.

After a while, though, he knew he had to stop – or he wouldn't stop. He stood up and looked down at Kitten's quivering body. She turned her head and closed her eyes as her breasts rose and fell with the effort of her breathing. He sighed deeply and savored the taste and smell of her. *It has to be now.* He pulled out the small drawer attached to the table.

"You're beautiful, Kitten," he said. He took out two sets of handcuffs. She didn't open her eyes but flinched at the sound of the cuffs. "You've been very, very good. I hope you'll continue to be." He cuffed her right wrist to the table comfortably and smiled when she finally opened her eyes and looked at him with those big, brown, inquiring eyes. "You're not resisting," he said with a bright smile. "I'm impressed."

She hesitated when he reached for her left wrist, but then her arm relaxed and her breath quickened. Secured in her handcuffs, he reached out and traced her nipple with his index finger. His dick twitched when her sigh filled the silence. Next, he blindfolded her, which added to the already-intoxicating tension in her body. Caleb was surprised she hadn't said a word or resisted him in any substantial way – he couldn't decide whether or not he had wanted her to be so pliable.

"What are you thinking?" he asked. He slowly reached for the machine that would deliver the surprise he had planned.

Kitten licked her lips. "I'm thinking," she whispered as she undulated against her restraints, "how badly I want you to finish what you started."

Caleb chuckled. "Trust me. I intend to." He flipped the switch on the machine. It made an ominous humming sound, not unlike a generator.

Kitten tried to move all at once, her efforts resulting in nothing more than the clanging of handcuffs against her railing.

"What is that?" she shouted.

"Do you want me to gag you, too?" Caleb asked. Kitten shook her head violently. "Okay then – let me finish."

Kitten strained against her bonds when his fingers grabbed hold of her sensitive clit and affixed a padded clamp. She wiggled her bottom, trying to shake it loose, but it wouldn't move.

"I wanted you to be nice and ready for this. And you are – you're so close." He sucked hard on her nipple and despite her growing fear, she arched her back, trying to push more of her tit into his mouth. It was tempting, but Caleb pulled away and clamped her nipple snugly and repeated his efforts on the other breast. When he finished, he stepped back and took in the graphic picture she made – blindfolded, bound, and clamped, with thin cables running between her legs. "I think I'll gag you anyway – I wouldn't want you waking anyone."

Kitten seemed on the verge of protest, but Caleb put a swift stop to it by placing a soft piece of cloth into her mouth and securing it behind her head. Not much of a gag, really, but it would muffle any sounds coming out of her mouth and make her words incoherent.

"Shh," said Caleb in the crest of her ear. "This next lesson is probably the most important and most difficult to learn." He stroked her hair. "Pleasure comes to you only when your Master desires it. In the meantime, you'll hunger for it, ache with it, and suffer through it – much like you are now. I'm going to bed. If you continue being a good girl, maybe I'll let you come for breakfast."

Kitten was in the middle of a muffled tirade when a surge of pulsing electricity simultaneously zapped through her clit and nipples. Caleb watched as her body became paralyzed with panic and intense pleasure. The current was low enough not to hurt, but strong enough to make her body contract. She strained and pressed toward the sensation. She arched her back, lost in the sensation of the clamps gently pulling on her nipples as little tremors were sent through them. Her hips pumped gently into the air looking for release when the sensation abruptly stopped. She screamed with frustration, no way to alleviate her need – either by finding release or letting it ebb into nothingness.

Caleb gave her one more lingering look and then he made his way toward the stairs. He called behind him, "It's going to be a long night. Good luck, Kitten."

Out of the wine cellar, Caleb pressed his back against the door and let out a sigh to fight the urge to run downstairs and bury himself inside of his beautiful, cock-starved virgin.

"Fuck," he said on a rush of air and headed toward his room. Tired, Caleb checked his watch. It was late – or early, depending on how you looked at it. He undressed and turned out the light. In the darkness of the room and his mind, she came to him. He held his erect cock firmly and an image of Kitten came to him.

He imagined her downstairs, with her legs spread wide and her pussy open and wet. His cock throbbed hotly in his fist. He gripped it tight, squeezing out warm precome. He smeared it over the head. He fantasized.

He used his thumb to gently pry the small inner lips of her slippery little cunt and watched her moan. Then he slid his cock up and down her slit, covering himself in her juices, preparing them both. He leaned forward, and the warmth of her breasts pressed against his naked chest.

Outside the fantasy he audibly moaned as his pace increased.

"Make love to me," she whispered, and they were suddenly in her bedroom. He reached down, pulled up her nightgown, and pushed against her

285

with his cock. He was gentle, patiently waiting for her to relax and for her legs to drop open before he pushed again.

"I love you," she said, with tears in her eyes. She kissed him and tangled her fingers in his hair, urging him deeper inside of her. She kept saying she loved him. He pushed himself fully inside her.

Faster and faster he stroked himself. His balls pulled themselves closer to his body, ready to release the orgasm he'd been holding in for far too long.

He pumped in and out of her hot tightness, and she moaned and screamed her appreciation.

"I'm yours," she panted, "only yours."

It felt wrong to fantasize about such things – but Caleb didn't care. Fantasies were all he could have, and no one could take them from him. He grunted loudly as his orgasm erupted into the air, coating him in warm, sticky semen.

16

Day 10: Evening

"I have to pee," I say to Reed. He makes a face but doesn't comment. "What? People have to pee sometimes, Reed."

"Yes," he says drolly, "I'm aware. I just don't understand why you feel the need to give me the specifics. A simple, 'I need a break' would have sufficed."

I laugh and hop down from my bed to walk into the lavatory. Reed is a little stiff as I walk past him. He's avoiding my eyes and purposely staring out the window. He can be such a weirdo, but I can't help but wonder about him. I wonder what he's like when he isn't so wrapped up in his FBI persona.

You know what they say about the quiet ones.

I've been talking for hours. My mouth feels bone dry. I remove the plastic wrap from one of the cups and take a drink of water from the tap. It tastes like shit, but I swallow it anyway.

Somewhere far away in my mind, I know I should feel emotionally drained, or even weepy and sad. Mostly I just feel…nothing. I'm not sure why. I guess it's because I know how the story ends, and with every word I utter I know I'm preparing myself for the eventuality of what's to come. It's like I'm telling a story that happened to someone else.

I love Caleb. I love him. I don't care anymore

287

about the awful shit he put me through – what matters most is the fact my love for him exists. No amount of talking or therapy will change what happened. It won't change how I feel.

He's gone, Livvie.

There it is. There's the pain. It's an ember forever burning in my heart. It's a reminder Caleb will live forever.

I've cried so much over the last ten days. I've been living in so much agony. I know when all is said and done, when Reed has heard everything, when he and Sloan move on – I'll be all alone with my pain and my love. But today – today I'm fine. Today I'm telling the story as if it happened to someone else.

I conclude my business in the bathroom, wash my hands, and open the door. Sloan is standing in the room with Reed when I come out of the bathroom. The atmosphere seems thick, but with what, I'm not certain. Sloan is smiling, but Reed looks like someone ate his lunch out of the community fridge.

Sloan holds up a large, brown sack with grease stains on the bottom. "I brought dinner," she says to me.

"Awesome!" I say, surprised by the gesture.

Sloan smiles at me, warmly. "I know how you *love* the hospital food, but I figured you might appreciate some greasy burgers and fries instead." My stomach growls in response and Sloan lifts a smug eyebrow. "Agent Reed, I know you try to stay away from the junk, so I brought you a grilled chicken salad. I hope that's okay."

I take the bag from Sloan and set it on the rolling bed tray so I can get to my damn burger. Otherwise, I might try to eat through the bag. I reach in and grab the loose fries at the bottom and shove them into my mouth.

"Hawt! Hawt!" I say, but I keep chewing the salty deliciousness in my mouth. To hell with first degree burns – the fries are amazing! I'm so busy stuffing my face with loose fries, it takes me a moment to realize no one else is talking. I look up and see Reed and Sloan are having some sort of awkward staring contest. I think Reed is losing. *Interesting.*

Reed finally clears his throat and looks toward his briefcase. "Actually, I have to go. I have some emails to answer and some calls I have to make. Um, thank you, though – for the food." Reed begins gathering his things in a hurried fashion. I've never seen him so...flustered, I guess is the word.

Curiouser and curiouser.

"Matthew," Sloan begins and falters when Reed stops gathering his things just long enough to glare at her. She holds up her hands. "Agent Reed, I can't think of anything so time sensitive it can't wait until after you've had dinner."

Reed sighs deeply, but doesn't stop getting his papers together. "Thank you for the food, Dr. Sloan. I don't mean to be rude or sound ungrateful, but I really do have work to do. And yes, it is time sensitive. Offices in Pakistan should be opening soon, and they have information I need."

Sloan falters, pursing her lips briefly. "Oh. I didn't realize. I'm sorry."

No one even notices I'm here in the room and I feel like a voyeur. *Fascinating!* I think of Felipe and Celia's little surveillance hobby and blush. Whatever is going on between Sloan and Reed really isn't my business.

"Here!" I say loudly, letting them know they are being watched. I raise Reed's salad triumphantly and eat the loose fries on the lid. "You can take it with you."

Sloan gives me a grateful smile, as though relieved I broke their uneasy connection. She reaches for the container and takes it from my hand. "Yes, please take the salad. You have to eat something."

Reed looks at the salad as if he's never eaten one before, then at Sloan and me. He is angry, and it has nothing to do with anything. He is just pissed off. He wants to be angry at Sloan, but she hasn't given him a reason, hasn't said or done anything revolting. Still, he's choosing to be angry with her. Finally, he sets his briefcase down on his chair and takes the container. "Thank you," he says.

"You're welcome," Sloan says, in that soft way Caleb would use on me when he was feeling fanciful. Sloan watches Reed's face, and then her gaze skids away when he glances at her and quickly averts his eyes.

Ooooh...she likes him. It surprises me, and yet not. I tend to see Dr. Sloan and Agent Reed as robots, like they have no lives. It's interesting to see them in a new way.

Reed's face looks a little red. I can't believe he's blushing. He actually looks adorable. I don't want him to leave. I want to sit on my bed and watch the two of them squirm under my scrutiny. I mean really…it's only fair.

"Come on, Reed, stay." I pat the spot at the foot of my bed, grinning. He looks at me silently. *If looks could kill…* "You said you'd listen to the rest of my story, remember?"

"I really can't, Miss Ruiz," he says, "but I'll be back later. In the meantime," he says as he opens his briefcase and removes his recorder, "tape it for me?"

Sloan takes the recorder and nods, careful not to look at anything. "Of course."

Reed nods tightly and closes his briefcase again before practically running from the room. I really can't believe what I've just seen.

"What the hell's going on between you two?" I ask Sloan around a mouthful of fries. She turns her head away from the door and looks at me, startled. I wiggle my eyebrows and she laughs.

"Nothing, Livvie. Nothing at all," she says, her voice shaky. "Now stop eating my fries and give me those." She reaches into the bag and takes out a burger and a container of fries before she sits in Reed's former seat.

"Mmm," she says when she pops a fry into her mouth.

"Mmm," I mimic and do the same. When I'm done swallowing, I jump straight to the good stuff. "So…did you really come to see me or Agent

Reed?"

Sloan smiles and shakes her head. Her mouth is full, but she tries to answer me anyway. "You, of course."

"Liar," I tease.

Sloan shrugs. "I'm not here to talk about Reed."

"Don't you mean...*Matthew*?"

"Livvie," she says in warning.

"Janice," I say sarcastically. "Come on, Sloan. I've been telling you both some pretty deep shit. I think I'm entitled to a distraction and some gossip. Reed's hot. I understand."

"There's nothing to tell," she insists, but she's getting pink in the face. No matter the age, what I feel is universal. You can't fight who you're attracted to. Sometimes fate gets it right, and then makes you pay for it.

"Whatever. I know something's going on. Caleb used to get upset when I'd use his name in front of other people, but in private? Whole other story. I saw Reed's face when you called him Matthew. He was giving you the business."

Sloan chokes on her burger and greedily takes a sip from her drink to clear it. "Livvie!"

"Fine, fine," I say and pick up my burger, so disappointed. The burger is so greasy, and I can already feel the grease running through my veins. I moan as I chew. "You don't have to tell me, as long as you bring me another one of these tomorrow."

"Deal," Sloan says and takes another bite.

We eat in companionable silence for several minutes, the occasional moan and gluttonous eye-roll as our only means of communication.

Afterward, Sloan and I talk about how I'm feeling. *Fine.* She asks if I might be ready to talk to my mother. *No. Definitely not.*

"What could be the harm?" Sloan asks. "She misses you very much."

I look down into my lap. I'm not sad. I'm embarrassed to look Sloan in the eye and admit the truth. "I want her to suffer."

Sloan is quiet.

"The last few months have been awful," I continue. "I've been beaten, humiliated, and forced into situations no person should ever have to suffer." I pause, brooding and getting angry at my mother. "Still, I'd live it all again if I could change the past eighteen years with my mother. I've spent so much time already trying to make her love me, understand me. I've spent so much time giving a fuck about what she thought. I'm done, Sloan. I'm done caring. It's time for me to live my own life, my own way, and I don't want her to be a part of it."

"What is your way?" Sloan asks. There is no emotional quality to her voice. If she's judging me, I can't tell. If she agrees with me, it's also a mystery.

"I don't know. I have no idea who I'm supposed to be anymore. I only know I don't want to be who someone else thinks I should be."

"Good," Sloan says.

Sloan and I talk for a while longer before I tell her I'm tired and want to lie down. I let her hug me goodbye, and perhaps...I hold on to her for just a little longer than I intended. Sloan doesn't seem to mind.

Once she's gone, I turn down the lights and get in bed with Reed's recorder. I turn it on and start talking.

***

Another surge of electricity pumped through me. I was starved for release. I screamed behind my gag and struggled against my tethers, but all it did was heighten my suffering. I lifted my ass, trying to find a way to move and create enough friction to send me into orgasm – but it was crushingly useless. I whimpered and let the tears flow when the pulsing stopped. The door opened and a sigh of relief swept through me. Caleb had finally come back to end my suffering. I knew he would.

He approached me slowly and I made soft, pleading sounds to beg him to make it stop. As if reading my mind, his warm hand cupped my face and I inclined toward it, pressing my wet cheek against his wrist and crying pitifully. Had I been able to see, perhaps I would've been more embarrassed and prideful. Instead, I was simply lost in my misery and eager to be free of it.

His hand traveled down my neck and chest as another pulse hit me. I arched. I wanted to come. No – I *needed* to come. The table shook as I struggled. Caleb's hand caressed the soft flesh under my breast, which only made it more intense. I only needed a little more, just a little more. It stopped. I cried harder.

I pleaded behind the gag, but Caleb said nothing.

Instead, his hands cupped both my breasts and then pulled the clamps off my nipples slowly. Blood rushed to my nipples and I screamed behind the gag. It hurt, but it also made me ache for more. He massaged my breasts and I almost cooed as I tried to press more of myself into his hands. Abruptly, the warmth of his mouth kissed around my left breast, and the soft tickle of his hair caressed my chest.

"Yes," I sighed.

Caleb's mouth was achingly gentle; his tongue swirled around my taut flesh – no teeth, no violent sucking, just soft licks and kisses that made me want to touch him. As he repeated the process on the other breast, yet another jolt of electricity assailed my poor clit.

"Please!" I screamed behind the gag. "Please!"

He stood back until the pulsing stopped, and I feared he would leave me again. I heard him unzip his pants and I had to stop myself from nodding fervently. *Yes, I want this. Please, I want this.* His fingers pulled down the gag, and I immediately began begging him for respite.

"Master, please make it stop. Let me come. I'll be good. I swear. I'll be good." When he said nothing, I whimpered. "Caleb, please!" The heat of him radiated close to my face, followed by the soft press of his cock against my lips. I didn't hesitate; I opened my mouth and took him in.

Shocking realization hit me – this wasn't Caleb. He felt all wrong in my mouth. I tried to pull back, but the stranger held the back of my head firmly in place – and despite my instincts, I didn't actually want to bite him.

Another pulse hit and assaulted me from every conceivable angle. I moaned around the stranger, while simultaneously trying to fuck the air and back away from him. I wasn't as afraid as I should've been. Perhaps it was because he fucked my mouth slowly, without violence. Yes, the stranger made it obvious he wouldn't allow me to turn away, but he was far from rough. The pulsing stopped and I let my hips drop to the table. I struggled to breathe steadily with the stranger's cock in my mouth. In the quiet stillness, I heard his soft, guttural moans as he glided in and out of my mouth.

He withdrew without coming, and I immediately felt the awkwardness and shame I should've felt earlier settle to the forefront. I wanted to ask who the fuck he was. I wanted to scream for help, for Caleb, but I said nothing.

"Beautiful," he said with a soft Spanish accent. My entire body blushed then. I could feel the warmth of it.

"Felipe?" I asked timidly, on the verge of fresh tears.

"Yes, my sweet girl, but you should not speak unless you are asked," he said gently. "I know your Master has tried to teach you better. Still, I can't blame him for being so lenient with you. I let Celia get away with too much," he chuckled. "Though, I don't know why he allows you to use his name. It's so intimate. Are both of you intimate?" I didn't reply. I was in too much shock. "Answer," he said softly. I opened my mouth then, but the only thing to come out was a long, throaty moan as the electricity once again assaulted me. He stepped away and there was a clicking sound. The pulsing stopped.

"Oh! God!" I moaned. "Thank you!" My heart didn't have a chance to slow down.

Felipe's fingers stroked the inner lips of my pussy almost immediately. I tried to shift away, but all I managed was to move my hips up and down, which seemed only to further his efforts. A stutter of "noes" flowed out of me when I felt one of his fingers trying to worm its way inside me, but he quickly silenced me with a firm tap on the side of my face and an equally-firm call for silence. It didn't hurt, but it was effective.

"I'm only looking," he said. He pushed against something painful inside of me. I started to cry, and much to my relief, the finger withdrew.

I wanted Caleb. *How could he leave me here like this?*

"You get really wet for a virgin," he said, and again my body flushed with heat and embarrassment. "Nothing wrong with that, though." Was he smiling? Fear tapped across my insides. I hoped this man would leave soon and Caleb would come back to let me go. A long silence followed, punctuated by my low sobs and occasional intake of breath as I tried to keep my crying quiet.

Finally, he spoke. "Don't worry, sweet girl. I'll be gone soon and I won't hurt you. I was only curious. Perhaps when your real master allows it, I can better explore my curiosity." I tried to focus on the fact he'd said he wouldn't hurt me and sighed

297

with relief, willing myself to calm and let the tears dry away.

"Caleb is very…*enamored* of you," he said and laughed low. It seemed a private joke I was not privy to. "Do you love him?" he asked casually.

I didn't respond. I was too tired, shocked, and scared to answer.

"I could always reconnect the machine," he said.

"No!" I shouted before I could stop myself.

"I thought you might say that," he said.

"I don't know," I whispered.

"Explain."

"I've never been in love before. I wouldn't know."

Felipe guffawed. "Everyone knows, my dear. You know. Do you love him or not?"

I didn't know what to say. I didn't know enough about Felipe to guess whether or not he meant me or Caleb any harm. Aside from Celia, I was never alone with anyone but Caleb.

"Do you love Celia?" I asked instead.

Felipe sighed. "Clever girl. Answer a question with a question and you can never say the wrong thing. Regardless, I have my answer. It's a pity he doesn't know it."

"He does," I whispered.

Felipe laughed loudly. "One would think! Do you know how I met Celia?"

I shook my head.

"She is the daughter of my former rival. Many years ago, when I decided to make my name, I went up against her father and won. As a trophy…I took

298

Celia." His voice turned soft. "She hated me for many years, and I was not always so kind to her. Now...not a moment goes by I do not wish I could take back wasted time. I spoil her."

"By letting her clean your house and be your slave?" I asked, incredulous.

"I see why Caleb is so drawn to you. You're the type of woman who begs to be bridled and yet refuses to yield. Such women are the nectar of life," he said. "Believe me, Celia is quite happy. I give her everything she needs and more than she desires."

I kept my mouth shut and let Felipe have it his way.

"Will you allow Caleb to sell you?" he asked.

"I don't have a choice," I whispered.

"To live as a slave or to die on one's own terms is always a choice, sweet girl," he whispered. "Perhaps you should remind your current master."

"Why do you say my *current* master?"

"Didn't Caleb tell you? Rafiq arrives tomorrow. I suspect you'll both be leaving us very soon. It's a pity, though. I begrudgingly admit I've enjoyed having you both around. Caleb is an interesting man – a bit...drastic, but interesting nonetheless."

I felt as though someone had punched me in the stomach and knocked the air out of my lungs. Rafiq was coming for me, and Caleb wasn't going to stop him. It was over. I'd lost.

"Let me go," I whimpered. "Please, help me."

Felipe sighed. "I'm afraid it isn't possible, sweet girl. Rafiq...well, let me just say, he does not take kindly to betrayal."

299

As I tried to process what he was telling me, I heard his steps and cringed when he set the wet gag back into place and secured it firmly. I panicked when the coldness of the cables ran up along my body. I didn't want the clamps back on my nipples. I struggled with all my might. My torso was relatively free, so it was with some difficulty that he held me down with his weight to replace the clamps.

"No!" I screamed in frustration, but there was only his soft laughter in response.

"I'm sorry, sweet girl, but I can't have your master find you in a different position. It's rude."

I whined pitifully. I had finally come down from my heightened arousal. My clit ached, and my nipples did too – but I was glad to feel somewhat normal again. I wasn't sure I could handle more torture.

"I'll give you a gift before I go," said Felipe.

I shook my head passionately, but it didn't stop him from placing his hand between my legs and caressing me. My body stilled, and against my wishes, he stoked the flame of my desire, in no time making it burn hotly once more. Soon, I pressed myself toward him, looking for the release I needed so desperately. And finally, he sent me over the edge. He rubbed me harder and faster, and I screamed as my orgasm ripped me apart. I wanted more. As starved as I was, the powerful orgasm did little to ebb my passion. It was with deep dread I realized he was replacing the clamp taken from my clit. I begged for him not to do it.

Within moments of him leaving, my torture

began anew.

***

It was a very long time before the door opened again, and this time I wasn't going to simply be content with physical release. Unless, of course, physical release included punching Caleb in the stomach and then raping him into oblivion.

I growled when I heard footsteps coming near me, secretly praying it was Caleb I was directing my wrath toward and not another uninvited visitor. One smug laugh later, and I knew it was him. I couldn't help but feel a deep sense of relief.

"How're you feeling, Pet?" I would've liked to spew invective at him just then, but the machine went off again and it was all I could do to hold in my screaming. Over the course of the night, the charges had become less frequent. I wondered if it had been a mercy my mysterious visitor had imparted. Regardless, the pulses were powerful, and it had been going on for hours. They were both pleasurable and painful, with increasing tendencies toward the pain. When the charge finally released me, I couldn't help but sob softly behind the drenched gag in my mouth.

"That bad, huh?" he said, but I knew his words held absolutely no sympathy for what he'd done. I sucked in air deeply when he removed the clamps from my body.

"I hate you!" I yelled. Though the words were muffled behind the gag, I knew he could make them

301

out. He cupped my breasts in both hands and gently massaged me.

"I hate you, *Master*," he said with hungry lust lacing his voice.

He tweaked my nipples playfully. I winced and tried to shrink away from his touch.

"Sensitive?" he whispered softly in my ear. When I didn't respond, he pinched them a little harder and a yelp broke past my lips. "Answer," he said coolly.

"Yes, Master," I whined. My anger with him had grown as the hours had passed. I'd convinced myself that when he came to get me, I would really give him a piece of my mind. Of course, it's easy to be brave when the object of your fear isn't holding your sore nipples hostage.

"Good, Kitten," he said. He placed his warm palms against my stiff little peaks and pressed softly to massage them as he also kneaded my breasts. I moaned loudly. My head rolled to the side as he touched me exactly the way I needed to be touched. I never wanted the feeling to end.

His thigh pressed against the table near the top of my head as he worked his hands lower, from my breasts, to my ribs, to my surprisingly sore hips. He rubbed softly, and I couldn't help but moan and get lost in the surety of his hands and in the clean, masculine smell emanating from his body, which inevitably leaned toward me. I thought about Felipe. I thought about the way he'd pressed his cock against my lips, the way I'd so readily accepted him when I thought he had been Caleb.

Unwittingly, I undulated beneath Caleb's hands, my body telling him what I couldn't possibly say out loud. I needed him to make me come. He sighed audibly, and I knew he wanted me as badly as I wanted him.

I fought off the memory of what he'd told me after I'd offered him not only my body, but my heart. *"You thought what? You thought offering me a little pussy was going to make some kind of a difference?"* I recoiled at the memory and tears stung behind my eyes. I was thankful for the blindfold. Suddenly, I wasn't sure I wanted him touching me anymore – but what choice did I have? Felipe's options seemed far too extreme.

It occurred to me then, the one choice that was mine to make was to not to let him hurt me anymore – not where it mattered. My heart sank heavily in my chest for reasons I didn't want to acknowledge. I *had* thought my confession should make some kind of a difference.

I was lost in my self-pitying thoughts when he pulled me back into reality by running his finger along the seam of my inflamed sex. I jerked in my bonds.

"Sensitive here, too?" he inquired darkly and began his practiced assault on my clit. I groaned sadly in response and nodded. "Aww, poor Kitten. Would you like me to let you come now?" Tears leaked from my eyes and were immediately absorbed by the blindfold. I nodded. His voice had taken on a sinister edge – he was enjoying this, and I was in a strange sort of misery. He shifted his

303

position, coming around to my right as he stroked me at an easier angle.

"I want to hear you beg me," he said and pulled the gag from my mouth. I rotated my jaw, trying to get it to feel normal again and finding it difficult. "Beg me," he commanded. My heart raced at his steady touch, the tingling heat of impending orgasm spreading through my body. If he stopped me this time, I would die. I was sure of it.

"I'm…I'm begging you," I whispered. My voice was alien to my ears as I failed to keep my emotions out of my voice.

"I did think it was really cute when you said you loved me."

The orgasm tore through me with a violence I don't think even Caleb was expecting. I screamed at the top of my lungs, and my body arched as much as it could in its restraints. Every part of me tingled, throbbed, and burned with release. My thighs quivered, and my heart beat savagely in my chest, ears, and clit.

It washed over me in waves: my old life, meeting Caleb, my botched escape, Caleb's kindness that first night he held me, his smile, his hands, his smell, his kiss, the spankings, the torture, my declaration of love, his reaction…his reaction… his cruel fucking reaction. When the best and worst of it subsided, my hips hit the table with a wet thud and I lie there crying, as any number of emotions ran wild in my body while the aftermath settled.

"Wow," he whispered.

I was so tired. I hadn't slept all night. Caleb was

quiet and I was glad for it. I had nothing to say to him. Though I thoroughly hoped he was done torturing me for a while and would allow me to finally get some sleep – alone.

I started to drift away while he went about unfastening my thighs and legs. It was an odd thing to feel so drowsy and satiated, while at the same time jittery and anxious over being released. His warm palms touched my ribs, and my drowsiness disappeared – but my anxiety mounted.

"How are your ribs feeling?" he asked with a degree of thoughtfulness.

"A little sore," I said, so softly I almost doubted he heard.

"Is it bad?" He seemed concerned.

I hated when he was like this. I would prefer him to always be a cold-blooded bastard. At least then, I could forgive him for the things he did. Instead, he showed me bursts of his humanity. It was worse, knowing he knew the difference between kindness and cruelty and chose the baser of the two. I shook my head.

He undid the cuffs on my wrists. I immediately tried to sit up. Not really as a show of defiance – it just seemed like the natural thing to do. My hips were agonizingly stiff and sore. It took Caleb's awkward help to lift my legs out of the stirrups. After too many hours apart, I could hardly close them.

I sat for a moment, my legs dangling off the table and my hands over my breasts. I hoped he wouldn't remove the blindfold and I wouldn't have

305

to look into his eyes. He stood in front of me. Our bodies weren't touching, but I felt him everywhere. Then the warmth of his fingers smoothed against my cheek, and something in my chest began to burn. Slowly, he pulled the blindfold away, and I rubbed my puffy eyes as I adjusted to the soft light.

He looked gorgeous, as usual, though his customary smile was not present – only a look of seriousness. It occurred to me I must look like garbage, with my ratted hair and puffy face. Meanwhile, Caleb stood in front of me – sexy as hell.

I couldn't look him in the face. I rarely ever could. I focused on his lightweight, button-up shirt, khaki pants, and casual shoes. I focused on his large hands as they reached up and rubbed my thighs. I let out a startled gasp he didn't acknowledge.

"Are you hungry?" he asked ominously. I nodded, looking down into my lap. He slapped my thigh loudly, and I had to fight every impulse to push him away. Heat crept up into my face, but I maintained my composure.

"Yes, Master," I said through clenched teeth. "I'm hungry."

"Good," he said, no humor in his voice. "You can get down on your knees and eat my cock."

I stared at him incredulously for a moment, waiting for him to say something further – though what I expected him to say, I didn't know. Strangely, the longer I looked at him, the more I became aware I was doing so without his permission. I also felt, as I often did, that he could read my mind. I took a deep breath and looked away quickly, in the hopes he had not read too much. Out of the corner of my eye, I saw his hands slowly reaching for his belt. A sense of impending doom spurred me into action, and I reflexively placed my right hand over his.

"You aren't going to whip me, are you?" I didn't look up. My fingers trembled. If he wasn't already, then I probably planted the idea in his mind. *Stupid, stupid, stupid.*

"Would you like me to?" he asked. I shook my head emphatically. No, I did not. "Then get your hands off of me. I didn't give you permission to touch me." I retracted my hands and waited for him to speak. "Good. Now get down on your knees and put your hands in your lap. You're not allowed to touch me."

I swallowed hard and fortified myself to do as I was told. Avoiding his gaze, I attempted to lower myself from the table onto my shaky legs. My legs gave out, but Caleb reached out to steady me. I almost grabbed hold of him to stop myself from falling, but I managed to prevent the reflex and hung in his arms like a rag doll as he lowered me onto my knees.

"Thank you," I whispered.

He stood. "You know what, Kitten?" he said. "I think I *will* whip you. Ask me what for."

My eyes were already misted over with fresh tears when I looked up at him. "Why?"

He smiled and shook his head, just before he grabbed the back of my head and pulled my hair hard enough to let me know I was in trouble. "How

307

about for talking when you weren't asked to speak, touching me as if you have the right, looking at me without being told, and most importantly, for consistently addressing me improperly?" He gripped my hair tight. I whined sharply behind my closed lips and my eyes reflexively shut. "Now, you tell me, Kitten, do you deserve to be punished?"

There could not possibly be any good answer to his question. Even silence would be thought of as another infraction. My mind raced to find a way out of the situation, but I knew the damage had been done.

I cried miserably, but I opened my mouth and replied, "If it's what you want, Master, then yes." I kept my eyes closed, mindful not to look at him unbidden, and he released my hair.

"That's a good answer, Kitten. Later, I'll show you exactly what I want. In the meantime, show me how much you want to make me happy."

17

He made me walk – with traces of his semen on my chin and neck – naked, sobbing, and on shaky legs up the steps of the dungeon and out into the civilized surroundings of the mansion above. I hesitated strongly at the top of the steps when I heard the unmistakable murmur of people in conversation. Caleb pressed his hand firmly against the curve of my bottom and urged me forward, but I only leaned back and tried to step down. Propping me up with one hand, he delivered a powerful, ringing slap across the delicate flesh of my ass, and I couldn't help but cry out loudly and lurch through the door. Six sets of eyes turned toward me at once. They displayed a mixture of surprise and amusement.

The strong desire to run surged through me, but Caleb held my hair cruelly in his grasp. As I was forced to kneel at his feet, I instantly grabbed hold of his pant leg and hid.

"Well, this entire day just became more interesting," said an unfamiliar voice with a southern drawl. His comment was met with resounding laughter.

"I apologize," said Caleb. "She's not quite house broken yet."

I was too scared to be outraged. Above my head, sitting at a table, was a group of men and women. They didn't seem to have a problem with a man

309

dragging in a naked and crying woman. I couldn't imagine a more horrifying scenario.

When the laughter subsided, a familiar voice spoke. "Will you both be having breakfast with us?" It was Felipe – there was no mistaking the strong, assured inflection of his voice, and of course, there was the Spanish accent. My heart skipped a beat. What would happen if he told Caleb about last night? Had he told Caleb about last night? What if it was a test – and *I* was supposed to tell him?

"No, not this morning – but perhaps for dinner. I need time to make her suitable." He finally let my hair loose. I made no attempt to move; cowered against his legs, I felt oddly protected.

"Of course," said Felipe. "Celia will help you."

Caleb made me travel the rest of the way upstairs on my hands and knees, while the others looked on and remarked on how obvious it was I was new and how fun it would be to get a hold of my sexy ass.

Heat crawled all across my body, but I kept my head down and focused only on getting as far away from this emerging situation as possible. Somewhere in the back of my mind, I also worried about what was going to happen to me next. I realized my deepest hope was for Caleb to take me upstairs, bathe me, feed me, and hold me as he filled my ears with reassurances. I wanted him to remind me he would never let anyone hurt me, but as he forced me past the door to my room, my hopes seemed more and more unlikely.

A little further down, we rounded a corner and my knees were finally given respite as they met with a small, carpeted alcove. Caleb stepped in front of me and opened the large wooden door. I hesitated for only a moment, not knowing why, but then crawled across the threshold. The room was not what I expected. If ever I imagined a room for Caleb to call his own, it would have been this one. It seemed inundated with his ominous taste.

The carpet was a deep burgundy. It was so dark I almost mistook it for black. The bed sat high, covered in the blackest of spreads, turned down to reveal crimson silk sheets and pillows. The headboard was black as well – a large, tall, square thing. It gave the bed an obviously-masculine tone, and attached to its center were two thick metal loops. The door shut behind me and the room was drenched in darkness. I swallowed hard.

A small clicking sound and the light of a bedside lamp scarcely lit the room. I dared not make a sound or movement, though the urge to turn and look at Caleb was intense. My eyes stared forward, catching sight of a leather-clad bench of sorts. There was no television, no stereo, and no phone, but there were books. I noticed them in a corner bookcase, their spines showing they'd been thoroughly read and enjoyed. I suddenly ached to know their titles. I wondered what he read, what made him happy. There was also an odd piece of furniture standing in front of the stark curtains. I knew from a glance I was best left unaware of its purpose. It formed the shape of a large X, and at the top of each corner rested the same metal loops as the headboard. I shuddered in spite of myself.

"You embarrassed me down there." My entire body tensed at the sound of his angry voice.

"I'm sorry, Master," I whispered low. I struggled desperately to stay perfectly still. I treated him as the sort of predator to only attack moving prey. I heard the distinct sound of a buckle being undone and the swish of a belt being pulled from its belt loops. I started to shake.

"You're going to learn what is expected of you, Pet."

Everything in my body screamed for me to run, but somewhere inside my head a small voice whispered there was no escape – only obedience. *Only obedience will make him happy*. I nodded absently.

He didn't say anything further. He simply pressed my forehead to the ground and laid his belt down across my backside in quick succession.

At one, I clenched my jaw and forced my hands under my knees to keep from trying to take the belt.

At two and three, I was rocking as I wailed into the carpet.

Four, and I attempted to place my hands in the way of his belt by shielding my buttocks. My fingers brushed across raised welts.

Five, six, and seven, he held my hands tight against the small of my back.

Eight and nine left me screaming out loud and panting.

He stopped for a moment, long enough for me to tell him how sorry I was, that I would obey, that I would be good – I promised. A few more and he finally seemed satisfied.

He let my arms go, but I knew better than to follow my instincts to get up. I grabbed my wrists and held them at the small of my back, just as he had them. I heard his soft laugh over my sporadic whimpers and sobs, and for some reason, my body became slightly more at ease.

"Good girl, Kitten," he said. I sighed deeply with relief.

He dropped to one knee at my side and pulled me back firmly by my hair. I continued crying and fighting the urge to rub my behind as the real pain of the whipping set in, scalding hot and prickly.

"Does it hurt?" he asked.

"Yes, Master," I whimpered pitifully.

"Will you remember it?"

I managed to respond through my sobs again. "Yes, Master."

He stood, dragging me up by my hair with the effort. I arched my back and succumbed to my urges. I rubbed my behind forcefully with the palms of my hands. I only made it worse. He grabbed hold of my wrists and pinned them to the small of my back.

"Stay still!" he snapped. Instinctually, I pressed my forehead to the front of his shirt. I tried to straighten my legs. The feel of his firm chest pressed against my face did things to me I had come to expect. *Why do you always smell so good?* After a moment, the pain became secondary to thoughts of my naked body pressed against his clothes. I stood still, but I could not bring myself to pull away from him. He let my wrists go and I immediately wrapped them around his waist and pressed into him. He was hard, and soft, and strong, and he smelled like everything I wanted wrapped around me.

He tensed in my embrace and quickly placed his hands on my shoulders to urge me back. I looked up at him and saw the anger and confusion in his eyes, but I didn't care. Rafiq was coming for me. Caleb would either protect me, or he wouldn't. I couldn't ask him without giving Felipe away, nor could I ignore the feelings stirring inside me. Perhaps it was my exhaustion, or the long night of sexual torture he'd subjected me to, or perhaps it was simply the undeniable power he had over me – but whatever it was, I desperately needed to kiss him. I rose on the balls of my feet and inclined my lips toward his, begging him with my eyes to make this easier for me. If he was shocked, he didn't show it – he simply stayed immobile as I finally touched my trembling mouth to his.

His hands gripped my shoulders tighter when I traced my tongue along his bottom lip, urging him to open to my kiss. He obliged me and I almost wept at the taste of him. He finally softened and inclined his head by the slightest of degrees. I delved deeper into his mouth, shaking in my need to be touched by him.

He lifted his hand to the back of my head and kissed me with all the passion of the previous morning.

I couldn't stop the moan that broke past my lips. I had never felt anything like this. Never had I wanted to laugh, and weep, and fuck, and devour another human being until there was nothing left of him – until we were one person and I could feel peace. I grabbed his face in my hands and kissed him all over. My loud panting was echoed by his softer sounds. I sought his mouth over and over. I wrapped my leg around him, trying to climb onto him as he straightened his body. Abruptly, he broke the kiss and pushed me to the floor. I stared up at him, my heart laid bare at his feet. His chest rose and fell with anxious breath, but his words were steady and calm.

"That's the last time you'll ever do something without being told. And it's the last time I'll ever kiss you. I hope you enjoyed it." Through a mist of my tears, I thought I saw a flicker of hurt in his eyes. I dismissed it as my broken heart trying to reclaim some of its dignity.

"Please, Caleb!" I sobbed loudly. "Don't do this. Take me and let's go. Let's leave!"

He slapped me. Not savagely, but it stung, and the heat of my shock crept across my face and down my neck. I placed my hand on my cheek. It was hot to the touch. When the initial moment of shock wore off, I thought it strange I should feel the pain of his slap in my chest, but I did – and it hurt more than I ever thought possible.

Caleb's eyes held a glimpse of shock I'd never seen in his eyes before. He turned his back on me and walked through one of the doors in the room.

I heard water running.

He walked back out. "Clean yourself up and wait for Celia," he spat and walked out of the room.

I cried openly once the door shut, but I did as he asked.

315

***

An hour and a half later, I sat sobbing on the edge of the tub while Celia gently brushed my hair and tried her best to soothe me.

"I'm sorry, Kitten," she whispered. I sobbed harder. I nodded meekly to appease her. In all honesty, my tears had little to do with her or the fact she had painfully waxed all the hair on my body, with the exception of a small 'strip' at the apex of my pussy. Though, the pain would not easily be forgotten. Mostly, I cried because I could not shake Caleb from my thoughts. He didn't give a shit about me, and somehow I had fallen in love with him. He'd never kiss me again. That's what he'd said – never. I'd trusted him. I'd done everything he'd asked of me in the hopes he'd spare me. His loyalty had never rested with me, and I'd been foolish to believe I could win him over.

I couldn't help but replay the moment over and over in my mind. Even knowing the pain I felt was emotional, I physically hurt all over.

"Celia?" I finally managed to speak through my sobs.

"Sí, mi amor?" she said.

I spoke to her in Spanish. "Why does he treat me so badly? One moment he smiles at me and the next…" A hard lump formed in my throat, making it difficult to swallow, let alone speak.

"Don't cry, sweet girl," she said. It reminded me of Felipe, but I didn't mention it. She set the brush aside and held my head to her chest. I held on to her

316

tightly, flooded with the need to be held. She stroked my hair with her hand and spoke. "I think there are things you don't know about your master. Perhaps he seems unpredictable, but he is filled with passion for you. My master is always pleasant, even when he punishes me – yet I know nothing of what he feels." I could make out the pain in her voice. She was in love with Felipe and believed he didn't love her back.

I thought about my interaction with him in the dungeon and I had to disagree. Felipe was head over heels for Celia. It seemed ridiculous she didn't know. However, it wasn't my place to tell her.

"So many years together," she said in a soft whisper, "and he has never shown a flicker of interest one way or the other." She gave a wry smile. "Except, of course, when he wants to fuck me…or watch someone else fuck me." Her statement shocked me.

"I'm sorry," I said in sympathy.

"Oh, don't fret, little one. I don't mind. I always enjoy it, and when he makes love to me after," she sighed, "he makes sure I never feel ashamed, or dirty, or any of those other things. He just makes me feel like I've made him happy, and it makes me happy." I looked up at her and saw she had tears in her eyes. She smiled at me and quickly wiped them away with the back of her hand.

"I'm sorry I was cruel to you, Celia…you know…that night." Her smile grew wider.

"I'm sorry I was so reckless. I didn't know he meant so much to you. I couldn't say no to him, but I didn't have to flaunt my pleasure with such abandon." I think we both blushed. I gripped her hand and she sat next to me.

"Celia, do you ever...ever think of running?" She didn't pretend not to understand my meaning, though her eyes filled with a tempered panic and she instinctually looked around the room.

"You must never say such things, Kitten – not even to other girls like us. They'll turn on you for no other reason than to see you punished. But no, I could never leave Felipe. Perhaps he does not love me, but he cares for me. He gives me everything I desire without my having to ask. I love him. Before him...I don't remember what I lived for, what I liked to do – none of it matters to me now." I nodded slightly, though I didn't really understand what she meant.

The door opened. Celia and I startled guiltily. Caleb paused, his gaze penetrating my skin, even as I looked down into my lap like a scorned dog.

"Celia," he said after a moment, "go downstairs."

"Sí, Señor," she replied shakily and scurried from the room.

"Come here," he said to me.

Instinctively, I went to stand.

"In here, you are always on your knees unless told otherwise," he said.

Shaking, I went down on my knees and followed him as he walked into the bedroom. My heart pounded wildly in my chest, and between my thighs, my newly-bared flesh made me all too aware of my nakedness. My curiosity over what he would do next turned my stomach in knots, yet I followed him almost eagerly in the hopes he would be kinder than he had been.

He led me to a small 'bed,' consisting of a few thick, silken comforters set on the floor near his bed. "Stand near the bed. Leave your arms at your side," he ordered dispassionately.

Reluctantly, I did as I was told. On the bed in front of me lay some articles of clothing – some of them I was familiar with, others I was not. Devoid of any emotion, he lifted a pair of black translucent panties from the bed and motioned for me to step into them. I did so without comment, but when I lifted my leg to step in, I lost my balance and put my hands on his shoulders to steady myself. He tensed under my hands and I withdrew them. The black stockings didn't go on any steadier, but I let my arms go out for balance.

He stood and eyed the panties and stockings as my skin warmed under his scrutiny. I dared not look directly at his face to see if he appreciated what he saw. Perhaps not surprisingly, the panties caused a strange and overwhelming surge of desire. The newly-exposed skin of my pussy sprang to life at the feel of the smooth and silky material. Suddenly, I'd never been more grateful to be a woman. Our desires could be hidden, whereas a man's could not. Still, it was with some difficulty I didn't press my thighs together.

I'd never worn a corset before, so I was ill prepared for the snugness. Made of smooth black leather, it sat below the soft weight of my breasts and encased my entire abdomen. I let out a loud grunt when he cinched the back in one swift and devastating pull. He stilled a moment, and I regained my wits – and my oxygen.

"Can you breathe?"

I gave a jerky nod. "Yes, Master."

"Good. If your ribs start to hurt, tell me immediately."

Another nod. "Yes, Master."

There were strange pieces of leather attached to the front of the corset. I quickly learned they were for my wrists. With my wrists securely fastened, I could not lift my arms.

"That should keep your hands where they belong," he said with a mild touch of anger. I flushed at the memory of my bold kiss and winced at the memory of what had come of it. I heard rustling behind me but resisted the urge to look.

"Bend over the bed and spread your legs," he said.

I turned and saw he held something in his hand, but I couldn't quite make it out.

"Do as I said!"

I struggled to obey, hoping I wouldn't feel his belt across my sensitive behind. As scared as I was, my heart twisted when I recognized his smell on the bedding. Tears stung the backs of my eyes. I almost whispered his name, but I knew only horrible things could come of it. I wished I had never told him I loved him. I wished I had handled his revelations differently.

"I don't want revenge, Caleb. I don't want to end up like you, letting some fucking vendetta run my life. I just want my freedom. I want to be free, Caleb. Not someone's whore...not even yours."

My heartache turned to panic when Caleb's fingers pried my buttocks apart. I stilled, willing the intrusion to go away. One of his fingers pressed upon the bud of my anus, while the others kept my panties to the side. There was no stopping him.

"Relax," he said. He slid an obviously-lubed digit inside me slowly.

I couldn't make a sound, but inside I screamed in shock. In...and out...in...and out, he slowly thrust. Despite the fear and apprehension inside me, the sensation brought about the now-familiar pull of desire low in my belly. My panties, already wet, clung to my naked flesh, willing me to undulate against the fingers. They were so close to my clit... so close.

"Feel good, Pet?" he whispered huskily. I tensed, and I was sure he felt it around his finger. He pushed his finger deeper inside me until my stomach pinched, and a moan escaped my lips.

He held me suspended on his finger, wrenching both tears of humiliation and lustful moans from me. "Yes. Yes, Master." I sobbed.

He withdrew slowly. I eased my hips back down, and again his smell saturated my senses. I wondered for the millionth time why I wanted him so badly when he was such a calculating bastard. While I panted for breath, Caleb prepared his second assault by reinserting his finger with even more lubricant.

He tried to push something inside me, something foreign.

"What are you doing?" I shouted before I could stop myself.

"Relax," he said.

Shocked into instant silence, I immediately willed myself to obey. Slowly, the object went in and I found myself filled just to the point of pain and on the precipice of intense pleasure. I could feel it in my stomach, and strangely, I could also feel it pressing against the walls of my pussy. I lay still, panting and moaning, trying to decipher what the hell just happened.

Caleb's warm body pressed against my back. His hot mouth sucked at my earlobe, and my muscles contracted strongly, surging with wetness. "Don't you dare push this out, or I'll whip your ass raw." As he said the words, he thrust his erection against me and shifted the plug inside me. I moaned.

"Yes, Master," I whispered. My voice was a wanton plea for more contact. He reared back, his left hand between my shoulder blades, his hips still pressed against mine. I sighed when he tugged my panties down to expose my ass. He reached between us to trace his fingers between my cheeks. I thrust back, urging him lower to the swollen bud of my clit, begging him to finish me. It didn't take long. He rubbed my clit gently with his fingers while the palm of his hand shifted the plug inside me. I came within moments, in hard, jerking motions involving my entire body. After, he helped me to the floor and told me to sleep.

18

I opened my eyes and stared into the semi-darkness, unwilling to move in the event Caleb planned to torture me further upon my waking. My sleep had been awkward. My wrists were shackled to a tightly-laced leather corset. It was difficult to breathe or lift my arms more than a few inches in front of me. I was also made to sleep on the floor – it was padded with bedding, but not anywhere near as comfortable as a bed.

I thought about the morning. After Caleb had made his somewhat-violent use of my mouth – which, strangely enough, had me both wanting and hating him – he denied me the measure of solace he'd up until now always given me after such ordeals: affection. I had to admit, it really hurt my feelings. Despite everything he'd put me through, he'd never made me feel cheap. Even in the beginning, when he'd been even more of a calloused bastard, he'd managed to allay my fear and anxiety when he was done with me. I feared those days were gone since the moment I had told him I loved him.

Playing the day over in my mind did little to urge me into waking, but I couldn't sleep anymore. Not only had I slept most of the day, but my stomach begged for something to eat. Then, as if on cue, the door opened and Caleb strode into the room. My heart instantly sped up and skipped a beat as I took in the sight of him in a tuxedo. His thick and

323

gorgeous blond hair, often worn in a style of organized dishevelment, was now combed away from his face. The intensity of his blue eyes at once felt like both a punch to the stomach and a soft, hungering caress.

He seemed endlessly calm as he approached me. I remembered myself and looked away. He knelt next to me. I let out a sigh I didn't realize I'd held when he reached out and traced my chin with his long, smooth fingers. He cupped my chin and tingles spread throughout my body. I shivered in spite of myself. He turned my face toward his, and I could no longer resist looking into his eyes.

"Did you sleep well, Kitten?" he asked so softly, I ached.

"Yes, Master," I whispered.

"Good. It's time to go downstairs and introduce you to the rest of the guests."

My stomach twisted, though at this point it had less to do with my hunger and more with my anxiety. I said nothing and didn't resist when he helped me to my feet. As I stood only inches away from him, his smell once again surrounded me. For a moment, I couldn't help but close my eyes and imagine a situation different than this one – one where I could just be myself, and he would adore me for it. He smoothed my hair back, unraveling the snags formed in my sleep and working them through quickly and deftly.

"There," he said, more to himself than to me, "that looks a lot better."

An awkward silence fell between us. I kept my

eyes focused on the cleanly-pressed shirt in front of me. He sighed, and I couldn't help but notice it was the kind of sigh someone let out when they were preparing themselves to do something difficult. I knew it had to do with Rafiq, somehow, but I couldn't ask him. I couldn't accept my fate just yet. I had to hope the Caleb I had grown to love was thriving inside the version of Caleb in front of me. Hope was all I had left.

With no further ado, he turned me around and swept the bulk of my hair over my left shoulder. My entire body shivered. I heard him pull something from his pocket. I tensed when I felt the smooth band of leather circle my throat.

"It's not the same collar you wore before. I like this one much better. It's softer, and it won't dig into you," he whispered.

Were my hands free, I might have reached up to touch the loop attached to the front. But they weren't free – like me, they were bound by circumstance.

"I want you to know," he said matter-of-factly, "there's going to be a lot of people downstairs. These people are important acquaintances of mine. I expect you to behave. Do exactly as I say, keep your eyes lowered, and it should be an enjoyable evening for the both of us. Understood?"

I swallowed thickly and managed to whisper, "Yes, Master."

"Turn around," he said. "I have a little something to ensure your obedience." As I turned, I couldn't help but meet his eyes. He pulled me close, holding me in place by way of his hand at the small of my back. His other hand cupped my breast just inside my corset. He put his mouth on my nipple and sucked.

I couldn't hold in a powerful sigh. I was wet, but his affection was to be short lived. Just as soon as his mouth released me, firm pressure took hold of my nipple. While I swooned, he repeated the perfunctory process on my other breast and then stood back to admire his work.

I looked down at my breasts through a haze of tears to notice the delicate clamps adorning my nipples. A thin, gold chain joined them and led directly into Caleb's hand. As I took stock of my predicament, I couldn't help looking up at Caleb with a pleading expression. He tugged gently, as if to say my pleading was meaningless. My body stiffened and a jolt of pain and sensation drilled down through my belly, ending between my legs. The plug in my ass moved, exaggerating the sensation. In midstream, the pain changed to something pulsating, something near pleasure. Like a puppet, my body relaxed as Caleb released the tension.

"Are we clear on the rules of obedience?" Caleb asked, and then not waiting for my answer he continued. "This is a test of sorts, Kitten. Don't disappoint me." He turned his back to me. "Follow behind on my left, keep your eyes lowered, and there should be no need to test the sensitivity of your nipples."

"Yes, Master," I replied, not able to keep the tremor from my voice. Tears clung to my lashes and my body quaked, but I followed Caleb as directed.

We walked the pace of a parade. A slight murmur of low voices reached the top of the stairway. Candlelight from the room below glimmered across the marble stairs, lighting our descent in living color. The warm glow eased some of my quaking, along with Caleb's care of the chain joining us together.

At the bottom of the stairway, Felipe greeted Caleb. "Good to have you join us, my friend. I see you have your lovely Kitten in tow. Everyone is looking forward to seeing her."

"Felipe," Caleb acknowledged. I couldn't help but notice Caleb didn't sound too pleased.

Our eyes met over Caleb's shoulder, but he did not let on about my disobedience. In fact, he winked at me. We were sharing yet another moment, unbeknownst to my master. I flushed deeply.

"I thought you should know the boy is here with Mr. B tonight and will be part of the evening's entertainment," Felipe added in a whisper loud enough for me to hear. The statement had a mocking edge, as if he were poking fun at Caleb. I didn't like it.

"Interesting," Caleb replied, simple and abrupt. Caleb lifted his head and scanned the small gathering of people. Instinctually, I scanned the room as well and promptly received a continuous tug of shooting pain through my nipples for the effort.

"Eyes down," Caleb said over his shoulder to me, his voice riddled with undisguised anger.

"Yes, Master," I said in a jagged whisper. I wanted to scream from the pain torturing my nipples, but the tension on the chain lessened, and my breath spun out in a heavy sigh of relief.

Caleb moved past Felipe. I followed, fearful of the damn chain he held. We stepped off the marble stairway onto carpet and crossed the room. The soft touch of the plush carpeting massaged the bottom of my stocking feet.

"Well, look what the cat dragged in," came a man's Southern drawl, followed by a low whistle. "She's a beauty. I'd love to test drive her, especially if she handles anything like this one Felipe gave my wife to try." The man moved back for Caleb to look.

I dared raise my eyes only a bit, my head still bent toward the floor. From the corner of my eye, I saw a boy near my age standing on his knees. He was perhaps the most beautifully handsome boy I'd ever seen. Still, I could not shake the notion I knew him somehow. He raised his dark blue eyes just enough to connect with mine. My breath caught and my eyes opened wide.

"Kid!" I exclaimed before I could stop myself. Pain quickly overturned surprise as my nipples burned from incessant pressure.

"Eyes down, Kitten," Caleb snapped.

I was slow in my obedience. I'd known Kid had been captured, but I hadn't seen him since the night Caleb and I had arrived at the mansion. I wondered where he had been all this time. His hair was longer, his body leaner, and his demeanor signaled just how deeply he'd been broken down. Despite everything, he looked healthy – perhaps even happy. I didn't know how to feel about seeing him. Kid reminded me too much of what had happened to me with the bikers. I tried hard to remember he had been the one to stop his friends from beating me to death.

Caleb tugged again, this time with only as much force as was necessary to demand my attention.

"Yes, Master," I finally whispered, and Caleb held me still to untie my wrists.

"Keep your hands behind your back unless you need them for balance."

Forced into close proximity, I couldn't help but take in the sight of Kid dressed only in a loin cloth. His wrists were tethered, and he had clamps on his nipples. Around his neck, there was a collar with a leather leash attached. His body radiated heat against my legs. I wanted to cry out from the injustice of it all. I began to pant with anxiety – maybe even panic.

"Oh, she's a feisty one. I think I'd like to play with her for a while," Mr. B added, and a chuckle rumbled out, sounding like it came from the bottom of his belly.

"That won't be possible," Caleb said. His tone was somewhat harsh, and I couldn't help but notice the way those near him stared at him. "Kitten is meant for other things."

I raised my eyes slightly, looking through the fringe of my lashes as he led me toward a table dressed in white linen. Candelabras bathed a warm glow over the two couples at the table enjoying cocktails and conversation. They wore suits and gowns – aristocrats dressed up for an expensive night out.

A woman, dressed similar to me, sat on her knees near the table. Her body was poised, yet relaxed. Her eyes were cast down and her hands were folded over her thighs. Caleb stopped near her, dropping the chain into her hands. He pressed my shoulders down. I bent down to rest on my knees and the plug in my ass shifted. Sensations pulsed through my body, making me shake.

"I'll be right back, Celia. Make sure Kitten remains here for a few minutes."

I gasped, not recognizing Celia, but kept my eyes down. As soon as Caleb walked away, I raised my eyes slightly to get a better look. Celia looked exotic and beautiful. I knew, of course, she belonged to Felipe, but I had no idea she was subject to participating in anything like this. Last time, she had wielded the crop, but tonight, she was a prisoner like me – and, apparently, Kid.

Another couple, a tall woman and a short man, both dressed in white, approached. They were pulling a red-corseted woman behind them. The woman wore nipple chains, red silk stockings, and a red lace thong, with a red ribbon weaved through her long dark hair. The couple settled at the table, and the woman in red sat on her knees next to the man.

The classic formalwear and respectful murmur of voices intertwined with a gentle tinkle of laughter. Theirs was a different world from the one I was used to. Men with smiling faces, women dripping with sparkling jewelry and long polished nails, tugging behind them corseted half-naked women. I noticed Kid was the only male prisoner.

"Everyone, please find a seat. We are ready to serve your first course," Felipe announced from the end of the table. Gentle music began playing in the background and more candles were lit around the room. Caleb came to get me at the same time Felipe came for Celia.

"Come on, Kitten, let's have some dinner. I'm sure you're hungry." Caleb moved slowly so I could keep up crawling along on my knees the few feet to the table. He sat down at the table, positioning me next to him on the floor.

Servers dressed in scant uniforms, barely covering their breasts or backsides, placed platters of appetizers down the center of the table. Some refreshed water glasses, and others refilled wine glasses.

On the other side of me sat Felipe, Celia close to his side on the floor. The woman in white sat next to Caleb.

"Kitten, you're behaving exemplarily tonight," Felipe whispered and gently touched my shoulder. I remained in position, though his touch sent a shiver of mistrust down my arm. I turned my head slightly to see if Caleb noticed.

"She's had her moments," Caleb added, as if I weren't there. His attention was drawn to the woman in white sitting next to him. From my position on the floor, I watched her polished fingers slide up the middle of his thigh and stop short of the bulge between his legs.

"So good to see you again, Caleb," her silky voice purred loudly enough for me to hear.

"Have we met?" Caleb asked and placed his hand over hers, preventing it from going any farther up his leg.

"Regrettably, no. I was here when you and your lovely girl first arrived. I admired you, and I was sure to find out who you were," she all but purred.

"I see," said Caleb. "Well, it's a pleasure to meet you, Miss…?"

"J," she said. "*Mrs.* J, but don't worry – Mr. J is well aware of my extra-curricular activities." She gave a short, flirtatious laugh. Her fingers moved up to cup Caleb's bulge.

I fought the urge to swat her hand away. *Mine! You fucking bitch.*

Caleb pressed her hand to him and then moved it back into her lap. "Thank you for the compliment, Mrs. J, but I think your attentions would be best spent on someone else." Caleb's voice carried down to me, even though it was a whisper next to Mrs. J's ear.

"You're not available?" She sounded disappointed.

Seething with jealousy, and with the memory of Caleb and Celia in my thoughts, I inclined myself toward Caleb and rubbed my head against his thigh. To my surprise, Caleb's hand landed on my head in a soft and reassuring caress before he urged me away.

Caleb chuckled low, and I watched his hand squeeze the top of Mrs. J's thigh through her satin gown. Her legs parted, and she pulled his hand toward her center.

"You're hungry. We'll make sure you get your fill." Caleb caressed her deeply with his fingers then slipped from her grasp and moved his hands above the table. He grabbed a plate of the appetizers and piled a few on her plate as well as his own. "That should get you started." His voice held a promise, and I had to wonder what he planned for later.

Tears stung the backs of my eyes. Not that he noticed. My heart hammered in my chest and I swear the ringing in my ears blasted out for everyone to hear. My breath came in pants, and Felipe's hand brushed my upper arm.

"Relax," he whispered.

Caleb reached down with a succulent shelled shrimp in his hand. "Open, Kitten."

My eyes automatically rose to his level. Before I settled an appropriate glare at him, my nipples received a burning tug that stole my breath. My mouth dropped open, quite by accident, but Caleb used the opportune moment to plop the morsel into my mouth. Mortified, I could do nothing but chew. My stomach appreciated the attention.

All of the chained ones ate from their master's hand. It appalled me, but I remained submissive. I promised obedience. It made Caleb happy, and my survival ultimately depended on his happiness. I still hadn't seen Rafiq, but I had come to expect surprises.

When the last course was finished, Caleb pulled away from the table. "You need to relieve yourself and freshen up."

Felipe interjected. "Celia can take her to the slave quarters, if it's all right with you, Caleb."

"I'll take her over with Celia. Then Celia can show Kitten what's expected."

Caleb helped me to my feet. The plug shifted, creating another tremble through my body. Felipe gave Celia's chain over to Caleb, and he led us away.

He handed Celia my chain at the door. The room was shiny and sterile white. A row of tubs lined the floor to the right of me – some large, some small. To the left were private rooms. Farther down, I saw a large mosaic featuring a young Mexican girl bathing outdoors and touching her nipples while a man watched in the distance. It provided the backdrop for the shower room, which featured a row of shower heads, drains in the floor, and a few toilet stalls.

"What is this place, Celia?" I whispered. My voice held both wonderment and trepidation. Unconsciously, I reached for her hand and she held it.

"It's just a room, Kitten."

She leaned in close to my ear and whispered, "Everything we say is recorded. Motion sensors, microphones." I nodded.

"Go on and use the ladies. I need to grab some towels."

After I relieved myself, Celia took me to a small, private, and curtained room. There was a sink and a set of towels. A cabinet sat next to the sink was laden with toiletries.

"I'm going to freshen between your legs." She slid my silk panties down, along with my silk stockings, and I let her. She'd cleaned me up so many times before, I held no embarrassment. "Once I've done it for you, you'll understand what you need to do the next time you are told to freshen up." She lathered up a cloth with some special soap smelling of almonds and honey. "Stand on this towel and open your legs for me." I did as she asked. She was amazingly gentle, as always. I could almost understand how women swayed over to women. Celia didn't touch me inappropriately, but her demeanor was so gentle it lulled me into relaxing.

It wasn't long before we were back out to Caleb. He walked Celia over to Felipe, who then handed her off to one of the first couples I saw sitting at the dining table. Celia went without rebelling, even when both the man and the woman touched her breasts.

Caleb tugged on my chain, creating another shot from my nipples to my pussy. I closed my eyes and held back a plea. "Let's not keep people waiting," he said.

Caleb tied my wrists to the loops at the front of my corset. We moved close to another area in the same large room. Couches and low tables with candles and wineglasses were strategically placed in an area close to a stone fireplace wall. Flames licked the piled wood within the hearth.

335

We stopped beside the couple we'd met earlier. Their names for the evening seemed to be Mr. and Mrs. B. A cursory glance, and I realized Kid sat on his knees next to them with his head bowed and his hands behind his back. I would have felt sorry for him, but I was too concerned with my own situation.

I wondered what Caleb had planned for the evening. So far, it had a very *Eyes Wide Shut* atmosphere. I wanted to be alone with him. I wanted to explain how much he truly meant to me. I wanted him to understand my feelings for him had nothing to do with manipulating him or trying to gain my freedom.

I didn't want to be Caleb's whore, that much I wouldn't take back. I also didn't care for revenge. I wanted Caleb. I knew it was stupid. I knew he was a terrible person who'd done terrible things. I knew he didn't deserve me or my love. I didn't care. During the course of our time together, I'd fallen in love with my captor. I'd fallen in love with his smell and his taste, his smile, kindness, and yes, even his cruelty, because I knew it was a part of him.

I wanted him to know. I wanted him to know everything, and I wanted it to mean something to him. I wanted him to choose me and accept me. I wanted him to leave everything behind and love me.

"Kitten..." his forehead pressed hard against the nape of my neck, "you ask for impossible things."

I didn't care.

I was lost in thought when Caleb's hand, warm and reassuring, landed on my shoulder. I looked up at him, and I let my longing for him show. He smiled, but it struck me as sad. Caleb's sad smiles never boded well for me.

"Down," Caleb said, gesturing toward the spot next to Kid.

I let myself sink into the command. I wanted to comply. I wanted to make Caleb happy in any way I was able, in the hopes he would never be able to let me go.

"Ladies and Gentlemen, dessert is about to be served." Felipe's low, accented timbre silenced the small group. Chairs slid across the carpeted area near where I lay – the sound of people getting comfortable. I wondered why Caleb didn't pull me up in preparation to eat.

Abruptly, Caleb's hand was in my hair and pulled me close. He whispered in my ear, "I know how difficult this is going to be for you. It's going to be difficult for me, too. That said, I expect perfection, Kitten. Do you understand?"

My pulse quickened; my vision blurred. "Caleb...."

"Shh, Kitten," he reprimanded. "Obey."

I pulled back when he let me go and our eyes met. He gave me another sad smile, and then, for reasons I couldn't possibly know, Caleb pushed my face down into Kid's lap. My butt rose off the floor and Caleb pushed against the plug in my ass with his knee. Again, to my mortification, the plug shifted. Beneath Kid's loin cloth, something else stirred.

Caleb, sounding strained, added, "I wondered how these two would respond to each other." He

removed his knee from my derrière, and I sprang
backward, falling on my ass. My bent knees splayed
open as I lie on my back, unable to push myself up
with my wrists tethered.

"Well, by the looks of the kid's cloth there, I'd
say he's pretty pumped up." Mr. B laughed out loud.
The sound carried over the quiet murmurs of the
other guests.

I closed my eyes, embarrassed, and waited for
the nipple pain. Guests shuffled around us, and I
squeezed my eyes tighter, afraid of where to look in
this position. Suddenly, a warm, trembling hand slid
up my nylon stocking, just on the inside of my calf,
slowly over my knee, and up the inside of my thigh.
It stopped, but then hesitantly burned a path back
down the inside of my leg to the arch of my foot.
The hand gently massaged my foot before moving to
the inside of my other leg and sliding its way toward
my thigh. Fingertips, ever so lightly, brushed the
small patch of silk between my legs.

The persistent hand rubbing my leg became two
hands and both brushed between my legs at once.
Muscled thighs pushed my legs farther apart. I could
no longer fight the urge to open my eyes. I dared to
peek through the fringe of my lashes and saw Kid's
shoulder-length, blond hair. It was combed away
from his boyish beauty. His cheeks burned with
embarrassment, mirroring my own, as he positioned
himself close to my center and continued rubbing
my thighs.

His eyes remained closed as he assailed my body
with his touch. I imagined Kid getting a tug on his

nipples as reprimand for opening his eyes. The tip of his tongue slid across his full bottom lip, and for some reason a sensation rippled along my center.

I wanted so badly to see Caleb that my eyes opened wider. A searing pressure on my nipples told me he remained close. My eyes closed and the pressure subsided. It was proof he was watching me intently as another man touched me.

So, this is what will make Caleb happy. My heart pinched at the betrayal. *Fine, he wants to pretend there's nothing between us? I'll give him a show to remember.*

Kid definitely knew what he was doing. His hands created a burning desire – not just where he touched me, but throughout my whole being. In fact, it was tough to keep control. Part of me strove to hold on to my pride, or what was left of it, and another part of me wanted to let go with reckless abandon.

Kid's gentle and warm caresses stoked something deep inside me. I was breathless, tingly, and so wet between my legs the silk settled into my folds. His hands laid trails over my thighs, hips, and belly...*damn corset.* Suddenly, a different set of hands pulled me back and stood me upright.

There was another rumble of laughter from Mr. B., who took control of Kid. With a great deal of effort, I kept my eyes down. Caleb pressed me back into his erection. I was unable to stop a soft moan. To my shock and surprise, Caleb unbound my wrists and began unlacing my corset. My entire body tensed in a silent plea for him to stop. He pressed his lips softly to the shell of my ear. "Obey," he whispered with enough intensity to almost stop my heart.

I remained still as he completely unlaced my corset. My breath caught with its removal, and I heard the heavy intake of breath from the others around me through the ringing in my ears. A blindfold was slipped over my eyes. Both clamps were released from my breasts, and my nipples burned as blood rushed into the starved areas. Caleb released me, and I stood feeling alone and exposed.

Where is Caleb?

My pride dropped away, and my heart filled with sadness while my head filled with embarrassment. The stillness in the room was palpable, punctuated keenly by the lone sound of my anxious breath. There was a soft rustle, then the feel of smooth fingers rolling one of my silk stockings down my thigh. I desperately fought my urge to resist.

This is what he wants. Be brave.

My sex pulsed as my left stocking was rolled down my leg. I reached my hands out to feel and gasped when they were quickly gathered up between my breasts. My body was hoisted into the air. I kicked out with my legs, but someone grabbed them firmly. They placed me on a hard surface, which I knew instinctually to be one of the linen-covered dining tables.

I panicked, and at once Caleb's voice was in my ear telling me to obey. "Steady, Kitten. I won't let him inside you. I won't let *anyone* inside you." Through my panic, I almost missed the possessive nature of his words, but the part of me that thought of him as mine wanted to recognize it as an admission. I relaxed by the barest of degrees.

My wrists were tied together and held over my head. Within moments, soft, feathery touches along the top of my silk panties assailed my senses. Despite my apprehension, a shudder ran through me. Those hands, those warm, trembling, and wonderful hands, activated something. A charge ignited within me as my panties slipped down and away. My head swam in the smell of lust, the taste of it. I suddenly wanted satisfaction. I needed it.

Muscular thighs pressed between my legs. Palms pushed against both of my inner thighs, splaying my legs wide and opening my pussy. My hips rose off the table and a finger slid down and back up my crevice. My hips rose higher, begging. A moan and a sob fell from my lips. My hands were pushed harder into the table.

Hands cupped my buttocks from between my legs and lifted my hips higher, pushing the plug in my ass right against my throbbing sex muscle. Another moan left my lips. I was panting.

Without warning, a tongue, so masterful, thick, wet, and slightly rough, licked and lapped my nether lips. The mouth on my pussy pulled me in, sucking until another moan left me breathless. The tongue spread me apart, laying me open. A gentle nip on my clit ignited a thousand flames within my body.

Other hands massaged my breasts, rolling my sensitive buds between fingers. *Please be Caleb.* Waves of fire begged to be released inside me; my body trembled with need. The concentrated sucking and licking on my swollen clit swept me over the edge. Panting turned into screams and a flood of sensation carried me away.

My butt was placed back on the table and I lay there spent, tears wetting the blindfold, my legs still trembling and splayed open. The room filled with applause.

"If this enthusiasm is any indication, I see no reason why we shouldn't have a second course of dessert," Felipe said, breaking through the applause in the room.

I'm dessert? Nice of Caleb to make me part of dinner. Bastard!

I struggled to raise myself, pulling my legs together and bending my knees up so my ankles hid my swollen sex. My back remained stuck to the linen cloth. My wrists stayed pinned to the table over my head.

Caleb's voice filled my left ear. "It's your turn to reciprocate, Kitten."

What the hell does he mean?

My body was pulled up to sitting. Again, the plug shifted. A spasm shot through my pussy, making me gasp. My wrists were loosed and my hands placed on Kid's loin cloth. The blindfold remained in place. His upper body heat reached out to me. He smelled sweet, but unnatural, as though someone had covered him in something scented. I preferred the way Caleb smelled.

I moved one hand around to feel Kid's position. His knees stuck out in front; his buttocks sat on his ankles. I slid my hand down his muscled arm to find his wrists had been tied behind his back. My fingers traced his chest and released the clamps from his nipples, tossing them away. His heavy exhale moistened my face.

So, this is what I'm supposed to do? Perform?!?

I was apprehensive in the extreme. I had only done this twice before, and only with Caleb. I couldn't believe he was going to let me do this – *make* me do this. I could feel my lip tremble. I could feel the tears waiting in my throat, but then I thought about Caleb and his night with Celia.

I remembered my jealousy and my rage. I wanted Caleb to feel those things. I wanted him to watch me give to someone else what I felt in my heart had been reserved only for him. If he cared for me at all, I knew this was a sure way to find out. I took several deep breaths and prepared myself for what I was about to do.

"I guess you do *want revenge,"* Ruthless Me whispered.

You bet your sweet ass, I do.

Kid's chest pounded beneath my trembling right hand. His hardness throbbed against my left palm. I slid my legs underneath me and raised my upper body to meet his. I pressed my breasts against his chest and his breath caught. My left palm felt a shift, a thickening, his cock barely contained. I licked his chest, his nipples, as far up as I could reach on his neck, until he bent down to me.

Our lips touched ever so gently. The taste and smell of me lingered in his mouth as his tongue slid

343

between my lips. I shuddered, and he pressed his chest harder into mine, our lips taking in each other.

We were only kissing for a few seconds before my head was snapped back by my hair and Caleb's voice filled my head in a growl against my ear. "No kissing on the lips." He pinched my buttocks so hard I couldn't help but cry out.

I jerked into Kid and nearly tipped us both over. Kid's strength steadied me. I paused, resting against him, before I slowly resumed kissing him. I let my mouth travel along his chest, shoulders, arms, and nipples before making my way up to his neck. I felt him bending his head down toward me, and I pushed him back with both hands against his chest.

The kissing show is over, buddy!

Kid's hips rutted against mine, his loin cloth totally deformed. My arms went around his waist, my fingers followed the thong of the loin cloth, and my breasts molded against his belly. It tied in the back, which only took seconds for me to untie. The thong immediately opened and released his penned-up cock. My hands felt its throbbing length and width. His balls rested against the pouch of the loin cloth. I carefully pulled the cloth away.

We froze. *Am I really going to do this?* I couldn't believe how far I'd come. Over the course of a few months, I had gone from being afraid of sex to performing a sexual act with a stranger in front of an entire room of derelicts. Kid groaned and pressed his warm cock against my hand in a wordless plea for me to set him free from his sexual purgatory. How well I knew the feeling.

Kid sucked in his breath when I kissed the tip of his cock. He tasted different than Caleb, but it probably had more to do with the fact he had been prepared. He tasted sweet, as if someone had covered him in some sort of spicy cinnamon concoction. It wasn't unpleasant. I spread a bead of precome with my lips and tongue, and he became both salty and sweet in my mouth. As I slid my tongue down the length of him, Kid's body shuddered. He let out a deep breath and moaned. His hips rocked toward my mouth.

Is this what you want, Caleb? I hope you're watching, you son of a bitch. I want you breathless with want. I want you to see how I please a man. Will that make you want me?

The blindfold made it easy for me to imagine Caleb in Kid's place. I imagined hearing his ragged breath in my ears, his body trembling with desire and need for me. My body responded, my beaded nipples yearned for attention, and my sex pulsed to the rhythm of Kid's thrusting hips.

My lips surrounded the head of Kid's cock, and my tongue played with both the underside of its rim and the slit at the top. Kid panted heavily, his hips thrusting harder, until his cock slid further into my mouth and my tongue touched it everywhere. His body stiffened, his breath sucked in, and so did the breath of the room. For a moment, time suspended. Then, he moaned.

I made my move. I squeezed my fingers around his cock low and pumped him in time with my mouth, drawing him in and out. He gasped, and I heard hands kneading and rubbing his chest. He thrust into my mouth faster. My mouth sucked, my tongue stroked, and my pussy screamed for its own release. My hips gyrated against the air, until someone splayed my legs apart and slid a hand through the back of my thighs, squeezing my nether lips.

It stopped me for a nanosecond, until a couple fingers found my clit and began rubbing. My hips thrust to match Kid's. His cock pulsed; he thrust a final time and spilled into my mouth. I milked him dry as waves of heat spun through me. A palm pressed against my ass, shifting the plug, and I screamed with my lips still around Kid's cock. The wretched fingers continued rubbing my swollen clit.

Oh god, Caleb! Yes. Please, keep going.

Wave after wave of sensation touched every part of my body, but Caleb's fingers on my clit and his palm against my ass were relentless. My body heated up again, as did Kid's. He heard me, felt my tongue, my breath, and my moans of ecstasy against his still-throbbing cock. His hips thrust a little more, and I squeezed and sucked a little more, imagining Caleb in front of me – as well as behind.

Kid moved his cock in and out of my mouth. I could barely hold it with my hands, he moved so fast and rough.

I rocked against Caleb's hand, matching Kid's rhythm. My breath came quick and hard. I was barely able to breathe, but I didn't care. My mouth was full. My ass was full. My clit was ready to explode. Caleb's fingers were skilled. They knew my pussy. I came in a fit of tears.

19

There was no applause – just the sound of Livvie's broken sobs and Kid's muted pants.

Caleb felt...well, he didn't know how he felt. He only knew he wanted Livvie. He wanted her close and away from all the prying eyes around them. Rafiq had not arrived, and Caleb was overwhelmed with anger and regret in addition to an influx of emotions he had no time to analyze.

"I'm taking her upstairs," Caleb said, gathering Livvie's naked and quivering body into his arms. He noticed Kid's eyes, glazed with unshed tears and harboring a more than guilty expression. If Caleb didn't know better, he'd say the boy was smitten in the worst way. The very idea seemed to incite his anger and yes, his jealousy. Caleb was teeming with jealousy. If he didn't get away from Kid soon, Caleb worried he'd be unable to control himself.

She kissed him, he screamed in this head.

She'll kiss Vladek, too.

Caleb couldn't think about it. His thoughts were too dangerous. His emotions were too raw and logic was quickly fleeing. Devoid of reason, he could find no cause to keep him from taking Livvie upstairs and fucking her senseless. He wanted to scrub every trace of Kid from her body and clear every memory of him from Livvie's mind. Caleb wanted her to think only of him, to *be* with him.

You can't do it, can you? You can't let her go. Find a way, Caleb. Find a way to make Rafiq understand.

Caleb's thoughts ran wild as he held Livvie to his chest and walked toward his room. His heart pounded a sharp tattoo he could visibly see shifting her in his arms.

Once upstairs, Caleb gently placed Livvie onto his bed. In the short time it had taken him to get to his room, she had somehow managed to sob her way into a kind of sleep. Her eyes were closed. Every so often, she would take in a deep breath, and her chest shuddered before she exhaled. Caleb looked down at her sleeping form and wondered what she dreamed about in her passed-out state of slumber. Her body jerked, twisting her over onto her back, her nakedness open for the taking. He wanted to take her. His erection pressed into the zipper of his pants, begging for release.

He closed his eyes in order to relax, still standing next to the bed. Her smell permeated his senses, a fragrance light, musky, and all her own. It had pulled him to her earlier tonight. Like a sea siren calling to a sailor, her need compelled him to act. Without thought, he had rolled his sleeves up and dived in with both hands to quench her thirst.

Mine.

The word was a declaration. It rocked him to his very foundation. It was a truth he'd kept hidden for far too long. Caleb didn't know anything about love, or loving anyone, but he knew…Livvie was his. He owned her. He possessed her and he knew, with everything he was, he couldn't give her away.

Mine!

Mine!

Mine!

Rafiq will understand. I'll make him understand.

Caleb was far from rational. Deep down, he knew Rafiq wouldn't understand. He would see it as the deepest betrayal. He would demand the impossible of Caleb. Rafiq would try to hurt them both. Caleb pushed those thoughts away.

Before common sense could return, Caleb gently raised Livvie's hands and untied her wrists. Livvie sighed, and Caleb lied down on top of her in time to watch her eyes flutter open. He stared into her deep, chocolate-colored eyes and saw himself reflected in their depths as she focused on him. A myriad of feelings passed through him – jealousy and possessiveness at the forefront. He needed to make her his: unequivocally and irreversibly.

Livvie's expression turned inscrutable. She lay under Caleb, her arms limp at her sides, her expressive eyes cold and distant.

Caleb wanted nothing more than to know what she was thinking, but he was too terrified to ask. The feeling of terror was foreign and unwanted. The last time he'd felt it, Livvie was in a house, bleeding, broken, and barely holding on to her life. He'd been terrified then, and he'd barely known her. The way he felt for her then paled in comparison to the new feelings he harbored. He dared not ask what was in her heart. He knew he couldn't bear to hear it.

"I can't stand the smell of him on you," Caleb sneered.

Tears sprang to Livvie's eyes and trailed down her temples. She closed her eyes and turned her head away from Caleb.

He put his hand on her face and forced her to face him.

Don't ask.

Don't ask.

Fuck! I'm going to ask.

He needed to know. He needed to know if her love for him was real. He needed to know hope was not lost and he could still, against all odds, repair the damage he had done.

"Did you enjoy it?" he asked. He tried not to make it sound like an accusation, but he knew he fell short. Livvie raised her hands to her face, covering her eyes and mouth as she began weeping. Again, Caleb refused to let her hide. He reached for her hands and pressed them into the bed above her.

"Tell me!" he snapped.

"I don't know what you want me to say!" she cried.

"Tell me the truth! Did you like sucking his dick? Did he eat your pussy better than I do?" Caleb's thoughts were suddenly murderous. He had meant to be kind, he had meant to be gentle, but it just wasn't his way. He no longer knew what 'his way' was.

"Yes!" Livvie screamed. "Yes, you son of a bitch. I liked it. Isn't that why you made me do it?

351

So you could parade me around like a trained fucking poodle?"

Caleb saw red. He squeezed Livvie's wrists until she cried out in pain, and he forced himself to let go. Her words hurt him.

Mine! You're fucking mine!

Caleb pulled away from Livvie and reached for his belt. He unfastened it quickly and pulled it free in one swift jerk. Livvie gasped, scrambling backward across the bedspread. Caleb caught her ankle and dragged her back toward the edge of the bed. She folded her knees and crossed her arms over her breasts.

The plug in Livvie's ass was clearly visible and the sight sent the strangest series of emotions through him, not the least of which was lust. He leaned forward above her and braced his arm across her legs to keep her bent. He chanced a glance up at her face and saw the terror in her eyes as she strove to remain perfectly still.

He reached down and pressed his palm against the plug. Livvie groaned and shut her eyes but made no move to stop him. Caleb knew it was cruel to keep her in such a position, but his anger and lust kept him from gentling.

Caleb's fingers traced the rim of Livvie's hole, stretched around the plug. "How about this, Kitten? Do you like this? Should I invite everyone downstairs to watch?"

Livvie closed her eyes and turned away with a whimper.

"Look at me," he said and tugged gently on the plug until she complied. "Do you want me to take this out?"

"Yes, Master," she whimpered. Tears ran down her temples.

"Ah! It's Master, now, is it?" he said. "You're so much more obedient when you've something rammed up your ass." He tugged again.

"Please, don't! I only did it because you told me to!" she sobbed.

"Quiet! You don't want to provoke me," he said. His body trembled with rage.

You're scaring her, you idiot. You won't get to her this way.

Caleb knew he was hearing the voice of reason in his head, but he seemed unable to help himself. His fingers traced the edges of the plug, over and over until he could feel Livvie's hips rocking on their own.

"Tell me you like this," he said. Lust edged his voice.

"I like it," she whispered.

Caleb continued his gentle but sadistic exploration. He watched as Livvie's tears wet her face, but her teeth nibbled on her lip. She felt pleasure, but she also felt shame. It was a feeling Caleb understood all too well.

Slowly, he pressed on her muscles and pulled on the plug. He wanted it out. He wanted all evidence of the past twenty-four hours stripped away from her body and from his mind.

"Relax," he snapped when he felt her tighten up. "Push the plug out," he ordered.

"I can't," Livvie sobbed.

"Push, now!" he said and spanked her upturned ass. It wasn't much of a slap, but his point was made. Livvie squeezed her eyes shut and pushed at the same time Caleb slid his finger in around the plug to loosen the suction created by Livvie's ass.

Slowly, he wiggled the plug back and forth as Livvie pushed, until finally it popped out. "Oh!" Livvie cried out.

As Caleb dispensed with the toy, Livvie turned onto her side and wept into his bedspread. He returned shortly, at a loss for how he wanted to proceed. He needed to make her his. He pulled her up off the bed and turned her toward it. His heart ached when she didn't resist.

Easy, Caleb. Don't break her. Win her.

Caleb wrapped his arms around Livvie and pulled her close. He needed her close. She trembled in his arms, her chest heaved with sobs. Caleb buried his nose in her neck and shut his eyes tightly.

"I'm sorry," he said. "I know. I know you only did it because I told you to." Livvie gasped and squirmed in his arms as she tried to turn around, but Caleb held her in place. He needed to say things to her, and he couldn't do it unless his eyes were closed and her body was pressed against his. *That* was his way.

He'd confessed so many things to her in the dark. He'd whispered to her as she'd slept. He'd held her close to him and fantasized about all the things he wanted and yet felt could never be his. He'd discovered a secret place inside himself in those moments.

He was done fantasizing. He wanted his desires to become reality.

"I'm fucked in the head, Livvie. I know it. I know I'm wrong," he whispered and held her tighter. She was frozen in his arms.

"I felt like I didn't have a choice. Felipe's been watching us since we got here. He has cameras everywhere," he continued. Livvie gasped. "But I did have a choice. I could have told him to go fuck himself. I could have killed him right then and there – but I didn't."

"Rafiq will be here soon, and I…. I needed a way to let you go. I needed a way to remind myself I can't keep you." Caleb could feel himself getting choked up. His skin crawled with heat and shame. He was weak to express so much, but now the floodgates had opened – he could do nothing but hold tight to Livvie as he was battered against the rocks.

"I've lived a horrible life. I've done terrible, unspeakable things. You have to know, I'm not sorry. I've never killed anyone who didn't deserve it. The scars on my back are the least of what I've suffered. And it's only because of Rafiq I'm alive."

"No, Caleb," Livvie whimpered.

Caleb squeezed her again, too roughly. He loosened his hold when Livvie whined, but he couldn't let her go. "I don't know how to make you understand. I don't know how to tell you how much

I owe him. I owe him everything! But God help me
– I can't…."

He couldn't say it. He couldn't tell her how
much she had come to mean to him. She could
destroy him with her rejection. If she had feigned her
feelings for him, if he'd bought into her lies and her
quest for freedom…he wasn't sure what he would
do. He could hurt her.

Mine!

"I couldn't stand to see you with that
motherfucker downstairs. I wanted to beat him
unconscious. Even now, I can smell him on you and
it makes me sick!" He growled.

Livvie cried. She struggled in Caleb's grasp until
she freed her arms. She placed them over his hands
and squeezed them. "I didn't want to," she sobbed.
"But…you're just…you're all over the place! One
minute, I think…you *must* feel something. You *have*
to care! But the next…Caleb, you're awful. You're
cruel and you…you break my heart."

Caleb held her as she sobbed in his arms and
never had he wished he could just let go so much.
He wished he were capable of letting everything
come out of him. He wanted to cry. He could feel the
tears in his throat. Everything hurt – his heart, his
throat, even his eyes as he kept them tightly closed.
His arms ached with the intensity of his hold on
Livvie, but he couldn't let it out. He'd trained
himself for far too long, and unlike the job he'd done
with Livvie, he'd trained himself much too well.

"I can't take it anymore, Caleb. I've tried, but I
can't," she sobbed. "Every time I think you're

coming around, every time I let myself hope – you crush me. You rip everything out! Sometimes I think I fucking hate you. Sometimes I know I hate you. And still! Still, Caleb – I love you. I put my faith in you. I believe you when you say it's all going to be alright.

"I'm done," she said with a determination capable of stopping Caleb's heart. "I'm done, Caleb. I'll kill myself!"

Mine!

Pure rage slammed into Caleb. He turned her in his arms and pushed her onto the bed. His body came crashing down on top of her and he held her down. "Don't you dare! Don't you dare say shit like that to me. That's the coward's way out, and you know it," he spat.

Livvie's eyes burned with a rage to match Caleb's own. He could see it. He could feel it. "You're the coward, Caleb. I'm not afraid to tell you how I feel. I'm not afraid to admit that despite everything you've done to me, I love you."

She loves me.

"Do you have any idea how stupid I feel confessing to you?" she continued. "You kidnapped me! You've humiliated me, beat me, nearly gotten me raped, and just a moment ago you had me suck a complete stranger's dick in a room full of twisted perverts. I love you, but I'm not the coward, Caleb. I deserve to live or die on my own fucking terms."

Caleb stared down into Livvie's face, and the steel he saw behind her eyes shook him to his foundation for the second time. Livvie was no coward. He knew it, had even told himself he'd never accuse her of such a thing again, and this had been why. Livvie would do it. She would end her own life. Caleb couldn't breathe.

"I'm sorry," he whispered. It seemed to be all he could say, all he was capable of saying. He relaxed his hold on her and rested his head next to hers on the bed. He made himself breathe past the pain, past the anguish lying in wait in his throat. Slowly, deeply, he breathed.

They lay in silence for several minutes. Caleb could feel Livvie's tears as they slid down her face; they wet his own. It was as close to crying as Caleb could get, and for a moment he imagined they were his tears. They were his confession. They said all the things he couldn't...because he was a coward.

Slowly, Livvie stirred. Caleb wasn't sure what to expect, but then he felt her arms slide around him. Caleb's stomach dipped; his heart felt squeezed. She shouldn't be holding him. He knew it was his place to comfort her, since he was the one responsible for all of her suffering. Still, Caleb was selfish. He let her be the one to comfort them.

"I thought about you," she said numbly, "while he was touching me. I thought about you." Caleb pressed into her in a silent plea for her to stop talking. He didn't want to hear this, but Livvie was done listening to him and he knew it. "I wanted to make you jealous. I wanted to make you feel even a *fraction* of what I felt the night you fucked Celia in front of me."

Caleb winced. His heart felt even tighter. He hoped Livvie's words meant he hadn't lost her yet. Somehow he'd find a way to make it right with her and Rafiq.

"I was insanely jealous," Caleb offered in supplication.

Livvie squeezed him for a moment then loosened her hold. "I know. It should make me happy, but it doesn't." She sighed.

"Why?" Caleb asked softly into her warm, wet neck.

"I'd rather make you happy, Caleb. I'd rather see you smile. Sometimes you smile, and I…" she paused, overwhelmed, "I forget about everything that's wrong with you."

Caleb wasn't sure what to say, so he simply told her the truth. "I'd rather see you smile, too. In the beginning, when I didn't know you…you seemed so sad. I watched you cry one day, and I thought, 'I want to taste her tears'. I have a thing about them. I confess, I've made you cry just to see your tears. I've gotten off on your suffering." He swallowed.

"But now," Caleb said, "I never want to see you cry again. I wish I could go back to the day on the street, the day you thought I'd saved you from the guy in the car, and just…let you believe I was your hero. You smiled at me so sweetly. You thanked me. I wish I'd just let it be."

Caleb could feel Livvie taking deep breaths.

"I know it's what I should want, too," she said, "but I don't. I accuse you of being fucked in the head, Caleb. The truth is… I wonder if I'm not fucked up, too. I should hate you, Caleb. Now I've decided what my fate will be, I should want to kill you. I don't. I can't imagine never having known you.

"Maybe it's fate," Livvie said, "if you believe in that sort of thing. Maybe you were supposed to meet me that day. You asked me once if I'd choose some other girl to take my place. I wanted to say yes."

"You said no," Caleb whispered. He thought about how it might have worked out with another girl – if he'd have the feelings he had for Livvie for someone else. He'd been conflicted from the start. He'd been ready to leave his life as Rafiq's right hand behind until Vladek had resurfaced unexpectedly. Perhaps his emotions had less to do with Livvie and more with his desire to move on from his past. Nonetheless, he doubted it. Livvie was unique to him. Irreplaceable.

"I did, but I wanted to say yes, Caleb. If I had believed for a second you'd let some other girl suffer in my place...I think I might have said yes," she said dully. "I'm fucked in the head, too. Even before I met you."

Caleb let her words sink in for a moment. He didn't believe they were true. Livvie was far from fucked up, especially while he was the standard. However, if Livvie chose to see some greater purpose behind their relationship and therefore not hate him, he was too weak not to let her believe it.

As the silence stretched on between them, Caleb became more aware of Livvie and her nudity. He ached to touch her, to make love to her, but there were more things he had to say first.

"I can't erase my debt to Rafiq," he said. Livvie tensed, but Caleb hurried his words along. "It's not something I expect you to understand, but I can't just leave."

"What do you mean, Caleb? What does it mean, for us?" Her words were said without emotion, but Caleb knew how much she held in check.

"It means I have to make him understand. We'll have to find another way, maybe another girl…" he began.

Livvie pushed at his shoulder and sat up. "Are you fucking kidding me, Caleb? Another girl? How could I live with myself?!?"

Caleb's anger was returning. "You just finished saying…."

"That was before!" Livvie shouted. "I could never put someone through this. Never! Please, Caleb, see reason. Let me get dressed, and let's get the fuck out of here and never look back." She reached out with both hands and held Caleb's face in a vise-like grip. "Please, Caleb. Please."

Caleb stared into Livvie's pleading eyes and for a moment he thought he might open his mouth and say yes.

"I expect obedience, Caleb. I expect your loyalty. Anyone who betrays me will only do it once. Do you understand?" Rafiq had said ominously.

"Yes, Rafiq, I understand," Caleb had replied.

361

"I want to, Livvie," Caleb whispered. "Aside from my revenge, I can honestly tell you, there is nothing I desire more than to take you away and find out what this thing between us is all about." He reached for her hands and placed them in her lap before he stroked her hair affectionately.

"But, this is who I am. I repay my debts. Nothing comes before family, loyalty, duty, and honor. Rafiq is as close to family as I can remember, and I owe him. If you're asking me to betray him...you can never accept who I am."

Livvie shut her eyes tightly, seemingly processing the pain Caleb's words had caused. He felt stupid and naïve. He should have known Livvie would be incapable of understanding him or his motives. Livvie was no monster, and she wouldn't become one simply because Caleb was.

"Why does this guy need to die so badly, Caleb? What did he do? What is so horrible you'd dedicate your life and sacrifice your happiness to kill him? Help me understand, Caleb," Livvie whispered.

Caleb looked at Livvie. Had he seen any trace of condescension, he would have told her to go to hell. But the only thing expressed in Livvie's eyes was concern. He was surprised he even recognized it. Rafiq had never really been concerned for Caleb.

Rafiq had been Caleb's salvation, his tutor, mentor, and sometimes friend. He'd clothed him, provided shelter and food. He'd nursed him from a traumatized whore into a dangerous man. Yet, Rafiq had always demanded his due. At the slightest hint of uncertainty on Caleb's part, Rafiq never hesitated to remind him of his place. Caleb's life had always been conditional. Rafiq's favor had always been conditional.

Caleb had never questioned Rafiq's methods or his authority. It had never mattered to him that Rafiq demanded blind obedience. He had always believed he was lucky to be alive and been grateful for Rafiq. Caleb was still grateful and always would be, but until Livvie, Caleb had never known how it felt to have someone care, truly care, for him.

"I think…" Caleb said as his heart hammered hard in his chest, "he sold me." His flesh felt like it was on fire, like it would burn, crackle, and molt right off his bones.

"Sold? As…as in…?" Livvie seemed at a loss for words.

Caleb looked her dead in the eyes and steeled himself. "It didn't happen last week, alright!" he said angrily. "I was young. I don't even remember how young I was. I have no memories of my life before Narweh. Sometimes, I think I remember something, but I can't be sure. Even my early years with Narweh get mixed up. I wasn't born a monster, Livvie."

Livvie's face crumpled and she seemed to explode with tears. She wrapped her arms around Caleb's neck, squeezing him with all her strength. "Oh, God! Oh, Caleb. I'm so sorry I called you that. I'm so sorry."

Caleb's emotions were everywhere. He didn't want her pity. He never wanted pity. Still, he seemed to need Livvie's arms. He didn't have it in him to push her away.

"I wasn't alone. There were six of us," Caleb said. He held Livvie tight to his chest. "I don't remember being sold. There wasn't an auction or anything. I think I came in a box. To this day, I can't stand cramped spaces – or boats. I hate boats."

"Things…" Caleb struggled, "happened to me. Narweh liked to beat me…among other things." Caleb felt Livvie's arms tighten around him.

Mine!

"I was getting too old, I think. I was tall compared to the others. I had hair on my balls and under my arms. The men who...." Caleb swallowed hard. "They wanted boys, not men. I think Narweh meant to kill me."

"Stop," Livvie sobbed into Caleb's neck. "I can't listen anymore."

Caleb felt something slide loose inside him: shame. Pure, uncut shame rolled through him. "Don't love me now you know I used to be a whore?"

He pushed Livvie away and she flopped backward onto the bed. Her red, puffy eyes fixed on Caleb with disdain. "You're an idiot!" she said and sat up. "I can't listen anymore because I can't stand the thought of you being hurt!" She crawled toward Caleb slowly, wary.

Caleb wanted to run, but he remained immobile as Livvie's words tried to settle into his mind. "It was a long time ago. I made him pay." Caleb met

Livvie's eyes and saw a flicker of realization light her features.

"The bikers," she whispered.

"Yes," Caleb said. He cleared his throat, trying to keep calm when all he wanted was to destroy something in a fit of murderous rage.

Livvie nodded. "Those men deserved to die." Caleb reared back, incredulous. Livvie continued, "Narweh deserved to die, too. And I...I get why you can't let this go."

"You do?" Caleb's heart thudded in his ears.

Livvie smiled, but it didn't reach her eyes. "Yes, Caleb."

"But...?" Caleb prodded.

Livvie's mouth turned down in the corners. "I can't let you replace me. I couldn't live with myself, Caleb. I couldn't live...with you."

"Maybe it's not up to you!" Caleb snapped.

Livvie held up her hand, her fingers curled under as she reached for Caleb. She approached him slowly, as one would a wild animal.

Caleb had the desire to push her hand away, but the sorrow on Livvie's face gave him pause. He let her touch his face, and he marveled at how much affection he could feel in her simple yet complex touch. He closed his eyes and let himself feel loved, just for a few seconds to commit it to memory. It hurt to think it might be the first and last time anyone ever touched him in such a way.

"I can't wait two years for you to come get me, Caleb. I'm done being the damsel in distress. I don't need anyone to save me," she said. Her voice was calm, resolute.

"Livvie…" Caleb began, but she put her fingers to his lips.

"I'll do it, Caleb. I'll go to the auction and I'll be perfect. I'll make the son of a bitch want me," her breath shuddered, "and when we're alone…I'll kill him for you."

Caleb's eyes flew open and he shook his head. "What the fuck are you talking about?"

"You want him dead, right?" Livvie said. "What does it matter who kills him or when? I could poison him or something."

Caleb couldn't help but smile, even as he knew he would never let her do such a thing. The fact she would even offer…

"I thought you weren't interested in revenge?" Caleb teased.

"I'm not interested in *my* revenge, Caleb. But for you…." Livvie whispered, and her eyes said the rest.

Caleb lunged toward Livvie, toppling her backward onto the bed. When Livvie gasped in surprise, he took the opportunity to kiss her. He wished he couldn't taste Kid in her mouth, but he refused to let it stop him. He needed this. He needed Livvie and her love. His heart had never felt so flooded. He felt he could burst open with the strength and force of it. Nothing but need and desire would come pouring out of him.

He put everything he felt, but couldn't put into words, into his kiss. His hands held on to Livvie, pressing her closer, deeper into his body. His inability to touch every part of her at one time seemed a great injustice.

Closer!

Mine!

He broke away from the kiss, only because he needed her permission. He was done taking anything from her she wasn't willing to give. "Can I…." *Fuck you?* Didn't seem right. *Make love to you?* So fucking cheesy.

"Yes, Caleb! For fucksake, yes!" Livvie cried and pulled Caleb back down into their kiss.

Caleb chuckled softly into her mouth but quickly regained his bearings. He wanted this to be perfect. For the both of them. Despite how his own body protested, he pulled himself up and off the bed. He held out his hand for Livvie before he spoke. "I want to take a shower. I've waited a long time for this, and I just want it to be us. I only want to smell *you*."

Livvie blushed but didn't say anything. She took Caleb's hand and followed close behind him as they entered the bathroom to wash all traces of the other man away.

Beneath the flood of warm water, he kissed Livvie. Only hours before, he'd told her he would never kiss her again. What an idiot he'd been! Pressed against her, his bare skin against hers, he regretted every horrible thing he had done to Livvie. He decided he would do anything to make it up to her. He would beg her forgiveness. He would bare his soul. He would bleed and die if he had to, but he would never hurt Livvie again.

"I love you," she said between kisses.

"Shh," Caleb whispered against her mouth. He knew she wanted him to say the words. He wanted to say them as well, but he didn't want to lie. Caleb was a monster. Monsters didn't love. He cared. He hungered. He lusted. He felt more than he ever dreamed possible, and yet…he couldn't be sure it was love. He wouldn't lie.

Caleb went to his knees, kissing a trail across Livvie's body as he went. He sucked water from her nipples, drawing her taut flesh into his mouth in long, greedy pulls. He licked under her breasts and down her ribs. He worshipped her hips and belly. Finally, he parted her legs to find the source of her womanhood.

He could smell her arousal, see the redness of her swollen clit as it peeked out from under her hood. Pushing her legs farther apart, he stared at the open petals of her inner lips. Soon, his cock would be sliding past them and into the heat of her. She would be his – irrevocably. Caleb leaned forward and kissed her lips as he would her mouth.

She moaned and her hands moved toward Caleb's head, pushing him closer. It was exactly where Caleb wanted to be – closer. He teased her lips gently with the tip of this tongue, letting them part slowly as her arousal and his mouth made Livvie wetter. As she rocked on his face, he pushed deeper, tasting her inside.

"Oh, Caleb," she sighed. "Oh, god. You feel so good."

Caleb's hands weren't idle. They traveled up and down her legs, sometimes spreading her thighs, other times scratching up the backs of her legs, forcing her up on her toes. He let them keep traveling as he licked, sucked, and even fucked Livvie with his tongue.

"I'm gonna come," Livvie panted. Caleb grabbed her ass with both hands, holding her in place as he moaned into her pussy and she came on his tongue.

"Caleb!" she shouted and fisted his hair. She couldn't move her hips, so she pulled him close.

Once Livvie had finished shivering, she let go of Caleb's hair. It had hurt, but he was okay with pain, especially under the circumstances. He stood slowly, letting his knees work out the pain from having been on the shower floor for so long, and turned off the water.

Livvie reached out and grasped his cock, startling him. He was hard and her touch made him eager. As quickly as was safely possible, he led the way out of the shower and back into the bedroom. To hell with towels.

"I want you," Caleb said. He slid against Livvie in a preview of what was to come.

"I want you, too," Livvie said and spread her legs. She shivered, her hair and body soaking wet.

Caleb reached down to Livvie's pussy and rubbed her with his fingers, loving the sounds she made and the way she undulated against him. Assured of her desire, Caleb slid his index finger into Livvie's tight, wet hole.

"Oh!" Livvie sighed. She rocked back and forth.

Caleb's head swam with desire. She was so tight inside. Her muscles sucked on his finger, drawing it deeper inside. There was no way he'd fit inside her if he didn't prepare her well enough. He dipped his head down to her nipple and trapped the little bud between his lips. When her hips rocked up, he slipped another finger inside.

"Ow!" she said, followed by a moan as Caleb laved her nipple.

Caleb waited for her to relax and for her legs to drop open again before he slowly began moving his fingers back and forth. Her muscles loosened in degrees, stretching around his fingers, lubricating them with her desire.

"This is going to hurt a little. You know that, right?" Caleb said. He stared down into Livvie's chocolate-colored eyes and saw her trust. He didn't want to betray it again.

"I know. It's okay," she said and pulled him down toward her mouth. The kiss she placed on Caleb's lips was sweet and full of warmth.

Caleb felt the barricade of her virginity with his fingers. "Put your hands over your head," he said. Livvie complied instantly and Caleb used his left hand to pin her wrists. He pushed deeper with his fingers, slowly turning them width-wise.

"Caleb!" Livvie tried to push away from his fingers, her face a twisted mask of pain.

"I know, Livvie. I know it hurts, but it'll be over soon, I promise." Caleb kissed her lips gently, not offended she wasn't kissing him back because she was too wrapped up in her pain.

"Please," she whimpered.

"Relax, Livvie," he encouraged. His thumb made circles around her clit as he continued to push against the wall of her virginity. Finally, he felt it give way. It seemed to dissolve as if it had never been.

"Ow," Livvie whimpered and rubbed her head against Caleb's outstretched arm.

"Shh, it's done. I think that was the worst part," he whispered and kissed her trembling lips. He let her wrists go, and he sighed when she wrapped her arms around his neck and started kissing his neck.

Caleb cautiously slid his fingers out. Livvie whined and stopped kissing him. They both looked at his fingers and noticed her light pink blood on them. Caleb couldn't hear past the sound of his heart beating in his ears.

Mine!

He spared a glance toward Livvie and saw she was embarrassed. Meeting her eyes, Caleb placed his fingers near his mouth and licked her virgin blood off of them. Livvie's face went from embarrassment to horror.

Caleb didn't care. "There. Now you're part of me, forever. You're mine, Livvie. I hope you understand."

Livvie swallowed audibly, her eyes flicking from Caleb's to his fingers and back. "I'm yours," she said, but then added, "only yours. And you're mine, only mine."

Caleb could only smile. He couldn't have said it better himself.

"Ready?"

She ran her hand down his face. "Yes."

Caleb reached down and grabbed his dick. If he'd ever been this hard, he didn't remember it. He was glad this was Livvie's first time, because he wasn't going to last very long and perhaps it would keep her from getting too sore. He rubbed the head of his cock through her wetness, deliberately sliding it over her clit every once in a while.

"Caleb, stop it. Just do it already," she moaned. She was trying to get onto his cock herself, but Caleb kept moving his hips back.

He laughed. "Greedy little pussy, you have."

"Mmm," she moaned. "All the better to make you come."

Caleb almost lost it. He'd never imagined Livvie to have such a dirty mouth. He liked it. "Well, we'll see, won't we?" He pushed into her pussy. He didn't thrust himself inside, but he wasn't too slow. He wanted her to get to the part where the pain was a memory and she could appreciate the pleasure he wanted to give her.

"Oh, god!" she shouted. Her legs wrapped around him in an attempt to hold him still, but Caleb simply lifted her weight and rocked. With her arms and legs wrapped around him, she hung like a pendulum and her momentum forced Caleb deeper.

"Please," Caleb whispered in Arabic, "I want to be all the way inside you."

"What?" Livvie said through gritted teeth.

"I said your pussy is amazing!" And damn it, it was! Caleb sat back on his heels and wrapped his arms around Livvie. He pushed in the last few inches, grunting loudly when he felt Livvie's ass on his balls.

He waited. Livvie held him tightly, leaving kisses on his face, mouth, and neck. She sighed when her muscles finally relaxed and Caleb settled into her.

"I love you," she repeated. "I love you so fucking much."

Buried inside of Livvie, Caleb experienced nirvana. If ever there were a time to repeat Livvie's words, he knew it should be now. He couldn't. He hoped in time, he could. All he could do was caress her, kiss her, and slide in and out of her in the hopes she could feel everything he wanted to express.

"You're mine," he said.

"Yours," she repeated.

Livvie was too tight, too wet, and too fucking incredible inside for Caleb to hold back. He held Livvie in his arms and rocked his hips under, sealing himself against her wet flesh, and he started to fuck. Up and down he bounced Livvie on his dick. He wanted to yell out every time he went balls deep, but he settled for whispering filth to her in a language she didn't understand.

"Oh. Oh. Oh, god," was all Livvie seemed capable of getting out.

Caleb felt heat at the base of his spine and he knew it would be spreading. He was going to come any second and as much as he wanted to, he knew he couldn't come inside Livvie. He laid her down on the bed, fighting her arms as she clutched at his shoulders and back.

"Arms over your head, right now," he ordered.

"Yes, Caleb," Livvie moaned.

Livvie's enthusiastic obedience was enough to push Caleb over the edge. He sucked Livvie's nipple into his mouth. He sucked hard, forcing her to cry out before he pulled his cock out of her and came against her thigh.

Once he was done panting, Caleb held Livvie's trembling body in his arms. He'd never felt happiness like he felt it then, but Livvie was crying. "Are you hurt?" Caleb whispered. He was mortified to think he'd taken more pleasure than he gave.

Livvie reached up, touched his face, and smiled. "I'm okay," she said sheepishly.

Caleb wiped at her tears. "Then why are you crying?"

"I don't know," Livvie said. Her shaking hands stroked Caleb's hair away from his forehead. He closed his eyes, enjoying the proprietary way she touched him. "I think I'm just happy," she whispered.

Caleb let out a short laugh. "Strange response to happiness, but okay." He leaned down and licked at one of the salty tears trailing toward Livvie's ear. He smiled when he felt her try to wriggle out from under him.

"What are you doing?" she asked and laughed.

"I was curious," he whispered.

"About what?"

Caleb looked down at Livvie in wonder. He had done so many terrible things to her, things he could never take back. And still, she loved him. Of all the tears he'd made her shed, these were his favorite. "If happy tears taste the same as the sad ones," he said.

A rush of tears rolled down her face, but her smile widened. "And?" she croaked.

"I think they're sweeter," Caleb whispered. He kissed her lips and discovered what real sweetness was. "But it could just be your face."

Caleb knew he could never undo what he'd just done, and he was glad.

20

Once upon a time, Caleb held me captive in the dark – now he used it to seduce me. His fingertips traced patterns on my skin, while his lips found their way down my spine, leaving goose bumps in their wake. I sighed and arched beneath him, begging him.

"You're spoiled," he whispered at the base of my spine.

"I've earned it," I sighed into the bed. One of his large hands palmed my ass cheek and I found myself lifting my hips. I never wanted to leave Caleb's bed again. I could be content to live out my life being touched, kissed, and made love to by him.

He swatted my behind playfully. "Careful, Kitten – if you put your ass in my face again, you're going to learn what a pervert I really am."

I stilled for a moment, not sure I wanted to play this game, but then I felt Caleb's teeth nibbling at the curve of my bottom and thought fled. Slowly, he sucked my flesh into his mouth and bit me gently. It was the perfect blend of pleasure and pain. His tongue laved each spot before he moved on to the next. Small gasps escaped my mouth with each bite.

"Like that, Pet?" he whispered. He blew gently across my damp skin and I moaned.

"Yes, Caleb," I sighed. He had called me by my name earlier, and while it melted my heart to know Caleb saw me as a person and not a thing, I was just as happy to be his Kitten. For better or worse, Caleb had instilled his tastes in me.

I liked knowing the only thing I had to do to make Caleb happy was exactly as I was told. There was no wrong way to touch him. He took charge and knew what to do. In all the humiliations he had put me through, the one thing he had never done was make me feel bad about my body or my inexperience.

Caleb shifted, and his hands positioned me to suit him. His cock rested against my left leg, while my right was moved up on the bed. I blushed, knowing how exposed I was from behind, but I didn't stop him from exploring. If Caleb wanted something, he was sure to get it one way or another. I chose the path of least resistance and greatest pleasure.

I gasped when his finger stroked the seam of my pussy. I was sore inside, but his soft, skillful touches on my clit were magic. They always had been. As his finger circled my clit, my hips found their own rhythm, sometimes chasing Caleb's touch, others trying to pull away from the intensity. I didn't want the frenzy of orgasm. I was content to languish in the lazy pleasure Caleb cultivated so easily. Caleb resumed his love bites, and I could do little more than writhe and moan.

"Tell me again whom you belong to," he whispered.

I moaned, loudly and unabashedly. "To you, Caleb. I belong to you," I sighed.

"Mmm," he groaned and bit me again. I gasped

but didn't pull away from his mouth. "I wish you weren't sore. I'm dying to get inside you again."

My stomach flipped, and I sounded breathless when I replied, "I want you, too." Instinctively, I raised my hips toward his face. Caleb's arm wrapped around my right hip, holding me in place as his tongue delved into the last place I was ever expecting.

"Caleb!" I screamed and tried to get away from his mouth. I moved like a cat trying to escape water, but Caleb had me where he wanted. The feeling of his tongue sweeping across the bud of my sphincter was an alien and shocking sensation.

"Stop moving," he commanded.

I opened my mouth to protest when his tongue pushed at the entrance to my hole and sound escaped me entirely. I froze out of pure instinct, letting Caleb fuck this secret part of me with his mouth. My muscles ached under the strain of staying so still. After a while, though, I relaxed into Caleb's touch.

He rewarded me by loosening his hold on my hip and returning his fingers to my neglected pussy. At the first touch of his fingers rubbing my clit, I came. It was too much to resist when Caleb's domination of me was so thorough. Just the thought of him having me pinned face down with his tongue in my ass and his fingers stroking my clit was enough to push me over the edge a second time. I dropped like a rag doll onto the bed.

Caleb rolled me onto my back with a sense of urgency and scurried to the top of the bed. He lifted my head onto his knee. I opened my mouth to his cock and swallowed everything he had deigned to give me. Caleb had taken my virginity gently, but this was the version of him I knew I could expect moving forward. I licked and sucked his glorious cock until he told me to stop and he gathered me into his arms. It was the first night in close to four months I felt safe, sated, and loved. I slept like the dead.

Rafiq had been delayed by some unforeseen event and Caleb wouldn't tell me what it might be. For two days and two nights, it had been glorious. We had two entire days of being ourselves, of being free of obligations and thoughts of revenge. Two days of making love every night in Caleb's bed.

Caleb was still a kinky bastard, and I was glad to know his taste for imaginative torments had not abated. The specter of my virginity long gone, Caleb felt free to indulge. He liked to make me beg. Over his knee, with my ass in the air, he'd slide his fingers into me and make me beg to come. I would have done it gladly, but the catch involved letting him spank me until I came. In the end, I could never resist and the begging became as real as my orgasms – and the sting of his palm. Afterward, he'd fling me onto the bed and fuck me into another orgasm before he came. We split most of our time between the bed and the shower.

The third morning, Celia came into the room to open the curtains, a suspicious but playful smirk alight in her features. I hadn't spoken to her since the night of Felipe's party, and when I tried, both she and Caleb seemed opposed to the idea.

"She belongs to Felipe, and for all we know she's here to spy on us. She isn't your friend, and neither of us can afford to trust her," Caleb ranted after Celia left.

"She doesn't even want to talk to me. If she was a spy, wouldn't she be trying to – I don't know – pump me for information?" I said sarcastically.

"Don't be so naïve, Kitten. Your face alone gives away everything between us. You can't hide a thing because your emotions are written all over your face for anyone interested to read," he said angrily.

I couldn't help but smile; I was happy. I didn't want to have to hide it. I knew the situation remained dangerous. "What do you expect me to do, Caleb, just ignore her? She's seen me spread-eagled!"

"I expect obedience; I expect loyalty."

Caleb was apparently less inclined to smile, and I knew it had to do with Rafiq. Caleb continued to struggle with what he called a betrayal. I understood now why the situation was so difficult for him, but my need to survive, my need for both of us to escape, was far more important to me than Caleb's need to make things right between him and Rafiq.

"I'm loyal, Caleb. I can't make any promises as to the rest. You've said it yourself – Rafiq is dangerous. He'll kill anyone standing in his way – that's us. It's us or him at this point, Caleb. It's you who needs to decide where your loyalties lie."

Caleb glared at me for several seconds before his expression softened. He sighed heavily and nodded. "I have to get you out of here, Kitten. I promised to keep you safe and I will, but I've already told you…I can't betray Rafiq any more than I already have. I have to talk to him, convince him there's another way. Then I can come for you."

I scrambled toward him and wrapped my arms around his neck. "I can't leave without you, Caleb. What if you never come back? I'll be out there on my own and anything could happen. What if…what if he kills you? How will I live with myself?" Tears ran down my face as I struggled to find the words to convince him to leave with me and forget about his debt to Rafiq.

"I'm capable of taking care of myself, Kitten. No matter what, I can't leave this unfinished. If we run, he'll never stop looking for us. What then? I have no plans to live my life in hiding. I have to finish things one way or the other," Caleb said. He stroked my hair and tried to be reassuring, but his words left me cold and numb.

"I won't go," I whispered.

"Felipe is having another party tomorrow. There will be lots of people and, I'm hoping, plenty of distractions. You're leaving, Pet. It's the only way I can keep you safe." Caleb hugged me so tightly I didn't have breath to cry.

One more night – it was all we could have. I was determined to make the most of it. I pulled back from Caleb. I wanted to see his face. I wanted to memorize every curve, every eyelash. I looked into his Caribbean-blue eyes and the things I saw stirred my soul, but broke my heart.

"Tell me you love me, Caleb," I whispered.

He kissed me, refusing. "I wish I could, Kitten."

***

I heard pounding – loud and frantic pounding. My eyes flashed open and the dark surrounding me only helped to exacerbate my panic. Caleb was already out of bed.

"Get down on the ground and don't move," he said in an urgent whisper. He went to the closet and flung it open.

I reached for the bedside lamp and turned it on. "What's happening?" I asked. I threw the covers back and scrambled to the ground. Caleb threw something at me and it collided with my chest. He'd given me clothes.

"Put those on, now!" Caleb said. He was climbing into a pair of pants, buttoning them urgently. He fumbled with a box before he got it open. He removed his gun and cocked it.

Adrenaline pounded in my veins. Something bad was about to happen.

"Abra la puerta!" Celia shouted from the other side of the door. She was in a panic of her own and I didn't know what to make of it.

Caleb rushed toward me and slid onto the floor. I wrapped my arms around him, pulling him close. His hands dug into my wrists as he pulled me away. Something cold and hard made its way into my hand. I looked down and saw Caleb's gun.

"Get dressed and stay here. I'll knock two times before I come in. If anyone else comes into this room, you fucking shoot to kill. Do you understand?" he asked.

My panic made me deaf and blind. I didn't understand. I had no idea what Caleb was trying to tell me. He stood and tried to walk away. I grabbed on to his leg. "Caleb! Don't go; don't leave."

"Do what I tell you!" he shouted and pulled free with so much force I was afraid my arm had come out of its socket again. Caleb was at the door before I could catch him again. He held a big knife at his side and stood to one side of the door. He unlocked it slowly.

Celia burst into the room, but she didn't have a chance to say anything before Caleb grabbed her around the neck with his arm and put the knife to her throat. She struggled, but Caleb subdued her quickly and held her still.

"What's going on?" he snarled.

"I came to warn you," she said. "Rafiq and his men are here. They're downstairs with Felipe. They want to see you." Celia's hands held tightly to Caleb's forearm around her throat. "*Por favor*," she sobbed.

"Caleb, let her go," I sobbed. "She came to warn us."

Caleb squeezed Celia's throat until even her sobs couldn't escape. "We don't know, Kitten. She could be here to separate us."

"You're going to kill her!" I urged. I didn't believe Celia would sell me out, but I had no reason to believe she wouldn't. I raised the gun in my hands. "Let her go, Caleb. I'll keep her here."

Caleb stared at me. His eyes weren't his own and

reminded me more of an animal than a man.

"Please, Caleb. Let her go," I begged.

Slowly, Caleb's arm around Celia's throat loosened and she collapsed on the floor, sobbing as she held her throat. I looked up at Caleb and saw the horror in his eyes as he looked down at Celia.

"What's the plan, Caleb?" I said to refocus his attention. As much as I liked Celia, I liked living even more.

Caleb nodded as he fisted a handful of hair at his nape. "I need to go meet them."

"You can't! What if they're just waiting to kill you?!"

"If everything is as Celia says, then there's no reason I shouldn't go downstairs." Caleb went down on one knee and held the knife to Celia's throat.

"No," Celia pleaded, "Felipe sent me to warn you."

"Why would he warn me?!" Caleb insisted.

"Felipe knows what's been happening between the two of you and hasn't said a word to Rafiq. He doesn't want to deal with the fallout. You've been here for months, instead of the few days Rafiq originally promised. The last thing he needs is bloodshed in the house," Celia cried. She rubbed at her throat; it was red, but the damage seemed relatively benign. She could speak clearly and there weren't any bruises.

Caleb stood. "You stay here with her until I get back."

This was my worst nightmare come to life. Caleb was going to walk out the door and never come back. I just knew it. "Caleb, please don't go. Let's leave. Right now."

"I'll get her out if there's trouble," Celia suddenly offered. Caleb and I stared at her incredulously. "There are passages in the walls. Felipe had them built in case we needed to escape. I'll get her out, I promise."

"Why would you?" Caleb asked. He seemed to be coming around toward Celia.

"Not for you," she spat. "I don't want her to suffer."

Caleb nodded. "Thank you, Celia. I'm in your debt."

"If anything happens to Felipe, I'll be sure to collect," she said.

"Understood," Caleb whispered. He grabbed a shirt from the closet and put it on. "The library?" he asked. Celia nodded, and with that, Caleb left the room.

I wanted to scream. Caleb was gone and he'd left me to fend for myself. He'd panicked and perhaps threatened Celia when he didn't have to.

"Why would you bang on the door?" I asked Celia. She sat on the floor, rubbing her throat and wiping tears from her eyes.

"I didn't want them to come looking for you. Felipe barely stopped Rafiq from coming up here himself," Celia said calmly.

I felt the gun, warm from my hand and wet with sweat. "Caleb says Felipe's been watching us. He said *you've* been watching us. Why would either of you help?"

"Felipe trusts no one, Kitten. I'm sorry I didn't tell you, but Felipe means more to me than you. I love him, but he's an opportunist," she said.

My head was spinning. "Did you really come to warn us, Celia? Is Caleb walking into a trap right now?" I tried to sound contrite. I tried to appear like a friend asking for another friend's advice, but truthfully, I wondered if I had it in me to shoot Celia if I had to. The answer terrified me.

"I swear I came to warn you. As far as I know, Caleb is meeting his friends and nothing more. The worst thing you could do right now is panic," she said.

I saw the pleading in her eyes and my instincts told me I could trust her. I wasn't sure my instincts were worth a damn, but the alternative left me cold. Celia was right; I was panicking. If Rafiq had wanted us dead and nothing more, he could have gunned us down in our sleep.

"I believe you," I whispered and set the gun down on the bed. Celia's eyes cut to it, but she remained in place. I started to put on the clothes Caleb had left for me.

"What are you doing? Get undressed. If they come up here and find you wearing Caleb's clothes, they'll know you were planning to escape," Celia said.

"What if something happens and I need clothes?"

"You won't need them, Kitten. I promise. The danger was in Rafiq finding you both together in a compromising situation."

Again, I believed her. Perhaps I would believe

386

anyone who told me I had no reason to kill and no reason to suspect the worst. Perhaps Celia was telling the truth. I chose to believe the less horrific of the two. I quickly removed the shirt I had just put on.

Abruptly, there was a knock at the door. "Celia?" asked a male voice.

I reached for the gun.

***

Caleb struggled for calm as he approached the door to the library. Tucked into the back of his pants and sheathed was his large hunting knife. He wondered for a moment if he was doing the right thing by meeting with Rafiq. He had hoped he could convince him their plans for revenge could still prove fruitful without sacrificing Livvie. He still hoped for that particular outcome, but having Livvie in the house was less than ideal.

Upstairs, Livvie was vulnerable. If anything were to happen to him, he knew she stood little to no chance of escape. Caleb had fucked up, plain and simple. He had let his emotions get the better of him and he'd acted rashly with Celia, who perhaps would sell him and Livvie out the moment the opportunity presented itself. For all he knew, she already had.

There was only one way to find out though, and Caleb was determined to see things to their conclusion – one way or the other. He opened the door and stepped into the library. Four sets of eyes turned to greet him and they belonged to Felipe,

387

Rafiq, Jair, and Nancy. Each of the men had a drink in hand and sat near Felipe's desk chatting about benign things. Nancy knelt at Rafiq's side, her eyes on the floor. She trembled slightly, and Caleb wondered if it was fear or cold causing it but didn't care either way. Caleb breathed a sigh of relief but still felt worried about the situation upstairs. He hoped Livvie could keep her head and not do anything drastic in his absence.

"*Khoya!* Were you sleeping? You look exhausted," Rafiq said with a smile.

"I was," he said cautiously. "I wasn't expecting you so soon."

Rafiq eyed him curiously. "Why would you? I told you I wasn't sure how long it would take to resolve the situation."

Caleb often neglected to take into account Rafiq's political ties to the Pakistani government. From time to time, his job as a military officer took precedent over his more illicit activities. In those circumstances, not even Caleb knew what Rafiq was involved in, and he'd never really cared. If Rafiq wanted to maintain separate lives, it wasn't Caleb's place to meddle.

"I thought you'd contact me is all. If I'd known to expect you, I would have greeted you at the door," Caleb said without bite. Rafiq let Caleb speak candidly in private, but in public, there was a protocol to be followed. Rafiq was older and, as Caleb's mentor and former guardian, in a position commanding respect. To publicly disrespect Rafiq would be folly of the worst kind.

Rafiq smiled. "No worries, *Khoya*. You're here now and so am I. Come," he gestured toward another chair, "have a drink with us."

Caleb managed a smile. "Of course, but let me go upstairs and put on some shoes first. I wasn't sure what to expect and I rushed." What he really wanted to do was go upstairs and give Livvie some relief.

"Where is Celia?" Felipe interjected. His tone was light and jovial, but Caleb saw the way his eyes narrowed and his mouth twisted.

"Upstairs with Kitten. I didn't want to leave her alone," Caleb offered with a warning glance of his own.

"Does she still require constant supervision?" Rafiq asked disapprovingly.

"No, but I thought it best not to leave her alone, just the same," Caleb said before Felipe could offer his own thoughts.

"Hmm," Rafiq replied and took a sip from his drink. It looked like scotch. "Well, have a seat, Caleb. Don't put on shoes on my account. We'll all be retiring soon. I'm tired from so much traveling."

"Of course," Caleb said and took the drink Jair offered him before he sat next to him. Jair smirked, but said nothing, and Caleb decided it was best not to make a scene.

"So, Felipe tells me the girl has been making excellent progress. He says she's even participated in one of his sordid parties," Rafiq said with a smile. "He assures me the girl's involvement did not compromise her virginity."

Caleb swallowed all the liquid in his glass and

winced as the amber liquid burned down his throat. "Yes, that's right." Inside his chest, his heart took up a rapid beat.

"Glad to hear it, *Khoya*," Rafiq said. "Jair had his doubts, but I told him you would never betray me. Not for the sake of one girl."

Caleb turned to scowl at Jair in open disgust. "Of course not, Rafiq. I'll never understand why you listen to anything this pig has to say."

Jair stood and flung his chair back, but Caleb was prepared to meet him. As Jair lunged, Caleb used his upward momentum to push the other man into the air and slam him to the ground. Caleb took advantage of Jair's stunned state and landed a satisfying punch across his face.

"Caleb!" Rafiq admonished. "Get off of him, now!"

Caleb landed another punch and Jair lost consciousness. Caleb couldn't stand the son of a bitch, and regardless of how things turned out, he wouldn't suffer Jair a moment longer. He reached back for the knife in his pants, determined to plant it in Jair's chest, but then felt two sets of hands pulling him backward.

"Caleb, no!" shouted Felipe. "Control yourself in my home."

A flat hand collided with the side of Caleb's face and he knew instantly it had been Rafiq who slapped him. As Caleb struggled to regain his bearing, he heard a gun being cocked just before Rafiq's foot landed on his chest, winding him.

"Jair does what I ask him to do. If you have a

problem with it, you can take it up with me, Caleb. I won't tolerate your disrespect. Apologize to Felipe, or so help me, you will walk with a limp from this night forward," Rafiq shouted.

Behind Rafiq, Nancy was weeping. Caleb held up his hands in surrender. "I'm sorry! I lost control." Rafiq's eyes burned with anger and Caleb knew he wouldn't hesitate to follow through on his threat.

"What the hell would possess you, Caleb?" Rafiq spat, literally.

"He's been begging me to put a knife in him since we met, Rafiq. Do you honestly expect me to let him disrespect me? In front of you? You've never doubted me before. Never! And suddenly, his word means more to you than mine?" Caleb's chest heaved beneath Rafiq's foot.

Rafiq sighed deeply and shook his head. "I never said such a thing, *Khoya*." He removed his foot from Caleb's chest and cocked his weapon one more time to take the bullet out of the chamber. "Things are…."

"I know," Caleb whispered. Their revenge was close at hand and Caleb had jeopardized it. Rafiq had every right to shoot Caleb where he lay. The pain in Caleb's chest suddenly had nothing to do with being held down. He had betrayed the one person who'd never judged him for the things he'd done, for the sake of the one person who loved him in spite of the person he'd become. "I'm sorry," Caleb said again, knowing Rafiq couldn't yet guess how deeply his apology went.

He realized there would be no reasoning with

Rafiq, no compromise over his fate or Livvie's.
There was only one option left, and Caleb had
always known it might come down to it all along.
One of them would have to die.

***

"Celia?" the man repeated. I held the gun in my
hands but didn't know what I meant to do. I looked
toward Celia.

Her eyes were wide as saucers, but she held up
her hands and kept calm. "It's Felipe. Please, put the
gun down."

"Caleb said not to let anyone in. I think that
includes Felipe," I said. I felt faint, my world blurry
at the edges as I considered shooting my way out of
the room.

"Please, Kitten! Don't be an idiot. Felipe will
never let you out of here alive if you don't put the
gun away," she pleaded.

"Tell him to go away," I hissed.

"He'll know something's wrong. I would never
tell him what to do," she said.

Loud knocking and a string of Spanish came
through the door. "Celia, come to the door now or I
will break down the door."

I nearly vomited in my mouth as I considered
going up against Felipe. I looked to Celia and she
frantically wiped tears from her eyes. "Go to the
door," I said.

"What will you do?" Celia sobbed.

"Ask him where Caleb is," I urged.

Celia nodded and slowly crawled toward the door. "I'm in here with Kitten," she said. Her voice seemed calm, and considering her face was puffy with tears, I was impressed.

"Why is the door locked?" Felipe's angry voice asked through the door.

"Caleb was worried," she said. "Where is he?"

"Downstairs with Rafiq. Open the door," he said. It sounded like a command.

Celia looked toward me with a pleading expression. I weighed my options for a few seconds and decided to let Celia open the door, but there was no way I was giving up the gun. I put it on the ground next to me. "Open the door," I said.

"Be calm, Kitten," Celia said, "Felipe won't hurt you unless you make him. Trust me." She waited until I nodded and then turned the lock. She opened the door slowly and Felipe, gun in hand, stepped inside to the side of the door.

"What's going on?" he asked Celia but kept his eyes on me. I was still on the floor, taking cover next to the bed.

"Tell her Caleb is alright," Celia said. She placed herself between me and Felipe.

"Why have you been crying, Celia? What happened here?" Felipe asked. His tone was deadly and calm.

"Nothing, my love. I've just been keeping Kitten company. She's scared, Felipe. Tell her Caleb is alright. She's worried about him," she pleaded.

"He's fine. He and Rafiq are having a drink. He should be up here shortly. We can all wait for him," he said but didn't lower his gun.

"Why didn't he come himself?" I screeched.

"He couldn't, not without raising suspicions. As it was, *I* suspected something might be happening up here. Why were you crying, Celia?" Felipe asked. His tone hinted at his anger.

"It's just girl talk, Felipe. Please don't make a fuss. She was terrified you were coming to hurt her and it made me think about…" Celia's voice trailed off. Slowly, she raised her hand and caressed Felipe's face. "Don't you remember what it was like in the beginning?"

Felipe's eyes turned sad. He lowered his gun and kissed Celia's forehead. "I'm sorry she made you remember," he whispered. "Especially when I've tried so hard to make you forget."

"I have, Felipe. I promise you, I have," she whispered.

Celia still stood between us, and while I didn't necessarily trust Felipe, she had proven herself a friend by remaining between me and certain death. I remembered my conversation in the dungeon with Felipe. He had taken Celia as a trophy and, by his own admission, had not treated her kindly. Looking at them now, it was difficult to picture a time when Felipe was cruel to Celia. Then again, I didn't know either of them very well. Celia didn't seem to have a clue as to how much Felipe loved her. It looked fairly obvious to me.

Felipe nodded and pulled Celia into his arms. She sobbed loudly into his chest as he stroked her hair and whispered reassuring things. Seeing them made me ache for Caleb.

"I'm sorry," I said, "I didn't mean to cause any problems." It was true. I didn't want to cause problems. The only thing I wanted was a way out for me and Caleb.

Felipe looked up at me. "Go wash up, sweet girl. Your master should be coming back any minute and I suggest you're ready for him when he does. You don't have much time together."

"What do you mean?!" I blurted.

Felipe gave me a wry smile. "I wish there was more I could do for the two of you. I've enjoyed watching your relationship unfold. Good luck to you, Kitten."

As I sat, stunned and with my mouth agape, Felipe led Celia out of the room and shut the door behind him. I had surrendered my hostage. I had surrendered my guide. I had surrendered to whatever fate awaited me once the door opened.

21

Day 10: 11pm

Matthew had had a sick feeling in his stomach for the better part of the last hour. The feeling wasn't necessarily new – it had accompanied him many times on certain cases. The world was a sick, fucked-up place and he dealt with it more than most, but this case was shaping up to be a nightmare he'd remember forever. Every agent had a case that haunted them. Olivia and her Caleb would be his.

Some interesting hits had turned up via facial recognition, nation-wide records searches, and the Homeland Security database. Matthew, along with a few other agents, had started putting the pieces together over the last five hours.

"I think Karachi makes the most sense given the intel," Agent Williams said. She'd flown in from Virginia once the sensitive nature of the case became clearer.

"I agree. The boys at the FIA aren't going to like what we have to say, but it looks like Muhammad Rafiq has been making use of military resources to cover up his human trafficking ring," Matthew said.

Karachi was a coastal city, accessible by air and sea. It was an ethnically and socio-economically diverse area, capable of camouflaging rich and poor alike. According to information from SSgt Patel, who had access to the passenger manifests and air traffic control documentation, several high visibility persons of interest would be arriving in the next two days. Many were already in the city. Unfortunately, none of the names on the list were Vladek Rostrovich or Demitri Balk. Still, Matthew reasoned, he could be traveling under a different alias. One thing was certain though – Muhammad Rafiq would be in attendance.

He thought about Olivia Ruiz and everything she had been saying over the last several days. She had no idea how deep Rafiq's involvement in the slave trade ran. Based on the pile of information on Matthew's desk, he was beginning to suspect Caleb had no idea either. Rafiq had been in it for the money for a very long time. The evidence suggested he'd been a key player since 1984.

Matthew held up a picture of Vladek Rostrovich and Muhammad Rafiq taken in Pakistan that same year. Rafiq wore his military uniform and pointed to a table full of Russian weapons, his arm slung over Vladek's shoulder.

Matthew's best guess was that Muhammad Rafiq had acted as Vladek Rostrovich's arms broker during his missions in other parts of the world, most notably in Africa, Turkey, Afghanistan, and Pakistan. Perhaps guns had begun the connection, but it hadn't ended there.

Another photograph from 1987 showed Rafiq and Vladek at a Pakistani military dinner. Vladek sat at the officers table with Rafiq; also in attendance was Bapoto Sekibo. He was notorious for razing entire villages, killing men, women, and children in the pursuit of natural resources and valuable territories for corporate projects coming in from other countries. Some of the corporations even had roots in the U.S. In fact, all three men had been photographed at one time or another with U.S. Senators or CEOs of major companies.

Matthew wasn't surprised sex, guns, and money were interconnected. Even Vladek's African diamond mines didn't come as a shock. No, the most shocking piece of information was an unsolved missing person's case from 1989 sitting on the pile. He couldn't resist picking it up and staring at the picture paper-clipped to the file.

"Pretty fucked up, huh?" Agent Williams whispered from across the desk.

The sick feeling in Matthew's stomach flared and he rubbed his stomach. As he stared at the photo, he wondered what, if anything, he should do with the information. "Yeah. It is."

"You okay? When's the last time you ate?" Williams asked.

"Hours ago, and just a salad. Been on a steady stream of coffee since then," Matthew said and offered a watery smile. It was nice working with someone, even if Agent Williams was a little too young and bright-eyed for his tastes. She still got excited about the job and didn't hide it very well. Matthew didn't really get excited anymore – solving cases was an obsession, locking the bad guys up, satisfying – but he'd stopped being excited a long time ago. No matter how many cases were resolved or how many villains were brought to justice, there were always new cases and new bad guys. It was a vicious circle.

"That stuff'll kill you," Agent Williams said through a smile. "I still have half a turkey sandwich in the fridge if you want it?"

"No, that's okay. I'm not hungry," he said.

"You keep staring at that picture?" she hedged.

Matthew couldn't stop thinking about Olivia. She was mourning the loss of a man she didn't really know, and for the first time, Matthew was beginning to understand why she fought for him so strongly. "The witness says he died helping her escape. I'm wondering if it should just stay there. I mean, I wish I didn't know this. I can't imagine how the mother would feel."

"I try not to think about that stuff. Not really our priority, you know?" Williams said. "It's going to be a bitch getting a team into Pakistan. I'm trying to just focus on one thing at a time. Some kidnapped kid who turned out to be a serious prick isn't really on my radar."

Matthew looked up at Williams. "How old are you, Williams?"

She stiffened. "Twenty-four," she answered. "Why? Are you going to give me shit about my age?"

He held up the photograph. "James Cole was a few months shy of his sixth birthday when he was taken. Just try to imagine your life the past eighteen years and how different it was compared to the hell this little boy had to live through."

Williams stared long and hard at the photograph

before she turned away to mess with the files on her own side of the desk. "It's sad, Reed. I know it's sad, but there's nothing we can do for that kid. And the man he turned out to be? He's better off dead," Williams said.

"I'm not trying to defend him. Trust me, I've spent the last week doing exactly the opposite. It's just…she has a way of making me think about things. She basically talked her way out of being sold at the auction." Matthew smiled. Olivia was certainly unlike any person he'd met in his thirteen years on the job. He would never forget her or Caleb, and the boy he'd been. He would never forget this case, and for whatever reason, he felt the need to take a moment and preserve the memory of it correctly.

"Pretty smart girl. Except for the falling in love with her captor part," Williams said. "*Although*, if you're going to fall for any kidnapper, good *gawd*, he should be as handsome as this son of a bitch." Williams lifted Caleb's surveillance photo from a few years back and waggled her eyebrows.

Matthew laughed. "You're sick. You know that, right?"

Williams shrugged. "I don't get out much."

"Why's that?"

"Eh, the job, I guess. I don't really get off on dating other agents, and normal guys can't deal." She shrugged again.

"Do you think we should let his mother know we found him?" Matthew asked.

"It's been twenty years, Reed. She's probably

thought he was dead for a long time. I don't think telling her we found her son and he just so happens to be a human trafficking son of a bitch who died in a botched escape attempt is exactly consoling," Williams said, wryly. She and Matthew sat in silence for a few moments before Williams added, "She's better off believing her little boy died innocent, you know?"

Williams had a point. "Yeah. I just wish...I wish I'd been in the Bureau back then. Maybe I could have found him before it was too late." He thought about Olivia and her grief. It was sad, knowing she was the only one who would miss Caleb. She was the only who would mourn him.

"Wait!" Williams said suddenly and startled Matthew.

"What is it?"

"Well, it's not really relevant, but..." She handed one of her files over to Matthew. "Vladek went to college in the U.S. He went to the University of Oregon," she whispered.

"So?"

"So, check the date," she added grimly.

"He didn't finish. He was there '80 to '82." Realization was slowly dawning on Matthew, and he felt bile crawling up into the back of his throat. "James Cole was born in 1983. In Oregon."

"You don't think?"

"Olivia Ruiz mentioned Rafiq wanted revenge against Vladek, something to do with his mother and sister. Apparently, Vladek killed them, or so Rafiq says. I'm starting to think everything out of the

401

guy's mouth is bullshit."

"Do you want me to pull James' birth certificate?"

"Yeah, do that. Did you already call the Deputy Director to let him know we think the auction is taking place at the military cantonment in Karachi?"

"I told him an hour ago – figured he could get started on organizing the op. That SSgt Patel doesn't seem like the cooperative type. Holy fuck, Reed…do you honestly think Vladek would sell his own fucking son?!"

Matthew wanted to start punching things. "No. I think he was collateral damage." It was all starting to come together. The pieces of the puzzle were slowly forming in Matthew's mind. There were still huge pieces missing, but Matthew thought he could make out the picture just the same.

"Well, we already know where the auction is. Everything else is just gravy at this point. Let me finish pulling these records, and then I say we pack it in for the night. If we get the green light, we could have Rafiq in custody in the next seventy-two hours. We can get our answers straight from the source," Williams said.

Matthew could hear the anger and determination in Williams' voice. He admired her fire, but he'd been around long enough to know fire could get you burned. "I doubt we'll even get a crack at him, Williams. Be prepared."

"What do you mean? We have a mountain of fucking evidence and a witness," Williams spouted.

"What we *have* is a high ranking military official

from a foreign government accused of crimes in a completely different country. I want this guy. I want him bad, but I've been here before, Williams. Sometimes…they get away."

"Then why are you here, Reed? Why have you been working this case so damn hard?"

"Olivia Ruiz was the original perpetrator. She caused an international incident when she decided to cross the U.S.-Mexico border waving a gun. She didn't become the victim until later. I had no idea this case was going to become the juggernaut it is. I've worked the case, Williams. It's all any one of us can do," Reed said.

"Yeah, well…it's not over yet, Reed."

"Never said it was, Williams."

"Ugh!" Williams sighed.

"What is it?"

"I have James Cole's birth certificate. His father is listed as 'Vlad,' with no known last name. There's a death certificate here too, seven years after James disappeared. That's pretty standard, I guess. Let me see what I can find on the mother, Elizabeth Cole." Williams shook her head. "She died in 1997. Coroner's report reads self-inflicted gunshot wound to the head."

Matthew's heart felt like it was sinking. James Cole had been kidnapped when he was five and sold into slavery. It had most likely been an act of revenge against his father, Vladek Rostrovich. He'd been beaten and abused most of his life, and according to Olivia Ruiz, the only person he had ever trusted had been the one to ruin his life in the first place.

"This is depressing the hell out of me, Reed," Williams whispered.

"Yeah." Matthew cleared his throat. "Me too. I just thought I could give the poor woman some peace, but it looks like she found it on her own."

"We should get some sleep. Chances are, we're going to have a full day tomorrow. If everything goes well, you'll be on a plane to Pakistan to lead the raid. *Do* try to remember the little people when you're promoted." She smiled impishly and fluttered her lashes for effect.

Matthew managed a short laugh. "I'll try, Agent…?"

"Williams."

"Right. Williams." Matthew continued to go over the stack of files on his desk as Williams got ready to leave. He knew he should be doing the same, but he couldn't let it go quite yet.

"Why do I get the feeling I'm going to see you sitting there when I come back in the morning?" Williams said as she slung her laptop bag over her shoulder.

"I'll be out of here soon. I just want to poke around a little more. I couldn't sleep right now anyway – been drinking coffee all night, remember?"

"Yeah, yeah, likely story. I'll be in around seven if we're not called up sooner. I'll bring you something to eat and maybe some coffee that won't eat through your stomach," she said.

"I like the coffee."

"Suit yourself," Williams said as she stepped into the elevator.

Matthew stood up and grabbed the files on Williams' desk. He'd done his job. The rest would fall to the Bureau and the justice department. Regardless, the puzzle wasn't solved, and he couldn't stop putting it together. Olivia deserved to know the truth.

Three hours later, Matthew had a list of events and possibilities. He'd learned a lot of things about the major players in the case but had just as many new questions as he did answers:

1960: AKRAAN Arms Co. Est in Russia by?
- Vladek's father?

1961: Vladek Rostrovich, born – youngest of 3

1963: Muhammad Rafiq, born – eldest son (younger sister?)

1980-1982: Vladek, U of Orgegon (no major?)
- Meets Elizabeth Cole (student?)
- Father, 2brothers die in car accident (Dec '82, Vladek becomes heir)

Aug 3, 1983: James Cole, born. (Vladek?)

1983-1988: Vladek/Rafiq – arms dealing, trafficking
- Diamonds?
- Look into '87 thru '89

Mar 14, 1989: James Cole, kidnapped (no suspects)

405

- Kidnapped by Rafiq? Motive?
- Look into Rafiq's mother/sister death (motive)

1992-1994: Rafiq, Desert Storn
- Stash Cole instead of kill? Ransom? Collateral? What am I missing?
- James Cole kept in brothel (Narweh – deceased?) Check years 1989-?
- Narweh (no known last), need death cert
  - Pakistan? Review Ruiz statement for other possible

1997: James Cole (Caleb) 'rescued' by Rafiq
- See: Ruiz statement about seeking revenge 12 yrs
- Why would Rafiq come back for 'Caleb' (age 14)

2002: Balk Diamonds goes public
Why deleay btwn 1987-2002? Reivention or hiding?
Vladek knows about son? No current offspring.
James Cole is sole heir?

2009: Olivia Ruiz, kidnapped
James Cole 'Caleb' deceased?
Balk suddenly interested in slave trade? Motive?
Balk – location unknown. ?????

22

Caleb swirled his scotch in his glass but didn't take a drink. His thoughts were with Livvie. Felipe had gone upstairs, despite Caleb's best efforts to stall him and get there first. Fifteen minutes had passed and he hadn't heard a gunshot – or any screams. Good news, but his worries were far from dispelled. He wanted his wits about him if things suddenly took a turn for the worse. In many ways, they already had.

Caleb's mind felt ravaged over how to deal with Rafiq. Their relationship had always been complicated, but it remained the closest Caleb had to family or friendship. Rafiq had been Caleb's salvation and so many other things over the years… and now he contemplated killing him.

Caleb knew he couldn't run away with Livvie. Rafiq would hunt them down to the ends of the earth, and while Caleb could take care of himself, it was no life for Livvie. She deserved better. He had considered separating himself from her, but he knew if Rafiq couldn't find Caleb, he would find Livvie again and use her to get to him.

Rafiq deserved his revenge. Livvie deserved to live her life. That left Caleb thinking about what he deserved: nothing. He'd fought so hard to live, to survive, and he didn't relish the idea of ending it all, but he would…for Livvie, he would. He'd lived a meaningless life that would culminate in him destroying every meaningful relationship he'd ever had. At the very least, he thought, he could have meaning in his death.

"What has you so troubled, *Khoya*?" Rafiq asked in Arabic, now they were alone. He had sent Jair away once he'd regained consciousness, and Felipe had used the opportunity to excuse himself from the room. Nancy remained, but she seemed unaware of her surroundings as she huddled on the floor and supported Rafiq's legs on her back.

Caleb gestured toward her with his drink. "Is that really necessary?"

Rafiq smiled. "No, but she's here, so why not make use of her? Answer my question – what has you so troubled?"

Caleb's heartbeat accelerated and heat traveled down his spine, but he attempted nonchalance. "Things are moving quickly now. I keep going over things in my mind."

"Yes, it's been a long battle. I don't know which of us has sacrificed more to see Vladek suffer. The auction is only the first step. It will be up to you to earn his trust, but it will be worth it when everything he has belongs to us, even his very life," Rafiq said. He took another drink of scotch and Caleb noted it was his third.

"Yes," Caleb replied, but his tone hinted at his unease.

"You've been strange these last few months, Caleb. I would have thought you'd be happier to have your vengeance so close at hand," Rafiq said. He sounded irritated.

408

"Why can't I just kill him, Rafiq? I would do it. Gladly and in front of everyone, I would kill him. We're wealthy men. We don't need his company, or his money," Caleb said and instantly regretted it.

"It's not about the money, Caleb! It never has been. I want it because it's the only thing he loves as far as I can tell. If you knew of the things he's sacrificed for his precious billions, it would be all you could do not to find him now. Tonight! He has no wife, no children. He trusts no one! And he has taken everything from me. Death is not enough. Torture is not enough. I thought you of all people would understand!"

Hadn't Caleb said something similar to Livvie? It seemed like ages ago, the night he'd rescued her from the bikers and informed her of her fate. She'd asked him why?

"I have obligations, Kitten." He swallowed deeply. "There's a man who needs to die. I needed you...need—" He paused. "If I don't do this now then I'll never be free. I can't walk away until it's done. Until he pays for what he did to Rafiq's mother, to his sister – until he pays for what he did to me." Caleb stood abruptly, his chest heaving. He ran angry fingers through his hair and fisted his hands at his nape. "Until everything he loves is gone, until he – feels it. Then I can let it go. I'll have repaid my debt. Then, perhaps...maybe."

"I do, Rafiq. I do understand. For twelve years, my life has been nothing but our quest for revenge.

I'm just tired, Rafiq. I'm tired and I want it to be done. I want him dead and I can't wait for him to die slowly. I'm ready to move on," Caleb said. It was the truth. He was ready to move on with his life and he wanted it to be with Livvie. He wanted what could never be.

Caleb stared at Rafiq; the man wasn't well. His hair seemed grayer, his face harder, and his eyes lacked the slightest glimmer of compassion. In the entire time Caleb had known him, he had never taken a slave for his own. Trained them, yes – kept them, no. The fact he'd kept Nancy alive this long and broken her down so thoroughly spoke volumes about his mental state.

Caleb continued, momentarily resigned to his fate. "Have you no thought for me? *Brother.* All those years I spent as a whore? No one knows better than you everything I suffered. Did you never think I might want to forget? All those years of being your shadow, learning how to kill, and training whores for the very men who would have used me – did you never think I might want to just walk away from it and be…I don't know! Something more!" Caleb felt as though a floodgate had been opened in his soul.

"I was finally going to show her she was wrong about me…"

"You *are* something more, Caleb. *I* made you something more. I made you a man. I delivered you! I made others quake in fear of you. Who were you before me? *Kéleb!* That's who you were! A dog."

Rafiq slammed his glass on the end table near his chair and kicked Nancy over for good measure. Nancy's sobs quickly filled the room, but she held her hands over her mouth to stifle them.

Pure, uncut rage thrummed in Caleb's veins, and he'd never wanted to strike Rafiq so much. Only his thoughts of Livvie staid his hand. Her life was in danger and it remained Caleb's responsibility to keep her safe. "I know who I am, Rafiq. I know *what* I am. And I know I owe it all to you. You've spoken to me so much about loyalty, but only minutes ago you were willing to maim me to protect Jair, of all people. Where is the loyalty?"

"I told myself you couldn't help yourself. I told myself something happened to you to make you this way, to make you as fucked up as me, but you're even more fucked up than I am. And in the strangest corners of my mind I thought..."

Caleb remembered Livvie's fear, her despair. She'd been brutalized by several men, beaten and bloodied. She had thought Caleb was her savior. Caleb was no one's savior. He looked at Rafiq and saw the worst parts of himself reflected in the other man.

"That you could fix me? What's more, that I could fix you? Well, sorry, Pet, I don't want to be fixed."

Rafiq leaned forward, the devil in his eyes. "We've known one another for a long time, Caleb. You understand how important this is to me. I won't tolerate anyone interfering with our plans – not even you."

"You ran. I went to collect my property. End of story. In two years, maybe less, I'll have what I want – revenge."

For Rafiq and Caleb, it had always been about revenge. It had been the only thing that had *ever* mattered. Not friendship. Not loyalty. Not justice. It seemed so trivial now, so small when weighted against the price: Livvie. "I want to kill Vladek and I want it to be the end," Caleb whispered.

Rafiq let out a derisive snort and sat back. "This is about the girl, isn't it?"

Fear quickened Caleb's pulse. "No! This is about us. It's about our partnership and how much it has always been weighted in your favor."

"We proceed with the plan, Caleb," Rafiq said resolutely. "You've overstepped your boundaries and taken advantage of the love I have for you for the last time. You're tired and not yourself, and so I will try to forget the things you've said tonight – but I will not tolerate your disrespect again. Consider yourself warned."

Caleb took a moment to regain his calm. He was tired and tonight could very well be the last time he and Rafiq talked as friends. Sadness crept in around the edges of his anger. "I'm sorry, Rafiq. I haven't been fair. For twelve years you've looked after me when you didn't have to, and I don't want to sound ungrateful. I was an angry and willful boy, and it couldn't have been easy to take me in. I would be dead if not for you...or worse. Forgive me."

Rafiq seemed to soften. He sat back in his chair and thoughtfully eyed Caleb. "You're forgiven, *Khoya*. Perhaps I wasn't always kind or considerate of you, either. You've earned your keep and my respect." Rafiq stood and poured himself another drink and tilted it toward Caleb. "Drink with me, to loyalty."

Caleb raised his glass with some effort. "To loyalty." The liquid burned his throat and sat heavy in his stomach where it met with his shame and conspired to make him retch.

"We leave the day after tomorrow. I've arranged for a pilot and a private plane to fly us home. It will be a longer journey, avoiding customs, but I don't trust the girl. I'm not taking any chances. I'll resume her training in the morning. I want to be sure she's ready," Rafiq said. He seemed in higher spirits.

Caleb's heart sank. "Wouldn't it make more sense for me to maintain control of her training until we land in Pakistan? She's frightened of you, and it might prompt her to behave rashly."

Rafiq's brows furrowed. "You've coddled her enough, *Khoya*. It's time she understood her place."

"Have you thought about what might happen to her after we're done with her?" Caleb asked while trying to remain respectful.

Rafiq smiled. "Ah! You do want her, then?"

413

"No, Rafiq. Not after Vladek has had his way with her. I'm only curious if you have any plans for the future."

"I'll leave it to you, *Khoya*. Consider her your reward for a job well done. *When* it's done, of course," he said with a smile.

Caleb offered a smile of his own, though all he felt was anger and despair. Caleb stood slowly and embraced Rafiq as he said goodnight. In his heart, he knew it was also a farewell.

"Will you miss me, Caleb?" Livvie put her arms around Caleb. He held her in place.
"Yes," he said simply.

On his way back to his room, he ran into Felipe in the foyer.

"My, don't you look serious tonight." Felipe's accented words brought Caleb to a halt. Felipe walked over to him and led him toward one of the temporary bars he had set up for the party the following evening. "I believe you could use a drink, my friend."

Felipe walked behind the bar and poured them both a short glass of bourbon. He handed Caleb a glass and then lifted his, saying, "To a long life filled with love." He drank and then set his glass down on the bar when Caleb didn't reciprocate.

"I realize I owe you my gratitude, but I'm short on gratitude at the moment," Caleb said.

Felipe smiled. "Yes, that was close."

"Why would you help me?" Caleb asked, suspiciously.

Felipe shrugged. "I'm romantic. Also, I have no interest in having blood spilled in my home. Too messy." Felipe's expression turned quizzical. "What will you do, Caleb?"

Caleb didn't trust Felipe. "Rafiq insists on taking over Kitten's training. We leave the day after tomorrow. That should make you happy."

"Hmm," Felipe said and poured himself another glass of bourbon. "Rafiq insists on a lot of things, doesn't he? He's expecting a virgin."

Caleb bristled. "What exactly is your relationship with Rafiq?"

"He says we're friends, but I'm not sure I would put it quite that way. We're in business together. I'm surprised you didn't know, or at least that you didn't ask me sooner."

"What sort of business?" Caleb asked. His curiosity was piqued.

"This and that – it doesn't really matter, Caleb. I was only surprised you never asked the question. I suspect Rafiq never cared for questions. Are you truly going to give him the girl?" Felipe lifted an inquiring brow.

Caleb narrowed his eyes. "I don't have much a choice, do I?"

"There's always a choice, Caleb."

"What do you want, Felipe? You say you're in business with Rafiq – why are you so interested in me and what I'm doing?"

"Can I trust you?" Felipe asked with a smile.

415

"I'm trusting you to keep quiet about everything you've seen on your nasty little cameras. The most trustworthy relationships involve collateral."

Felipe chuckled. "Well, I *have* enjoyed watching you. Why not take the girl and run?"

"What do you want?!"

"I want Rafiq out of my business," he said as he swallowed his bourbon, "permanently."

"I could kill you for saying that," said Caleb.

"You could. Then you'd never know the truth," Felipe countered. He sighed and waited for Caleb to reply. When he didn't, Felipe said, "I've waited a long time for you to come forward to me with your past. I'd hoped we could be friends."

Caleb stared across the bar at Felipe, stunned. "You know my past? Wait...no. You heard me on the camera." He glared at Felipe with murderous intent.

"I know you were in Tehran. You never said *that* on camera," Felipe said.

Caleb's vision was blurry and his heart was racing. "Rafiq could have told you. You could have overheard our conversations."

Felipe became gravely serious. "Collateral, Caleb. Tell me a secret. One you've never told anyone and could cost you your life."

"Why the fuck would I, Felipe? You're not making any goddamn sense," Caleb growled. The world shifted beneath his feet, or so he thought.

"What I could tell you would change everything you have ever believed, and I need to know you can be trusted to do the right thing," Felipe said ominously.

Caleb didn't want to know. Whatever Felipe had to say wasn't going to be good, but he *had* to know. It was Eve and the apple all over again. Knowledge was the forbidden fruit, and once tasted, it could damn ones soul – but it was in mankind's nature to bite. "Felipe," Caleb choked out, as anger came to the surface. His body shook and his skin burned.

"A secret, Caleb," Felipe whispered and leaned forward.

There was nothing left to lose, except the girl. "I can't."

Felipe shook his head, "Then I can't help you. Goodnight, Caleb." He turned to walk away and Caleb grabbed his shoulder.

"Tell me," he growled.

"You first." Felipe gripped Caleb's hand and flung it off his shoulder.

"I...assure me the girl will be safe," Caleb said, and it felt like yet another betrayal. The implications alone were a death sentence for him and Livvie. Of course, Felipe already knew what she meant to him.

"What would you do for the girl, Caleb? Would you die for her? Would you kill?" asked Felipe in a whisper. He looked around the room, and Caleb did the same. They were alone.

Caleb's heart thundered in his chest. "Yes."

"Would you live? Could you live knowing your entire life has been a lie?"

Caleb was one second away from throttling Felipe and forcing him to talk. He still had his knife tucked into his pants, and already he was thinking of his plan of attack. "Tell me…now!"

Felipe sighed. "Follow me into the dungeon. I'll tell you everything, but you won't like it."

"Where's Kitten?"

"Upstairs and unharmed. If you care for her as much as I believe you do, I would suggest you keep your wits intact. If all goes as I hope it will, the both of you can leave this place together and never return." Felipe said.

"Why? Why now? All this time and you've never dangled information in front of me," Caleb said through gritted teeth. Felipe wanted Caleb to do something. It meant he couldn't be trusted. Caleb's mind was already churning with ideas on how to get rid of him. Still, Caleb wanted to hear what Felipe had to say. Perhaps he could use it to sway Rafiq.

"I'm a businessman, Caleb. One does not achieve my level of success without first being able to spot an opportunity. Twenty years ago, I saw an opportunity to stop being a lieutenant and become a general. Rafiq was useful then. Six years ago, I saw an opportunity to expand my business by eliminating my competition. I own half of Mexico now and do business around the world. Rafiq has become…less useful, and as I said, he insists on a lot – too much. You provide me an opportunity, Caleb. In exchange, I can give you the truth about who you are and where you come from."

"Admitting you want Rafiq out of your way doesn't give me a reason to trust you," Caleb said in hushed tones. "Why would you need me to do your dirty work?"

"Appearances, Caleb – they're everything. I've had plans to get rid of Rafiq cleanly, without inciting the loyalty of our mutual friends. However, I've been watching you…and the girl. I know what love can do to a man, and I know how desperate you are."

"Fuck you! I'm not desperate!"

"Aren't you? I wasn't sure at first. When you allowed the girl to play at my party, I thought your loyalty to Rafiq knows no bounds. But I saw how it affected you, how jealous you became. I know you took her virginity. Did you think you found all the cameras?" Felipe smiled smugly. "I didn't have to come to you, Caleb. I've put myself and Celia in a compromising situation, and I don't do it lightly. I'm offering you vengeance. I'm offering you a chance to live out your days with Kitten. Do you want it or not?"

Caleb thought about everything Felipe said. Felipe knew everything between him and Livvie and hadn't said a word. Caleb knew nothing about Felipe's plans until now, and the fact he'd offered the information himself only solidified his trustworthiness. Caleb had nothing left to lose and everything to gain. "Lead the way," he said.

As Caleb followed Felipe down the dark wooden stairs, he contemplated pushing him. However, he'd made up his mind to hear what the man had to say. He could always kill him after. Caleb reached for the light and turned it on as they descended.

He thought of the last time he had been down here. He'd strapped Kitten to an exam table and watched her play with her pussy. He smiled to himself.

When they arrived at the bottom, Felipe pointed to a chair near the wall. "I'll need you to sit there, and I'll need to tie you up."

Caleb's steps faltered and he reached for his knife. He held it out in front of him, blocking the stairs. "You've lost your fucking mind if you think I'm going to let you tie me up."

"Don't be a child! Your anger makes you stupid and I don't need you acting rashly. What I have to tell you is going to boil your blood, and I can't have you loose in the house!" Felipe shouted.

"Tell me what you have to say! Or you die now! I'm tired of your games, Felipe," Caleb said.

Felipe's eyes shone with fury as he held up his hands and backed away from Caleb. Abruptly, he reached behind him and pulled out his gun. "Sit. Now."

Adrenaline surged through Caleb's veins, but he knew he was at a disadvantage. He'd played directly into Felipe's hands. He weighed his options and was horrified to discover they were few and ended in his death. His only true concern was for Livvie.

"Swear to me the girl is safe," Caleb whispered and he realized it sounded like a plea. It had been a long time since Caleb had begged for anything.

Nothing left to lose, Caleb. Fuck your pride.

"I swear it," Felipe said evenly.

Caleb swallowed. "You can keep the gun on me. There's no need to tie me up."

"Come inside and sit down. I'll leave you free, but if you attempt to get by me, I *will* shoot you, Caleb. Do you understand?"

"Yes," Caleb said and did as Felipe asked.

"Did Rafiq ever tell you how his mother and sister died?" Felipe asked.

Caleb's heart felt like it might burst clear out of his chest. His mind was fixated on Livvie, on seeing her again, on getting her to safety. Felipe's questions seemed strange, and Caleb suddenly wished he'd never agreed to listen. "Vladek killed them."

"Did you never wonder why?"

Caleb *had* wondered, many times, but Rafiq had explained it all away by saying Vladek had been a criminal, simply passing through and fixating on his sister. "Get to the point!"

Felipe sighed heavily, "Very well. Rush me if you must, but keep your mouth shut and listen. *Rafiq* killed them."

Caleb's face contorted in disbelief. "You're lying!" He stood and took a step forward. He stopped when Felipe drew the hammer back on his revolver.

"Sit down! It's only the beginning," Felipe's accent was thicker when he was angry. Caleb sat. "I met Rafiq and Vladek in the 80s. The two of them were dealing in stockpiled Russian weapons. My boss at the time was accepting shipments from them in exchange for cocaine and heroin. Over the years,

421

all of us became…friends. Rafiq and Vladek were especially close."

Caleb felt dizzy, but he maintained his bearing.

"The stockpile eventually dwindled, but by then, Vladek had become the heir to his father's company in Russia. His father and brothers…met with an unfortunate accident. Anyway, things were good for a while, but nothing good lasts forever, as they say."

"Again," Caleb shouted, "get to the fucking point!"

Felipe smiled. "I'm tempted to put a bullet in you, Caleb. Shut up!

"Rafiq's father died, leaving him in charge of his mother and sister. Rafiq loved them very much and doted on them, especially his sister, A'noud. We were all young men then. Young men are stupid. Vladek stuck his dick where it didn't belong."

Caleb felt as though he'd been hit by lightning. "Rafiq's sister," Caleb said. Memories were strange. No matter how much time elapsed, or how a memory could change, a person still trusted their own mind. Caleb, the boy, had trusted Rafiq implicitly. It only made sense for Caleb, the man, to trust him as well. Still, the information, while surprising, was not damning or life changing. Caleb could understand why Rafiq would be angry.

"Yes," Felipe said. "When Rafiq discovered his sister was pregnant and Vladek was the father, he strangled his sister in a murderous rage."

"I don't believe you!" Caleb hissed. Rafiq wouldn't murder his own family, no matter how angry he might have been.

"Don't interrupt!" Felipe said. "It will all make sense to you in a few minutes. Rafiq's mother tried to protect her, and she met the same fate. Rafiq was riddled with guilt, and he blamed Vladek. Rafiq was out to find him, but Vladek was gone, so he went after their business contacts."

"How do you know all this?" Caleb asked. He was increasingly suspicious.

"My boss wouldn't help him, so he came to me. In exchange for what I knew, he helped me rise to power. I've always been an opportunist, Caleb. I thought he would lie in wait for Vladek, but what he did instead was…well, I'm sorry."

"For what?" Caleb snorted. "I still don't see what this has to do with me. Rafiq lost his temper – he wasn't himself. Vladek still deserves to die."

"It has a great deal to do with you, Caleb," Felipe said.

Caleb studied Felipe and the unease in his eyes set the hair on Caleb's body on edge. "What did he do?" Caleb asked, and for the first time, a tendril of pure fear raced down his spine.

"Vladek had been a bit of a ladies' man. Women swooned over his blond hair and blue eyes, but I remembered he once spoke longingly about an American woman he'd met at college. She'd left him suddenly, and V had said she was the one who got away. I pointed Rafiq toward her." Felipe paused, apparently lost in thought.

Caleb had heard enough. Felipe had said nothing to sway Caleb's loyalty and Livvie was waiting upstairs. Their time together had dwindled to a few precious hours and he was done wasting them. "So, Rafiq was a killer long before I knew him. So what?" Caleb stood. "Keep your secrets, Felipe. And keep mine as well, at least until tomorrow night. I promise to do the same."

"She had a son!" Felipe spat. "The spitting image of Vladek: blond hair, blue eyes."

Caleb slowly sat back down. He swallowed bile and broke out in a cold sweat. He didn't want to hear anymore. "Wait. Stop." He waved his arm.

"No one knew. Not even Vladek, I think. When Rafiq couldn't find Vladek, he went after the boy as a means to flush Vladek out."

Not fucking true. He's lying, Caleb. Kill him. He's lying!

Felipe didn't relent. "Vladek went deep into hiding. He had heard about A'noud and knew Rafiq was searching for him. He never came to claim his son, even after Rafiq put him to work in a brothel."

"Stop!" Caleb said.

"No!" Felipe insisted. "The truth, Caleb. Hear it."

"It doesn't make any sense! He's the one who saved me," Caleb insisted.

"All he's done is claim Vladek's son for his own and use him to carry out his ultimate revenge," Felipe whispered.

Blond hair. Blue eyes.

Images of Vladek flashed through Caleb's mind. He was older, and his hair had turned grey, but his eyes were blue.

He's Russian! They all have blue eyes!

424

Caleb had always wondered why he'd been taken. Why he'd been dragged so far away from home to be a whore. Why Rafiq would save *him* and not the others. Why?

"You're saying…" Caleb couldn't get the rest out. It was too unspeakable to even consider what Felipe was saying. Caleb's chest felt tight and his stomach churned.

"He left you there, Caleb. You were his revenge. Everyone knew it. The war came and he left you there to rot. No one crossed Rafiq after that, not once they knew what he was capable of. Even criminals love their families, their children."

Caleb felt himself burst open like a dam. Every emotion, every memory involving Rafiq sifted through his mind. There was nothing Rafiq wouldn't do to have his revenge. Nothing. Caleb fell to his knees and vomited. For the first time in years, Caleb cried. He couldn't stop. He screamed and he cried. He heaved for breath.

He rescued me. He clothed me. He fed me. He calls me brother.

"Liar!" Caleb cried. He reached for his knife and lunged toward Felipe, intent on cutting out his lying tongue.

23

Caleb woke. His head hurt, but it was nothing compared to the pain inside his chest. He pushed himself back onto his heels and raised a hand to his head. It came away bloody. He stared at the blood on his hand. There had been so much blood on Caleb's hands over the years.

He sobbed.

"He left you there, Caleb. You were his revenge. Everyone knew it. The war came and he left you there to rot. No one crossed Rafiq after that, not once they knew what he was capable of. Even criminals love their families, their children."

He wanted to tell himself there was absolutely no truth to what Felipe had told him, but he had to admit…it was possible. Rafiq had lied to him about how he knew Vladek. With all he and Rafiq had shared, Caleb couldn't think of a reason for Rafiq to keep such a thing from him. Unless he had a very good reason.

Vladek is my father.

Caleb shook his head. He couldn't think about that.

He looked around the room and saw it was empty; Felipe was gone. Caleb had gone toward him with his knife, intent on killing him, but his anger had made him sloppy and Felipe had struck him with the gun. The fact he didn't shoot Caleb only gave him more credibility.

Caleb wished he'd pulled the trigger, but he knew why Felipe had left him alive. He wanted Caleb to find Rafiq.

No! I can't.

He hunched over, the pain too much to bear. There was no way he could possibly survive this betrayal. His entire life had been a lie. He had not been abandoned. He had not been rescued. He'd been taken from a mother who loved him and had tried to protect him by running away from Vladek. He'd been kidnapped by the only real father he'd ever known.

Rafiq.

Rafiq had cared for him. He'd taught him how to read, how to speak five languages. Rafiq had stayed up late and spoken with Caleb because he'd known about the nightmares Caleb used to have when he went to bed alone. He'd taught him how to defend himself. And the entire time…

He knew what he'd done to me. He listened to me recount the way Narweh used to rape me. He'd held me when I cried.

Caleb screamed toward the ground.

I'll kill you! I'll kill you for what you've done.

"How could you?" he said aloud.

He must laugh at me.

An image of Rafiq and Jair popped into his mind. Their entire relationship had been suspect until that moment. If Rafiq was concerned about Caleb learning the truth, it made sense to have

427

someone around to watch Caleb. He wondered if Jair knew the truth and bile crept into his throat.

Kill them both.

Slowly, Caleb stood from his balled position on the floor. He looked around him and picked up his knife. As he held it in his hand, he shook with rage. Things would end tonight.

He trudged up the stairs, his bare feet slapping against the wood steps. His heart felt both fast and shallow. He had hungered for vengeance for so many years, never knowing the source of all his suffering had held his hand and pointed him toward his own father.

Vladek was not without guilt. He'd known what Rafiq did to him and still had not come for him. He had sacrificed his own flesh and blood for the sake of what? Money? Power? Cowardice?

Caleb had been a pawn since he was a child. Nothing he knew could be trusted – even his memories manipulated him. There was no such thing as truth. The truth relied heavily on perception and Caleb's had been fucked with since the beginning.

The door was open at the top of the stairs. Caleb didn't hear any sounds within the house. He suspected Felipe and Celia were long gone. He wondered if they had taken Livvie.

Livvie....

Caleb shut his eyes tight and forced her from his thoughts. He couldn't think about her. If he went upstairs and found her missing, he would lose any composure he had left. If he found her waiting for him with Felipe and Celia, he risked showing a side of himself he didn't want her to see. And if he found her hurt...or worse...he would simply turn the knife on himself and Rafiq would live. It was best he didn't know. Not yet.

Felipe's home was enormous, filled with many rooms and hiding spaces. He walked slowly, testing each door as quietly as possible. As he walked, his memories wreaked havoc on his soul.

"Why me, Rafiq? I'm no one. I don't even know who Vladek is," Caleb said. He sat on the floor with his legs pulled up toward his chest. It was almost time for bed, but he didn't want to go. He didn't want to risk having another nightmare.

Lately, he'd been dreaming about the night he killed Narweh. Caleb had shot him and his face was half gone, but Narweh didn't die. He sat up and jumped on top of Caleb, his open face dripping a river of blood onto Caleb's.

He could never go back to sleep after that.

Rafiq sat at his desk, writing. "Men like Vladek have no reason for their callousness, Caleb. They see something, or someone, they like and they take it. A'noud was beautiful." Rafiq paused and smiled. "She was sweet. She used to wrap her arms around me and refuse to let go unless I spun her around. My mother used to complain she'd never find a husband because she'd never want to be away from me." Rafiq's gaze was distant, as though he were reliving a fond memory.

Caleb looked toward the imaginary spot containing Rafiq's memory of his sister and he wished he had one of his own.

"Do you miss her?" Caleb asked in a whisper.

Rafiq's expression turned grim and he returned to his papers. "Much of the time. My hope is that once Vladek is dead, I can give my sister and mother some peace."

Caleb nodded. "Do you think...? Never mind." Caleb pulled at the rug with his fingernails, at a loss for what to say.

"Ask, Caleb. There is no room for secrets between you and I. We are in this together," Rafiq said. He smiled at Caleb warmly.

"I wouldn't keep secrets from you. I promise. You saved my life and I owe you everything. It's just...do you think...I have a family? I mean, I must have had one...before." Caleb's face felt hot.

Rafiq sighed. "I don't know, Caleb. I'm sorry."

Caleb shrugged and picked at the carpet some more. "It doesn't matter. You're the only one who came looking for me. If I have a family, they must not care very much."

Rafiq stood from his desk and got down on one knee in front of Caleb. He lifted Caleb's chin, forcing their eyes to meet. "We are orphans, Caleb. We make our own families."

Caleb's chest swelled with emotions he didn't understand. He pressed his lips together and nodded. He felt relieved when Rafiq let him go and ruffled his hair. Caleb didn't want to cry in front of Rafiq. He wanted to make him proud.

430

"Let us see what sweets are in the kitchen, Caleb."

Caleb smiled brightly and jumped up from the floor, trailing behind Rafiq.

His first impulse was to throw open the door and start stabbing anything within arm's reach, but he'd made enough mistakes to last him a lifetime. He was determined to get it right this time.

"Hold the gun steady, Caleb. It's very powerful," Rafiq said. He smiled and lifted Caleb's arms parallel to the ground.

"I can do it!" Caleb whined. He tried to shrug Rafiq away.

"I'm trying to teach you, Caleb. Listen."

"You've been talking forever. I just want to shoot."

"Patience," Rafiq said. "Widen your stance and try to pace your breathing."

Caleb scowled. He was tired of talking. He pointed the gun toward the tin can in the distance and squeezed the trigger. The force of the gun bent his elbows. The gun cracked him in the forehead and threw him toward the ground.

"Ahhh! Damn it!" Caleb rolled on the ground while holding his head. He kicked with his feet as he tried to assuage the pain. He could hear Rafiq laughing uproariously.

"I told you! You silly boy!" Rafiq stomped his foot as he laughed.

Caleb shut his eyes again and tried to breathe through the pain. He would give anything to return to the moment Felipe had offered him the truth and deny he wanted to hear it.

You knew it could come to this, Caleb. Only now, you don't have to feel guilt. It's a gift.

Caleb shook his head but gripped the knife tighter. He couldn't lie to himself. He had known it might come to this. He had hoped to sacrifice his own life, but in the back of his mind, he knew the survivor in him would fight to the bitter end. Rafiq had to die.

He took a deep, steadying breath and knocked on the door.

The beating of his heart swayed his body by the barest of degrees, building his adrenaline and his anxiety.

Caleb heard cursing, followed by rapid steps toward the door. He braced himself and a shiver ran down his spine.

The door opened and Jair stood in the doorway naked. His swarthy chest was slick with sweat.

"What do you want?" Jair sneered.

Caleb tried to remain calm, but all he heard in his head was: *Kill.*

"Where's Rafiq?" Caleb inquired urgently.

Jair registered Caleb's demeanor, his gaze focusing on the blood on Caleb's forehead. "What happened?"

Caleb swallowed. "Felipe attacked me. I have him tied up downstairs in the shower room."

"Does everyone hate you?" Jair turned into his room with a sneer in Caleb's direction.

Caleb spoke in Arabic. "He was planning to kill Rafiq. He wanted me to help him."

Jair turned his head toward Caleb as he pulled on a pair of pants and replied in the same language. "Why would he ask for your help?"

"He thought he had something to offer me. Obviously, he doesn't know how deep my loyalty runs. Where is Rafiq?" Caleb asked again. He was having a difficult time restraining himself. Nancy was tied face down on the bed. He could see her shaking and had no clue how he felt about her plight.

"Everyone seems to question your loyalty, Caleb. Perhaps there is something to question." Jair put his arms through a shirt.

"Fuck you, swine. Where is Rafiq? I won't ask again."

"Fuck you, Caleb. You and your little whore." Jair turned to retrieve his shoes and Caleb could no longer hold himself back.

As soon as Jair's back was turned, Caleb kicked the back of his knee and threw his weight onto Jair's back. He pushed his knife between Jair's ribs and into one of his lungs.

Jair bucked wildly, shock and adrenaline making him strong as an ox. Caleb wrapped his left arm around Jair's throat and held onto the knife in Jair's side as he was flung to the left and right with incredible force. Caleb didn't dare do anything but use his strength to stay on Jair. He could hear Nancy whimpering, but she had yet to scream.

Jair crawled, staggering across the room on his hands and knees while his blood soaked his shirt and Caleb's hand.

"No!" Jair gurgled. "No!" His arm reached back for Caleb, trying to drag him off.

Caleb shifted the knife in Jair's side, his body sliding against Jair's sweat and blood. He shut his eyes and listened to Jair's death rattles until he fell forward onto the floor. Caleb held on for a minute... waiting. There was nothing. He loosened his arm around Jair's throat and one last whisper of breath escaped him. Jair was dead.

Caleb shifted, straddling Jair's limp body, and pulled out his knife. He could hear Nancy crying into the bed and trying to quiet her panic.

"I'm not here for you," Caleb whispered. Nancy wept harder. Caleb lifted the knife and looked down at Jair's lifeless body. He stabbed him twice more to be sure.

Slowly, he stood and approached Nancy. She flinched, her chest rising and falling to the rhythm of her panic.

"Please!" she cried. "I'm so sorry. I'm so sorry for what I did. Please, don't hurt me. No more. Please, God, no more." She sobbed and shook her head.

Caleb sat on the edge of the bed. "Are you sure you want to live?" His voice was wooden and detached. He felt so many things, but they were distant. This was not bloodlust. There was no satisfaction in what he'd done, or what he was about to do. "You won't forget," he continued. "Every time you close your eyes…it will be waiting there. Every time a man touches you, you'll struggle not to cry out. Are you sure that's what you want?"

Nancy wouldn't stop sobbing.

"I can make it fast. No pain. I promise."

"Please," she pleaded, "let me go."

"Do you know where Rafiq is?" he asked, his tone cold and far away.

"L-l-ast time, we…" Nancy sobbed, but kept going, "we stayed in this guest house out by the pool. He…he didn't want anyone to hear me SCREAMING!" Nancy wailed into the mattress and pulled on the restraints holding her down.

Caleb couldn't stand to listen to her misery. He felt responsible for it. He had brought her into his world. No matter what she'd done, she didn't deserve the price she'd paid. He leaned over her body, wincing at the way she screamed in horror. He cut her loose.

Nancy didn't move – she simply continued to scream and cry on the bed.

"Good luck," he whispered. He stood and searched Jair's things and found his knife and gun. He picked them both up and walked out of the room.

It was warm outside, even in the dead of night. Caleb walked toward the guest house with a high level of trepidation but an even greater sense of determination.

Part of him wanted to simply go inside and kill Rafiq as he slept. It would be over quickly. Caleb would never have to confront Rafiq's betrayal. He would never have to face the man he had thought of as a father, brother, and friend and ask him what had been real between them and what had been a ploy. He would never have to see Rafiq's eyes lose the spark that meant he was alive.

Still, Caleb knew he had come too far not to learn the full truth. He needed to know for certain. He needed to hear it from Rafiq's lips and see it in his eyes. A part of Caleb ached to learn it had all been a lie from Felipe.

He was shocked to see Rafiq swimming in the pool when he approached, gun raised. His heart hammered wildly in his chest and he felt a little dizzy.

I can't.

I can.

I can.

I can.

Rafiq emerged from the water and wiped his face. It took him a moment to see Caleb standing near the edge of the water. He smiled for a fraction of a second until he registered the gun in Caleb's hand.

Rafiq glared and shook his head. "I wish I could say I'm surprised, *Khoya*."

Caleb shut his eyes for a moment. When he opened them, he returned Rafiq's anger. "I am not your brother, Rafiq. I doubt you ever saw me as such."

"You're bleeding," he said. His tone was casual and unafraid.

Caleb wiped at his forehead. "I had a talk with Felipe. It didn't end well."

Rafiq smiled. "Is that all? I don't care if you've killed him, Caleb. Put the gun away," he ordered. He was always giving orders. He'd always believed he had the right, especially when it came to Caleb.

"I didn't kill him. I killed Jair," Caleb said through a smile.

Anger swiftly came over Rafiq's features. "And now you're here to kill me?! You ungrateful little whore. I should have let you die in Tehran!"

Caleb felt heat race down his spine and he straightened. "Get out of the water, Rafiq. Slowly, or I'll shoot you where you stand."

"Do it! I don't fear you, Caleb." Despite his words, Rafiq stepped back toward the steps of the pool. Caleb followed him around the edge until Rafiq stood out of the water.

Without hesitation, Caleb shot Rafiq in his right knee. Rafiq yelled out into the night, his wet body thudding against the concrete.

Rafiq's hands shook as he held his knee; fragments of bone lay around him, along with copious amounts of blood. "I'll kill you!" he screamed.

Adrenaline coursed through Caleb's veins. "How do you know Vladek?!" Caleb yelled over Rafiq's curses and wails.

"Fuck you! Give me a towel before I fucking bleed to death!"

Caleb reached for Rafiq's towel on one of the lounge chairs and threw it in Rafiq's direction. Rafiq shivered as he applied pressure to his destroyed knee. He was fighting shock.

Caleb felt sick to his stomach. When he was able to keep his nausea at bay and speak, his voice was broken. "Did you make me a whore, Rafiq? Did you take me from my mother?" It hurt to say the words. It hurt to look upon Rafiq and instantly know the answer.

It was in the way the anger disappeared on Rafiq's face. There was a glimpse of shame, but only that – a glimpse. When it passed, Rafiq was once again filled with a self-righteous rage. "How dare you! How dare you ask me such a stupid question, Caleb! After all we've been through and all I've done for you. *This*," he motioned to his bloody leg, "is how you repay me? You make me sick." He spat on the ground.

Caleb broke.

He fell to his knees on the concrete and hung his head. His sobs shook his chest and robbed him of breath. His mind raced with images of his torment. He relived the rapes and beatings. He felt the loss of his friend upon learning he'd been burned alive. But the worst…were the memories of Rafiq and the life they had lived together – good and bad.

"It's not too late, *Khoya*," Rafiq said softly. His voice trembled. "Help me inside."

Rafiq's words brought the world back into focus for Caleb. He stared into his lap, saw the gun lying limply in his hand, and made a decision. He went into the guest house and found what he needed before coming back outside to Rafiq.

Rafiq wasn't doing very well. He shook badly, and the color was drained from his face. "What are you doing, Caleb?" he asked. For the first time, there was fear in his eyes.

Caleb ignored the question. He stretched the length of cord he'd brought out and gestured toward Rafiq's hands. "Give them to me."

Rafiq shook his head. "No. You're not yourself, Caleb. Don't do this!"

Caleb held the cord taut in his hands and reached around Rafiq's head. He pulled back with both hands, dragging Rafiq into the house by his neck. A trail of blood followed them.

Rafiq didn't thrash around the way Jair had. He was too well trained as a soldier to make such a mistake. He placed his hands around the cord, taking tension off of his throat.

Once inside, Rafiq reached back for Caleb's arms, bracing the weight of his body, and rolled toward Caleb. It was enough to throw Caleb off balance. Rafiq dragged himself on top of Caleb and punched him in the same spot Felipe had struck with the gun.

Caleb's head snapped back and his vision blurred. He felt Rafiq's hands wrap around his throat, his thumbs pressing along his windpipe. Caleb lifted his leg and kicked at Rafiq's injured knee. It was enough to regain the advantage. As Rafiq instinctively recoiled and went for his knee, Caleb rolled on top of him. He kept punching Rafiq in the face until he went unconscious.

***

439

When Rafiq opened his eyes, Caleb could see he was instantly afraid. Caleb had tied him down on one of the lounge chairs that had been by the pool.

Caleb felt dead inside, but his thirst for vengeance had not abated. He had waited his entire life for this moment, and it could not be denied.

He sat on the ground next to Rafiq. His knife sat delicately on his knee and was still gory with Jair's blood. "You're going to die tonight, brother. I want you to know that," Caleb whispered. "I can kill quickly if you tell me the truth." He paused. "Or I can use my knife and practice all the things you've taught me about torture."

"Caleb…" Rafiq's voice shook.

"That's not my name, Rafiq. I don't remember my name. It was taken from me," Caleb said dully. "Do you know why?" Caleb looked up at Rafiq, his expression hard.

"You don't want to do this, Caleb," Rafiq said.

"No," Caleb replied and shook his head, "I don't want to do this." He picked up the knife and poked at Rafiq's knee.

"STOP!" Rafiq yelled. "Stop!"

Caleb returned the knife to his knee. "I never wanted to hurt you, Rafiq. Never! But you have to suffer for what you've done."

Rafiq's body shook violently. Sweat covered his body. "And what is it you think I've done?"

"I'll ask the questions. I'll start with the most important one: Did you give me to Narweh?"

Rafiq stared at him for a long time.

Caleb felt a tear race down his cheek and he wiped it away quickly with the back of his hand. He didn't know he was crying. It had been so long since he'd cried and he suddenly seemed unable to stop. He cleared his throat. "Your silence betrays you, Rafiq. I had hoped you would deny it. I almost killed Felipe for even suggesting it."

"It's not true, Caleb. Felipe is a liar," Rafiq whispered.

Caleb shut his eyes and wiped at his face again. He unexpectedly laughed. "You're late. And unconvincing. But thank you, for trying."

"I raised you," Rafiq implored.

"You did," Caleb nodded. "I think that's what makes your betrayal so much worse. I worshipped you as a boy. You were my savior."

"I treated you well, Caleb. I gave you everything your heart desired." There was sincerity in Rafiq's words.

"I always wondered why you came for me. At first, I thought you took pity because of what Narweh had done. I thought you rescued me because you were too late to save your sister. Felipe tells me you killed her…and your mother. Is that true?"

Rafiq turned his face away. "You don't know about the things you're saying," he grated.

"Explain it to me, then. You're about to die. Unburden your soul," Caleb said numbly.

Rafiq took a deep breath and released it slowly. "And my wife and children? What's to become of them?"

Caleb felt nothing. "Will your sons come after me?"

"They're too young for that, Caleb."

"I was about their age the first time I killed. Even younger when…" He couldn't continue.

"They're not like us. Swear to me you'll leave them alone, and I'll tell you what you want to know." Rafiq turned his head and looked at Caleb.

He nodded. "I swear it."

Rafiq also nodded. Tears swam in his eyes. "Thank you, Caleb." Rafiq turned his gaze toward the ceiling. "I know you won't believe me, but I have always regretted what happened to you. I was in pain and I…. I tried to make it up to you."

Caleb felt a rush of hot tears but managed to scoff. "As if anything could make up for what was done to me! You *know*! You know what they put me through, the pretty American boy who everyone called Dog." Caleb picked up the knife and stabbed it into Rafiq's thigh, twisting the blade.

"Caleb!" Rafiq shouted. "Please!"

"Yes! Please! That's how I begged, too. I said it so much, Narweh used to taunt me with the word."

"I gave you vengeance!"

"Vengeance will never undo what was done! Your betrayal is worse than anything Narweh *ever* did. He never betrayed me. He raped my body, but you…. *You*…I loved."

Rafiq was delirious with pain and blood loss. "*Khoya,*" he croaked, "I'm sorry."

"It's too late, Rafiq. Much, much too late."

Rafiq shook his head. "Vladek is a monster. He ruined my beloved A'noud. He turned her against me. My father had died and my sister was carrying Vladek's bastard! I was sick with grief. We fought and my mother got in the middle. I never meant to hurt them. They were my life! Vladek took them from me!"

"You killed them! You are responsible!" Caleb pulled the knife from Rafiq's thigh and listened to him weep. Caleb had never seen Rafiq cry and it did things to him he did not expect. He wanted to feel nothing but hatred, but he couldn't.

Caleb had done things too. He had killed and tortured. He had sold women into the very life he condemned Rafiq for thrusting him into. Caleb was no better than Rafiq. He deserved no better. Caleb had told Livvie he was sorry for what he'd done. He had meant it, but his apology could no more erase his actions than Rafiq could erase the past.

If Livvie could show forgiveness, Caleb could try.

Caleb got up on his knees and put his hands on Rafiq's face, turning his head toward Caleb. Rafiq met his gaze and Caleb saw sorrow and, perhaps, remorse. Caleb leaned down and kissed Rafiq on both cheeks before he looked at him steadily in the eyes. "I forgive you," he whispered.

Rafiq smiled weakly and shut his eyes.

Caleb slowly reached back for his gun and shot Rafiq in the heart.

Afterward, he washed Rafiq's body. He removed errant blood and dressed his wounds with strips of

443

cotton sheets. He wept as he wrapped the body tightly.

With great difficulty, he carried him out toward one of Felipe's gardens and buried the only family he had ever known.

24

"Are you hurt?" Caleb whispers. His blond brows are creased in concern. I've never seen him look like this. He's so happy, at ease.

I reach up and caress his beautiful face. "I'm okay."

He swipes at my eyes. "Then why are you crying?"

"I don't know," I say and continue to run my hand across his face. "I think I'm just happy."

He smile., "Strange response to happiness, but okay." He leans down and I feel him lick one of my tears.

I squirm. "What are you doing?" I laugh.

"I was curious," he whispers very seriously.

"About what?"

"If happy tears taste the same as the sad ones," he says.

His words make me cry even harder. I can't control them. I'm just so overwhelmed with everything. "And?" I manage.

"I think they're sweeter," he says and kisses me, "but it could just be your face." We dissolve into peals of laughter.

I hear voices.

I bolt up in bed. For a few seconds I have no idea where I am. The room is small. There are grates on the windows. The bed isn't Caleb's.

"I can't come back in three hours. I need to speak with her now," a man says. The voice is familiar, but I don't know why. I'm having trouble placing it.

It's Reed. Caleb's not here, remember?

I feel tears rolling down my cheeks and clogging my throat. I'm awake now. I remember where I am. I'm in the hospital. Caleb is gone. I'm alone in the dark again.

Only a few seconds ago, I held Caleb in my arms. I touched him. I smelled him. I tasted his flesh in my mouth. And now, he was gone. I'd forgotten.

The pain of remembering knocks the wind out of me and I take a deep breath. When I exhale, the sound coming out of me is pure grief. He was just here. He was just in my arms and I lost him.

"Help me! Please!" I beg. I'm not sure whom I'm begging. Maybe it's God. Maybe it's the devil. I just want the pain to go away.

The door to my room bursts open.

"Olivia?!?" Reed yells.

I don't acknowledge him. I'm on my knees with my head pressed into the bed and I'm sobbing. I shut my eyes tightly, willing myself to go back to sleep. I want to go back to my dream, back to Caleb. I can't fucking breathe! I can't breathe without him. I don't want to.

"What's wrong?" Reed asks urgently. "Are you hurt? Talk to me!"

446

Go away, go away, go away.

"This is a hospital, Agent Reed! Please, put away the gun!" a woman says.

"I love you, Caleb. I love you! If you care for me at all...please, don't do this! Please, don't leave me. I don't know how to live without you. Don't make me go back to trying to be someone I don't know how to be anymore."

"Livvie...."

"No!"

I scream in my sorrow. I can't help it. I would if I could. I know they're watching me. I can feel their hot stares against my back. They don't get it. No one does. I'm all alone and it's Caleb's fault.

"Please," I beg. "Please make it stop."

"Miss Ruiz?" Reed says cautiously. "Livvie?"

"Step back, Agent Reed. She's having some sort of break right now and she could hurt you if you get too close. Wait for the orderlies," says the woman.

"She's not going to hurt anyone. I'll take my chances," Reed says.

"Sir —"

"She's a witness in a federal investigation and I need to talk to her right the fuck now. I don't want her doped up. Get out!" Reed yells and his presence is beginning to penetrate the fog of my grief.

I keep telling myself to breathe. I keep reminding myself I've been here for days. Caleb has been gone for days. He wasn't here. I never touched him. I never held him.

"Live for me, Kitten. Be all those things you'd never be with me. Go to school. Meet a normal boy and fall in love. Forget me."

"I can't!" I yell into the void.

Breathe!
Breathe!
Breathe.
Breathe.

I hear the door open and shut. I wonder if I'm alone, but I can't will myself to look up. A tentative hand touches my back and I sob.

"Livvie?" says Reed.

"Go away," I sob.

"I…can't leave you like this," he says. He sounds uncomfortable.

"I'm fine. Please, go."

"You're not fine. You're a wreck," he says angrily.

"Why are you here?" I whisper. Talking to Reed is pulling me further away from my dream, my grief. I'm not sure I'm ready. I'm too raw and I can't face him.

"There's been movement on my case. It's all happening fast."

"What does that mean, Reed?" I'm exhausted and my tone reflects as much.

He sighs heavily, as if he's struggling under a tremendous weight. It makes me curious, despite myself. "I came…to hear the rest of your story."

My heart starts to race. Movement on the case, he'd said. I know Reed is lying, but about what?

Caleb!

I sit up fast, dizzy for a moment, and Reed steadies me. I grab his suit jacket and pull him close. I'm frantic. Reed's hands grab my shoulders and he pushes me. Hard. As I'm falling backward, he reaches for my forearm and quickly jerks me onto the bed. I rail against him, slapping and kicking, but before I know it, he's pinned my arms to my chest and sat on my legs.

"Get off me!"

"Calm down!"

I look at Reed for the first time since he's come in. He's panting hard and his dark hair is a disheveled mess that mirrors the state of his shirt and jacket.

"Did you find his body?" I whisper. I don't know what I'll do if he says yes.

"What? No. No!" Reed says. His expression has gone from anger to pity.

The news is a relief, but I can't stop crying. Reed slowly lets me go and I roll onto my side with my back to him. Reed rubs my back, but then seems to realize what he is doing and he walks away. I hear him sit in the chair.

"What's wrong?" he asks after a few minutes.

My sobbing has died away and I answer. "Bad dream. Well, not really. The only bad part was waking up and realizing…." I couldn't continue.

Reed is quiet for a while. I'm quiet too. It's the middle of the night, and his presence is a dark omen. Something has happened, and as much as I want to know – I don't want to know.

Finally, Reed clears his throat. "If it be thus to

449

dream, still let me sleep," he whispers. I'm not surprised he knows Shakespeare. Reed is a very smart man.

I smile in spite of the sorrow I feel. "*Twelfth Night*; Sebastian says those words to Olivia."

"I know. I attended the eleventh grade," he says. His smile is wry.

"Wasn't that like a million years ago? I'm surprised you remember it," I whisper. My face feels crusty with dried tears and I'm sure my face is a mess, but I'm finally starting to feel a little better. My thoughts and memories of the last several days are organizing themselves in my head, and clarity is returning. I've heard it said that time heals all wounds, but if a dream can pull you so deeply into your past you can't remember the present, I'm not sure my wounds will ever heal. Caleb lives in my dreams.

"I remember it just barely, Miss Ruiz," says Reed.

I roll onto my back and stare at the ceiling. My flickering bulb has long been replaced, but I can still hear the hum and follow along: *on-off-on-off-buzz-on.* "Why are you here, Reed?" I whisper. I stay focused on the ceiling, focused on my breathing, and try to prepare for what I'm about to hear.

"I told you – to hear the rest of your story," he says rather seriously.

"It's not the only reason though, is it?"

"No. It isn't." He clears his throat again. "Does the name James Cole mean anything to you?"

I'm confused. "No. Why?"

450

"It came up and I needed to know, that's all," Reed says. "Never mind. I guess it's not important."

"You wouldn't ask if it weren't important, Reed." He's piqued my interest and I struggle into a sitting position so I can see his face and gauge him better. He looks like he hasn't slept in days.

Reed leans forward with his arms rested on his knees. "I came to tell you the charges against you are being dropped." He says it in a rush, flat but full of something else. "Once you're cleared by your doctor, I've been instructed to debrief you. Sign some paperwork and you should be able to leave today."

"What!?!" I exclaim, my mind reeling. The news is a shock to my system. I'm not ready to go. I'm not ready to start over. I'm not ready to accept Caleb is gone and I have to face the world alone.

"We know where the auction is being held, and we know some of the persons attending," he says. "I wish I could tell you more, but I've been instructed to keep it in-house. All I can say is that it's over, Livvie. You're free. And you're safe. You get to have your life back, and so do the other victims."

My heartbeat feels erratic. I can't let Reed leave without knowing everything. I need him to understand. My information, my testimony, was my only bargaining chip. Without his need for it, I'm at a loss. "H-how do you know where the auction is?" I ask frantically.

Reed looks at me. "Why do you say it like that?" he demanded, eyes narrowing. "What is it you're not telling me?"

451

"Please, Reed. You have to tell me what you know. I've been spilling my guts to you for over a damn week. Please don't keep me in the dark. I deserve to know!" I'm begging him, but I don't feel ashamed.

"This case is more complicated than anyone could have expected, Miss Ruiz. It's out of my hands at this point. The Federal Investigation Agency in Pakistan has agreed to lead a joint task force." Reeds face becomes sour. "Oh, but I've been assured my involvement will be mentioned in the report!" Reed stands up and starts to pace. His anger and frustration is plain, but I don't understand where it's coming from.

"What does that mean, Reed? What happens once they arrest everyone?" I want to get off the bed and follow Reed as he paces the small room, but I know it will only annoy him and he might not tell me anything.

"It depends," he says through gritted teeth. He stands still for a moment, thinking something over. When he returns from his thoughts, he looks at me and I see regret in his eyes. My heart almost stops.

"There isn't going to be a trial," Reed says. He starts pacing again, a fist at the nape of his neck. "I knew it could go down this way. I didn't want to believe it, but I knew. I've been arguing with my boss for the last few hours. There's just…" Reed seems at a loss. "There'll be plenty of arrests, I'm sure. The people meant to be auctioned will undoubtedly be given sanctuary, but…there won't be any justice. Not the kind those victims deserve."

"How can that be?" I sob. "How can you let that happen?"

"Rafiq is a high-level military officer in the Pakistan Army, Livvie. His government isn't going to allow a scandal to get out. They've agreed to let our government be a part of the raid in exchange for keeping their people out of it. When the dust settles, they're the ones to decide who was there and who wasn't — that's how international politics work."

I feel like someone has hit me in the chest with a battering ram. For the second time in my life, I understand Caleb's thirst for vengeance. I could kill. I've done it before, and I don't feel bad about it. Some people deserve to die.

Tears are running from my eyes without ceasing; I'm soaked through with them. I'm not sad, though. I'm filled with rage and I have no way to let it out. There's no one to kill, nothing to hit, and nowhere to go.

"Reed," I sob, "I have to tell you something. Please, please try to understand. I need your help." My hands are clasped together and I'm holding them so tightly to my chest I can feel my thumb leaving a bruise.

Reed scrubs his hands over his face. "Please don't tell me something incriminating, Miss Ruiz. There's nothing I can do right now and if I have to put you back under arrest, it's going to seriously put a shitty end to an already shitty day. All I have is my integrity. Don't make me choose between it and you."

"Please, Reed! I have to tell you the rest of my

story," I plead. It's the most important part, the part I've been saving until I knew I could trust Reed. I just hope I'm not too late.

"I've heard all I need to know. My job was to investigate the border incident. You've been cleared of charges. My job was to locate the auction – done. I did my job. I came here to tell you you're free to go, and I was willing to listen to the rest of your story if it would give you closure – but if you're just going to incriminate yourself, I don't want to hear it. If I hear it, I'll act on it. Do you understand?"

Reed is angry, but I don't care. Caleb is too important. He's sacrificed so much for me, even to the point of protecting me from myself. I would have followed him anywhere, done anything he asked of me, but he'd cared enough not to let me. For all I knew, he would be at the auction, trying to kill Vladek and getting himself killed in the process. It was my turn to save him.

"Please," I beg, "you have to help him. If you arrest him, I know he'll live. There's no telling what will happen to him if he's in Pakistan. You said it yourself – Rafiq has a lot of power over there. Please! Please, Reed! Help him."

Reed stands deadly still, but his chest rises and falls harshly with each breath. "Are you telling me Caleb is alive?" Reed hisses.

My heart is racing. "No. Not yet. But if he were? Could you help him?"

"Goddamn it, Livvie!" Reed kicks the chair. "You lied to me!"

"*Maybe!* Maybe I did," I plead. I don't know if

wording things hypothetically changes anything, but I have to try. I have to know if Reed can help me. I have to know if he will. "I needed time, and you weren't giving me any," I sob. "You came in here, asking me all kinds of questions and calling me a fucking terrorist. What was I supposed to do?"

"You were supposed to tell me the truth! That was the deal. You tell me the truth and I help you," Reed says and resumes pacing.

"I did tell you the truth! I told you everything you needed to know. I helped you find the auction, but here you are – telling me there's no justice! So who's the liar, Reed?" I cry.

Reed turns and glares at me. He looks a lot of things: angry, exhausted, and sad. Finally, he looks away and collapses into the chair.

"Reed?" I hedge closer.

"There's nothing I can do, Livvie. The team is already on its way and the FIA is calling the shots," he says.

His words play in a loop in my head until they're reduced to their true meaning: I'll never see Caleb again. I feel dead inside. Empty. Hollow. Vivisected.

"There…has to be something," I croak.

Reed shakes his head.

In my head, I can hear myself screaming. I can see myself clawing at my skin and tearing at my hair. In reality, I'm motionless – no tears, no screams, no flesh being torn from my bones.

Reed is silent. He can't help me. No one can.

My thoughts turn to Caleb and the last days we spent together.

455

***

Caleb had been gone for hours. I sat on the floor, next to his gun, waiting for something to happen – anything to happen. Several times, I thought about leaving the room and searching for him but kept talking myself out of it. Caleb had said to wait. I waited.

A feeling of dread began to settle over me when I saw light peeking in around the curtains. The sun was coming up and Caleb still hadn't returned. I wondered if Celia might come back, but I doubted it. Our bridge was well and truly burned. My only solace was in knowing she would keep Felipe from hurting me.

Suddenly, there was a hard thump on the door, then another. My heart felt like it had leapt up into my throat, but then I remembered Caleb had said he would knock twice. I reached for the gun, just in case.

I watched as the handle turned, and when the door swung open, I could barely process what I saw. Caleb stood in the doorway. He was covered in dirt. He was smeared with blood.

"Caleb?" I managed to whisper but still couldn't move.

He wouldn't move from the doorway. He just stood there, his eyes fixed on some distant point. He looked like he'd been crying. His blue eyes were ringed with red and swollen. He had a cut on his forehead and blood dripped onto his eye. He didn't blink.

Instantly, I was in tears. Something terrible had happened. Something awful! Slowly, I stood up. I grabbed the shirt Caleb had left and pulled it on over my head. We had to go, and it was going to be up to me to get us out. I scrambled for a pair of pants and found a pair of Caleb's boxers instead.

Caleb never moved.

"Caleb?" I whispered and came a little closer. His mouth turned down briefly, like he'd been about to cry, but then his face returned to a catatonic state. "You're scaring me, Caleb. Please, say something," I sobbed.

Tears fell from his open eyes.

It was more than I could bear to see him in so much pain and not know why. I rushed forward and wrapped my arms around him. "Please, Caleb! Wake the fuck up!"

His weight collapsed on top of me and we fell. As I lay flat on my back, Caleb pulled me close and released an agonized wail into my chest. The sound terrified me and I wrapped my arms around him, holding him as tight as he held me. It was all I could do. His entire body trembled and shook with the force of his gut-wrenching sobs. I felt like a knife was buried in my intestines and someone kept turning the blade. The only thing I could do to keep from screaming was hold him.

My hand shook as I stroked his hair. "Shh, Caleb. Shh. It's okay. Whatever it is, it's okay." I sobbed when he pulled me tighter and tried to bury himself deeper into my chest.

His hair was stiff and brittle – gritty with sand.

457

He's been digging. He's covered in blood.

"Shh, baby," I whispered and kept stroking Caleb's hair. He was barely allowing me to breathe, he gripped me so tightly. "Whose blood is this?"

I felt him shaking his head, fast, angry. He accidentally nudged my chin and I winced. "Okay. It's okay. I don't need to know."

I was at a loss for how to reach him. The man in my arms wasn't Caleb – he was a shell of a human being. Primal and stripped bare. I had my suspicions about whose blood Caleb wore, but I didn't dare say it out loud.

He killed his only friend. For me.

My chest shook with the force of the sobs I kept trapped in my chest. Caleb needed me and I couldn't help him by falling apart. "We have to go, Caleb," I whispered. "It's not safe for us here."

Caleb moved fast. He lifted himself off my chest and caged me in with his body. He looked predatory, and I knew instinctively not to scream. His eyes raked over me, moving quickly from my eyes, to my mouth, to my neck, all the way down to my feet. I wasn't sure he even knew who I was.

My fingers hurt after being ripped away from his hair so abruptly. There were several strands intertwined with my fingers. Without moving, I let my eyes cut to my hand. Caleb followed my eyes, and when I slowly lifted my hand, he watched it intently. I put my fingers to the wound on his head, wiping away the blood. He needed stitches. Caleb closed his eyes and let me touch him.

"We have to go. Please…let's go," I repeated.

458

Caleb's eyes flew open and narrowed on my face. For several seconds, all he did was stare.

"Mine," he whispered.

"Yours," I said.

Caleb brought his mouth down on mine with such ferocity I almost pushed him away. The timing was terrible. Our lives were in danger. But Caleb needed me. He needed to be close and I owed it to him to give him what he needed.

I put my fear aside and opened my mouth to him, letting his tongue invade my mouth. He groaned when I wrapped my arms around him and pulled him down on top of me. I pulled at the filth-covered shirt he wore and broke our kiss just long enough to pull it over his head. Sand and, I was sure, blood fell onto my face, but I brushed it away with the back of my hand and went back to kissing Caleb.

His hands seemed to be everywhere at once, touching my hair, pulling me close, squeezing my breasts. His knee planted itself between my knees, prying them apart. I opened my legs and let Caleb's lower belly press against me. I could feel his cock, trapped inside his jeans, against my inner thigh.

As we pawed at one another, some of Caleb's primal behavior seeped its way into me, and before I knew it, I was pushing him off of me and to the side. He grabbed hold of my shirt and made a sound I took as a warning.

"Yours, Caleb. I promise," I said. I grabbed the hem of my shirt and pulled it over my head, exposing my breasts to Caleb. His mouth latched on, forcing me to cry out and hold him to my breast. I

459

straddled his hips, grinding against him through the fabric of our clothes.

For all of Caleb's animalistic intensity, he wasn't hurting me. He might have, if I'd given him a reason, but I was as open to him as water to a pebble. When his mouth pulled away from one nipple, I fed him the other.

"I love you," I said and stroked his hair. He whimpered.

Caleb would never regret the sacrifices he had made for me. I would make sure of it. For the rest of my life, I would dedicate myself to giving Caleb every ounce of love I had in me to share. I was his and he was mine and it was everything.

I pushed at Caleb's shoulder, urging him back toward the floor. I followed him down, resting my weight on him. His hands found the waistband of the shorts I wore and shoved. I reached back, and together we pushed the fabric down and off my legs.

I hated the feel of Caleb's dirty jeans against my bare skin. "Take these off," I said. I helped him push his pants down to his ankles. His feet were bare and caked in dirt, but I was more preoccupied with getting as close to Caleb as I possibly could.

Caleb's cock sprang up between us like a living thing. We reached for it at the same time, his hand over mine, and guided it between my legs. I was sore, but wet, and Caleb's cock slid into me with minimal effort. Caleb gripped my hips, pulling me down as he thrust.

"Oh, God," I cried out. My fingernails dug into his chest, scoring his skin, but Caleb only groaned and thrust into me again. And again. And again.

I fell forward, my hands bracing me above Caleb's head. I was adrift in a sea of pleasure and all-consuming lust. Arching my back, I teased Caleb's mouth with my nipple and he pulled it into his hungry mouth. I felt my pussy getting tighter around his cock. I whimpered as my orgasm approached, and Caleb fucked me harder, sucked me deeper into his mouth. I didn't have the breath to make a sound. I froze on top of him, letting him keep fucking me as I came.

His mouth pulled away from my breast with a loud pop and then Caleb's sounds filled the room as his come filled my pussy. Pulse after pulse of hot come flooded my insides and I couldn't get enough. I wanted Caleb inside me forever. I collapsed on top of him, loving the way my body rose and fell with each of his breaths.

"Livvie?" he whispered.

I forced myself up on my elbow and stroked his face with my other hand. "Yes," I said. My tears made him blurry, but I could tell he was back now, from wherever he had been.

"Are you okay? Did I hurt you?!" He sounded frantic.

"I'm fine, Caleb. I'm fine. I'm more worried about you," I said. I bent down and kissed his lips. When I pulled back, my heart ached to see him turn his face away from me.

"Don't look at me, Livvie," he whispered.

"Caleb, no." I tried to make him look at me, but all at once he sat up and put my head on his shoulder where I couldn't see him. I could feel him sliding out of me, his come aiding in the effort.

"I can't deal with it, okay? I —" His words sounded stuck in his throat.

"Okay," I whispered and held him in my arms for just a few more seconds.

"We have to go," he said.

Slowly, we reclaimed our bodies from one another. Tears stung the backs of my eyes, but I wouldn't let them free. Caleb needed me strong, and I was determined to give him everything he needed.

Silently, we went about prioritizing. Caleb pulled up his pants with a grimace and started barricading the door. I made myself useful by finding a bag and tossing in anything I thought we might need: the gun, clothes, a first-aid kit I found in the bathroom. It wasn't much, but it was something.

Caleb walked into the bathroom and turned the shower on. I didn't think we had time for it, but I knew better than to ask questions. With shaking hands, he removed his pants and stepped beneath the water. Blood and dirt quickly coated everything.

I thought about stepping in, but one look at Caleb and I knew he needed time alone. The water was steaming hot, clouding the bathroom. I turned on the fan but remained an otherwise-unobtrusive presence. At one point I heard him sob, but I remained on the floor, keeping silent vigil.

He'd been in the shower less than ten minutes before he turned the temperature down and stepped out. He silently grabbed a towel and walked out into the bedroom. My shower didn't last nearly as long, but by the time I stepped into the room, Caleb was more like himself.

"Time to go, Livvie," he said and gave me a smile. It was feigned, but I appreciated the effort. I tried to make my smile more convincing.

The house felt empty – *eerily* empty. No Felipe. No Celia. No Rafiq. Caleb offered no answers and I asked no questions.

It was hot outside, even early in the morning. I realized it had been a long time since I'd walked outside, beneath a glaring sun. I was wearing clothes. I was…free. My steps faltered as the realization hit me. FREE!

"The truck isn't far. Keep moving," Caleb said numbly.

I could feel myself getting choked up, excited laughter bubbled out of me. "Where are we going?" I asked with joyful tears in my eyes.

"Please don't ask. Just come with me."

I looked at him, the pain on his face palpable. This was not the time to argue with him. Whatever he was doing, it was a very big deal. It would change everything between us, but he'd asked me to come with him – and when the man you love asks you to go with him, you go.

We walked for less than a mile, but I marveled at the sheer size of Felipe's estate. Whatever he was into, it was certainly profitable. Finally, we found the old truck we had arrived in. I was surprised it started right up.

Caleb hadn't said much, and though he seemed in much better control of himself, I knew whatever had happened still weighed heavily on him. I reached for his hand across the seat and to my surprise, he not only held my hand, but squeezed it. As we left Felipe's house, I stared at the gravel road in the side view mirror. It was really happening. We were leaving – together. I wiped tears from my eyes for nearly twenty minutes.

We traveled for several hours before I forced Caleb to break his silence. "I'm hungry, Caleb." I looked at him and rubbed my stomach.

"We can get some food and water when we stop for gas. I want to keep moving for now," he said. His eyes never left the road, but his thumb moved back and forth over my hand.

"Okay," I said. "Will we…be driving long? You know, before we get wherever we're going?"

Caleb squeezed my hand and closed his eyes for a second. "We'll be on the road for about sixteen hours, maybe less. We can stop for the night once we're close."

I didn't like his tone. It was too…sad and distant. "Where are we –?"

"Kitten!" he admonished. He shook his head, "I mean…Livvie. Please. Stop."

Anxiety churned in my stomach. I didn't like this at all. I squeezed his hand. "You don't have to call me Livvie if you don't want to, Caleb. To be honest, it's kinda scaring me. *You're* scaring me."

Caleb's face seemed to crack for a second, and I caught a glimpse of his sadness before he relaxed his features. "Don't be scared, Kitten. Everything's going to be fine, I promise. You won't ever have to be scared of me again."

"What do you mean, Caleb?" I whispered.

"It means I'll take care of you," he said.

"We'll take care of each other. I'm stronger now, Caleb. Whatever happens...whatever *happened*, we can handle it together. Okay?"

He was quiet for a long time before he replied. "Okay."

"I love you," I said.

Silence.

We didn't make any unnecessary stops. We went to the bathroom and picked up food whenever we needed gas. Getting Caleb to talk was a bit of a chore, but he seemed very interested in my life before we met. I avoided talking about my family – my brothers and sisters, my mom. I knew I'd never see any of them again and thinking about it hurt too much to talk about. I had Caleb now and he needed me.

I talked about my favorite books and movies. I mentioned my dream of writing a book I would later adapt into a screenplay and direct myself. I was going to be a triple threat. Caleb smiled and said he'd love to read anything I wrote. I suddenly felt a lot more optimistic about Caleb's and my future, but I kept seeing signs for Laredo, Texas.

"What's in Texas?" I asked.

"Besides cowboys?" Caleb said. I glared at him. "I have business there, Kitten. Okay?" He was suddenly very serious again.

"Okay," I relented.

We'd been driving for close to ten hours when fatigue finally caught up with Caleb. He could barely keep his eyes open, and I convinced him we needed to stop because I didn't know how to drive. Caleb laughed at me but pulled into a motel for the night. The place wasn't much to look at, and quite honestly, the people in the parking lot were scary. This was definitely not a tourist destination.

"They're probably going to steal the truck. You know that, right?" I said.

Caleb shrugged. "I'll steal another one in the morning." I laughed; Caleb didn't.

I wanted to make love, but Caleb had fallen asleep while I was in the shower. I didn't have the heart to wake him. In the middle of the night, he reached for me. I barely knew what was happening before I felt his mouth on my sore pussy. I propped myself up on my elbows and watched him lick me until I came on his tongue.

By the time he entered me, I had forgotten about how sore I was. I was too full of Caleb's cock to care. I moaned my pleasure to the rafters, uncaring if anyone heard me. Caleb didn't seem to care either as he came inside me with a yell. There was a fleeting thought about protection, but then all I thought about was Caleb and the tiny thrusts he was making into my pussy as he rode out the aftershocks of his pleasure.

After we managed to clean up, we slept with the windows open. I slept in his arms, safe, secure, and content beyond belief. I didn't care where we were going, as long as he was with me.

25

I had just finished buttoning my shirt when it happened. There was a loud bang and something hit me in the face. I reached up to touch my cheek. My breath left me in the span of a heartbeat. Caleb was on top of me, shouting, but I couldn't hear what he was saying. I couldn't seem to hear *anything*.

My head hurt. I'd smacked it on the ground when Caleb tackled me. Debris was flying everywhere.

"Livvie!" Caleb yelled and shook me. It penetrated the silence in my head.

BOOM! Another torrent of debris flew toward us. Caleb lay on top of me, shielding my face with his arms as he tucked his head near my shoulder.

Someone was fucking shooting at us. My eyes cut to the door, and I could see large gaping holes where wood used to be.

We rolled behind the bed. My entire body was shaking and I had no idea what was going on. Caleb was shoving me and I cried out in pain.

"Get in the tub!" He shouted. He shoved me again.

I managed to get on my hands and knees. I crawled the few feet to the bathroom and scrambled into the tub. I realized Caleb wasn't with me.

467

"Caleb!" I screamed. The bathroom door slammed shut. I was too scared to move.

"He's going to die out there, you stupid bitch! Do something!" Ruthless Me screamed.

I couldn't move. I couldn't, fucking, move. My entire world was moving in slow motion and there was nothing I could do to speed it back up. I felt something wet on my face. My hand came away bloody when I touched it.

"Caleb!" I screamed again.

A loud bang rattled the bathroom door and I threw myself back in the tub. I couldn't stop screaming or crying.

"You fucking coward, Livvie! I'll never forgive you," Ruthless said.

I slapped my hands over my ears, willing the voice to go away. I could still hear her screaming, begging me to do something. I could hear yelling just outside the door – a struggle. The door shook repeatedly as something was slammed against it.

"Help him!"

"What do you want me to do?!" I screamed out loud.

"Stay down!" I heard Caleb yell.

"Help him!"

Hearing Caleb's voice, knowing he was fighting to stay alive only a few feet away, seemed to clear some of my panic.

"The gun, Livvie. The gun. Where is it?" Ruthless said.

I took several deep breaths, frantic breaths, as I tried to remember. Where was the gun? Where was the gun? In the bag!

"Good, Livvie. Where's the bag?"

I sobbed loudly. "I don't know."

A string of loud and angry shouting came through the door. I didn't understand it, but I knew it was Arabic. They'd come for us. Rafiq was here to kill us.

"The bag!" Ruthless screamed.

Images. They flashed through my mind's eye in rapid succession: I brought the bag in. I set it down on the table. Caleb picked it up and took it into the bathroom. He needed a butterfly stitch for his head. It was in there when I showered.

I looked around the bathroom, but I didn't see it.

It was there when I went to bed. Caleb and I had sex and after, he wanted clean underwear. Next to the bed on Caleb's side.

"Get there, Livvie. Get to the gun," Ruthless said.

I shook my head back and forth as I sobbed. I didn't know what was out there. If I opened the door...

"They already know you're in here! You're going to die. Caleb is going to die. Please!"

I scrambled out of the tub. The bathroom was tiny; my foot still touched the edge of the tub as I put my hand against the door. I could still hear Caleb fighting someone on the other side.

"I'm coming out!" I screamed.

"No!" Caleb yelled, and there was a loud crash.

I gripped the handle of the door and pulled it open. The clothing rack was directly across from the bathroom, creating a little square alcove to the side of the bedroom. I could see Caleb on the floor, grappling with someone.

"Run, Livvie!"

I stood up and tried to run past them and get on the bed. A hand reached out and grabbed my ankle. I fell face first onto the floor, but the pain didn't register. I kicked with my legs, blind to what or whom I was hitting. The hand let go.

I looked back and saw blood. Caleb's head was down. There was a loud, panicked scream and the person under Caleb pulled at his hair to wrench him backward. Caleb's mouth opened on a scream and blood came spurting out.

The screams continued, one after the other.

I froze. The screaming. I couldn't take the screaming.

Caleb's body was suddenly thrown toward the alcove. I didn't recognize our attacker. His face gushed with blood and a flap of skin hung from his cheek.

I screamed.

The man was still screaming as he threw himself on top of Caleb. He was beating his head into the floor.

I forced myself to move. I scrambled toward the bed, frantically running my hands underneath and feeling for the bag. It was there! I pulled it out and dumped it out on the floor. The gun came toppling out and I gripped it. It went off. I hit myself in the face with the back of my hand.

"Livvie!" Caleb yelled. The sound was a wet gurgle.

I regrouped quickly and held the gun in both hands. I pulled the hammer back and my hands trembled as I pointed it at the man on top of Caleb. "Get off him! Now!"

He turned to look at me, the flap of skin on his face just hanging there as blood gushed out, one heavy spurt after another. He rushed me and I squeezed the trigger. The force toppled me. My vision blurred for a couple of seconds. I scrambled backward on my hands, searching for the gun behind me.

I'd shot him. Our attacker lay on the ground, his body twitching and shuddering. His hands clawed at his chest. There was blood everywhere.

"What did I do?!" I screamed.

"What did I do?!"

"What did I do?!"

"Caleb, Livvie! Focus. Focus on Caleb. Where's Caleb?" Ruthless asked.

Somehow, I registered the situation. I looked toward the bathroom. Caleb wasn't moving. *No. No, no, no, no, no!* I saw red. Nothing but red! I found the gun and picked it back up. I crawled over and put the barrel on our attacker's chest. He tried to fight me while I pulled back the hammer, but he was weak, and my rage made me strong. I screamed as I pulled the trigger and blood sprayed my face, neck,

471

and body. When I opened my eyes, I stared directly into his wide-open chest.

"Caleb!" I yelled. When he didn't answer, I crawled toward him, terrified of what I might find when I reached him. He wasn't moving. He was covered in blood and he wasn't moving! I pulled his head into my lap and tapped the side of his face, "Caleb? Wake up, baby. Wake up! We have to go." There was no reaction. "Please. Please, God!" I put my hand on his chest. He was breathing.

I could hear shouting from outside. People running and squealing tires leaving the parking lot. Cops would be here soon. I put Caleb's head down and grabbed his shirt to sit him up. "Wake up! Please!" I shook him. His head fell forward and he coughed blood onto my pants. "Oh! Oh! Thank you!" I pulled him to my chest, running my hands all over him.

"Livvie," he said. And then he really woke up. "Livvie!" He pulled back and stared at me in shock. He pushed me to one side and looked behind me, then back to my face. "Are you okay?" he asked frantically.

I nodded, tears streaming down my face.

"We have to go," he said. "Now. Get up." He pushed me up and I helped him stand. He grabbed my hand and stooped down to scoop up the gun.

I ran to the pile of things next to the bed and found the keys. I shoved everything else inside in one huge ball.

"Get to the truck, Livvie," Caleb said. He seemed much too calm.

I ran across the parking lot, surprised to discover there were no people out there anymore. I managed to get the key into the lock and open the door. I scrambled inside and slammed it shut.

I heard another gunshot and ducked. Nothing happened for several seconds, but then the truck shook and I heard a loud thud. I squeezed my eyes shut. The cab door opened.

"It's me, Livvie. It's me," Caleb whispered. He found the keys in my hand and pried them loose. He peeled out of the parking lot as I shivered and cried on the seat next to him. After a while, I felt his fingers in my hair, gently stroking my head.

I had killed a man. I was covered in his blood. *I had to do it. I'm not sorry.*

And I wasn't. I wasn't sorry the son of a bitch was dead. I'd known he was dead after I shot him the first time. There was no way he could have survived the wound I'd given him. I had shot him the second time because...I wanted to. He had tried to kill me, but it was seeing Caleb's motionless body that had ultimately filled me with rage. Caleb was mine. I was through letting people take things from me.

We drove for a few hours. I had no idea where we were and I didn't care. I kept my head on Caleb's lap and let him touch me. Everything in my world made sense if Caleb kept touching me.

Eventually, Caleb stopped the truck, but he asked me to stay put while he took care of the body in the bed. The final shot I had heard was Caleb shooting

473

the guy in the face. He didn't want him identified. The guy in question had been Jair's cousin, Khalid.

I wanted to ask about Rafiq and the others, but then I remembered the way Caleb had come back to the room, shell-shocked and devoid of life. Some things were better left unsaid. Caleb and I were alive. We were together. Everything else? I didn't need to know.

Caleb got back in the truck faster than I would have expected. "It's done," he said.

"You buried him?" I asked doubtfully.

"No need. The animals can have him," he said. He reached across the seat and pulled my forehead toward his lips. "I killed that man, Livvie. Do you understand?" he whispered.

"What? No."

"Livvie! Listen to what I'm telling you!" He looked me dead in my eyes. His expression was hard and cold. "I killed him." He nodded his head until I mimicked him.

"Okay," I whispered.

"Good girl," he whispered and kissed me. Our agreement was sealed.

***

I should have known what Caleb was planning. There had been plenty of signs. I should have questioned him more about what had traumatized him back at Felipe's mansion. I should have demanded to know the plan when I kept seeing signs for Texas. At the very least, I should have asked more questions about the piece of paper Caleb demanded I memorize. He said anyone with the pass codes and account information could gain access, and it was important only he and I knew the information. I had felt so special. I thought he trusted me. I had felt like a spy when I burned the piece of paper and threw the ashes out the window.

I didn't ask questions. I didn't demand answers. Instead, I had been completely blindsided when Caleb stopped the truck and shattered my entire world by saying our time together had come to an end.

We were both silent for a long time. I didn't want to be the first to speak – I was afraid I couldn't. Caleb finally cleared his throat and broke the silence. "The border is just a few kilometers up the road. I can't go any closer." He gestured to the blood all over him.

"What makes you think *I* can? I killed –"

"You didn't kill anyone!" he shouted. "You were kidnapped. You've been trying to escape, and for months…I've…I kept you prisoner. I raped you," he said.

His words were a knife in my heart and I slapped him. Hard. "Don't say that! I know how we started out, Caleb. I know! But, please," I begged. "I love you."

Caleb's eyes welled up with tears, but he smiled and rubbed his face. "You slapped me," he laughed. "Again!"

"Why are you doing this, Caleb?" I asked as calmly as I could, but already my throat was thick with the sobs I was trying to hold inside.

He looked at me and I could see the faintest trace of something resembling the pain on my own face. "Because…it's the right thing to do."

"Why can't you let me decide for myself what the right thing is? I want to stay with you." I choked out. My heart raced, and I could no longer hold back my tears. He was giving me my chance to go home, to go back to my life, to go back to everything I said I wanted – but all I could think was none of it mattered if it meant I'd never see him again.

He gripped the steering wheel tightly and pressed his forehead against it. "You don't know what you want, Livvie, and what you think you want, you've been brainwashed into wanting." I immediately took a breath in order to protest; he held up his hand to stop me.

"I've been doing this a long time – manipulating people to get my way. That's why you think you love me! Because I've broken you down and built you back up to believe it. It wasn't an accident! Once you leave this behind…you'll see that."

I could barely see him through the mist of tears clouding my vision. Caleb believed everything he said. I could hear it in his voice – but he was wrong. He hadn't manipulated me into loving him. He'd tried to do the very opposite.

"So, that's it? You think I'm just some idiot that fell for your bullshit? Well you're wrong! I fell in love with you, Caleb. I fell in love with your sick sense of humor. I fell in love with the way you protected me. You saved my life!"

"I went to collect my property, Livvie," he said solemnly.

"I'm not Livvie anymore! I'm yours! Isn't that what you said? Isn't it what you promised? What we swore!" I wept.

"I don't want to own you. I want you to be free, and as long as you're with me...I'll always see you as my slave," he whispered.

I couldn't stand the sight of Caleb's head bowed in shame. He was much too proud a person. "I was never your slave, Caleb. You tried, I'll give you that, but we both know you belong to me as much as I belong to you. If you'd really been able to break me down and build me back up, neither of us would be here. No matter how fucked up the circumstances, I genuinely fell in love with you...and...and believe it or not...you love me too."

"Kitten," he said, "monsters can't love." He swiped at his eyes. "Now, get out of the truck. Walk toward the border, and don't ever look back."

Unable to control myself any longer, I wrapped my arms around him as tightly as I could. "I love you, Caleb. I love you! If you care for me at all... please, don't do this! Please, don't leave me. I don't know how to live without you. Don't make me go back to trying to be someone I don't know how to be anymore."

His arms gently guided me back, and when our eyes met, I finally saw the emotions he tried so hard to keep hidden and the resolve with which he said, "Live for me, Kitten. Be all those things you'd never be with me. Go to school. Meet a normal boy and fall in love. Forget me. It's time for you to go, Kitten. Time for us both to go."

"Where will you go?"

"It's best you don't know."

My heart sank, but I knew I had lost the argument and there was no stopping this goodbye. I wanted to kiss him then, just one last kiss to remember him by, but I knew kissing him would only be torture. I wanted to remember our last kiss as being one of passion and connection, not one of sadness and regret.

I let him go and opened the door.

"Take this," he whispered and pushed the gun toward me. "It's how you escaped."

I stared at the gun for a long time. I even contemplated taking Caleb hostage with it and forcing him to drive us somewhere else. But he'd hurt me. His rejection stung more than anyone's, and my pride wouldn't let me beg him anymore.

I picked up the gun and stared at his perfect profile as he stared out the windshield without a glance in my direction. He'd made his choice, and it wasn't me. I stepped out of the truck, slammed the door, and started my trek toward the border.

As I walked, I could feel his eyes on me, the way I could always feel his eyes on me. Tears ran down my face unabashed, but I didn't move to wipe them away. I had earned those tears, and I would wear them as a symbol of everything I had been through. They represented all the pain I had suffered, the love I felt, and the ocean of loss sweeping through my soul. I had finally learned to obey and never looked back.

I was covered in blood and bruises when I arrived at the border. In shock over everything that had happened with Caleb, I didn't respond well to the border patrol officers screaming at me with raised weapons. I had a weapon of my own and I wasn't afraid to fucking use it. And if I died? Who the fuck cared?

I put the gun to my head and demanded to be let through.

The fucktards shot me.

I thought I would die, bleed out as they wrestled me to the ground and handcuffed me. I didn't know they had shot me with rubber bullets.

26

Day 14:

Matthew sat across from the former Miss Olivia Ruiz. She looked like hell. Her long, dark hair was pulled away from her face into a severe bun. She had dark circles under her eyes and she hadn't been eating much. Her lack of food intake had kept her at the hospital an additional 72 hours, but they couldn't keep her once she had decided she wanted to leave.

Agent Sloan was also in the room. The revelations of the case had been difficult for her to swallow as well, and Matthew wished there were some way to comfort her without leading her on. She had come to his room after visiting Olivia at the hospital and learning about his and Olivia's last conversation. They spoke about the case for a while, but then she had wanted to talk about the night they'd had sex, and he had to let her know in no uncertain terms it had been a one night affair. She'd called him a coward. He'd called her worse.

"Is this the last piece of paper?" Sophia Cole asked.

"Yes," Matthew said. "Once you walk out of this room, you'll be Sophia Cole. In exchange for your silence on the events of the last four months, the Bureau has dropped the charges against you and given you a new identity. We will cover your accrued medical expenses, and you will be provided with the airline ticket you requested. In addition, your mother will receive the sum of $200,000 to be paid over five years. You understand, should you violate the terms of your agreement with the U.S. Government, you may be treated as a terrorist under the provisions of the Patriot Act and subject to a $250,000 fine and potential imprisonment. As a suspected terrorist, you may not be granted access to a lawyer or be formally charged. However, your case will be reviewed every three years to make a determination on whether or not you pose further threat. Do you understand the terms of this agreement?" he asked.

"Yes," Sophia whispered dully.

"Do you agree to the terms of this agreement?" he asked.

"Yes," Sophia said. "It's not like I have much of a choice."

Matthew sighed heavily and his eyes briefly met Sloan's. She shook her head slightly, letting him know how much she hated what was happening. Matthew hated it too, but his hands were tied on the issue. "The U.S. Government has given you all the things you've asked for, with the exception of returning into your care the S&W Model 29 revolver confiscated when you were first apprehended," Matthew said.

"And the bad guys go free. Don't forget that part, *Agent* Reed," Sophia said coldly.

Matthew was just as pissed off about that, but he'd done his job and he'd bent as far as he could. "Your assailants were never recovered at the auction in Karachi, Miss Cole." It felt wrong to call her by that name, but it was the one she had chosen and Matthew would respect it. "The U.S. Government sees no need to damage its relationship with Pakistan based on unsubstantiated allegations. However, it will be mentioned in the report that your statement led the joint task force to the auction and resulted in the freeing of over 127 human trafficking victims and the arrest of 243 potential traffickers."

"Whatever, Reed. Are we done here? I'd like to go," Sophia said. Matthew didn't take her disdain personally. He knew the real reason for her distress, and it had little to do with the deal she was making – the deal she'd asked for. She was still grieving over Caleb's –*James*'– death.

Matthew suspected he was still alive, but as far as he, or the Bureau, was concerned, James Cole had died in Mexico of gunshot wounds he sustained while aiding in Olivia's escape. The shooter, Khalid Baloch, was still at large. Matthew had closed James Cole's kidnapping case as well, but not before he reached out to Demitri Balk's personal assistant and was told Mr. Balk had 'no surviving children'. Mr. Balk himself was unavailable.

"Yes, Miss Cole, we're done," Matthew said. He could almost feel Sophia's sorrow from across the table, and it seemed to work its way into his own frame of mind. He had wanted things to end differently. Not just for Sophia, but for him as well. He'd been losing his faith in the system for quite some time. He had hoped by solving this case and putting the bad men in jail, he might regain some of the fire he'd once had for his job. Instead, the victory had been bittersweet. Over a hundred women were free from sexual slavery, but only a fraction of their traffickers would see the inside of a jail cell. Most of them would simply pay fines and go free. 'Bittersweet' was a lackluster description of what had happened in Pakistan.

"Come on, sweetheart," Sloan said to Sophia, "I'll walk you out." She stood and gathered up her papers, putting them into her briefcase.

Matthew watched Sloan intently. Her red hair was gathered in a French braid, and her face was scrubbed clean of all make-up. She wore a grey suit that covered up all her sexy curves. She was somewhat of an enigma. Matthew wondered how she was able to change like night and day. As a social worker, she seemed empathetic and somewhat devoid of interesting facets in her personality, but Matthew knew, first hand, what she could be like when she took down the mantle. He almost regretted not taking her up on her offer of more sex. He'd never been with a woman so attuned to his needs. Then again, she terrified him a little.

Matthew stood and offered Sophia his hand. "Goodbye, Miss Cole. Please know…you can contact me if you ever need anything. You have my card, and I'd be offended if you didn't use it."

Sophia smiled at him, but tears shone in her eyes. "Thanks, Reed. I know you did your best." She shook his hand.

"Thank you, Miss Cole," he said. It didn't feel like enough. It probably never would. Matthew turned toward Sloan and extended his hand. "Thank you for all your help too, Agent Sloan."

Sloan raised an auburn brow but took Matthew's hand and shook it. "No problem, Agent Reed. Let me know if you need any help with the final report. I'm leaving for Virginia tomorrow night, but until then…my phone's on." She smiled and Matthew felt his face heat up.

"I should have everything, but thank you," he said stiffly.

"You two should just fuck and get it over with," Sophia said without humor.

"Livvie! I mean…let's go," Sloan said.

Matthew didn't have a chance to respond before the two women left the room. He smiled to himself and shook his head. He was definitely going to miss Livvie and her crass sense of humor. He hoped she would seek the help she needed and make a full recovery one day. It would be a shame for such a beautiful, intelligent, and brave person to lose faith in the future.

Matthew picked up his recorder and turned it off. It was an archaic contraption and completely unnecessary considering everything in this room was recorded by the surveillance cameras, but he liked to maintain his own evidence. Things had a way of getting lost. He put it in his briefcase, along with his files, and headed out the door.

As he walked toward the elevator, he glimpsed 'Sophia' exchanging a tearful embrace with her mother. Matthew didn't exactly like the woman after all he'd learned about her, but he was happy she was finally getting the opportunity to see her daughter and perhaps apologize for everything she'd put her through. As part of the agreement, Sophia's family would be relocated and her mother would be offered her choice of training and employment. It was more than she deserved in Matthew's estimation.

Matthew would be heading back to an empty apartment in South Carolina until he was assigned to a new case. He hoped it would differ greatly from this one, and he was fairly sure it would. In the meantime, he'd decided he wouldn't give up on getting in touch with Demitri Balk. The guy was dirty, and despite all evidence to the contrary, he wasn't untouchable. Perhaps, in time, he would also lead him to Muhammad Rafiq and the rest of his cohorts.

James Cole deserved justice.

"I don't want revenge, Caleb. I don't want to end up like you, letting some fucking vendetta run my life. I just want my freedom." – Livvie

27

Day 287: Kaiserslautern, Germany

He'd learned the hard way that there was no future when all he could see was revenge. The only thing revenge had ever given him was a brief moment of satisfaction, followed by an empty abyss. He was through with revenge. He wanted to feel full instead of empty – loved, instead of feared.

Love, Caleb reminded himself. Love was the purpose of all this. He'd been dreaming of this moment for nearly a year, but now that his moment had arrived, he hesitated. Was it the right thing to do? Should he take his own advice – leave and never look back? He wasn't sure.

As a slave trainer, he had trained at least a score of girls. Some had been willing, offering themselves as pleasure slaves to escape destitution, sacrificing freedom for security. Others had come to him as the coerced daughters of impoverished farmers looking to off load their burden in exchange for a dowry. Some had been the fourth or fifth wives of sheikhs and bankers sent by their husbands to learn to satisfy their distinct appetites. He had trained so many, he had forgotten their names.

He knew them all by heart now. Ojal Nath had ended up in Turkey; her master had died and passed her off to his son. Caleb had paid a king's ransom to set her free. She was safe at home with her family now, and she had enough money to support herself and her young daughter.

He'd been too late to save Pia Kumar – she had been dead for nearly five years. She had been beaten to death by her master's new wife. Caleb had made sure to bury the both of them together. Alive.

Isa Nasser, Naba Mazin, and Jamila Awad had refused their freedom. They had come to him willing from the first, and they lived happily with their respective masters/husbands. They'd been more terrified of Caleb than of remaining in their servitude. He'd wished them well and vowed to keep an eye on them.

His years spent with Rafiq had built him a reputation, and Caleb took full advantage of the fear he'd cultivated as Rafiq's 'loyal disciple'. A lot of blood had been spilled in the last ten months – some of it even belonged to Caleb – but it didn't buy redemption. Caleb knew he could never be redeemed, and he'd made his peace with it. He couldn't right the wrongs, but he could offer a better future to those he'd wronged for the sake of his own selfishness.

It wasn't about revenge. Caleb had had enough revenge to last him several lifetimes. The things he'd done to Rafiq and Jair in Mexico hadn't given him solace. They'd given him nightmares. For Caleb, it had become about love. He loved Livvie. Through

her, he'd learned what love could make a person do
and it drove him forward. She had given him a gift,
and while he didn't deserve it, he tried to make sure
it had not been wasted.

His work was far from over, and he remained
dedicated to his task, but the road was long and
Caleb was only human. There was a hole in his heart
and each day it grew, threatening to pull him into a
pit of despair.

Caleb, from his vantage point diagonally across
the street, glanced at the girl he'd been observing for
the last thirty minutes. Her hair was pulled away
from her face, a heavy frown playing across her
mouth as she stared intently at the laptop sitting on
the table in front of her. She fidgeted sometimes,
alluding to a sense of restlessness she was unable to
hide. He wondered why she seemed so anxious. As
he eyed her beautiful face, he felt himself bursting
with hope and burning with shame.

After Mexico, Caleb had traveled farther and
farther south, until he could book passage to
Switzerland. He liked Zürich; he liked its diversity
and wealth, and he knew no one would notice him
there. He'd been putting his investments into
commodities and he had enough money now to live
as he pleased and travel the world to free the women
he had wronged. Still, it wasn't in his nature to
pursue being miserable, and so he'd looked for
Livvie.

At first, there had been plenty of information.
He'd simply had to get on his computer and sift
through the dozens of news stories from the weeks

following her rescue. Things had not been easy for Livvie once she'd crossed the border. She had been the target of a controversy-starved media. They followed her every move, and her reluctance to speak with the press only made her a more attractive target.

Her beautiful face had lit up his computer screen, but all he had learned was that she refused to speak to anyone. She had looked sad, and his heart had ached because he'd known it was his fault. Then, after a few weeks of coverage, Livvie had seemingly disappeared.

Caleb had called the bank in Mexico and was informed the account he had set up was closed several months back. The person who'd closed the account had left no messages with the bank.

His next plan of attack had been to find Livvie through her family. Caleb knew the FBI would be keeping a close eye on Livvie and had decided to hire a private investigator online. Livvie's family was gone, and the private investigator he'd hired couldn't provide him with any answers. Instead, the investigator had asked to meet in person, and Caleb had severed all communication.

He'd almost given up hope of finding her until he remembered she'd had a friend named Nicole. Caleb didn't know the girl's last name, and he'd had to go about finding her himself. She was attending university in California. He'd followed her for weeks, but saw no signs of Livvie.

His break didn't come until Nicole left her laptop unattended while she went off to play a game of

Ultimate Frisbee with her friends. Caleb had simply walked past the table filled with belongings and snatched it up, along with other things of value he could grab in a few seconds. He wanted it to look like a general robbery.

Livvie had not been easy to find, and at first he had been glad. However, as the months had passed, he'd become obsessed with knowing how she was. Nicole's laptop stood the best chance of letting him know how Livvie had fared. He'd told himself he only wanted to make sure she was safe and happy, but in the back of his mind, he'd known the real reason he wanted to find her again.

"I'm yours! Isn't that what you said? Isn't it what you promised? What we swore!" she'd cried.

Back at his hotel, he'd opened the laptop with shaking fingers and a racing heart. At first, he'd thought it was yet another dead end, but then he realized Nicole had been trying to make contact with someone named Sophia for quite some time. He followed the trail, opening each message Nicole had sent until, at last, he arrived at an email from Sophia.

To: Nicole <whitefish4568@...>
From: Sophia <cleverkitten89@g...>
Subject: Re: Where the hell are you?
December 23, 2009

Hey girl, long time, no hear – I know. I'm sorry. Even as I write this, I know you have every right to hit the delete button, but I hope you'll at least hear me out. It's almost Christmas,

490

and I'm lonely. I miss you. I miss my family (never thought I'd say that).

I've been wandering around Europe, seeing all the things most people won't get to see in their entire lives. The truth? It's not all it's cracked up to be. The French are truly assholes. I wouldn't suggest coming unless you speak fluent French, because they're pretty crappy to tourists. For the city of love, it's pretty damn lonely. I had to take the stairs up the Eiffel Tower and when I finally reached the top I realized I had no one to share the moment with me. I mean, it was crowded and people were pushing, but the view was truly gorgeous — but alone, it's just another tall building. Someone stole my wallet and I didn't notice until I tried to get something from the gift shop.

England is super expensive. Did you know it's like two dollars to every pound?!? I didn't stay there long. The money I have is great, but it won't last forever if I don't take care of how I spend it. The one great thing about England is the people are much nicer, but the men remind me a little too much of you know who. The accent makes me want to cry.

I miss him, Nick. I know it's stupid, but I do. I think it's why I couldn't talk to anyone after I left the hospital. I didn't think you'd understand. It's not that I don't trust you – I do. It's just that I love him and everyone else hates him and I can't deal with it.

Someday, I'll be ready. Someday, I'll stop loving him and seeing him everywhere I go. I'll stop hearing his voice in my head and dreaming of his kisses every night. Someday, I'll be able to see things the way I should and I'll hate him for everything he put me through – but not today. Not tomorrow.

You're angry with me and believe me, I get it. I would be pissed if you decided to fall off the edge of the earth and not reply to my messages, but I needed time. I still need time. If you're not there for me when I'm through this, I'll understand. Just know, I love you and I never wanted things to be this way between us. If I don't hear from you, have a Merry Christmas.

Hugs,

491

Sophia

Caleb searched the rest of the messages but
didn't find any dated after Livvie's email.
Apparently, Nicole had moved on, and Livvie had
let her. Perhaps, Caleb thought, he should do the
same with Livvie – but his heart had been claimed.
He needed to know if she still loved him, or if he'd
been right and everything she had felt for him had
been based on her need to survive.

He'd agonized over whether or not he should
seek her out. He knew her answer could destroy him,
but he needed to know. He needed to know if she
suffered without him, as much as he suffered
without her. If she loved him, he wanted to spend the
rest of his life trying to be worthy of her. If she
didn't, he could at least take solace in knowing he'd
made the right decision in setting her free.

Caleb looked at the girl sitting outside the café.
Did he even know her anymore? Could she sense her
life as she knew it hanging precariously in the
balance? Could she feel his eyes on her? Did she
have a sixth sense for monsters? The thought made
him sad.

He'd been here before. He'd done *this* before. He
shouldn't be watching her. He shouldn't be
contemplating thrusting himself back into her life.
He still had work to do, women to free from the
slavery he had subjected them to live through.

He looked at the girl one last time.

I love you, Livvie.

He put the key in the ignition and drove away.

***

Day 392: Barcelona, Spain

It's just a feeling, but I've been having it for a while. Someone's been watching me. I've been in touch with Reed, and he's dutifully put out some feelers to find out if I might be in danger. He's supposed to meet me in a few days, under the guise of following a counterfeiting case. In the meantime, he wants me to behave normally. He doesn't want whoever's following me to know I'm on to them.

Reed says he's heard reports of someone targeting Rafiq's known associates. Rafiq has been missing for over a year, and his government is none too happy about it. They think the FBI has something to do with his disappearance. Of course, they can't prove it. Reed doesn't seem too bent out of shape about it, though. The culprit is apparently some sort of vigilante. He's freed eighteen women from sexual slavery.

When I first heard the news, I immediately thought it might be Caleb, and my heart felt like someone had squeezed it in their fist. Reed didn't say it, but I thought he might suspect it was Caleb, too. It was in the way he asked me if I had any idea who might be responsible, or if anyone had been in touch with me.

"James Cole is dead," I had whispered.

"Yes," Reed replied, "I hope he has enough sense to stay that way."

493

I want to agree with Reed, but in my heart, I know what I really want. I want it to be Caleb. I want to know he's alive. I want to know he's out there trying to correct some of his mistakes. More than anything, I want to see Caleb again.

I'd contemplated killing myself early on, but then I'd hear Caleb's voice in my ear telling me to survive, that it was the coward's way out. So, I'd taken the money Caleb had left for me and decided to see the parts of the world I'd heard so much about and thought I'd never lay eyes on.

The last year has been a whirlwind. I've lost so much, and only now have I started to get some of it back. To date, I've seen four of the seven wonders, and I have plans to see the Pyramids before the year is out. I have a job, working as a waitress at an Applebee's of all places. Who comes to Barcelona to eat at an Applebee's? I don't care, though; it's work, and it pays for my classes at European University Barcelona, where I'm studying creative writing.

I don't like to rely on Caleb's money, so I have a financial advisor who invests it for me and looks after my affairs. Each month, I receive a generous stipend to supplement my income from working as a waitress.

Things were really hard at first, but it continues to get easier if I take my life and break it up into small increments. I wake up, take a shower, brush my teeth, get dressed, and go to work. I meet people, and I've even managed to make some friends. I met Claudia and Rubio in line for a screening of *The Rocky Horror Picture Show*. Claudia had been dressed as Colombia, and her boyfriend as Riff Raff. I didn't dress up.

They're great friends. They don't ask me questions about my past, and I don't offer any information. Mostly, we like to hang out after work and drink pitchers of sangria outside *El Gallo Negro*. They serve the best chicken/seafood paella I've found anywhere. After we get good and sauced, we usually go see the latest movie or go back to my place and play Rock Band on my PlayStation.

My friends may not ask about my past, but they're always interested in my present and future. They often try to set me up with their other friends, but I firmly resist. It isn't that I don't want a boyfriend, I do – but I'm not ready.

Caleb still fills my dreams and stars in each and every one of my fantasies. I still have the picture Reed gave me, and so I can still imagine his face with perfect clarity as I touch myself. Sometimes soft and slow, reaching for climax like one stretches after a good nap. Sometimes, I like it fast and rough. I pinch my nipples hard and rub my clit while I push my fingers deep inside my pussy and play Caleb's words in my head.

"Is that good, Pet?" he asks.

"Yes, Caleb," I answer.

I never mention Caleb to Claudia or Rubio. My memories and fantasies are my own business, but I think Claudia can tell whenever I miss Caleb. She smiles and reaches for my hand. She reminds me I don't have to be lonely.

I've been thinking about Caleb more frequently in recent months. Ever since I thought I felt his eyes on me one day outside of a café in Germany. I'd been sitting outside, typing on my laptop. Then again, I'd been writing about him.

I've been writing our story for over a year, every detail I can remember. I know I'm not supposed to talk about what happened with the public, but it's occurred to me how many people want to hear my story. Why shouldn't I be able to tell it? I'm not a complete idiot. I've changed all the names and locations. I've decided to market the book as fiction. And of course, I have a pseudonym. The important thing for me is people read it and perhaps understand why I'm still in love with the man who kept me prisoner.

I know all about James Cole. Reed can be a dick, but his heart is usually in the right place. He told me as much as he could. I've deduced the rest. At first, I felt gutted by everything I had learned. I had called Caleb a monster, but he'd only been doing the things he'd been taught to do.

I often think about the day he'd walked into the room, covered in dirt, smeared with blood, and devastated by whatever he'd done to get that way. There wasn't a doubt in my mind he'd killed Rafiq. I just wish he'd known his tears had been wasted. I wonder if the reason Caleb pushed me away was because he felt guilty over what he'd done to Rafiq to save me. Perhaps, if he'd known what a true monster Rafiq was, he'd have taken me with him instead of throwing me out of his life. Then again, maybe not.

"You have that 'lost in space' look again," Claudia says as she takes the seat opposite me at our table. "One day, you're going to have to tell me what that's about. I know it has to be a boy." She moves her eyebrows up and down.

I smile at her. "You're late. Where's Rubio?"

"He ran into his friend Sebastian. I think they'll be here in a bit."

"Claudia," I groan. "How many times do I have to tell you? I'm not interested in a hook up."

"It's not! I swear, it was a total accident. We were on our way here and they ran into each other." She quickly pours herself a glass of sangria and starts sipping. She's a terrible liar. "Besides, he's gorgeous. He's a student at EUB and he wants to be an artist. He's good, too – Rubi and I saw some of his paintings."

"I have to go," I say and start gathering my things. I am definitely not in the mood to deal with another 'accidental' blind date.

Claudia rolls her eyes and tugs me back down into my seat. "Don't be rude, Sophia. Rubi wouldn't set you up with a troll. Come on, stay for one pitcher."

"So, it *is* a set up then!" I scowl at Claudia and she doesn't even blush.

"Yes, okay – you got us. We're terrible friends for wanting to see you happy." She tosses her hands in the air sarcastically.

497

"I *am* happy, Claudia. I'd be a lot happier if you guys would stop setting me up." I cross my arms over my chest, but I know I can't stay angry.

"Excuse me, Sophia," interrupts the waiter. His name is Marco, and he knows our little group pretty well. He's asked me out a couple of times, but I always say no.

"What's up, Polo?" I ask with a smile. He hates his nickname.

"Very funny. Somebody asked me to give you this," he says and hands me a piece of paper.

"Ooooh, a secret admirer!" Claudia says. Both Marco and I blush, but only Marco has the luxury of walking away from an awkward situation.

"You're a jerk, you know that?" I say to Claudia, but she just smiles.

I open the note and I only have to read the first sentence to know who it's from.

I can't imagine what you must think of me...

I stand up so quickly, I knock over the pitcher of sangria and it shatters on the floor. My heart is beating in a frantic, but familiar rhythm. Claudia is up on her feet, trying to get me to acknowledge her, but I'm too busy scanning the crowd for him. He's here somewhere. He's here! I don't see him and I want to scream. I can't lose him again. I can't! Already, there are tears in my eyes. I look down at the note:

And I don't expect you've forgiven me. Still, selfishly, I have to ask you – are you glad I made you get out of the car? Was I right? Was everything you felt for me on account of my manipulation? If so, please know I am deeply sorry. That I will NEVER bother you again – I swear you'll never have cause to fear me. But if I was wrong, if you still care for me – meet me? Paseo de Colon, San Sebastia tower, eight o' clock tonight.
- C

"I have to go, Claudia," I say.

"Wait! What happened? Talk to me, Sophia," Claudia shouts after me.

I'm already half way down the block. As I run, I look around me. Is he watching me? Is it really him? Should I call Reed? It could be a trap, but I don't think so. Only Caleb would know about our last conversation. It's him. I know it in my fucking bones.

I'm in tears by the time I reach my apartment. I look at the clock. It's only four o'clock. I have four whole hours to wait. I've waited an entire fucking year, but these last four hours are going to be torture.

Epilogue

James swallowed thickly as the stared at the words on the screen.

> *As I walked, I could feel his eyes on me, the way I could always feel his eyes on me. Tears ran down my face unabashed, but I didn't move to wipe them away. I had earned those tears, and I would wear them as a symbol of everything I had been through. They represented all the pain I had suffered, the love I felt, and the ocean of loss sweeping through my soul. I had finally learned to obey and never looked back.*

The End

Sophia had written a very tragic love story, but it was a love story just the same. She had been very generous to him, painting a far better picture of the man he had been than he would have. She'd been working for weeks, sequestered in her little room upstairs. He wasn't allowed in there, and though he didn't like it, he respected Sophia's wishes. He respected all her wishes these days.

Several hours ago, she'd flown into the kitchen and thrown her arms around him.

"Why are you smiling, Kitten? Did you finally finish?" James asked.

500

"Yes! I finished," she said and followed up with a little dance. She'd immediately dragged him upstairs and planted him in front of the laptop so he could start reading. There wasn't another chair, so she'd gotten down on her knees and rested her head on his knee.

As he read, he stroked her hair. James had been scared to read everything from Sophia's point of view, but he was glad he'd made it through and discovered just how Sophia remembered everything. She loved him, he was sure of it, and while he still didn't think he deserved it, he was happy about it nonetheless.

He once again gazed on her sleeping form, unable to resist shifting her hair away from her face and behind her ear. Her mouth was slack, and he was sure she had drooled on him, but it didn't matter. She was the most beautiful thing he had ever seen. He couldn't help but stroke her. He loved the soft noises she made when he did. He didn't deserve her. He never did.

She'd been with him for over a year now, and secretly he always hoped she would tire of him and decide to leave. She told him she loved him often, and each time, it cut him down to his core. He didn't deserve her love. He couldn't bring himself to pretend he did.

When he'd learned she'd been writing their story, he helped her in any way he could. It was his outlet as much as hers. He needed to see it in black and white – the pain he put her through, the monster he had been. He never wanted to forget what he could never allow himself to become again.

Since the night Sophia had met him at the *Paseo*, the night he had decided to leave everything behind and integrate into mainstream society, so much of him had changed. Away from the horrors of his youth, away from blood and vengeance, he was just – James.

At first, he'd had no idea what to do with himself. All around him, real life was happening, and he was a spectator. What did he know about meeting people in cafés? About having friends that weren't killers?

But at night, in the dark, when he found he couldn't sleep because the world felt suddenly too big – there was Sophia.

Whenever he thought about running away and returning to the life he knew, he thought about the day he'd given her the note. She'd burst into tears and run away from the café. He'd thought she would call the FBI, and he'd been prepared to go to prison if they were the ones to meet him at the *Paseo*.

Instead, she had met him there. She stood, looking like a goddess among commoners. Her hair lay in soft waves down her back, occasionally being picked up by the breeze. She wore a black halter dress that hugged her breasts and bared her back. She also wore incredibly tall heels. They were dangerous, considering the cobbled streets. She'd wanted him to know she was a grown woman, and she wasn't afraid of him anymore.

He approached her from across the square. He was nervous. He wore jeans and a black cashmere sweater. The sleeves were pushed up to his forearms. He wanted her to know he was different. He didn't want to hurt her anymore.

Her back was to him as he approached, but the breeze suddenly died and she turned when she heard his steps approaching.

There had been no words. He simply stood in front of her with his hands in his pockets. Her breath caught, and for a while she only stared at him. She stepped closer, and he almost took a step back – but didn't. She was suddenly very close, and he couldn't help but inhale her scent and close his eyes. She touched his shirt and pulled him down. His head swam. Then she kissed him, and it was all that needed to be said.

He moved to Barcelona so she could still attend university. They never talked about the past. When people asked them how they met, she was quick to intercept the question and respond. They had met at the *Paseo de Colon*.

When they made love, he was surprised to discover Sophia's tastes had evolved. She wanted him to spank her. She wanted him to bind her arms. He felt sick about it at first. Her proclivities were obviously his fault. Still, their games turned him on to the point of physical pain.

He felt villainous, but what was done was done, and now he would do everything he could to give her what she wanted. He owed her much. Besides, it wasn't always rough. Sometimes it was vanilla – and he liked that too.

Carefully, James lifted Sophia into his arms and carried her to their bedroom. He laid her down on the bed, smiling as she shifted around, seeking some way to get comfortable. He undressed and got in bed next to her. Just touching her made him hard. He owed her so much.

Suddenly overwhelmed, he held her impossibly tight. She whimpered and whined until her eyes opened and she stared up at his face. "Oh my god, what's wrong?" she asked and stroked his distressed face.

"I love you," he whispered.

"I love you, too," she replied. Sophia's eyes welled up with tears and she tilted her face toward his.

She kissed him so passionately, so sweetly, that James thought if she never kissed him again, this was the kiss he always wanted to remember.

The End

About the Author

CJ Roberts is an independent writer. She favors dark and erotic stories with taboo twists. Her work has been called sexy and disturbing in the same sentence.

She was born and raised in Southern California. Following high school, she joined the U.S. Air Force in 1998, served ten years and traveled the world.

She is married to an amazing and talented man who never stops impressing her; they have one beautiful daughter.

Stalk her on Twitter @AuthorCJRoberts
www.aboutcjroberts.com

23995091R00274

Made in the USA
Lexington, KY
02 July 2013